**The Apples of Idu**
*Gods of the Rag*
MATT L
Editors: Clark Chamberlain, Fred Roth
Cover: Yocla Designs

Copyright © 2017 Matt Larkin.

Incandescent Phoenix Books
mattlarkinbooks.com

# MIDGARD

THULE

NIDAVELLIR

SVIARLAND

LAPPMARKEN

JAMTLA

DALAR

URSAL

NJARAR

LANDVIK SEA

OSTERGOTLAND

SKANE

MORIMARUSA

NORREVYSKE

CUBRIA

AGUS SJAELLAND BURGUNDAHOLMR

LAALAND

RIJNLAND

MENZLIN

XANTEN

HUNALAND

BAIA

SWABIA

STYRIA

VALLAND

AQUISGRANA

IDAVOLLIR

OUTER MIKLAGARD

BRETLAND

REIDGOTALAND

ANDALUS

KARJUBA

MIDDLE SEA

VANAHEIM

SERKLAND CALIPHATE

# CONTENTS

POHJOLA

KVENLAND

KALEVALA

SAMODIYTSIA

BJARMALAND

HOLMGARD

QAZAN

UTGARD

MIDGARD WALL

JARNVID

HALFHAUGR

KIOVIA

TARAZ

AUJUM

HYRKANIAN SEA

BLACK SEA

MIKLAGARD

MIKLAGARD

## EXTRA RESOURCES

For full color, higher-res maps, character lists, location overviews, and glossaries, check out the bonus resources here:
**https://tinyurl.com/y47j3gcj**

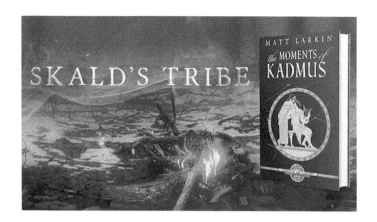

Join the Skalds' Tribe newsletter and get access to exclusive insider information and your FREE copy of *The Moments of Kadmus*.

https://www.mattlarkinbooks.com/skalds/

# PROLOGUE

*F*ire is life.

That aphorism had spread through the North Realms as thoroughly as the mists themselves. Fire could hold those freezing mists at bay. But all fires dwindled, and still the cold remained, hungry, waiting to devour man and beast.

And Loki was left alone to tend the flame. Fate bound him, hurled him ever forward toward a destiny of anguish and despair with only the barest ember of hope remaining. Hope for a better future than this dying world. The hope that for once, if he kindled the flame high enough, it might endure and offer a lasting bulwark against the cold and the dark. Likely, it was a delusion he clung to like a man wandering in a blizzard, convinced shelter lay just beyond the next pass.

A figure drifted in on the mist and sat across the bonfire from Loki. Few among the Realms of man still remembered Loki's guest. Those who did called him the Mad Vanr. The sorcerer king who had walked away from his throne after looking too long and too deep into the dark and losing himself there.

Loki could empathize with such a failing. Long ago, pyromancers had stared into flames such as these, seeking answers from the perilous future. Few remained with such talents, and those few, like Loki, felt the burden ever more keenly for it.

The Vanr cleared his throat as he warmed his hands before the fire. "I passed beyond the edge of the Midgard Wall some moons back." Mundilfari, his people had called him, in ages past when he sat upon the throne of Vanaheim. This wretched figure had once been the sorcerer who protected Midgard against the chaos and darkness—for which he lost his humanity and spiraled into depravity, falling ever deeper into the dark between Realms. "I passed into Utgard freely. There are cracks in the wall, fissures that widen with age."

Loki poked the fire with a stick. "Naught lasts forever." The Vanir—most of all Mundilfari himself—had raised a mighty wall out of the mountains, a barrier to encircle most of Midgard, separate it from the lands of the jotunnar. That very act, calling upon such forbidden depths of the Art, might have been the point that sent this Vanr plummeting toward the abyss of madness. Now, uncounted centuries later, the sorcerer had fought his way back from the edge. But to use his Art once again, he'd risk falling deeper than ever and, like as not, find himself becoming a vessel for some horror of the Otherworlds.

So he had visited Utgard, perhaps needed to see for himself how the World had changed beyond the wall. In Utgard, chaos reigned. The very nature of chaos ensured all boundaries designed to occlude it would eventually succumb to entropy.

"Maybe the jotunnar will soon pass through the wall."

Loki shook his head. "Some of them already have."

Mundilfari groaned and let his head fall into his palms. "All that I have done, all I wrought for Midgard is failing."

Every such salvation represented a temporary reprieve from Fate. The Vanr may have bought Mankind time, but that time had dwindled with each passing winter, just as the flames dwindled. "Naught lasts forever," Loki repeated.

Mundilfari stared up at the night sky as if some answer might lurk there, among stars hidden by clouds and mist. "I hear whispers from Vanaheim. A wind sweeps through my mind and claims that some few precious, perilous treasures have vanished from the islands. When is gold worth more than gold?"

"Idunn has taken some of the apples with her."

Mundilfari might have gone mad, but the wind in his mind spoke some truths. The flames had told Loki much the same tale.

"What will she do?"

Loki crooked the hint of a smile.

"Fine. What will you do, fire-bringer?"

The flames danced, writhing as if in response to the Vanr's question. Loki rose. "As ever, I will do whatever the future demands of me. I have to keep the flame alive."

Fire is life.

# PART I

Year 117, Age of Vingethor
Fourth Moon, Winter

## 1

*F*lames from the pyre leapt high into the night, banishing mist and preserving the living, even as they consumed the dead, as they devoured flesh and dreams and hopes.

Father.

Odin stood at the forefront of the gathered crowd, staring into the flames, unwilling to look at the mass of people who had come to bid farewell to Borr, the great jarl. All the nearest Ás tribes had come. The jarls decked in their fine embroidered furs and golden arm rings, their thegns clad in fine mail, and even völvur—witches learned in secrets forever denied to men. All had come to pay silent respect to the greatest Aesir in living memory. The World was lesser now. The flames were a failing defense against the ever encroaching cold. One day, all fires would burn down to cinders. One day, the World would die.

One day soon, most like.

Odin's two brothers looked to him now, looked to see what he, the eldest, would do, what he would say. He had already spoken in their father's honor, his voice almost breaking. But his brothers, the rest of the Wodan tribe, and even the other tribes' jarls all waited for more of his words. As if some speech, some feeble gesture or deficient sentiment, might preserve the tenuous peace Father had struggled to hold between the tribes. All words would fall short, so Odin had none to offer.

How disappointed they would be to learn the son could not match the father. Would not, if he could. Father's dreams of a united people smoldered and turned to ash around his broken body. Someone had betrayed him, murdered him. Tyr, his champion, had found his body rent asunder and crushed almost beyond recognition. A body left out in the mist might rise as a draug, damned to wander Midgard somewhere between life and death. Not Father. Too little remained of the man for that. His head, torn from his shoulders, had lain far from his body.

And yet, his murderers had not claimed his spear, Gungnir. That had remained lodged in a tree trunk. The sacred weapon of the jarls of the Wodanar, granted to them by the Vanr Idunn during the Great March. It fell now into Odin's keeping. When he held it, he felt both strong and unworthy, filled with righteous wrath and the implacable need to avenge this wrong. By Frey's flaming sword and the spear of his father, he would do so! Odin would slaughter any and all who had so dishonored Borr and he would leave their carcasses to the anguish of mist.

Odin had borne Father's head back himself, in trembling hands, unwilling to accept a litter for it, no matter how heavy it grew over the miles. Head and body both burned now, on a mighty pyre just outside the town wall.

Fists clenched at his side, Odin stood motionless until that pyre had dwindled down to embers. The others had left, he knew, drifted away one by one, leaving him alone with the cinders. Only ravens perched upon the trees accompanied him in his grief. In the town, his brothers threw a feast in Father's name.

Odin had no mood to feast. Not this night.

Footfalls crunched on the snow behind him. A hand fell on his shoulder. Jaw tight, Odin turned to see Tyr there. A powerful man with long dark hair and a trim beard, Tyr was taller than Odin—and Odin was a large man. Tyr bore the scars of a hundred battles, more perhaps. But he hadn't been at his jarl's side in the end. Odin fixed him with a glower and did not speak. Naught remained to say.

"Valkyries have taken him to Valhalla by now," Tyr said. "Borr feasts with the Vanir."

Odin shrugged the man's hand off his shoulder and turned once more to the pyre. If only he could believe Tyr. But surely his father's spirit did not rest easy, not while his murder stood unavenged. Thousands of ghosts dwelt in the mists, lingering just beyond firelight, wandering in eternal torment. Father would not rise as a draug, for such things inhabited their own corpses. But some other kind of ghost ... perhaps. A fevered specter or wraith, watching as his son did naught to end his suffering.

But then, whom could he take revenge *against*?

No one in the village of Unterhagen had survived to tell the tale. When Father did not return from some secret meeting, Tyr had tracked him to the village. Odin followed with a small war band. The slaughter and savagery they found in Unterhagen suggested trolls—except trolls didn't usually kill the women, preferring to claim them as wives. Men, women, children—all lay dead, battered and beaten, their corpses spread across the village.

Odin had walked there in agonized torpor, fearing what he'd find. Unterhagen lay in a small valley, only nine homes cluttered in a wooded valley a few days from Eskgard. A snowstorm had swept in and blanketed the massacre, forcing Odin and Tyr and the others to dig through the snow to even find many of the corpses.

And they had found them. No corpse could be left to rot, for fear of the draugar. So they had dug through the snow until at last they had found a severed head. Father.

They burned the bodies of the freemen and slaves in three large pyres. But Borr was noble, of the line of Loridi, and thus deserved a funeral fit for such venerated blood. And so they brought what pieces of him they could find and waited. Waited while the other tribes braved the winter storms to come and pay last respects to the greatest of the Aesir.

"You must speak to your guests," Tyr said.

Odin scoffed. He had questioned all he could, trying to learn who his father had gone to meet. Searching for an answer, searching for the path to vengeance. No one had those answers. Not the völvur, whose useless visions told him less than naught. Not the jarls nor their thegns. No one.

"You do not well remember the Njarar War—"

"Of course I don't fucking remember it. It was twenty winters back, I was four."

Tyr scowled at his interruption. "You may not remember it. I do. By the end, more than half the Ás tribes, the better part of all Aujum ... it was *drowning* in blood. If not for Borr, Njord knows what would have become of this land. Your father ended the war. Brought peace between us."

Relatively speaking. The Aesir tribes still raided against one another, from time to time. Father did—*had done*—his best to direct their aggression back north, into Sviarland. Njarar was one of seven petty kingdoms there. Father had spoken more than once of turning from raids to conquest, of bringing the northern kingdoms under Ás control. He might have done it, too. But still, not all the Aesir cared overmuch for Father's attempts to unite them. Some claimed the man thought he was Vingethor himself, thinking to be king. No one had stood as king since then, not in the five generations since the Great March out of Bjarmaland. Maybe no one would ever be king again. None of it mattered. Not compared to the weight on Odin's shoulders. His first duty was to his father's honor. Blood called out for blood, and he would bathe all Aujum in it to avenge Father.

One of the other jarls must have planned this, tired of Father's attempts to direct them—the slaughter, the barbarism, a mere ruse to distract from the truth.

"Odin, you must see to the guests," Tyr said. Persistent man, Odin would have to grant him that.

Odin spat in the snow. "Yes. I will see to them, thegn."

"Hold them together. Hold the tribes together. Let Borr's life mean something."

Odin lunged at him before he knew what he was doing, snatched up a fistful of Tyr's fur cloak, and jerked the man closer. "His life meant something. It meant *everything*!"

Tyr growled before he answered. "You are not the only one who loved him."

Oh. Oh no. Odin shook his head, almost choking on his rage. "He took you in. But he was *not* your father."

"I did not say he was. He was a great man. Many loved him for it. I ask you to be worthy of that legacy."

Odin shoved Tyr away and stormed off, back toward the town and his feast hall. The guests awaited.

The jarls of the Hasding, Didung, and Godwulf tribes had come, though each sat apart from the others, surrounded by their own men and shieldmaidens. Smoke from numerous braziers choked the feast hall, mingling with the smell of roasting mammoth. Between the braziers and the press of bodies, the hall remained warm despite the freezing winds just outside.

Lodur, jarl of the Diduni, clapped Odin on the shoulder and offered a solemn nod. Naught remained to say, really. Odin's father had fostered Lodur for two winters, and in that time Lodur had tried often to best Odin in every feat of strength and arms. The Didung won oft as not, too. Lodur's grief for Father was real, Odin had no doubt, but it was a candle next to the raging inferno consuming Odin.

Odin wandered the hall, finding no solace in any who had once been his friends. He wanted neither friendship nor condolence. He wanted vengeance. He wanted blood. And to get it, he needed someone who knew something of Unterhagen and what had befallen it.

Decrepit Jarl Hadding of the Hasdingi had no sons, so his daughter sat by his side, speaking to others about the great Borr. As if she might begin to imagine.

Hadding's long beard and longer hair had both gone gray, and Odin guessed the jarl had seen at least fifty winters, probably more. That was an age few men reached, and fewer still among warriors. A man of honor would have fallen in battle long ago. Hadding didn't care for raids, always hiding behind his fortress walls. But that fortress, Halfhaugr, lay at the heart of Aujum. All the tribes came there to trade, to share stories, to take respite from the mist. And that meant many tales reached Halfhaugr.

Trying not to glower, Odin stalked over to the table where the old craven sat. He almost tripped over one of the numerous elkhounds seeking warmth inside the hall. Grumbling, Odin ruffled the hound's ears to show he meant no harm. Father always said, trust the hounds, that they smelled when aught was amiss—that's when you brought out the iron. Iron to ward, iron to slay.

Hadding lacked the stones to have betrayed Father. Ironic, that his weakness made him one of the few men here Odin had little reason to doubt. While the Wodanar— indeed, all the other tribes here today—migrated around Aujum every few years, the Hasdingi cowered behind their fortress, trusting in dverg runes and the goodwill of others to keep them safe. They had grown fat off Borr's peace and would not have wanted that to end.

Odin slumped down on the bench across from the other jarl. Hadding did not rise to greet him, instead clearing his throat with a thick cough.

His daughter stood, though, and inclined her head. "Jarl Odin Borrson. You honor us." She was young, clad in a vibrant green dress, her long, auburn hair worn in elaborate braids. What was her name again? Frigg?

He inclined his head to her. He had imagined himself bedding her, at least briefly. But a jarl's daughter was not like to give in easily, and he had no time for pursuing her. He had plenty of slaves to fulfill his needs.

"We grieve with you," Hadding said. Again the man coughed, slapping a hand to his chest. The thickness—it must already be filling his lungs. Odin pitied any man forced to endure such a death. One more reason to seek the end on a battlefield and find the embrace of valkyries. Dying like that, Hadding had naught to look forward to save the gates of Hel.

"Thank you," Odin said. The old man seemed almost sincere. Without Father's watchful eye, other tribes might look to seize Halfhaugr for themselves.

"Will you eat with us?" the girl asked.

Odin motioned to a slave to bring him the drinking

horn. He took a long swig of mead before handing it to the next man—one of Hadding's thegns, no doubt, aging himself. The whole damned tribe would probably find themselves eating from Hel's table within a winter or two. Odin cleared his throat. "Jarl Borr went to Unterhagen for a reason. Someone knows why, knows who he went to meet. I want information." He thumped his forefinger on the pine tabletop. "I want it now. Father's ghost has languished too long already. I feel his grimace cast upon us from the shadows."

Hadding rubbed his chest. "Maybe. But as yet, men speak of other things. They speak of war. We face dangerous times, and when winter breaks …"

When winter broke, Hadding would no doubt have any of the other eight tribes trying to seize Halfhaugr from him. Did he think Odin would do aught to protect him? Odin fixed the useless old man with a level stare. At the moment, the Wodanar themselves had no reason not to claim the fortress.

"What about the foreigner?" Frigg said.

Odin looked to her. "What foreigner?"

"A man came to us recently, someone from far away. Somewhere in the South Realms, maybe, he didn't say. But rumor claims he is a masterful tracker, wise in woodcraft, and nigh as learned as any Miklagarder, as well."

Hadding waved his daughter away. "The man is full of himself. You can't trust a man who talks like a völva and fills his mind with South Realmer learning."

That earned him a scowl from Frigg.

"Tyr already searched Unterhagen for tracks. With the snows, he found naught."

"Maybe," Frigg said. "But this man might know something else. He has a strange urd about him."

Urd? What did some jarl's daughter know of a man's fate? Still, he had naught else to go on.

"Then I will go back to Halfhaugr with you, meet this foreigner," Odin said. "If he can do as you say, you and he shall both earn my gratitude."

Almost as one, a number of the hounds perked up and stared at the doors to the feast hall. A moment later those doors crashed open. Then even the people began to fall silent. Men rose from their benches to move toward the newcomer.

A crowd quickly surrounded her, and she took each into her gaze. When her eyes met Odin's, he stumbled. She wore her long, brown hair loose, flowing around her shoulders. Her skin was rich, deeper in color than any he'd ever seen, and now that he'd drawn nigh, he could see the flowing red gown she wore beneath her furs. The material shimmered in the light of the braziers and was sheer enough to give a hint of the delicate flesh beneath. Odin had no doubt that every man in the circle eyed her with lust, even as he pictured himself carrying her off to his own bed in the back room of the hall.

"Dangerous lands to walk alone," he said. "Especially at night." Especially for an unarmed woman.

Visitors from another tribe were not uncommon, but no one traveled in the dead of night unless desperate. The deathchill was the *least* one needed to fear at night, and that could easily bring down a man. Beyond that, trolls and vaettir, especially the vilest ones like draugar, often grew more active at night. Sunlight thinned the mists and tended to drive its horrors into hiding.

The foreign woman smiled at him—or rather, she crooked half her mouth in a smile. "You are Odin." Her voice was light, her accent lilting and odd.

"I am," he said. "And who are you, my lady?"

"My name is Idunn."

A murmur rose through the crowd. Someone scoffed and someone else gasped. Odin caught himself glancing at Gungnir where it rested against his throne.

"Idunn?" The goddess of spring? One of the Vanir here, among them? The same who had given the spear Gungnir to his great-great-grandfather?

"Yes," she said, flashing a bit of teeth in her smile now. "Do your people still remember me? I'd hoped they would."

How coy. Every Ás remembered Idunn—assuming she was who she claimed to be. Beautiful, no doubt, but a goddess? Since when did gods come strolling into Aesir halls in the middle of the night? Though that was exactly where his ancestors claimed Gungnir came from. Regardless, there was only one thing a jarl could do when a guest came calling.

"Lady Idunn, I extend to you the full hospitality of the Wodanar."

With that smile, she'd have any man in the tribe eager to do her bidding.

## 2

*O*din had taken Idunn out into the night despite the cold. Tyr assumed he wanted to speak with her without prying eyes. Keeping others from following was probably the only reason he had allowed Tyr along. Hand resting on the sword over his shoulder, Tyr followed several paces behind the pair. One of the elkhounds walked at his side. Always best to take a dog if you could. Hounds smelled foulness in the mist. Let you know when aught went creeping about.

Like Odin, Tyr carried a torch. A man needed fire. Without it, the mist would seep into his body. Into his soul. Tyr had seen men go Mist-mad. They'd lose themselves. Have to be put down or banished for the good of the tribe. Besides, the mists sheltered ghosts, trolls, draugar, and other vaettir. All waiting to prey on the World of Men as soon as the fires dwindled.

"So," Odin said after walking through the town awhile.

The Wodanar were spending the winter at Eskgard. Reinforced old houses not used in a decade. When summer came, they'd abandon this place for better hunting grounds. Migrating in winter was left to the foolish and the desperate.

"So," Idunn answered. "Here we are."

This woman was like none Tyr had ever seen. Dark brown hair, exotic skin like some South Realmer. Graceful movements, confidence. And she had wandered the wilds alone. Did that make her a fool—or desperate? Or could she truly be one of the Vanir? Nigh to absurd. If the Vanir existed at all, they no longer walked the lands of Midgard. Not in ages. But then ... most would have said the same of jotunnar. And Tyr knew better on that count.

"Yes, here," Odin said. "Where you would have me believe a Vanr has come to call upon my people."

She shrugged. "Oh. Well, yes. I think so. I mean you should believe me. You still have Gungnir, don't you?"

Odin grunted. "What do you want of me?"

Tyr knew he ought to keep more careful watch, but he could not tear his eyes from the two of them. The one, a self-proclaimed goddess. Beautiful and outlandish enough that he could not quite dismiss her claim. And the other ... Borr's son. Borr had been a hero to many. He had saved Tyr from a wretched life as a raider enslaved to a more wretched master. Had taken him in. In time, Borr made him first a thegn and then his personal champion. Had even trusted him to help instruct his own sons with weapons. If naught else could be said for him, Tyr knew his way around a battle. Blade, axe, or bow, Tyr had mastered them all.

And Odin had grown up quite skilled himself, at least in weaponry. But he was not his father. Not by any measure. The young man had fire. But that fire stoked his pride more than his honor. Rage consumed him. Tyr did not *blame* him for wanting to avenge his father. Indeed, Tyr himself would have gone to great lengths to do so. But Odin was allowing

Borr's legacy to splinter around him while he quested for revenge against unknown enemies. Tyr had helped Borr forge this peace. Had waded through rivers of blood to do so. And Odin and his brothers saw none of that. Would not listen.

Idunn giggled. What kind of goddess giggles? "What a question. What do I want from you? Let me ask you—what do you think your father would want of you?"

"Vengeance." The man didn't even hesitate.

Tyr stifled a groan. Barely. The hound cocked one of his ears at Tyr. Asking if he had sensed danger. He had, though no danger he could explain to the animal.

"Truly? Don't you think he'd care about maintaining all he was building? Just maybe he'd want you to continue on the path he'd begun?" Goddess or not, Idunn had the right of it. Maybe *she* could talk some sense into Odin. If she did, his brothers would fall in line. Odin was eldest, and they looked to him.

Odin groaned, cast a glance back at Tyr. Tyr offered him a nod. "What of it?"

"You are jarl now. What would it take for you to be something more? To be a king?"

Tyr's foot snagged in the snow. King? Not even Borr had held such a lofty goal, despite the claims of other jarls. Mist-madness, if he'd ever heard it.

Odin stopped there and turned on her, forcing her and Tyr to pause as well. "We'd have to call an Althing, put it to a vote among the nobles of all nine tribes. Which is not going to happen. No Althing, no vote, and if there was, not one man everyone could agree on to be king. Least of all me."

"Oh? Can you think of some better way to honor your father?"

Odin folded his arms over his chest and shook his head. "What do you hope to gain from this?"

"Hmmm." She reached inside her fur cloak and pulled something out. It looked like an apple. A golden apple glittering in the torchlight. "Do you know what this is?" Odin shook his head. "This is immortality, my dear Odin. This sweet fruit tastes of the World itself. And I bring it to you, even as I once brought Gungnir to your ancestors."

"Wh-why?"

Tyr's mouth hung open. He could not quite manage to shut it.

Idunn withdrew the apple and stuck it back within the folds of her cloak. "This ultimate gift I could grant you. The power to live forever, to lead your people—all of the Aesir—forever. But you must do two great services for me."

Odin licked his lips. "Live forever? How am I even to believe such a thing?"

"The apple comes from the World Tree, Yggdrasil, the heart of Vanaheim, the source of all life. But then, you wouldn't really know until you tried it, would you?" She shrugged. "It's a puzzle. Sometimes you have to have faith. Sometimes you have to take a chance."

Tyr's heart pounded against his ribs. What she spoke of sounded impossible. Sounded like the prattling of a Mist-mad völva. And yet ... he wanted to believe. Her voice, like music, offering such temptations. And Odin had not quite leapt at the chance. Had Tyr underestimated his new jarl?

Odin released a shuddering breath. "Your terms, Vanr?"

"You must make yourself king of all the Aesir."

Odin spread his hands wide. "I'm not fucking Vingethor. And do you really think my father intended to become king? Do you think he could have? The other jarls wouldn't have bowed before him, and they sure as Hel will not bow before me. In any event, why do you care?"

"Mankind is dying, Odin. Slowly, yes, but with each generation Mankind's numbers dwindle. The mist suffocates your world, and the cold creeps ever closer, while petty kings and jarls fight each other for scraps. It's why I gave your ancestors Gungnir. Back then, I thought it might prove enough. It did not. If naught changes, there will be but a few more generations of life left in Midgard."

Her words left Tyr shivering. Völvur stories claimed that long ago, maybe thousands of years ago, this world was warmer. Before the mists. Now, each passing winter claimed more lives. Men froze. Murdered each other over scraps of food. Or because they could. And out in the mist, those who fell lingered. Grim, wakeful. Caught between life and death. Idunn spoke of the end times as a nigh certainty. And worse, as fast approaching.

Odin pressed his palms against his forehead, shaking his head. "And if I would or even could do such a thing, claim this throne ... what of your other request?"

Tyr had almost forgotten she had asked for two services. As if becoming king of nine tribes on the brink of war were not enough burden for the brash young man.

"Once you are king, I will come to you with another task. You will owe me then, and I will have your oath you'll do all in your power to grant my final request."

Odin scoffed. "You still have not told me what that request is."

Idunn giggled again. "I suppose I haven't. First make yourself king."

The jarl held up his hands. "No. No, I will not give an oath to any task without knowing what you ask. A man would have to be a fool to do such a thing. If you care so

much about Mankind's urd, *goddess*, you attend to it." With
that, he shook his head and stormed back toward the feast
hall.

"I am trying," Idunn mumbled.

Tyr took a few steps closer. "You truly believe that man
would make a good king?"

Idunn grinned now. A half smile, like a wicked child. "I
think he could be the greatest king the Aesir have ever
known. Beyond Vingethor, beyond even Loridi. Maybe. If he
can see past his own petty desires. And stop staring at my
tits."

Tyr realized what he had been doing and flushed.
Maybe she couldn't tell in the torchlight. His tongue felt
heavy in his mouth. What did a man say to a goddess?
Particularly one as odd as this. "I ... er." He cleared his
throat. "Borr worked his whole life to win and keep peace
between the tribes. Everyone respected him." Or feared him.
"But Odin is right. The other nobles wouldn't have
supported Borr as king. They certainly won't support his
son."

Idunn scratched the hound's head—and the animal let
her. "Hmmm. Well—not yet."

## 3

*T*he snows ran deep, five feet at least, covering all the North Realms. Farther north, men said it never melted. At least a thousand years of it, the völvur said. Once, long ago, they said, there was a time of warmth. A time of true summers, where green covered the world. A time before the mists that blanketed all Midgard and stole the minds and memories of men. Völvur said a lot of things. Odin suspected they knew far less than they pretended.

Crossing Aujum in winter meant sledges drawn by dogs, yipping, barking, surging forward as if they also knew it. The fewer nights in the wild, the better. Cowardice sent you to Hel's table. But if you forgot to fear the mists, you'd find yourself dead or worse.

If they pressed hard enough, they might make Halfhaugr in three days. Three days—but the nights, oh, the nights they had to huddle around the largest fires they could manage, desperate to ward off not only the cold, but the mist and the fell vaettir it brought with it. The Hasding thegn with Hadding—Agilaz was his name—he knew his woodcraft. Each night he found a sheltered campsite and got a blazing fire going. And then Odin and the others would gather round, trying to stay warm, trying to pretend they did not hear the fell whispers far out in the night. Shades or vaettir, no doubt, watching them, waiting for the fires to die. Waiting to consume their flesh or souls. Vaettir despised men, even as they envied them their warmth, or so völvur said.

One such fire crackled this night. Tyr sat across from him, roasting a squirrel Agilaz had shot. Odin had consented to bring his own thegn on this trek, had left his brother in charge of the Wodanar in his absence. No sense dragging half the tribe along with him.

A man had to be Mist-mad to travel in winter. A night without shelter was apt to drag a man into the deathchill, leaving naught but a draug behind. The cold could freeze a body solid in an hour—and those who met such an urd without fire would find no peace even in death. The damned wandered the mist for all eternity, preying on the living in a futile effort to divert their own agony and rage.

Odin knew about rage. About its futility. Some things which had been stolen could never be regained.

He spat out into the darkness. His vengeance would not be denied. If ghosts or draugar or aught else stood in his way, he would cut them down with Gungnir and send them screaming down to Hel.

"Jarl Borr called upon us several moons back," Hadding's daughter said.

Odin glanced at her. Frigg looked a few years his junior, but she carried herself with the refined elegance of a born noblewoman—head high, back straight, and eyes sharp. He looked back to the fire. Father had oft called upon all the tribes, endlessly working to avoid war, always making plans. Trying to save everyone. Except himself.

Head torn from his shoulders.

Body mangled beyond recognition.

Father.

A corpse, rent in half.

"He was a hero to many people," Frigg said when Odin didn't answer.

He grunted. Yes. Father had been a hero, sure enough. A master warrior, a good man. Generous with his allies, implacable to his foes. And always there for his sons. Odin clenched his teeth so tightly they felt apt to crack. And still he could not release his bite. The pressure would keep him going while his fury kept him warm, simmering, boiling. The waiting ate at his guts. No, he need not worry overmuch about deathchill. Not with such heat consuming him from the inside out.

Borr the hero. The warrior. The father.

Head torn from his shoulders.

"I understand your pain," Frigg said.

Odin snorted at that. His brothers—Vili and Ve—*they* could understand. Perhaps Tyr might begin to. The thegn had been closer to Borr than any man, probably looked at him as a kind of foster father. No one else could know.

"You see, I lost my mother two winters back. I remember the hollowness, the consuming apathy toward life that threatened to bury me like a blizzard."

Apathy. No, Odin knew naught of apathy. His heart was an inferno, blazing with the need to act, to destroy and wreak revenge upon the entire World. So hot did he burn, he wondered that fire did not seep from his eyes, having no other outlet. He glared at the woman who dared think herself capable of knowing his loss. Apathy!

"He left a legacy behind. A very fragile hope of peace between the nine tribes. In recent years, he had been helping arrange marriages to tie every tribe to every other. A web of alliances that ..."

Odin stopped listening to her. She meant to ask whether he was worthy of his father's legacy. How could he be? How could anyone? Father had walked with the purpose and stature of one like Vingethor, like Loridi. A legend in his own lifetime, his fame spread across Aujum like a winter storm, touching every living Ás. And Odin, a mere man, had naught to offer next to such grandeur. Naught save vengeance. Father's ghost could not be allowed to suffer as others did, trapped on Midgard, trapped in the mists.

"And you must continue what he began," Frigg was saying.

"You fear for Halfhaugr," he snapped. "So you feign empathy for me in the hope I will protect you."

Frigg stiffened and Tyr growled, poking the fire with a stick. Hadding and Agilaz had turned to him now, both watching him.

"Was that my father's legacy?" Odin asked. "To guard those too weak to help themselves?"

"Boy!" Hadding coughed, choking on his own outburst. "I fought in the Njarar War while you were barely off your mother's tit. Agilaz fought beside me. And you ..." Another hacking fit of coughs interrupted him.

"Jarl Hadding risked travel in winter. Out of respect for Borr," Tyr said. Always chiding him. Like everyone else, he expected Odin to turn into his father. But no one could.

Still, he supposed he ought to *try*. Even knowing he could not live up to that legacy, he must come as close as he could. He was the eldest son of Borr, after all. Odin waved the others to calmness. "You need not worry. I will uphold any oath my father made."

"Borr did not make us an oath, exactly." Frigg laid a

hand on his forearm, then jerked her arm away as if Odin truly were aflame. "I ..."

"Daughter?" Hadding coughed again. "Are you well?"

"The weight of urd crashes upon us ..." Frigg's face had turned ashen, eyes staring off at something beyond sight.

Urd? Now she spoke of Fate. She talked like ... Frey's flaming sword! "You're a fucking völva."

For the jarl's oldest daughter to be a völva—she must have had some natural gift to be chosen for such a calling. Völvur didn't marry, not often, so the jarl sacrificed a valuable political asset. But some women were born with unnatural insight. You couldn't trust them. They were always messing with strange plants, speaking to ghosts. And they could bespell a man's mind with their beguiling seid.

Let a völva get her legs around you, and she'd ensorcel you. A völva's trench was as dangerous as a troll's fist.

Frigg blinked, shook her head, then scowled as if suddenly aware of him once again. "You say that as if it were a bad thing. Do the Wodanar not rely on their own völvur?"

His father had. He had looked to Heidr for guidance. But the völva had not foreseen his death or betrayal, or had not warned him of it. She had failed her jarl. Odin would not make the same mistake of trusting in such Otherworldly insights.

Hadding's daughter was dangerous.

**4**

———

*A* low fire simmered in the pit in Frigg's room, its embers nigh burned out even as Sigyn huddled close, warming her hands. Sigyn's half sister had returned from the Wodan town, and returned with the new jarl of that tribe, no less. Like any völva, Frigg did what she did with a plan, though she oft kept close-lipped on the details. The völva wanted Sigyn's advice, of course, but had too much pride to ask for it or even to reveal her own endgame. Not that she had to.

Whenever they played tafl—one more game sat abandoned on the board nearby—Sigyn always won, much to her elder sister's chagrin. Frigg saw the board and the pieces, thought about her turns, and yet, somehow never quite wrapped her mind around the finite possibilities of such a game. A limited number of moves existed and, discounting moves made without logic, fewer still remained.

The Hasding tribe teetered upon a precipice, poised to collapse and be annihilated by any other tribe, be it the Skalduns, Godwulfs, or Itrmanni.

Sigyn's stomach churned at the thought of such a day.

Men would come with fire and lust, burning and raping, quick to enslave whomever they could and butcher the rest. Warriors, like her foster family, they would die. Noble women, like her sister, would be lucky to find themselves forced into marriage.

Even the Wodan tribe, those Frigg pled to for succor, had become a source of unpredictability. Their new jarl might embrace Borr's peace or reject it, and betray the Hasdingi to their enemies. It meant Frigg needed to sway this Odin and do so quickly, before he set his course. To win him to their side, the Hasdingi would need to seduce him, be it with silver, political power, or a more literal seduction, and the völva daughter of a jarl would know of all such means.

From the way Frigg sat now, eyes staring into the flames, Sigyn could guess how well any of those tactics had worked. Frigg's maid, Fulla, brought a bowl of soup to her lady, then offered Sigyn one as well. Unlike everyone else in the fortress, the maid had never looked on Sigyn with disdain. Truly, even from a servant, a woman had to appreciate that.

"Careful now," Fulla said. The maid had fiery red hair, a face full of freckles, and an over-quick smile. "It's plenty hot and more than fresh."

"How can something be *more* than fresh?" Sigyn mumbled, not really looking at the maid.

"Really, now, that's a silly question from such a smart girl. You just have to ask the cooks, you do, you tell them 'I want this extra fresh,' and they give it to you. With a smile. Most times you just have to ask for what you want."

Sigyn snorted.

"See now." Fulla pointed a finger at her. "You didn't leave the alfar their copper, did you? Now I told you twice, you just need to offer up a copper—in the right place, of course, in an alf stone—and they'd help you find yourself luck in love. But you didn't try it, did you now?"

"No man wants a wife smarter than she is," Sigyn mumbled under her breath. Freyja, she was tired of hearing her father spout that nonsense! She'd think the daughter of the jarl—even the *bastard* daughter—would have prospects. And yet, nineteen winters was already nigh past marrying age. She shook her head at Fulla. "If the alfar exist at all, why would they take the least interest in who a mortal girl married?"

Fulla opened her mouth, but Frigg answered first. "They exist, all the vaettir do, sister, just beyond the edge of our world. The Otherworlds touch ours in places. Do not forget that."

"*And*," Fulla added, "they'd care about your marriage if you paid them the copper, they would."

Sigyn rolled her eyes.

"Jarl Odin has a grander urd upon him than I would have first thought." Frigg looked at Sigyn. There it was, wanting advice, wanting to know how to plan her next move, but too proud to ask for it.

Sigyn folded her arms. "You've had one of your visions." She made special effort to keep any disdain from her voice. "But you don't know what it means, whether you saw some truth or whether your vision was the result of smoking nasty weeds."

"I do not smoke weeds, sister."

Sure. "If you are so convinced of your mystical abilities, why do you still doubt them?"

"I do not *doubt* my visions. I just ... Odin cares only for avenging his father and seemed more than taken aback to learn of my status."

Sigyn raised an eyebrow.

"Oh, I did not tell him I was a völva. He determined as much after I read him."

Sigyn sighed, then poked the fire. Tending it was Fulla's task, but Sigyn was used to taking care of such things herself. Not everyone grew up in the jarl's fortress. Unlike Frigg, Sigyn had learned independence from a young age. "Whatever you plan now will fail, not because you've chosen the wrong plan, but because you've chosen the wrong time. When you lost your mother, would you have received the advances of a man, political, sexual, or otherwise?"

Frigg frowned and rubbed her arms at the mention of Fjorgyn's death two winters back. Sigyn had comforted Frigg as best she could, but Fjorgyn had always despised Sigyn as the reminder of her husband's infidelity. Only with Fjorgyn's death had Sigyn even been allowed inside her father's hall. It made it hard to truly mourn the woman's passing. Her death did not make this place home, though, nor did it endear her to anyone in it. She came here for Frigg, because her sister needed her, even if she hated to admit it.

Fulla clucked her tongue. "Now why'd you have to go and bring that up? Here my lady was almost able to forget how her mother went and died like that. It's a hard thing you know, a hard thing indeed, losing a parent. Now I would know, see. I lost both my parents back in the war, and here I was a tiny girl, not even ten winters."

Sigyn fixed Fulla with a level gaze, but the maid didn't catch the barest hint of her intent. The Njarar War had cost them all a great deal. Sigyn's mother had died, too, and her father would have exposed her to the winter were it not for his thegn Agilaz taking her in. She sympathized with Fulla, of course, but the woman had the unending effusiveness of a girl of three winters and the credulity to match. "If you wish to win Odin to our side," she said to her sister, "help him avenge Borr. Then, while he is flush with victory, *then* you start making your moves."

Frigg frowned. "Yes, I told him about a tracker who came here, one Father has housed in the fortress."

Sigyn shrugged. "Good. How you help him doesn't matter overmuch, just that, if he succeeds, he remembers he owes you. And if he fails, still he knows you aided him as best you could." She rose, stretching.

"You won't stay here tonight?" Frigg asked.

Sigyn shook her head. Sleeping in Frigg's room she'd be safe enough, yes, but not even their father seemed to want her here. She had better places to be, places where people might relish her company, and where none would look on her with the contempt of Hadding's court.

5

———

*H*alfhaugr lay at the center of Aujum, and thus some might have called it the heart of Aesir lands. It earned its name from the hill it sat on, broken as if a jotunn had cleft it in half. A spiked wooden wall protected the town, with a single entrance by the river. Odin had visited here before, of course, and like now, he could not decide whether he ought to be impressed at the defenses or not. Yes, the strong wall and the fortress beyond probably kept the people safe within—even as it kept them prisoner in their own homes, slaves to the fears that surrounded them. Fears of the mist, of the vaettir, of even the other tribes of Aesir all too eager to claim this central location.

Odin's tribe traded the security of such places for the ability to pursue game as it migrated. The Hasdingi would have to send their hunters far and wide to feed themselves. These people were ruled by their fears. Whatever they feared ... they long ago had let it conquer them. And a people conquered once could be conquered again.

Still, the fortress itself was built of ancient stone, marked with strange runes perhaps only völvur could read. It stood tall, with a pair of ravens sitting atop its peak as if taunting him. Ravens fed on corpses, and taking this place would create a great many of those.

Jarl Hadding had given his guest a room within the fortress. Odin and Tyr awaited this foreigner now, sitting in a feast hall lit by too few braziers and no windows. The whole place was choked in shadow and stank of too many men, women, and hounds huddling too close together.

"I do not understand why you think some foreigner will find what I could not," Tyr said. "Your place is guiding your tribe. Not charging off alone on such a vain hope."

Odin shrugged. "Go back to them, if you will. I'll not let any chance to avenge Father pass me by."

The shadows half masked Tyr's answering scowl. Tyr cracked his neck. "I have no intention of letting the heir of Borr get himself killed."

They sat apart from the other Hasding warriors. A few had tried to approach, to offer mead or elk flesh for the night meal. Odin had accepted the food but ushered away company. He did not come here seeking companionship from the cowards hiding behind these walls.

"I'm not going to die."

Tyr thumped the table with his forefinger. "I fear you haven't given proper thought to our *own* guest. Idunn. She comes to you and asks you to fulfill Borr's legacy. To make yourself king of Aesir. How can you back away from such a calling? What better way to honor your father? If you were to unite the Aesir we could fulfill his dreams and more."

Odin rubbed the stubble on his chin before fixing Tyr with a level gaze. Surely his father's thegn knew better than that. Odin had a greater duty to his father. He had sworn blood vengeance, and he was damned tired of having to remind everyone of that.

A figure drifted toward them, moving in and out of fire-light and shadow. The man nodded at them as he drew nigh, and Odin motioned for him to sit. The stranger did so, staring at Odin with intensely blue eyes, almost like crystal. Deep, haunted, seeming to know too much. Like some damned völva. The stranger had reddish brown hair hanging down to his cheekbones, contrasting with the darker hair of his short beard.

"You are Loki?" Odin asked.

"Yes, Odin, I am."

Frigg must have told him about them. The man didn't talk like a foreigner, though the völva had referred to him as such. His skin tone was a bit deeper than normal, though perhaps not so much as Idunn's. "Where do you hail from?"

Loki laced his fingers together on the table, eyes refusing to release Odin from their gaze. "That's not what you came here to ask me, nor would names of far off lands hold much meaning to your ears."

"Miklagard?" The southern empire was more legend than place, at least to most tribes, but Odin had heard the Friallaf tribe had fought several skirmishes against them. They sailed the Black Sea in great longships every summer, seeking plunder and glory.

The barest hint of a smile quirked on Loki's face. "Would you not rather speak of the true purpose of your visit to Halfhaugr? Do the empires of the South Realms hold true interest for you now?"

Odin shrugged. "No. I want to know about Unterhagen. So unless Miklagarders were the ones to massacre the village ... Do you know of it?"

"I know it. I walked there the day after it fell."

Before even Tyr or Odin.

Tyr leaned forward across the table now, staring at the

foreigner. "Then how do we know you were not with the raiders who wrought this havoc?"

"You saw the ruins, did you not? And do you believe it the work of men? Men are indeed capable of the vilest of deeds, of terrible savagery, but there are forces of chaos in the wild possessed of far greater strength than men."

"You mean trolls," Tyr said, the warrior's disgust obvious in his voice. Odin had seen a troll only once in his life and had been fortunate enough not to have to fight it. The creatures were ungodly strong, and worse, had hides like solid rock.

No doubt trolls could have done it, but still ... "They killed the women, too. Trolls claim human women as wives."

Loki nodded. "Then it seems something other than trolls must have wrought the chaos. So then, what else could there be? When you think upon the wild, upon the lands beyond the Realm of men, what comes to mind?"

Odin folded his arms. The foreigner was playing some kind of game with him, one he did not much appreciate. "Speak plainly, man. If you know what else besides trolls might have ..." Beyond the Realm of men. Beyond the ... He shook his head. "No. If you are having a jest with me, I warn you I have no mood for it."

"Before the snows buried the tracks, one could see footprints too large for a man."

Tyr groaned. "You think a fucking jotunn did this?"

The jottunar were supposed to live beyond the Midgard Wall, banished into the outer Realm of Utgard by the Vanir. Supposed to, but then, he and Tyr knew of at least one on this side. Odin glanced at Tyr, who shook his head.

"Hymir dwells very far from here, in Bjarmaland," Tyr said. "I do not think he could have come here without someone learning of it." Bjarmaland lay far to the east, nigh unto where the boundary of the Midgard Wall supposedly lay, encircling the Realm of men and warding it against the greatest forces of chaos. The Aesir had lived there, genera-tions back, before King Vingethor had brought them here in the Great March. And Tyr was right: if the jotunn had left his kingdom in Bjarmaland, surely stories would have spread.

Loki stared at Tyr now. "There is another who has crossed the Wall. Older and more powerful than his descen-dant Hymir. One called Ymir."

The thegn scoffed. "I say this man is a liar, Odin. He could not possibly know the things of which he speaks. Even if he went to Unterhagen, even if he saw the tracks. You think *tracks* told him the *name* of their owner? If he speaks truth at all, it could only be because he serves the fucking jotunn."

Odin bit back his response. Tyr would know about serving a jotunn. In service to Hymir, Tyr had raped and murdered, plundered and razed his way through half of Aujum. Until Father had stopped him. But Father had asked Odin never to speak of that.

Loki did not immediately answer, as a slave girl came and offered them a fresh drinking horn. Odin took it, took a long swig of the mead, then passed it to Tyr.

As the girl left, Loki smiled, just a little. "Anger is apt to cloud perception, and ignorance to narrow the possibilities you can conceive of. So burdened, a man blinds himself quite easily. Forgets, perhaps, one might take independent pieces of information and from them cobble together a clearer whole."

Tyr drained the horn without offering a single sip to Loki, then belched before turning to Odin. "This man seeks to lure you with honeyed words. Like a skald. I cannot say what he wants, and for that alone, I say we leave him be. Go back. Talk to Idunn, give weight to her words."

At that Loki's smile slipped and he frowned. He did not speak, however, instead fixing Odin with that intense gaze of his.

Odin stared back a moment before answering. "Where do I find this Ymir?"

"In the peaks of the Sudurberks, not so very far from Unterhagen."

"My lord," Tyr said. "You cannot consider this. Even if he speaks truth, the Sudurberks cover half of Midgard. How will you search such a massive area?"

"I can track Ymir," Loki said.

Odin nodded. Yes. Finally, progress. Father would know peace.

"You cannot fight a jotunn," Tyr said. "They are larger and stronger than men. Than even trolls. It is Mist-madness taking you."

Odin slammed his fist on the table, drawing every eye in the feast hall. "Tyr! I tire of your complaints. If you are so enamored with the woman claiming to be Idunn, go back to her. And tell my brothers to meet me at Unterhagen. *We* will hunt down our father's murderer."

Tyr rose, mouth agape, stammering for a moment. "M-my lord? My place is by your—"

"Go!" Odin snapped. "Go and send for my brothers."

Tyr rolled his shoulders, then cracked his neck. His hand toyed with the arm ring Father had given him as a symbol of his loyalty. Loyalty that ought now to bind him to Odin's commands. "As you wish."

The foreigner watched as Tyr stormed out of the hall,

then turned back to Odin. "Your warrior wishes to do right by you."

Odin grunted. He knew that, and he sure as Hel didn't need some foreigner to tell him. "Right now, all I care about is Father. This jotunn took him from me, and for that I will send his soul screaming down to Hel. Anyone not helping with that is just in the way."

"Oh, I will help you, Odin. Count on that."

$\mathcal{M}$any winters, Sigyn and her foster family stayed in Vestborg, the hunting fort Hadding had long ago granted to Agilaz, but Sigyn's foster family also owned a house here at Halfhaugr. They had remained here all winter. Much as Sigyn welcomed the chance to spend more time with Frigg, she abhorred the true reason they had wintered in Halfhaugr. And, as usual, her opinion counted about as much as single snowflakes did in a blizzard.

Torch in one hand, she swung open the house gate. Their house hound, Shortsnout, rushed over and licked her hand with the enthusiasm and affection a woman found only in a dog. She patted the animal and whispered to him, before ushering him back toward the house.

Her foster brother, Hermod, stood in the barn, feeding Snow Rabbit. Agilaz had won the mare from a man who had enough mead to think he could outshoot the master archer, and ever since, Hermod had treated the horse as a member of the family. "You come back late. We already took night meal."

Sigyn shrugged. "Frigg has a guest."

Hermod had nigh unto six winters on her. Whereas Agilaz had taught Sigyn basic woodcraft and archery, he had taught his son all he knew, shaping him into a master hunter and a talented warrior. Sigyn had once asked Olrun to train her as a shieldmaiden, but her foster mother had refused, claiming a woman with Sigyn's mind and lineage could do more off the battlefield than on it.

*Lineage*. A bloodline that damned her every which way she turned, leaving her with no place in the halls of the nobility, nor quite one outside those halls. Just important enough to warrant respect, meaning men whispered about her only when they thought she couldn't hear. *Odd one, that Sigyn. Always flitting from one craft to the next. Never settling like a proper lady.* She knew she was beautiful—that wasn't the issue. She had long, blonde hair even Frigg envied, though her sister wouldn't admit that. Breasts, hips—all in the proportions any man should have wanted. She hated to believe her father had the right of it, but in truth, hiding her intelligence had become a matter of course, at least outside her family.

She tapped a finger to her lip, waiting to see if Hermod would say more, but he just nodded and went back to caring for the damned horse. He never scorned her the way others did, but then, he didn't exactly *see* her either. And soon, he'd never get the chance.

Sighing, she turned to head inside and almost crashed into Olrun. The blonde woman might have passed for Sigyn's real mother—they shared similar enough features, save Olrun's much more pronounced muscles, taut from years of swinging a sword. The woman put a hand on the back of Sigyn's neck and pulled her into an embrace. If her foster family didn't exactly know what to do with her, at least they always welcomed her.

The moment Sigyn broke away, Olrun pulled her inside.

Agilaz sat inside, by the fire pit, the ever-solemn expression on his face. He nodded at Sigyn, and then, at some look from his wife, rose and headed outside without a word. Not a good sign. Shortsnout hopped up and followed his master outside, leaving Sigyn alone with Olrun.

After dousing her torch, Sigyn sat, helping herself to what remained of a snow fox. No matter how hard winter grew, her foster father always managed to bring home something to eat. Unlike many in Halfhaugr, Sigyn rarely had to live with hunger.

Olrun slumped down across from her. Her foster parents were not nigh as old as her real father, but still, time had worn on them. Olrun did not speak of her past much, so Sigyn could only guess at her age. She had fought as a shieldmaiden in the Njarar War, and that had started twenty winters back, so Olrun must be fast approaching forty winters herself. Old enough she probably expected grandchildren soon. And now she'd finally get them.

"We need every tie we can get to the Godwulfs," Olrun said.

Sigyn stuffed more fox in her face so she wouldn't have to answer. Olrun was more perceptive than her son, it seemed. The woman had a secret Sigyn had never quite uncovered, and not for lack of trying. She had thought, once, to trick Hermod into revealing the truth, but he had only claimed his mother had once been a valkyrie, having a jest at Sigyn's expense.

"If the engagement fails, Hadding's brother will have one more reason to stake his claim to this place."

Sigyn nodded, doing her utmost to seem in total accord with whatever Olrun said. Hadding's brother Alci was jarl of the Godwulfs, but as a blood relative to Hadding, he did have a claim on Hadding's lands. Especially with his brother's health faltering and Father having no male heir. Hermod's marriage to a Godwulf noble's daughter would help ease the growing tensions between the tribes, or so Jarl Hadding had convinced himself. After all, the son of his most trusted thegn? Hermod was the best Hadding could offer—since Frigg was a völva and Sigyn was apparently worthless.

She swallowed a greasy bite. Don't say it. She should not speak, not now. "If Alci wants Halfhaugr, you really think marrying Hermod to someone not even directly related to him will stop him?" And she said it.

Olrun scowled. Yes, Sigyn should have kept her damned mouth shut. "It will *help*."

Sure it would. Sigyn tossed a bone in the fire pit. "Well, then, I want to help too. I'll ride with Agilaz and Hermod to meet the Godwulfs."

Olrun shook her head and sighed. "*Sigyn*. No good can come from your going, and I fear a great deal of misfortune might follow from it."

"Njord knows when or if we'll see Hermod again. I will go to bid my brother farewell."

Olrun scooted closer until her face rested nigh unto Sigyn's, and when she spoke, she did so in a whisper. "As long as you do so as a sister only. Do not confuse my son."

Sigyn sighed and nodded. She would not confuse anyone.

No one save, perhaps, herself.

## 7

*F*ool son of Borr. Placing his trust in some foreign wanderer instead of the goddess in their midst. Tyr knew better. You had to trust the gods. They were all that stood between man and chaos. The Realms of Utgard pushed against Midgard. Tyr had seen it, been part of it, before Borr. Before a jarl had saved him from the darkness, from the cold.

He had seen more than his fill of both.

Men were animals, until someone taught them honor. Tyr had been worse than any berserk or varulf.

Ve knelt nearby, stuffing his satchel with supplies for their fool endeavor. Tyr should go with them. He'd sworn to Borr to protect his sons. And if they went alone ... Blame Loki for this fuckery. You couldn't trust a man with a silver tongue.

"You know of the jotunnar, thegn," Ve said. "You've seen them."

Tyr grunted. "One."

"How is a man to face such a threat?"

A man was like to shit himself and die screaming. Boy

probably didn't need to hear that. "Try to catch him unawares. Strike fast. Strike hard. They have strength many times that of a man. Don't think to block its blows on your shield. All you'll get is a broken arm and broken shield."

The young skald shook his head, not quite hiding his fear. A brave man fought other men. A fool fought jotunnar. "The tales we'll have about this one."

Yes. Skalds might call it *The Fall of the Sons of Borr*. Njord watch over the fool brothers. Tyr spat in the snow and walked away. Odin had forbidden him to come. Had chosen that damned foreigner. Taken any choice out of Tyr's hands.

At least, he had no choice about the jotunn. Still, the goddess remained in Eskgard. Odin had granted her a house here. Jarl did one thing right. Tyr trod through the town, feet crunching well-packed snow. A pair of hunters drove a dog sled past him, hauling in a reindeer carcass. Good catch. They'd feed half the town with that. The best was always a mammoth, of course. But bringing one down oft cost lives, good men. They'd lost two last moon trying for a big mammoth. Beast escaped too. After that, Tyr had helped bring down another for Borr's funeral himself.

He shook his head. Idunn had said Mankind was dying. All he'd seen, he could almost believe it. Even if jotunnar and other forces of Utgard did not threaten Midgard, still, he'd believe it. You had to trust a goddess when she spoke.

At her house, he paused. How did you approach a goddess? He didn't know protocol from troll shit when it came to gods and goddesses. Treat her like a jarl? Without a better plan, he rapped his fist on the door.

"Enter."

He did.

Idunn sat in front of the fire pit. Three children rested nearby, looking at him like an intruder. She winked. "Come to hear to my stories too? A good tale transcends genera-tions while knitting them closer together. It's an art, Tyr."

"Skald's work." He shook his head. "I would speak with you. Alone."

"Hmmm. And as always, the children suffer. All right, go on then. I'll continue the tale after the night meal. The best stories are told after dark anyway."

The children groaned. One, a girl of five or six winters, cast him a baleful glare as they left. Tyr shut the door behind them.

"Your fame has spread through Aujum. Borr's great thegn. Men speak as though you have no equal with a blade in all the North Realms."

"Huh. Not sure about that." He sat down in front of her. Most men didn't know what a bastard he'd been before he met Borr. The jarl had held that secret close, to protect Tyr. Save him from well-earned revenge. "You told Odin to become a king."

"Oh, yes. For certain that must be the first step. He'll need the Aesir behind him, united against greater threats."

"What threats? Jotunnar?"

Idunn shrugged. "There are certainly ones who mean Mankind ill, yes."

Tyr grunted. What he knew of them, they didn't neces-sarily mean man ill. Not exactly. They were just happy to prey on men. Take whatever they had, devour or enslave them. Fell creatures, too at home in the mist.

"And you came here just to ask me if I meant what I said? That I wanted Odin to become king?"

"Uh, no. I wanted to know how we do it."

Idunn warmed her hands by the fire. "Yes. He does not seem well set on the idea, does he? One would expect a man to seize the opportunity for such fame, and yet he cast it aside, unable to accept the urd. Or perhaps unwilling to shoulder the responsibility that accompanies such glory. If only urd were so kind as to ask us our wishes, perhaps he would live a peaceful life. But that seems unlikely to me."

"You know a man's urd?"

She laughed. "I'm not one of the Norns, Tyr. I don't weave urds, but I can guess, read the signs. Sometimes a man chooses glory. Sometimes it is thrust upon him by necessity or by those around him."

"Huh." Borr's legacy was about to crumble in Odin's uncaring hands. While Odin was off chasing a jotunn, the tribes simmered in discontent. Come summer and the melting of snows, war was like to tear them apart. Unless someone held them together, as Borr had wished. "You think we can force it on him? Force him to accept the responsibility of kingship? Save the peace?"

"Were you so inclined to try, what would you do, Tyr? How would you secure a throne for Odin? Hypothetically speaking."

Tyr groaned. He cracked his neck. She was asking him? What did he know of kingship or politics? Tyr was a warrior, a killer. Better than he had been, yes, but still … men feared him for his blade, not his skill at tafl. "All I know is defending and attacking."

"And how many winters did you pass at Borr's side, watching as he held the tribes together, one carefully woven knot at a time? Did you see naught of the ties he tried to forge?"

He had been there, most of the time. True enough. He pinched the bridge of his nose. Such things made his head throb. "The Athra tribe in the north. Borr's wife came from them. Odin's cousin Annar rules the tribe. But he didn't come to the funeral. Strange, that."

Idunn grinned. "A potential ally. Family is complicated, Tyr. It's important to know where they stand."

He grunted. If Odin wasn't going to choose to save his father's work, Tyr would do it for him. That seemed to be what the goddess wanted of him. You had to try to understand the gods when you could. "I'll go, talk to Annar. Maybe he might support Odin at the Althing."

Idunn nodded. "Be careful, then."

Tyr was always careful. Kept you alive longer, at least on a good day.

**8**

———

*S*itting, waiting in Unterhagen—Odin knew he tortured himself even coming here—he could not look away. Could not stop staring at the ruined, snow-covered village. Could not quite still the voice somewhere in his mind that expected his father to step around a mound of snow, walk over, and embrace him. Ask why he was fretting.

Father did not come.

Not in the flesh, at any rate. Perhaps his ghost watched Odin now, waiting, as Odin did, his back to the fire Loki had built. The lamentations of so many murdered ghosts filled the air here. Not something he could hear—unless it were the howling wind—but he could feel it. Like the hunger of a man who hadn't eaten in days.

The foreigner spoke little, seemed to understand Odin's desire for solitude. If that was what he truly wished. Like the dead, he dwelt in isolated misery, unable to find solace in others. Because, like the dead, no living man could understand his anguish. Or so he was apt to think in bouts of melancholy that served no one.

"Do your parents still live?" Odin asked, without looking back at the man.

The foreigner did not immediately answer, but Odin could hear him poking at the fire. "All my family, and all I have loved, are gone now, lost in the march of years."

"I seem to have opened an old wound." Odin watched the snowdrifts. He had been wrong. Loki clearly did know suffering.

And still no one came. Father would never again walk by his side. Odin kept telling himself that, but his mind refused to accept it. Such a great man could not be snuffed out in an instant like a flame doused. It should have been ... different.

"Some wounds never quite heal," Loki said. "They scab over, perhaps, and we become so accustomed to the pain we may forget it's there. And the reminder of it does not cause the pain, just forces us to acknowledge it once more."

Odin grunted, then did turn back to face him. Loki was staring into the fire like a man looking into the eyes of his mistress. "You understand pain."

"Those who do not have not lived overlong in this world."

"And do you find your answer in the flames?"

Loki shrugged. "Fire is life."

Odin grunted. So he knew. "Yet I find myself weary of life, drawn ever to think on the fallen."

Loki shook his head. "There is a darkness pervading the Realm of the living, I grant, but do not mistake the Other-worlds as cleaner or clearer, Odin, for they are Realms of lies. Like memories twisted in the back of your mind, the dead *lie*." He pointed off in the distance. "Your brothers approach."

IN THE MORNING, they had set out south, toward the Sudurberks. Ve, the youngest of the three brothers, constantly yammered on with Loki. The foreigner did not *quite* engage Ve in his contests of poetry, though certainly he spoke with the authority of a skald, if not the grandeur. Not exactly.

"All who travel far are said to see much," Ve said. "Surely then, a wanderer such as yourself might enthrall us with tales of Miklagard or even Serkland. Speak, then, of wonders that we might know the glories of your wanderings."

Vili grumbled under his breath, as he so often did when their youngest brother got into his moods. "Man claims to have seen Miklagard, and you believe him? Fools, both of you."

Loki glanced at Odin, the hint of a wry smile on his face. "If I had seen Miklagard or Serkland or Nidavellir or even beyond, would it bear relevance to the task at hand? Or do you seek to distract yourself from the fears that prey upon you, from the threat you march toward?"

"You calling me a craven?" Vili demanded.

"I don't believe I did."

Vili grumbled again, and moved needlessly close to Loki, probably trying to intimidate him with his size. As a berserk, Vili was always torn in two—part of him human, part of him driven by a savage animal spirit. He looked the part, standing a full head taller than Odin.

If it bothered Loki, he gave no indication.

"What my brother wants to know," Ve said, "is how you can know so much about the jotunnar? About this one in particular, one of whom we have heard no songs nor stories."

"Oh?" Loki asked. He walked across the snow with ease,

not even relying on snowshoes. "Have you not heard the tales of Aurgelmir, the lord of the rime jotunnar? It seems a significant lapse in the education of any skald."

Vili spat. "What the fuck is Aurgelmir?"

Ve chuckled nervously. "Father of the frost jotunnar, at least according to some tales. Maybe a progenitor of their whole line. So you're saying this Ymir *is* Aurgelmir?" Ve scrambled a little closer to Odin, who rolled his eyes.

"Bah!" Their berserk brother spat again. "The foreigner makes you into a fool, little brother. Look at you, quivering at the thought of such a thing. You truly believe the father of all frost jotunnar exists, lives still, and came out to smash a small village on the edge of Aujum? Next you'll tell me you believe that troll shit about men and women coming from different trees."

Ve chuckled. "My brother, a poet you are not, in word nor soul. You doubt every tale right up until you find yourself enmeshed in it, then scream and chop and hew until the tale submits to your liking."

The berserk spat again, grumbling under his breath as they walked. His mumbles persisted until nigh unto sunset, while Ve continued to pry against Loki's wits. Odin found himself only half listening. His youngest brother had a clever tongue, but he seemed to have finally found a man he could not outsmart. Odin cared very little for these duels of wits, even before. Before such things became utter pettiness in the face of all-consuming loss and the need to avenge that loss upon the whole World.

As evening drew nigh, Loki directed them toward a ruined tower in the foothills beneath the Sudurberks. Though built from stone two feet thick, a breach twice the size of a man tore through the wall, allowing a thick drift of snow to pile up inside. The tower's peak had fallen, its rubble no doubt buried in the snows that blanketed the hill.

"Men must take what shelter they can," Ve said, "but vaettir are drawn to such places. Njord knows what kind of fell being might dwell within, and we brought no hounds to sniff them out."

Torch out before him, Loki kept pushing on toward the tower. "A long time ago, even before Njord was king of the Vanir, they built towers like these to watch the mountains."

Ve snorted. "Naught happened *before* Njord was king. Any skald could tell you that. Your illusion of wisdom falters, foreigner."

Odin glanced from Loki to his brother, then pushed on toward the breach in the tower wall. Who to believe? Certainly völvur seemed to agree with Ve, that one ought to avoid ruins when possible. Remnants of the Old Kingdoms dotted all of the North Realms, places once glorious, built to ward against the mist or each other. Now, though, trolls, draugar, and other vaettir lurked in such places, hiding from sunlight and venturing out at night. So völvur said. But then again, when facing a winter storm, sometimes a man had to take whatever shelter he could.

"So you think the Vanir themselves built this tower?" Odin asked.

Loki brought his torch close to the outer wall, then began to chip at ice crusted upon the stone. A large chunk of it fell free, and Loki brushed aside what remained with his forearm. The walls bore some kind of runes, but such symbols meant naught to Odin, nor to any man. Only völvur learned such arts. And how had Loki known to find one there?

"Before the rise of the Old Kingdoms, the Vanir waged unending wars against the jotunnar. Many of their foes dwelt in these mountains, so the Vanir built towers to watch for them, guard against them. Sometimes they succeeded, and sometimes the walls could not withstand the violence of such manifestations of chaos." Loki swept his torch around to indicate the breach in the wall. "The storm will get worse, and we ought to save our strength for the journey through the mountains."

Odin grunted, then climbed over the snow pile to reach the inside of the tower. A spiraling stair led to the upper regions, but he already knew those had collapsed. Still, the ceiling here remained intact, and a wide fire pit lay in the tower's center. He nodded. Loki was right. This place was the best respite they were like to find before nightfall.

"Vili," Odin said. "Go find whatever wood you can. We need to get a blaze going before the sun sets." Sparse trees—evergreens, mostly—covered these foothills, though none survived higher up in the mountains. This might prove their last chance to make fresh torches or rest safe by a fire. "Ve, sweep the tower and make sure we truly are alone." Besides vaettir, one always had to worry about cave hyenas, bears, and other predators. They all liked such places.

Loki drifted around the edge of this central room, inspecting shelves that lined the walls. Some of those shelves held what must be parchment. Men in the South Realms used such things. Bits of it crumbled as Loki touched it, and Odin scoffed. And that was why völvur carved their runes into stone and wood. Lasted longer.

The foreigner paid no attention, lifting a piece the size of his hand up close toward his face. Wait ... could he *read* the markings upon it? That sounded most unmanly of him. Odin folded his arms. Indeed, if Loki spoke the truth and the Vanir had built this place, how did the foreigner know that? How could he guess what had happened before the

Old Kingdoms? The most learned skalds Odin had ever known had a few tales, stories of the Vanir from the old times, but Loki spoke with more authority than that. Was his guide a skald himself? And one who could read?

Odin's brothers had distrusted Loki the moment they met him, as had Tyr. But Tyr was filled with suspicion and doubt, Vili never liked anyone, and Ve probably saw Loki as a threat to his own status as a skald. Still. He knew—or claimed to know—more than any man ought.

Such a man might well bring disaster among them by fumbling into eldritch lore not meant for man or even for Mankind. Such was the man with whom Odin had entrusted his chance at vengeance.

## 9

_T_he crunch of his snowshoes rang out louder than Tyr would have liked. Especially with evening drawing nigh. Still no shelter. Just the woods. On and on. Not the Jarnvid. He'd have known if he'd wandered into the twisted forest of the trolls. But woods covered much of Aujum. The Athra lived in towns in the north, by the Gandvik Sea. Whalers. Had to pass through all these woods to reach them. Woods, and lands held by the Godwulfs.

The only other way would have taken him through Skaldun lands, and Tyr would not go there. Not until he must.

Njord grant him a ruin, a cave, something. Somewhere he could kindle a flame against the encroaching night. He'd never get a blaze going in this snow. The crunch of ice sounded off, and he froze in place. Had that come from behind him?

Tyr spun, hand on his sword hilt. Naught back there but trees. Those, too, could house vaettir, watching. Angry at the trespass of a man in silent woods. Ash wives demanded sacrifices, and the only blood Tyr had was his own.

Fuck.

Traveling alone. Fool plan. Maybe he ought to have convinced Vili or Ve to come. Vili, especially. The berserk had good ears, a strong nose. Not like a varulf, but still. Better than Tyr.

The sun would set in moments. He couldn't keep wandering all night. In the dark he'd become too easy prey for the denizens here. Sighing, he stuck his torch in the snow, wedged it tight. He lit two more, placing each around the spot he'd chosen in a triangle. Then he began gathering pine leaves, branches, aught that might have a chance of burning. He had to try.

All those he flung into a pile, then wedged a fourth torch in their midst, low enough for the flames to touch the tinder. By now, the sun had set, leaving him in almost total darkness save the torchlight.

A howl broke through the night, seeming to come from all around him. The howl might have been a wolf. But just one made no sense. Wolves were pack hunters. Even the largest ones, dire wolves, always stuck together. A lone wolf meant something fell, rabid, or possessed by the mists. Or a lone varulf, somehow cast out of his pack. A varulf meant a foe with human-like intelligence and supernatural cunning. It would stalk him.

Tyr dropped into a crouch by one of the torches and slid his sword free. Wait here. Let the wolf come to him. Normal wolf, even a dire wolf, it might not approach the flame. Varulf, though, it would make him prey. Maybe even come back with more of its kind.

Hunt, or be hunted. He wrapped his palm around the torch haft. Carry that, and the varulf would see him coming a mile away. Without it, Tyr couldn't see five feet. Mist, tree cover, they didn't let much moonlight in. His grip tightened around his sword hilt. Make a choice.

The obvious choice. The one Hymir would have had him choose. Risk it all, and win. The jotunn was a monster, an eater of man. And a survivor. Tyr groaned. No choice, really. He released the torch and stalked forward, staying low to the ground as he passed from tree to tree.

Beyond the light of his torches, he paused. Fresh paw prints in the snow, definitely canine, and large. Large enough to be dire wolf or varulf. And it had passed close. Just outside the circle of his flame.

Another growl.

As he rose, Tyr's eyes met those of a wolf, not a few feet away. Watching him from the mists. Tyr froze in place, caught in its gaze. He dared not look away and invite the beast to charge.

The wolf growled, baring teeth far too long. Hot saliva dripped from the wolf's mouth, casting up steam as it hit the snows.

"Easy," Tyr said, keeping his voice barely audible.

The wolf advanced a step, its snarl deepening.

The sudden shift of its weight was the only warning. It flung itself forward, faster than a wolf ought to be able. Tyr tumbled backward as it collided with him. Barely managed to fling his arm up in its path. The wolf bit down, fangs rending his chain armor like cloth. It tore through flesh as it bore him down. Tyr screamed in pain, a flash of red. His sword fell from his grasp.

Too strong. Gnashing, growling, rending his flesh.

His screams of agony ringing in his ears.

Not like this. He had fought his way out of the darkness, out of the cold. Made himself a man instead of a monster. He would not end here in cold woods, alone.

He shoved forward, now heedless of the wounds the wolf inflicted. With his bloody arm, he pushed it back enough to draw a dagger from his belt. He thrust it upward, into the wolf's belly. The beast whimpered, immediately releasing his arm and falling over.

Tyr flung himself atop the creature and rammed the dagger into its skull. Bucking, thrashing, though it ought to have been dead. And then stillness. The creature shuddered. Fur receded back into its skin. Joints popped as bones shifted, the corpse slowly reverting to human as the wolf spirit fled, driven back to whatever Otherworld it came from.

The pain washed over him afresh, and he spilled forward. He needed to bind the wound. Groaning, he half walked, half crawled back to his makeshift camp. He grabbed his sword along the way.

Varulf had mauled his arm. Völva might have cut it off to save him. Fuck that. A warrior without his sword arm was better off dead. The kindling had caught aflame at last. Blood streaming out now. Whole fucking World spinning.

He thrust the blade into the flame. Then he emptied his satchel. Bandages. Couldn't be certain he'd stop bleeding though. Growling, he looked to the blade. Starting to glow hot. Fucking varulf.

It would hurt. A lot.

But Tyr had known pain. The jotunn had inflicted it. Forced Tyr to inflict worse still.

He grabbed the sword and pressed the scalding blade to his arm.

His screams echoed through the wood.

LOST BLOOD MADE A MAN DELIRIOUS. Twisted like the Mist-mad. Why wasn't he dead yet? Ought to have died from those wounds. Lost in the night. No, no. Tyr was fucking strong.

Forged in the cold by Hymir. Remade in the light by Borr. He wouldn't die like this.

Not like this.

Torch in his working arm, he stumbled, crashed into a tree and fell in the snow. Blood had seeped through his bandages and now stained the spot where he'd fallen. Die out here alone, rise again as a draug. Men said it, and Tyr had seen the vile creatures, denied death. Wakeful in eternal torment, and strong as a troll.

Ahead, a lodge. A small house of logs. Delirium?

Hunter's lodge. Godwulf hunter, most like. Maybe even the varulf he'd just killed a few hours back.

Or not. Could be another's.

Men didn't turn away guests. No one wanted to be left in the cold. At night, though, alone in the woods—only a fool would let a stranger in. Vaettir could come to your door, ask a boon. Take your soul.

He drew nearer. Plume of smoke rose from the lodge. Fire.

Fire was life.

And Tyr wasn't ready to die. And if the hunter wanted to turn him away?

He'd not die this night. If he fell, he could never fulfill his promise to Borr.

He stumbled over to the house, pounded on the door. No answer. But shuffling inside.

A simmering anger roiled in Tyr's gut. Maybe the hunter knew the varulf who'd attacked him. Maybe not. Either way … "Open the fucking door!"

"Be gone!" a woman shouted from within. "In Njord's name I cast you out."

"I'm not a fucking vaettr. Open the door!"

"Be gone, I say! There is naught for you here."

The heat in his gut filled his limbs. A surging rage born of delirium and hate. Tyr kicked the door. It shuddered on its hinges, wood splintering. He kicked again. It flew inward. The woman inside scrambled away, sword up before her.

"I need shelter."

She looked to his arm, dripping blood through the bandage. Then she grasped her sword with both hands and took a step forward.

Tyr growled, flung the torch at her head.

She shrieked and batted it away with the sword. In the moment, he launched himself forward, caught her wrist. Twisted. The blade clattered to the floor. She writhed in his grasp, so he punched her with his right hand, then used his good hand to grab her by the throat when her head flopped back. He hefted her off the ground, squeezing.

From the shadows cast by her hearth, Borr looked on with shame. Judged him for such a breach of all honor. He was doing this for Borr, for Borr's sons. Doing what? Murdering a hunter? Growling as much at himself as the woman, he slammed her against the wall then dropped her. She lay still on the floor.

"You wronged her," Borr said.

Not his ghost. No, just the delirium. Tyr snatched up her sword lest she wake and attack him again. Odd. Woven iron with an over-keen edge. No modern smith could make such works. Something from the Old Kingdoms or the dvergar, maybe. But how did a simple hunter woman claim it?

"You are like Hymir."

Tyr spun at the ghost. "Hymir would have fucking raped her and then eaten her!"

Of course, naught stood there. He knew that. It could not be. "And you want to do the same."

"Shut up! Silence!"

"How had you such strength, Tyr? Strength to heft her with one hand, to squeeze her unconscious. Strength like the very jotunn who forged you."

No! Anger, pain. They had given him strength. Naught more. "Go to Hel."

"She holds me because of your failure."

The words hit him like a blow, and he stumbled against the wall. "I ... I didn't ... You didn't tell me your plans ..."

"Petty excuses. No wonder your woman left you."

Tyr screamed in wordless rage and flung the woman's sword at the shadows. It clattered against the wall. He was done arguing with shadows. It was not Borr.

It was *not* Borr.

This huntress would have food, something he could use for fresh bandages. He'd tie her up, treat his injuries. Manage a few hours' sleep. And go.

A darkness settled in this lodge. One he'd best be free of soon as he could.

## 10

*T*oward evening, the Godwulf town came into view. They had made good time, Agilaz riding beside his son and Sigyn sitting behind him, pressed against a foster brother she might soon never see again. Snow Rabbit had carried them far each day, and they had needed spend only a few nights in the wild, to everyone's certain relief. Shortsnout trotted behind them all without complaint, though the aging hound collapsed with exhaustion each night. Agilaz had already convinced Hermod to keep the animal, saying he'd need a friend in his new home.

The Godwulf lands lay on the eastern reaches of Aujum, nigh unto where the Jarnvid formed much of the border with Bjarmaland. The tribe wandered, however, migrating with each passing summer, never wintering twice in the same place. Always, however, they remained around that accursed forest. They raided into Bjarmaland by skirting its edges, though no man, not even varulfur, would dare enter the Jarnvid. Skalds claimed trolls dwelt there in ancient burrows, and their tales engendered nightmares in every woman in Midgard. Trolls ate men, on that, every skald agreed, debating only on whether trolls cooked a man first. But they took women as *wives*, as some people referred to the abomination that befell such a woman. If she survived the rapes at all, she was like to be torn apart when an infant troll clawed itself from her womb.

And did trolls really exist, or rather, were they figments conjured up to frighten the gullible and keep women in line? Sigyn had spoken to no man—at least no man not swaying from drink—who had seen such creatures with his own eyes, and she had asked. In many a skald's tale, trolls were the misbegotten offspring of the equally fanciful jotunnar, the beings of chaos beyond the edge of Midgard. But then, she knew of no one who had seen Utgard, either.

A wolf howl rang out as they drew nearer the town of Kaldlund, drawing a growl from Shortsnout. Agilaz spoke softly to the hound, eyes locked on the direction the howl had come from.

The Godwulfs claimed to guard the Jarnvid lest the trolls emerge and threaten all the North Realms. Perhaps they even spoke truth, had indeed faced perilous fiends of the mist. More like, though, they used it as an excuse for their never-ending raiding, their own rape and plunder of foreigners and other Ás tribes alike. And varulfur *did* exist. They could plant their seed in a woman's belly, and, oft as not, the child would bear the traits of the father. Such were the men Hermod had been sent to live among.

She had drawn a little closer to him now. How could she not? Varulfur and berserkir could barely contain their aggression and lust when they *tried*, and most of them didn't bother, from what she heard. Agilaz had warned her against coming here, but she would not let go of Hermod without seeing him safe. If he was lost from her life, he ought at least to be able to live his own, even if it was among such savage brutes as these.

"Don't worry," Hermod said. "We are guests here. No harm will come to you."

"Mmmm." How was she to tell him she feared as much for him as for herself? Such a sentiment would insult his honor. And Olrun had spoken the truth—they did need peace with the Godwulfs, lest Hadding's varulf brother come to take Halfhaugr from them. If that happened, anarchy would fall upon the Hasding town. Frigg, their father, and everyone else Sigyn cared for would face a bloodbath.

Kaldlund had only a spiked wooden wall around it, no ancient stone wrought in times past. Scant protection against the mist and its denizens. A fur-swathed man met them at the gate, axe in his hand. He nodded at Agilaz, and her foster father rode up and dismounted before him.

"Agilaz Farshot." The Godwulf man beckoned them inward with a wave. "Jarl Alci bids you join him for the night meal."

"How did they know we'd be here today?" Sigyn whispered into Hermod's ear.

"Scouts have followed us for hours," he whispered back. The Godwulf had turned to stare at them. "And he can probably hear us."

Varulf hearing was *that* good? A fine blessing, though she'd not have wanted the savagery that accompanied it.

The guard pointed toward the largest hall, and Agilaz started off that way. Hermod helped her off the horse, then climbed down himself and began to lead the animal after his father.

"I want you to keep her," Hermod said when they neared the jarl's hall.

"What?"

"Snow Rabbit. I won't have so much time to ride or hunt now, I think. She deserves someone who can give her the attention she needs. So when you go from here, take her with you."

Her mind raced through a dozen responses, none of which seemed sufficient rejoinder to Hermod bestowing upon her his most prized possession. "Thank you." Brilliant. With such ingenious lines, she need not worry about outsmarting a potential husband. Freyja! Why wouldn't her tongue work properly when she actually needed it? It certainly got her in enough trouble when she ought to have stayed silent.

He handed the reins to a slave who had already taken Agilaz's horse. Hand on her shoulder, Hermod guided her toward the hall. Inside, thick smoke clogged the air, wafting among the rafters and choking her. None of the raucous men and women seemed bothered, all noisily boasting, feasting, drinking. Some of them wore almost no clothing, despite the chill creeping into the hall. A woman, shield-maiden perhaps, sat on a bench, topless, paying not the slightest attention to a man sucking on her breast as she downed great swigs from a drinking horn. Two men wearing not a stitch took turns punching each other in the face while others laughed and shouted encouragement.

Even through the smoke, the Godwulf hall stank of wolves.

The bare-chested jarl lounged upon his throne, one leg thrown over an armrest, his long hair flowing like a red river over his shoulders. Maybe Hadding had looked thus twenty or twenty-five winters ago, though she found it hard to imagine him with the sheer pompous, self-assuredness of his brother. Still, they shared enough in common, the set of their eyes, that calculating look in them, that she would have known him even had he not sat upon the throne.

Alci had seen them, though he gave only the slightest inclination of his head to Agilaz and none at all to her or Hermod.

Another man rose, his own brown hair streaked with gray, and beckoned them over. "Come. I am Hoenir, thegn to Jarl Alci." And father of the woman now intent on stealing Hermod away. Agilaz and Hermod sat on the bench where Hoenir indicated, and Sigyn squeezed in between them, rather than find herself wedged against any of the abhorrent warriors at the table. Hoenir pointed to a blonde woman across from him. A vicious scar ran down from her forehead, split the bridge of her nose, and reached the edge of her cheek. The woman had arms thick as a young man's. "This is my daughter, Syn."

A shieldmaiden. Hermod was marrying a fucking shieldmaiden. Of course he was. Olrun had been a shieldmaiden, won glory for herself and her family, so why would her son want any ordinary woman?

The woman licked grease from her fingers and stared at Hermod with greedy little eyes but offered not a single gesture or token of respect. A barely controlled bitch who ought to be kept with the elkhounds. Sigyn forced a pleasant smile to her face and nodded at the scarred shieldmaiden. Not a varulf, or she wouldn't have such a pronounced scar. She'd have to thank Freyja for small blessings.

Agilaz exchanged pleasantries with Hoenir and his men,

introducing Hermod all around and even Sigyn, though she found herself with little to say to any of these people. How many of them were varulfur? It didn't matter, she supposed. Even could they ever have turned back, that time had passed, and they were trapped here. Whether *these* men and women were varulfur did not matter, not when dozens, maybe hundreds, in this tribe clearly were. They had walked into the den of wolves, and one of them would not walk out.

H<small>OENIR</small> <small>GAVE</small> the three of them a room in his own modest house. After long hours of drinking that left Sigyn warm and swaying, they had retired there. She had almost let one of the warriors lead her away and ease her pain and frustration, if only for a moment. But she was not quite that drunk, nor would she let herself be. Not here.

Her foster brother had collapsed on the floor and now lay snoring in front of the brazier, their hound curled upon against his side. Agilaz, however, watched her, expression grave.

Fine. So he wanted to talk. She could talk. Maybe not as well as usual, but why should she fucking care anymore? She spread her hands, welcoming in whatever carefully placed shot he had planned for her.

Agilaz, however, never spoke quickly, never rushed. He believed in having a plan and sticking to it, and he had told her as much. Repeatedly. "I spoke to Olrun before we left. She believed you should not have come here."

"Yes, I guess she does. None of us should have. What good do you think sacrificing your son will bring the Hasdingi?"

Agilaz looked to where Hermod lay, then shook his head. "I am not sacrificing him. Olrun and I chose to make our lives in Aujum, with your father, because I judged Hadding a good man."

Did he now? "A man who would have exposed his own daughter."

Her foster father frowned. "Hadding made many mistakes, but such is life. He trusted King Nidud of Njarar, borrowed gold and finely wrought weapons to fight his enemies."

Sigyn shrugged. She knew of the Njarar War, of how it had torn the tribes apart. Two and a half summers of murder and revenge, war and discord, that engulfed half of Aujum before it ended.

"Nidud's son Otwin has called in those debts, Sigyn, called for payment Hadding doesn't have. And so, our enemies multiply, while our friends dwindle. We *need* Hadding's brother turned to our cause lest the Sviarlander king march against us. If word reaches the king of renewed love between the brothers, he would be like to turn his eyes elsewhere."

So it was not only the other Ás tribes her father feared, but foreign kings as well. And because of that fear, he'd make any bargain, cling to any hope, no matter how ephemeral. Just as Frigg, in her own desperation, sought to call upon Jarl Odin for aid, so had her father sent Agilaz to befriend Jarl Alci. The trouble was, neither of the jarls had overmuch reason to offer loyalty. That Hermod was not betrothed to a varulf girl came as a welcome relief on one hand, but on the other, it meant Alci had given up the daughter of one of the least of his thegns. She rubbed her eyes.

"If you are wrong, if Alci turns on us, who do you think the first to fall will be now?"

Agilaz sighed and looked again at his sleeping son. Did Hermod even realize the danger he had placed himself in? "Get some sleep, Sigyn. We'll have to leave in the morn."

Oh, but she did not think sleep would come easy this night.

## 11

*T*he mountain had no name. Not among any of the Ás tribes, not that Odin knew. The völvur said that to name a thing was to evoke it, and none would dare evoke the soul of such a behemoth. Least of all as they tried to scale it.

The slope they climbed disappeared into the night sky, the peak still a mile or more above them. None of his tribe had attempted aught like this. Such wild places housed vaettir, trolls, and Njord knew what else. Ahead, his brothers trudged upward, their steps not nearly as certain as those of their guide. Snow crunched under their feet, snow that reached gods-alone-knew how deep. On these mountains, maybe it had never melted.

"Just how big is this jotunn?" Vili asked. Vili was the only one smiling during this whole endeavor. Men said berserkir knew no fear. Perhaps he simply had the brains of a bear as well as the courage of one.

Loki paused, crouched atop a boulder like a bobcat ready to pounce. The pelts he wore only enhanced the image. He turned slowly to look at Odin's brother. "Six times the size of a man. This one is, at least. As they grow older and feast upon the flesh of men, they can grow larger. And Ymir is ancient."

And they were hunting it. This would be a long night.

Vili grunted, then looked pointedly at Ve. "Which man? Some men are *larger* than others. Ve's barely the size of a dverg."

In truth, Ve stood some perhaps five and a half feet tall, and his thick muscles, braided beard, and battle scars would hardly let anyone mistake him for tiny. As usual, Ve simply glowered at Vili. The burgeoning skald would have his revenge over campfires, Odin had no doubt.

"That's enough," Odin said at last, pushing past the rest of the group. This jotunn would be nigh. And soon it would know the bite of his spear. He ran his fingers over Gungnir's runes. Power seeped into him whenever he held the weapon. The power to rule his tribe. The power to destroy his enemies. "We're here to avenge Father, not bicker like lovesick maids. Shut your mouths or go home."

"Not large enough," Loki whispered as Vili passed him.

Odin smirked. None of the others could see his face anyway. With the damnable snow flurries, they probably couldn't have seen it even had he been facing them. It was as if Hel herself had stirred the winds of Niflheim to thwart his quest.

His torch sputtered in his hand. The firelight would give away their position before they were halfway up the damned mountain. Four little specks, advancing closer on Ymir, announcing their intent. "We have to douse the flames."

Everyone paused, turned to him.

"Brother, are you already Mist-mad?" Ve asked. "Skalds and völvur alike agree, fire banishes darkness, mist, and cold. It is the first and last gift of man, one to never be squandered."

"If Ymir sees us coming, we lose our one advantage." Odin scowled, staring up at the peak, barely visible through the snow. The storm was growing worse. "I will not allow Father to go unavenged over some völva's tale of the mist. A man doesn't go mad in one night."

Loki drew up close to him now, shaking his head. "Your brother speaks truth. Fire is life, and it was given to Mankind at great cost to the giver. It is our only ally out here. And as a frost jotunn, Ymir abhors the flames. If you cast it aside, you lose a shield and sword both."

"I will not be denied!" Odin snapped. "Not over some petty fear of the wild. What happens if he sees us coming a mile away? The jotunn can hurl boulders down upon us."

Loki sighed. "Or worse. These snows may well respond to his beckoning. Jotunnar can reach into the Otherworlds for the power to change the Mortal Realm. No easy choices lay before you, nor are any like to lie in your future, Odin."

Odin waved the foreigner's nonsense away. "Douse the fucking flames. Now." He drove his torch into the snow then grasped Gungnir with both hands. Odin's spear, handed down through countless generations, bore an engraved dragon coiling around the shaft. But it was the blade, an undulating point like a flame, that truly made the weapon a thing of the gods. Etched on one side of the blade, another faint dragon swiveled, not worn away despite the immeasurable age of the spear. His father claimed the blade had been forged with a dragon's soul, in the time before time. Now it would be forged anew, drunk on the blood of the frost jotunn Ymir.

Odin kissed its blade. "Gods above and below, grant us victory." Four men against a jotunn. And before this night was done, it would know fear. He pressed on, pushing out ahead of his brothers.

One by one, torches hissed out in the snow behind him.

❧

THE FLURRIES POUNDED them with the ferocity of a blizzard. Perhaps Loki spoke truth, and Ymir had some fell sorcery with which to turn the mountain against them. Or perhaps it was a mere winter storm. Either way, Odin couldn't see far.

Arm shielding his face, he grunted, driving against the blinding snows. The slope had turned steep, and even using Gungnir as a walking stick, his progress had slowed nigh unto a crawl. He glanced back. Vili growled, pushing on, but Ve was actually having to use his hands to pull himself forward. And where had Loki gotten off to? In the darkness, the damned foreigner had disappeared. Slipped away like a craven? It didn't matter. The foreigner had brought the brothers far enough.

Odin pushed on, but not five steps farther, his foot slipped on the ice-slickened rocks. The ground gave way, snow skidding down past him. Odin twisted while trying to shout a warning to his brothers. The movement cost him what remained of his balance, and he plummeted down the slope.

Rime-covered rocks tore through his fur trousers, ripping gashes in his shins. The ice scored a long gouge into his thigh, searing him like a burn. His pack tore free and plummeted back down the slope. His fingers grasped the edge of a rock, but they were too numb. His grip faltered. In an instant, Loki leapt onto the rock and snatched Odin's arm.

The foreign guide yanked Odin back onto the platform,

then slapped him on the shoulder. "Not an auspicious way to begin the hunt."

Odin glanced back at his younger brothers. The snow he'd disturbed could well have started an avalanche, but they'd come off easy, buried only up to their calves. He'd hear worse of it over the fire, no doubt.

As soon as Loki released Odin, Odin slipped down onto his arse. Hot blood streamed out over his trousers and stained the ice platform. He prodded at the wound on his leg. "Fuck."

The wind howled at him, like something calling out from Niflheim. Odin crawled to the edge, peered out over that platform. Through dark and blinding snow, he couldn't see aught below. Hel would have had him if not for Loki. As it was, Hel had his pack. His extra torches, his food.

Vertigo seized him, and he backed away, suddenly over-come by the magnitude of what lay before them. Odin coughed, choked. They stood moments away from a clash fit for one of Ve's tales. He had no time to let dread or the pain of his wounds weigh him down.

Ve scrambled down toward the platform where Odin had fallen, snow skidding beneath his feet. "Are you injured, brother?"

"No. I covered my trousers in red war paint."

The skald knelt to examine Odin's wound, shaking his head. "You cannot go on."

"Like Hel," Odin said, then spat into the night. "Father's murderer is out there, and every heartbeat he lives is an insult."

Ve shrugged. "Better to live with an insult than die of hubris."

Odin shoved him away. "Father named you a man nigh

ten winters back, and still you think like a boy." He forced himself up, unsteady as he felt.

A hand on his shoulder pushed him back down. Loki. "Whether you intend to go forward or back, I must bind the wound. You cannot walk like this. You'd bleed out over the mountain."

"Man really is a fucking völva," Vili grumbled.

Loki set to tying Odin's leg with bandages and foul-smelling herbs from his pack. He paid Vili no mind, which only further enraged the berserk.

"Not got a damned thing to say for yourself? You admit to unmanliness? Maybe you'd rather have a boy than a girl?"

"Just shut up, Vili," Ve snapped. "We don't have a völva here. If Loki can save Odin's leg, let the man try."

"Not a fucking man at all. Probably got a trench instead of a cock."

"I have to stitch this," Loki said, still ignoring the berserk.

Odin gritted his teeth and nodded. The foreigner knew what he was about, treating Odin's wound quickly, with as few stitches as possible. Would have been better if he'd had some mead. Would have been better if this had not happened. Fuck.

"It strikes me our guide must have seen a great many battles," Ve said.

Loki paused for the barest instant. "More than you can imagine." He bit off the stitch, then wrapped another bandage around Odin's leg.

"This stranger has brought this upon us," Vili grumbled. "The storm, the foul urd, all of it. He acts like a woman, speaks like a völva, and invites the wrath of vaettir. Doesn't know his fucking place."

Loki met Odin's gaze and offered no answer to Vili, which only further set the berserk to grumbling.

When Loki had finished, Odin stood, wobbling for just a moment. Gungnir gave him strength. Its power filled him, dulled the pain. With it, he could best any foe.

"We must turn back," Ve said. "The storm is getting worse, half our food is gone, and that injury will slow you."

Odin sneered. "Then go back, coward. *My* father was murdered by that fucking jotunn." He thumped a finger on Ve's chest. "He came down off the mountain and killed him and everyone else in Unterhagen." He thumped Ve again. "I will not allow Father's ghost to writhe in torment one more night. I will not!" He shoved the boy for emphasis. "If you will not fight, I will do it alone. But there is no turning back. Not for me."

Vili cuffed Ve on the back of the head and started to climb again.

Odin followed after him. No turning back. Never.

## 12

The Gandvik formed the northern border of Aujum. The Athra tribe occupied a half dozen small towns there. Fishing, whaling, hunting seals. Sometimes, they crossed the sea to Sviarland for trade. Or to raid. Borr had said all the Ás tribes once lived on the Black Sea as the Athra now did on the Gandvik. Closest to the ways of their ancestors, perhaps.

The largest town, Breivik, served as the jarl's home and had done so for over a generation. Tyr had come here oft enough with Borr. Once, before she died, Bestla had come here to visit her parents. A stone wall, crumbling but still thick, surrounded the town on all but the sea side. Tyr had not reached the gate when a man skied out to meet him.

Big man, thick, bristly mustache. A warrior for certain. Didn't go for a weapon, but archers stood up on those walls.

"Who comes here?"

"Tyr. Thegn of the Wodanar."

The man grunted. "Your name is known, champion of Borr. I am Geir, thegn to Jarl Annar."

"I need to see him."

Geir nodded and beckoned Tyr to follow. The man shed his skis once within the town wall. Tyr unstrapped his own snowshoes and left them by the gate.

"You're wounded," Geir said.

"Varulf attack."

"Many of those of late. Not so many men walking away from them, though."

Tyr grunted. Varulfur were men possessed by vaettir. They died harder than other men, but they died still.

Geir led him past the shore where men were cutting blubber from a seal corpse. Bloody, foul-smelling mess, but it would give them oil. Make for a safer winter than most tribes had.

"Ever hit finfolk?"

"Wereseals?" Geir grunted. "Those are real?"

Tyr shrugged. Far as he knew.

Geir shook his head. "Not in the Gandvik. Fishermen, whalers, they claim serpents live in the deeps. Few swear to have seen one. Most don't believe though. Who escapes a serpent, right?"

Tyr nodded. Even jotunnar feared dragons. Such monstrosities were best left well alone.

Annar occupied an old hall, one built of stone. Thanks to braziers spaced every ten feet or so on each side, the hall didn't seem oppressive. A balcony rimmed the main hall. Windows up there were shuttered now, but Tyr had seen them open in summer. At the moment, a cluster of women stood up there. Staring as he trod down the hall.

The jarl, son of Bestla's sister, did not sit on a throne but rather paced about his hall. Every time he reached the right side, he'd spin and fling a knife at a shield hanging from a pillar. Men stood about Annar, offering the occasional bit of insight. Enough to tell the Athra did not fare well.

"My lord," Geir said. "Tyr of the Wodanar."

Annar paused midthrow, looked to Tyr. Then he turned back to finish hurling his knife. It clattered off the shield and landed on the floor. Annar swung his fist in obvious frustration. Only then did he turn to meet Tyr. He strode over, clapped him on the shoulder, and guided him away from the main hall, into a back room.

The jarl frowned at Tyr's arm. "Eir!" he bellowed down the hall.

A moment later, a middle-aged woman shuffled in, took one look at Tyr, and then fled.

Annar beckoned Tyr to sit on a bench. "Gone to get her healing supplies. Best völva in Aujum, men say, though she denies it. Varulf?"

"Your völva?"

"Frey's flaming sword, no! Varulf did that to your arm, I'm asking."

"Huh. Yes. A few days back from here."

Annar clucked his tongue. "And you're still standing. Impressive, warrior. Always winning so much fame."

"How did you know about the varulf?"

The jarl sat in a chair across from Tyr. "Hairy bastards are everywhere now. Encroaching on our lands."

"Godwulfs?"

Annar spread his hands. "One or two stray wolves, even a pack, I might think them wild. Gone to the mist. No, this is deliberate, a challenge. As soon as Borr died, they began pushing their borders. We can't fight them at night when they become wolves, of course. And in day, they're armed with the finest weapons, with mail that can turn even a strong spear."

"Huh. I saw a huntress with a woven iron sword."

"You killed her, I hope?"

Tyr scowled and stared into the nearest brazier. Annar said naught else. The völva, Eir, returned. She began unwinding the crude bandages Tyr had wrapped around his arm. After a moment, she hissed at the mangled mess.

"Can't see how you warded off rot, save the luck of Vanaheim. Someone there loves you."

The Vanr ... Idunn. Could her power have helped him in his quest? He shook the thought away. The goddess was helping, but not like that.

"About Borr ..."

Annar sighed and pressed his palms against his eyes. "I know it, man. I would have come to his funeral given any such chance. Only, with the wolves pressing in on us ... Safe passage to Wodan lands would be hard to find. Worse, I'd leave my people without their jarl. Is that why you're here? Odin is angry? Of course he is. Please explain to him, I had no choice, and I meant Borr no disrespect."

Eir smeared some foul-smelling paste on Tyr's wounds. For an instant it stung like fire, then gave way to a welcome warmth.

Tyr watched Annar.

The jarl shifted, obviously uncomfortable under the scrutiny. "We've lost a lot of men, hunters, fighters. Fishermen even, if they tried to bring a catch ashore too late in the day or too far from the town. Surely Odin will understand."

Even the goddess Idunn herself seemed hard-pressed to predict Odin's actions or reactions. Offered the chance at immortality and kingship, the fool had scorned her. Favored the foreigner. But Odin *would* be king. Would fulfill Borr's legacy if Tyr had to carry him to his throne kicking and screaming.

And to be king, he needed his cousin. Needed Annar to owe him a great debt.

"I can help you," Tyr said. "If we hunt down one or two of these raiding parties, the Godwulfs may decide to look for weaker prey. Turn their eyes away from the Athra."

With luck, maybe they'd go after the Skaldun.

"You'd fight by our side?"

Tyr grunted. "With your blessing, I will lead your warriors to victory. But you, Annar, you will owe Odin and the Wodanar for this."

Despite the slight hesitation in his eyes, Annar nodded.

Good.

Kill a few varulfur, and one tribe might already support Odin at the Althing. Now there just remained the problem of slaying well-armed men with superhuman strength and durability. Small problem.

## 13

*E*very step sent a lance of pain through his wounded
shins and his thigh. Pain was good. Pain meant he
had life. It meant he hadn't gone numb from the cold. It
meant there was still time. He could not feel his face. Even
his thick fur cloak provided scant protection against the
scathing chill of this storm. Ice stung his eyes.

The path had leveled some. He dug Gungnir's butt into
the ground, heaving himself forward. Just keep going.
Father was counting on him. Father.

Father.

Was he watching?

The ground rumbled beneath him, nigh costing him his
balance. One hand on the spear and the other on an ice-
coated boulder, he steadied himself.

The mountain trembled again, as though it wasn't
finished with its little earthquake. It went still. Then it trembled again. A dusting of snow skittered off a rock precipice
above, almost blending with the flurries. Stillness. Then
another quake.

The four men exchanged glances. Loki pointed to a pass just beyond the next rise.

Ymir was here. Finally.

Valkyries could very well have their souls before sunrise. If so, Odin sure as Hel was not going to be the only one dying on this mountain.

Father. Watch.

He scrambled toward the precipice wall.

Vili and Ve didn't need to be told what Odin planned. They made for the pass, Vili casting aside his furs even as he ran.

More snow fell from the overhang, the barrage of hoar now constant, making Odin's climb nigh blind. Gripping Gungnir, he felt for handholds with his free hand. Aught that could support his weight. He had to get to higher ground. He would look this jotunn in the eye before he cut it down to size.

And his brothers—Odin spared them a glance. Vili's back arched. He dropped to all fours, roaring in pain and perhaps joy at the change. His muscles rippled beneath his skin, shifting, tearing at stomach-rending angles. Tufts of brown fur sprouted from him as he released the bear spirit inside him. Had the giant ever seen a berserk? If not, he was in for a nasty surprise.

A peak of the mountain *moved*, just beyond the edge of the pass. Not a peak ... a horn, at least five feet long. A horn of granite. Odin's handholds vibrated as Ymir rose above the pass. The jotunn turned, as if slowly taking in Odin's brothers. Clinging frost fled its mouth, like the mists of Niflheim that engulfed the world. Its skin was tinted the icy blue of a man in the throes of deathchill.

Vili, a full bear now, roared and charged the monster. Ve hung back, but only for a moment, before raising his battle-axe and rushing after his brother. And Loki ... nowhere to be found. Fair enough—their guide had agreed only to help them find the one responsible for Father's death. It fell to the brothers to avenge Father.

Odin yanked himself onto the plateau, then scrubbed frost from his eyes. He'd have sworn the jotunn sneered. He hefted something—a boulder. Or a hammer with a head the size of a boulder. Vili charged right in.

"Hel's frozen tits," Odin mumbled.

Ymir twisted, surprisingly fast for a being of its size. An underhand swing of its hammer slammed into Vili with a sickening crack. The bear flew through the air at least twenty feet before smashing into the mountain slope. The jotunn's laughter echoed off the mountain peaks, reverberating across what seemed the whole of Midgard.

Ve screamed wildly, hewing his battle-axe into the jotunn's leg. From Ymir's reaction, or lack thereof, Odin suspected his brother wasn't even cutting through the iron shin guards.

Fucking jotunn was going to splatter his brothers without breaking a sweat. Odin backed to the edge of the plateau. Even with a running start, he'd never make that jump. The jotunn was simply too far. And a few more heartbeats and Ve wouldn't be around to distract it. Odin reversed his grip on Gungnir. A good throw. A throw the skalds would tell stories of.

The jotunn swooped down and snatched Ve in one hand. Odin's little brother froze, caught in a fist bigger than he was. His face turned red. The jotunn was squeezing the life out of him. Crushing his bones to pulp.

Now or never. Odin took off running. His feet skidded on the ice. The pain in his legs threatened to tear them out from under him. Didn't matter. Just momentum. Just a moment. He flung Gungnir with all his might. The spear soared faster than it should have, faster and farther than any throw a man could make. The missile shrieked through the air, and Ymir turned at the sound. Too late. Gungnir shot right through the jotunn's eye.

The behemoth bellowed, releasing Ve, who plummeted to the icy slope below. Vili might survive such a fall, but Ve was only human, like Odin himself. His little brother. A pit opened in Odin's stomach, and time slowed as Ve fell. As Odin watched, powerless.

From the shadows beneath the plateau, Loki jumped forward and caught Ve in his arms, rolling as he hit the ground.

Odin's breath caught. He'd thought their guide had fled.

Ymir stumbled, pitching forward, headfirst toward the plateau. Odin had sworn an oath in Father's name. All three brothers had. Time to make good.

Odin drew a deep breath. Set his jaw. And he ran.

He leapt from the plateau onto the jotunn's shoulder, then caught the haft of his spear. His own weight yanked it from the bastard's eye. Ymir howled, clutching his face, then fell to his knees. The movement shook Odin free, and his boots slipped on the jotunn's blood-slickened armor. He fell fifteen feet and landed in a snow drift. White filled his vision as his weight flung him deep into the drift.

Could have been worse, he supposed. Could have been rocks down there.

Odin kicked the snow, doing little but burying himself further. It'd take him forever to dig his way out of this.

Ymir screamed again, this time the wail of a tortured beast needing to be put out of its misery. Odin clawed his way upward, snow giving way grudgingly, if at all. He was missing the damned battle. Some jarl he was.

And then a hand appeared before his face.

He accepted the proffered grip, and Loki pulled him out of the drift. Ve had hamstrung Ymir and was now hacking at the jotunn's elbow. Loki pointed at Gungnir, which was sticking from the snow several feet away. Blood and gore streaked down it, a crimson stain spreading across the once pure snow.

Yes. Time to finish this.

Odin's legs nearly gave out beneath him as he trod toward his ancestral weapon.

He yanked the spear free, cracking blood that had already frozen to the ice. Ymir turned his one remaining eye toward Odin as he stalked over, pace steady, if slow for his own wounds. In that eye, Odin could see the beast knew the truth. And he was scared.

As he should be.

"Father!" Odin bellowed, his voice echoing off the mountain. He thrust the spear through Ymir's forehead.

# PART II

Fourth Moon

## 14

*A*rm raised against the blinding snow, Odin pushed forward. Ice crystals stung his forehead, ears, and any other exposed flesh they could find. The storm had not abated with Ymir's death. In truth, the blizzard had worsened, as if rejecting the frost jotunn's demise—or feasting upon his soul and growing fat on it.

Odin couldn't see a damned thing. He wasn't even sure they still headed in the right direction.

"We need shelter!" Vili shouted.

"Loki!" he shouted. "Where is that damned tower?"

For a moment there was no answer, then the foreigner emerged from the snow ahead, crystal blue eyes like burning lights. "We came down a different slope. It's too far."

Odin grimaced. Every attempt at relighting the torches had proved futile. There had to be something. His leg had gone numb. Perhaps only Gungnir's power kept him upright. "Find us shelter, any shelter!"

Loki glanced off to the north, silent a moment, then

shook his head. "There is naught to be found." Was that hesitation in his voice?

"What is it?"

Loki straightened his shoulders, then stood with his hands behind his back, as if resigned. "A castle from the Old Kingdoms. We could reach it soon ... But naught mortal lives there now."

Vaettir? "What is it? Trolls? Draugar?"

"I cannot say for certain, now. Long ago it belonged to a kingdom called the Odlingar."

How could Loki know such a thing? Truth was, it didn't matter. In this snowstorm, they'd all be dead in an hour. "Just take us there."

Loki took in each of the small party before turning back to Odin. Then he spun on his heel and changed course.

Odin's brothers both looked to him a moment, before chasing after Loki.

Fuck all. Odin dug Gungnir's butt into the ground and pulled himself forward, one painful step after another.

Ymir was dead.

Father was avenged. He had done it. He had brought Father peace.

WHEN THEIR GOAL at last came into view, Odin's face had gone numb and his arms stiff. Through the curtain of snow, he could just make out the structure atop a hill. It was a castle, and more complete than any he'd ever seen. Arches supported wings of the castle, which spread out over the valley, off the hilltop. A giant spire connected by a skybridge might have granted a view for miles over the mist, if not for the damned blinding snow. Finely carved frescos spoke of another age. And ice crystals covered every speck of the place.

"Hel's frozen tits," he mumbled. This had not been what he'd expected. These Odlingar built places fit for gods. And if they were gone, surely somewhat else must now lurk here. But here they were, and it was their only choice.

Loki glanced at him and must have read the decision on his face, for the foreigner took off toward the castle. The grade up the hill was steep, and every step over the ice threatened to steal Odin's balance. Behind, his brothers followed. Odin spared a glance at Ve, who trudged on with a vacant stare. Half frozen to death, with Vili's occasional shove keeping him going.

Odin pressed forward. Farther up, steps had been carved into the hill, those also crusted in ice and slippery. Odin used the butt of Gungnir as a walking stick, following close behind Loki. His leg didn't hurt so much—now it almost wouldn't respond.

"Have you been here before?" The storm seemed to swallow his words.

Still, Loki answered. "No." He pointed at the main gateway—massive double doors over an arch.

Odin trudged up to it, grateful for even the hint of shelter the shadow of the wall provided. He rapped on the door with his spear, but no answer came. All right then. Odin pushed his shoulder against the door, but ice held it fast.

Odin took Gungnir in both hands and thrust it forward. It splintered the ice, sending a spider web of cracks across it, and kept going, punching through the door underneath. Odin tried to yank the spear free, but it held fast. Instead, he worked it 'round and 'round, cracking more ice. At last he beckoned for Vili to join him. As one, they slammed into the doors. The ice shattered, and the doors flew inward, Gungnir clattering to the floor beneath.

"Everyone inside," he called and reclaimed his spear.

Thick shadows swelled over a gargantuan interior caked with ice. With the doors open, snow quickly began to pile up in the entryway. They needed a fire—fast.

Ice crusted over every window, tinting what little light reached inside blue-white. Tapestries hung from the wall, even these caked with hoar. An upper balcony ringed the hall, and several archways led onward. Gods knew how long it would take to explore such a place.

While the others pushed the doors half closed to guard against the storm, Odin yanked tapestries down and shook the ice free of them. Moments later, Loki joined him. When the fabric was dry enough, they kindled a fire.

Odin crouched nearby, warming his hands. The fire should keep the cold and the gods-damned mist away. His leg had started to throb. Odin slapped his fist against it. Had to keep the blood flowing.

"Let me see," Loki said. The foreigner pulled away the bandages while Vili set about tending the fire and heating what little meat they had. A slab of frozen mammoth, and with Odin's supplies gone, they'd have to share.

"This fire won't last long. Not with just a tapestry to burn. Ve, get some more."

His brother stared at him blankly.

"Now!" Odin snapped.

The young man jerked, then rose and drifted off toward the wall.

"Luck favors you," Loki said. "Another hour in the cold and you might have lost the leg. But you'll recover."

Odin grunted. "Vili, help Ve."

"I'm fucking starving."

"So am I, but it can wait. I don't want the boy wandering this place alone. Could still be draugar or aught else here."

Grumbling, the berserk lurched to his feet and went after Ve.

Loki retightened the bandage on Odin's leg, forcing Odin to stifle a grunt of pain.

"Thank you. Brother."

Loki snorted. "Brother?" he asked, when Odin turned back to him.

Odin leaned back on his elbows, grateful for even the slight respite. "Without doubt. You saved my life and that of my little brother. You alone helped me uphold my vow. You may not have been born of the same woman as I ..." But what did that even matter? No one controlled what family they were born to, but there was no reason you couldn't choose others. Rolling to his side, Odin pulled a knife from his belt. Loki stared at it without any hint of alarm. Pity—Odin had expected to at least startle the foreigner.

Instead Loki raised his eyes from the knife to Odin's face. Steady one, this. Fearless? Or just not easily worried? No, he had stood with them against a jotunn. That kind of courage exceeded that of even most berserkir.

Odin drew the knife along his palm, opening a shallow cut. "We shall be brothers in blood, my friend, until the end of our days." He held up his dripping palm for Loki to see, then passed the knife.

The other man took it without hesitation, though he did watch Odin's eyes a moment before opening his own palm. "Some things cannot be undone." He set the knife by the fire, then offered his hand.

Odin clasped it, mingling their blood. "Nor should they." A sudden warmth passed through him, and then dizziness. Hunger and fatigue, no doubt. His eyes swam. "We will be united, always, now. I will never accept any ale unless it be brought for you as well. I will take no glory without you at my side, brother."

Loki's hand tightened around Odin's. The man was stronger than he looked. Though svelte, his grip was like iron. "You invoke old magic without understanding it, brother. But I will stay by your side, long as I am able."

In truth, Loki was the strangest man Odin had ever known. He knew far more than a man ought, but that had proved a boon time and again on this trek. Without him Father would still dwell in agony. And surely he must be free now. Surely. Free and gone ... No longer watching Odin. That thought hit him like a blow to the chest, one that stole his breath.

Odin shook himself and broke the grip. He looked at the foreigner. Loki claimed to have come from the far west, but Odin knew little of lands beyond Aujum. Some said the gods lived in the west, beyond the farthest sea, on islands that knew neither time nor winter. Vanaheim. Had Idunn truly come from such a place? It seemed too good to be truth. Odin's people—all Ás tribes, really—had lived along the Black Sea far to the east, before Vingethor led them on the Great March. Nine tribes, all wandering Aujum, some fishing the Gandvik Sea, some raiding into Hunaland or Bjarmaland.

He leaned back on his elbows. "You keep many secrets, brother. Will you not speak of your homeland?"

Loki watched him with those intense eyes a moment. "A man is entitled to secrets and privacy both."

"Just fucking move!" Vili bellowed from across the hall.

Odin and Loki both looked to him as he shoved Ve out of the way and yanked down a tapestry on his own. Ve stood there, staring at the berserk as if uncertain what to do. He had dropped his torch, which now lay sputtering on the icy stone.

Loki rose, grabbed a torch, and strode over there, forcing Odin to hobble his way over to where his brothers worked.

As Loki approached, Ve backed away from him and sat against the wall. Loki knelt before him, staring into his eyes. And Ve's eyes—those looked a touch too wild and confused for Odin's liking.

"What is this?" Odin demanded as he reached them.

"Fucking uselessness," Vili said. Odin's huge brother hefted the tapestry by himself—berserk strength at its finest —and hauled it off, back toward the fire.

Loki didn't turn from Ve's face. "What was your mother's name?"

Ve's eyes seemed to gleam in the firelight, though he cringed from it as though it pained him. He shook his head, eyes growing even wider.

Odin knelt before his little brother. What in the gates of Hel? Their mother had died birthing Ve. And the boy had never known her, but he certainly knew the name Bestla. Father's beloved wife, oft mourned.

So now what ... No.

This wasn't possible. Völvur said the mists could steal memories, but völvur said so many things. Odin hadn't thought ... He'd taken Ve, taken both his brothers up the mountain to fight Ymir, unwilling to allow them torches for fear of jeopardizing his vengeance. Every step had drawn these mists deeper inside his own brother.

No. It could not be. Not in one night.

"Ve?" Odin's voice cracked, still sounding raspy. "Brother?"

At last a look of recognition flashed over Ve's face and he nodded to Odin. Recognition and dread. Gods above, his

brother knew what was happening to him. And he was terri-
fied. Odin reached a trembling hand to pat his brother on
the shoulder. "Don't worry, Ve. You'll be fine. You just need a
good night's sleep. Some food in your belly." Odin hauled Ve
to his feet and guided him back to the fire where Vili had
left the mammoth flesh roasting.

Gods, what a fool he'd been. To find vengeance for
Father he'd brought his brothers up a forbidden mountain,
then denied them the life-preserving flames that might have
warded off the mists. Ve sat, much farther from the fire than
he ought to.

"Eat," Odin said.

Ve moved no closer.

Odin groaned and snatched the meat off the spit Vili
had fashioned. When he brought it to Ve, his brother tore
into it with a ravenousness that would have done Vili proud.
He'd be fine. He watched Ve a moment. Just fine.

Odin turned, then tugged Loki aside, out of earshot of
his brothers. Would Vili turn on his brother? Maybe not,
but the rest of the tribe would. At night, sometimes men
told stories about those whose minds were taken by the
mists. Some said those who went Mist-mad eventually
became wraiths, wandering the World and filled with
unfathomable loathing of all that lived. Odin had seen it
four times—men cast out from the tribe because of the
madness, because the tribe feared a warrior's soul lost to
Niflheim.

And one had come back. But not as a man. As a draug—
a revenant risen from the dead and bent on vengeance
against those who had cast him out. The creature refused to
die, tearing men to pieces even as they hacked away at it. In
the end, Father had pinned the creature to the ground with
Gungnir and Tyr had lopped off its head. Their völva had

built a pyre to send the creature to Hel, and they had fled that camp, declaring it cursed for all time.

"Tell no one of this," Odin whispered to Loki. A resigned sadness washed over the foreigner's face before he nodded. Maybe a völva would have known what to do to save Ve. Heidr—their tribe völva, maybe she could help. Or …

Loki. The foreigner knew things, talked like a völva himself.

"Can aught be done for him?" Odin asked.

"We should rest."

Odin clenched his fists at his side and leaned in close to Loki's ear. "I will not let my brother fall."

Loki sighed. "Odin, some things are not easily undone."

"No!" Fuck that.

He'd find a way to save his brother.

❦

ARMS LADEN with yet another tapestry, Vili stomped back over to the fire. "Should get us through the night. I say we leave this cursed place at dawn." He slumped down by the others, glared at them—probably vexed they ate before him —and snatched up the remaining hunk of mammoth flesh.

Odin looked to Loki, then to the entrance. "We can leave when the storm clears. Be that dawn or otherwise."

Vili growled, juice dribbling down his chin and beading in his thick beard. "If the jotunn's death brought this on, the farther we get from here the better."

Odin could not argue with that. But nor would he again take Ve into the cold without flame, much as his younger brother now seemed to recoil from the very thing that ought to have protected him. The storm howling outside trapped them in this place, this ruin of the Old Kingdoms. Trapped, sitting and watching Ve stare vacantly off into the darkness of the hall, never looking into the fire.

Hel. Would Father blame Odin for this? In his desperation to avenge him, Odin had let another son of Borr fall to harm. Groaning, he lurched to his feet, drawing strength from Gungnir. He had done it. He'd avenged Father. So why did he still want to rage at the sky and burn down the World? Should it not have brought *his* soul peace, as well as Father's?

Vili glanced at him, spat. "There's rune markings on some of the walls. Fell place, this. I wouldn't wander."

Odin glared at the berserk a moment before shambling off toward the back of the hall. Oh, but he wanted to wander. He wanted to be anywhere but sitting there, watching his brother lose himself. Like a Hel-cursed fool, he'd allowed himself to believe Mist-madness could not touch him. Not him, not his family. It was a distant threat, one that fell upon other people. Not his problem.

Loki fell in by his side, saying naught. Perceptive enough to know naught could be said. His new brother already knew how Odin had failed his other brothers.

A curving staircase led to an upper balcony, but Odin passed beneath it, to where a series of oak doors lined the walls. Loki drifted along behind him. The foreigner brushed away a layer of hoar to reveal some strange markings carved into the walls. How on Hel's frozen arse had frost covered the *interior* walls? Something fell and unnatural was at work. Loki claimed not to have visited here before, but he still knew much of this place.

The runes Loki examined meant naught to Odin. Such were the workings of dvergar of old, warding the ancient places against the mist, or so völvur claimed. They also carved the symbols on runestones, marking safer routes from the more perilous ones. And Gungnir also bore runes, perhaps carved by the Vanir.

"Who did you say built this place?" Odin asked.

"The Odlingar. One of the Old Kingdoms, all of which collapsed some eight centuries back."

"How does a people capable of building this," Odin waved his arm to encompass the majesty of the castle, "fall?"

"The same as all once great kingdoms—torn apart by strife from within and torn down by foes from without. A neighboring kingdom took advantage of turmoil within the Odlingar houses and betrayed them."

Odin grunted. "How does a man know what happened eight hundred years ago?"

Loki chuckled. "I'm a student of history." He tried one of the doors, but it didn't budge.

The foreigner moved on to another door, tried the handle, and then shouldered it open. Ice cracked off it. The room beyond was cast in darkness and reeked of must and ancient death.

"So no one has come here in all those years?"

"They may have entered. I'm not certain whether anyone ever managed to leave."

What the fuck did that mean?

"What is it you think lives here?"

Loki knelt by a mound of ice. Under a thin layer of hoar, a pair of corpses lay in each other's arms. A mother and child, perhaps, wrapped in a dying embrace, frozen to death in this room. The foreigner frowned, shaking his head. "I doubt anything *lives* here."

A wind howled through the castle, raising the hair on the back of Odin's neck. That had come from upstairs, but no window looked apt to let wind *inside*. A wise man would flee the castle now. Save for the killing blizzard raging outside. He looked to Loki, but the foreigner only returned his stare blankly. Letting Odin decide. Cower in the hall and hope whatever lurked in those hidden recesses left them to their fire. Or face it.

Not much of a choice. Ve stared into the dark like a man drunk and dazed. Because of Odin. Because his big brother had let him face danger he ought not have. Odin pushed out the door and strode toward the stairs.

Vili had risen, taken up his axe, but Odin motioned him to stay. Odin's pace slowed as he climbed those stairs. Each step shot tendrils of pain through his leg that reached almost to his spine. Gungnir's butt clanged on the floor, the sound echoing in the empty hall.

At the top, a freezing wind rushed over him, howling like a wolf. A fell whisper emerged from one of the archways beyond.

*Leave.*

Odin spun. Naught there.

Loki had followed, now turning about.

"Did you hear something?" Odin asked.

Loki nodded.

Not in Odin's mind then. Forward. The archway opened onto a hallway, long, probably to the great tower. Large windows lined the hall, letting in a crisscross of light through cracked ice. This must be the skybridge he saw outside.

Odin leveled Gungnir, shared a glance with Loki, and proceeded down the hall. Whatever lived here, vaettir or not, his brothers needed this place, and it was his job to get them what they needed. He'd protect Ve by whatever means necessary.

*Leave!* The voice seemed to come from all around them. Still a whisper, but one laced with fury.

"Who are you?" Odin called, continuing down the hall. "What do you want?"

No answer came.

"A wraith," Odin whispered, praying he was wrong. Some claimed wraiths were the most dangerous of all the vaettir. They were shades of the dead bent on the destruction of life, stripped of all that once made them men. There was no fighting a wraith, not really. With neither body to slay nor blood to spill, such a ghost could not be killed. If they were lucky, maybe it would fear Gungnir.

If not, they might as well take their chances with the snowstorm.

A look at Loki told Odin the man would continue on. Odin nodded at his new brother, who drew something from beneath his furs. A crude iron dagger. Loki said naught in answer to Odin's raised eyebrow.

At the end of the hall an archway led onto a landing of the great tower. Stairs ringed the outside, rising up to the other levels.

Odin blew out a hard breath and clenched his grip around Gungnir. This was the way. The only way. His heart pounded so hard he could barely hear anything else. Just keep going forward.

He'd stepped one foot on the stairs when another chill passed over him. He spun around to see a woman standing in the archway they'd just passed through. She looked naught like any wraith he'd imagined, though the ends of the black cloak she wore faded away into wisps of nothingness. Her face seemed almost solid, and, though pained, not vile. She had green eyes and long blonde hair that blew about, though no wind reached in here. By her side stood a white wolf, also translucent. A ghost hound.

"Be gone, vaettr!" Odin shouted.

"You dare ... command me leave *my* home ... mortal?"

Loki raised his torch out in front of him and the dagger to his side but made no move to advance on this spirit.

"Your home?" Odin asked. "Then who are you, lady?"

"I am ... I was ... the queen here, long ago."

"My lady, please. We need shelter from the cold."

The ghost's form flickered then vanished.

Her voice whispered in Odin's ear. *There is none.*

He and Loki both spun about so fast they nearly tripped over themselves, stumbling backward. The ghost stood behind them, her wolf with teeth bared, stalking closer. She flickered again, appearing beside Loki, her hand on his head. His torch and dagger both slipped from his grip, and he fell to his knees. In an instant his skin turned blue as deathchill.

Odin swung Gungnir at her, and she vanished again. He spun as she appeared some distance behind him. The wolf stalked around, circling behind. He couldn't keep them both in view.

Loki groaned, crawling away with the torch in hand.

"Please!" Odin said. "We beg your hospitality."

The ghost's body shimmered, as if fading out of this Realm, before popping back up even closer. "The last time I sheltered travelers they turned on me. Killed my people, left me this cursed existence. It is not a mistake I am apt to repeat. Least of all to those who come saturated in the mists."

What? What did she ... Ve? "My brother? You know what's happening to him?"

The ghost flickered in and out of existence. "What always happens to mortal men who breathe too deeply the mists of Niflheim."

The wolf snarled and lunged.

Odin rolled to the side, whipping Gungnir forward. The ghost wolf snapped its jaws around the shaft and pinned Odin to the ground. The thing had weight like a real animal, though its breath was cold rather than hot, inches from his face. Odin pushed against the animal, unable to dislodge it.

"Please! We are not your enemies!"

She drifted to his side and pressed her hand to his cheek. Even as she did so, the wolf released Gungnir. Odin's own grip on the spear went limp, and it clattered to the floor. As it fell, a sudden weariness and chill set in on him. Sleep. He needed to sleep.

"Please what, mortal?"

"S-save my brother from the mist."

Loki lurched forward, waving the torch. The ghost and wolf both recoiled long before he touched either, the wolf snarling. He bent to retrieve the dagger.

"Why?" She drew the word out so long it seemed to writhe in his ears.

"I'd grant any request if it might save my brother."

"Odin—" Loki began.

Odin silenced him with a glare. "I will avenge whatever wrong was done to you, spirit. But save Ve from this dark urd."

The ghost flickered again, appearing just before Odin's face. She drew a finger along the line of his jaw. Her touch was like the mists—icy and maddening, hungry to consume body and mind and soul. "On your oath ..."

"I ... I swear it."

"Swear on your blood to return that which was stolen, the Singasteinn." She touched a hand to her breast, then shook her head. "Return my amulet to me before the solstice."

"I swear! Where do I find this amulet?

She drew back, and warmth slowly returned to his limbs, though cold still gripped his heart. "Taken ... taken by the Niflungar."

Not an Ás tribe. But whoever they were, he'd find them if it meant sparing his own people. The solstice, during the sixth moon, was less than three moons from now. Still it ought to prove ample time to track down whatever people these were. He crawled over to his spear. "I swear, by my own blood." He drew his hand along the blade of Gungnir, opening his palm. "I swear to return this Singasteinn to you in three moons. And you must save Ve."

The ghost drifted closer still, close enough to place an icy kiss on his lips. A chill settled deep within him, clenching around his heart. He hadn't realized he'd shut his eyes, but when he opened them, the woman and wolf were gone.

*Fail to bring it within three moons, and your oath is broken. All you build will turn to ash, your children shall die, and your dreams shall burn.*

Odin shook his head from the voice echoing within it. One look at Loki showed the man had heard naught.

*Three moons.*

Three moons to save Ve, to undo his mistake. Even when he returned to the fire, Odin couldn't get that icy chill out of his heart.

## 15

———

*T*he crumbling tower might have once watched over the Jarnvid. Now, no one maintained it. No one watched the wood from its ramparts. If the Godwulfs had been half the protectors they claimed to be, they'd have garrisoned this place for the good of all Aujum. Instead, Tyr had found it abandoned, nigh the southern border of Athra lands.

Occupying it, lighting a brazier atop the tower—an almost direct challenge to varulfur looking to expand their territory. Here, men pushed back, claiming what might have otherwise belonged to the wolves. Annar had set four archers atop the tower. They all hunkered down now, hidden and trusting the smoke to mask their scents.

Two nights already they had passed like this. Surely the Godwulfs could not anticipate the trap? Savage beasts were cunning, yes. But driven by instinct and fury.

Annar and a few of his men dwelt in the lower floors of the tower. In daylight, they worked to begin restoring the foundations as if they intended to stay here long.

Tyr and Geir, however, and three of Geir's men, lingered

in a dug-out snow drift. Skin caked with mud to mask their scents. Hidden, so the wolves would think their numbers few. Plan had sounded better before spending two freezing nights huddled in the snow.

"Some of the mist is getting inside," Geir complained again.

"A torch would give us away." Tyr had told him that enough times it ought to have sunk in by now. Yes, Mist-madness. They all feared it. But if they didn't kill these varulfur, naught else would matter.

Grumbling, Geir stuck his hands under his armpits. "If our stones freeze rock solid, we're not like to care about werewolves either."

"Too late," one of the men complained, and the others snickered.

The sun was dipping low. A third night. If the wolves didn't come tonight, they'd have to rethink their plan. They had announced their presence already, and if the varulfur didn't take the bait, they had wasted their efforts.

Sometime later, a howl rang out through the woods.

Another followed, and another.

Tyr held up a hand to forestall any of the men from speaking. Varulfur had great ears. Like real wolves. Stronger than men, track you by scent, hear you breathing. Best hunters in Midgard. But Tyr didn't like being hunted.

A large black wolf loped toward the tower. It meant others lurked in the woods, waiting. Watching to see if men saw their scout.

Tyr kept his hand up. Not yet.

The wolf nudged open the main door. It didn't latch, and they had left it unbarred on purpose. A moment later, shouts rang out. Growls. Screams.

Not yet.

Geir tried to rise behind him, and Tyr shoved him back down.

The varulfur would not send *one* wolf after them. Never just one.

And then five more oversized wolves came charging from the woods, rushing for the tower. Geir pushed past Tyr and charged out, bellowing a war cry. At the sound, two of the wolves broke off and circled him.

"Up! Go!" Tyr shouted at the others.

He scrambled out of the snowdrift.

"For Athra!" Geir shouted, swinging an axe wildly at the wolves. One jumped back out of the way. The other leapt forward, bearing him down. Teeth closed on his throat and yanked. Tore it out, showering steaming gore on the snow.

An arrow caught that one. It yelped. Tried to fall back. Tyr charged it, slashing. The wolf ducked, moving with uncanny speed. Dodged again and leapt for Tyr. He whipped his sword back into place, and the wolf impaled itself. The impact sent Tyr toppling over backward, heavy canine form landing atop him.

The other wolf snapped at him, but Geir's warriors tore into it with axes and spears. Its jaws closed around a man's knee and ripped it out. Bastard fell wailing.

The corpse atop Tyr had become a man. Heavy, too. Tyr shoved him off, jerked his sword free. Archers had felled another wolf outside the tower, but more screams echoed within. Tyr raced over there.

A wolf charged him as he hit the threshold. He didn't have time for a proper swing, but he twisted his blade enough to shear off part of the wolf's ear. The beast fell, whimpering. Tyr kicked it, twice. Then raised his blade to run it through.

"No, wait," Annar said. The jarl was favoring one arm,

blood seeping out between the chain links of his shirt. "A prisoner."

"You want to try to hold a varulf prisoner?"

The whole tower had become a slaughter house. Blood coated every wall, every surface. Half of Annar's men lay dead or dying, many missing their throats. One poor bastard was clutching his guts, uselessly trying to pile them back into his torn-open belly.

"Prisoners have uses. Especially those cowed by a solid defeat."

Several of these dead must have come from the varulfur.

Tyr groaned. Annar had a point. He kicked the downed varulf again. Hard.

§

THE TOWER HAD A BASEMENT, one lined with rotting barrels. Contents long since turned to dust. Rat shit covered half the floor. Rusted manacles on one wall served their purpose though. Not ideal. A varulf might be able to break bonds. If he did, Tyr would run him through. The sun had forced the man back into human form, and they had bound him in that awful place.

Two archers stood, arrows nocked and readied, and before them, a spearman. And Tyr, sword in hand. Given half an excuse, he'd have run through this shapeshifting trollfucker.

He kicked him in the gut, drawing him into sudden alertness. A low growl from deep inside the beast.

"Tell us your master's plans, wolf," Annar said.

The varulf sneered. "My master?"

Tyr grabbed him by the hair and hefted him to his feet.

"We know you serve the Godwulfs. Do not waste our time denying it."

"The Godwulfs, yes. But Jarl Alci?" The varulf spat on the floor, dangerously close to Tyr's boot.

Tyr raised his eyes slowly from the thick phlegm to the half-man before him. "Do not lie to me."

"On my honor."

Tyr scoffed. "Honor? What honor, varulf?"

The man strained against his chains. Rust showered down from them, where links ground together. The varulf leaned his face as close to Tyr as his bonds allowed. "I serve my tribe. You have no idea what it's like to have this thing inside you. Driving you to kill. *Worse.* So you can go fuck a troll. But you can't judge me."

Annar advanced now, wending his way through spearmen and archers. "What do you want from us?"

"Me? Not a damned thing. Alci, though, he wants it all. Your lands, your tribute. Probably your life, if you're the jarl."

Annar folded his arms over his chest. "You have a name, varulf?"

"I do. Hallr. Hallr Stonecrusher."

Annar looked to Tyr. "How'd you fasten a name like that?"

"Bit off another varulf's stones when he challenged me over a mate." The varulf smirked. "Listen. You don't have to kill me. You want the raids to stop? I could do that. If I were jarl."

Tyr groaned. So being a murderous beast was not enough. This varulf wanted to betray his own lord. No greater breach of honor seemed possible. They ought to send the men back to Alci with word of his treachery. Let the jarl exact what justice he would.

Or ... Or maybe Tyr ought to just finish things here and now. Keeping a varulf in their midst was asking for Annar to lose more good men like Geir. He pushed the edge of his sword against Hallr's neck. "Is there any reason I ought not leave you to rot in this tower?"

"Tyr." Annar's arm on his wrist. "He may have his uses."

Tyr spat in disgust but lowered his blade.

"Tell me," Annar said. "Why all this? Only because of Borr's death? Was that all that held Alci back?"

Hallr chuckled. "Made it easier, maybe. No, this was already simmering. You think Alci takes it well, his weak and dying brother holding Halfhaugr? The greatest fortress in Aujum? So when the messengers of Otwin came to us, he leapt at the offer."

"What are you talking about?" Annar demanded. "Who's Otwin?"

"King of Njarar, come at last to collect on the debt Hadding owed his father. And when Hadding refused him, he armed Alci with blades and armor of the finest make. Rumor says Volund himself forged them in the war. Otwin wants his due, and he wants his vengeance. But I care not a troll's fuck for either, and even less about the Athra. And if you are so keen to save yourselves, help me take the throne from him."

"Why would anyone follow you?" Tyr asked.

"I'm a distant cousin to the jarl and a respected warrior in our tribe."

Tyr shook his head. "Not here, you're not. You're a traitor, betraying your oath and your kin alike. Annar, hang this man and be done with it."

Annar rubbed his beard a moment. Then shook his head. "Not yet. I need to know how far Odin will support us."

Tyr glowered. Odin didn't even know Tyr had come. He could offer no promises on the man coming to support his cousin, much as Odin did value family. Still, Tyr was going to have to tell him now, especially with Alci moving in on Halfhaugr. Besides which, he needed to see Idunn. Maybe the goddess could see a way through this mire of intrigue and betrayal. Tyr surely could not.

"I'll leave for Eskgard as soon as I've gathered supplies. Annar, heed me. Do not let this man out of your sight while I am away. You cannot trust him."

The jarl nodded. "We'll bring him back to Breivik. Chains stay on. Fare well, Tyr."

And swiftly, Tyr hoped.

## 16

The depths of Halfhaugr, of the fortress itself, delved deep into the ground, dug—legend claimed—by dvergar. According to skalds, the twisted vaettir once held many lands beyond Nidavellir but had long since withdrawn from the affairs of men. In tales, they had built this place and marked it with ancient runes now known to only the völvur. Some, not even they understood. Sigyn didn't doubt the dvergar existed as such; she doubted more whether they truly were vaettir, spirits from an Otherworld, or rather, simply an old people now nigh unto extinct and long departed from these lands.

Frigg worked in one of those deep rooms, denying access to any of her father's men but welcoming Sigyn. As if Sigyn would ever feel welcome anywhere in Halfhaugr. Her half sister ground up some rancid paste on a table while a cauldron bubbled with fulvous smoke Sigyn avoided drawing too close to.

"Is that going to save him?" They both knew the signs in their father, of the thickness saturating his lungs, and he was not like to live out the winter.

Frigg sighed. "I don't know."

"What do the runes say?" The ancient markings decorated this room, as they did the outer fortress, but here, the
dvergar had grouped their writings close together, recording
a tale now forgotten by men. Perhaps that had led Frigg to
choose this place to work her witchcraft. It ought to break
Sigyn's heart, watching her own father die. But a heart can
only be broken so many times before a woman stops
noticing an extra crack or two. Sigyn ran her fingers along
the runes, tracing the patterns. "What does this one mean?"

"You know I can't tell you that. It is forbidden." Desperation and frustration mingled in her voice.

"I might be able to help."

"You are not a völva." They'd had this conversation
before, of course. Too many times. Sigyn would keep asking
until Frigg's desperation outweighed any concern for pointless traditions of secrecy.

The völvur jealously guarded all their secrets, runes
included. Since she had first come to the fortress two
winters ago, Sigyn had resolved to unravel the threads, solve
this puzzle. And at the moment, she'd do aught to keep her
mind off of Hermod. Off the danger he faced. As if any
puzzle, no matter how elaborate, could make her forget.

The door swung open, slammed against the wall, and
made Frigg jump, spilling the paste all over the table. They
both turned to see Fulla standing there, flushed and panting, eyes gleaming.

"You don't know what news I've got, I dare say you don't,
now do you?" The red-haired servant bore a grin wide
enough her face ought to have split in half like that.

Sigyn tapped a finger against her lip, but Frigg answered
before she could say aught. "What's happened?"

"Jarl Odin came back, he did. Not afore killing a jotunn,

deader than dead down in the Sudurberks. Whole town is talking of it. The scouts, they wanted him to stay and feast, but did he now? No! That man just went tromping right on back to Wodan lands like he had an awful rush on him, not hearing of aught else."

"Deader than dead?" Sigyn asked. "Are you certain? Maybe the jotunn was just plain dead."

"Well I didn't see the body myself now, but I can say I'm nigh positive, still."

Sigyn rolled her eyes. A jotunn. Really. "The bluster of men often knows few bounds, and he's not the first to claim to have slain some mystical monster. But a jotunn, here? If they exist at all, they dwell beyond the Midgard Wall."

Sighing, Frigg swept the paste back into the mortar bowl. "So, he did not stop in the town at all?" His absence would make all Frigg's schemes more difficult. Hard to sway a man who was not here. In fact, had he come here half as flush with his victory as Fulla seemed to be, Frigg might have drawn him to her bed. "I suppose we'll have to go there, then."

"I don't think you want to do that," Sigyn said. "Go chasing after him, and you show your impuissance in a time when the appearance of strength could mean everything." Like herself, following after Hermod. Wanting to ride Snow Rabbit back there and rescue him from his urd, though he sought no rescue from her or anyone else. "He wishes to celebrate with his kin. Let him. When the revels fade, he will remember who helped him, or if he does not, then he wouldn't have proved a stalwart ally in any event."

"You don't know what I saw in his future."

Nor was she certain she should care. "Because you chose to keep it to yourself. Share if you wish."

"Oh now!" Fulla said. "That sounds a wonderful idea, it does, my lady! Why you just tell us all about your visions, and we'll help you understand them."

Sigyn snorted. "Yes. *We'll* help you understand."

Frigg looked from her maid to Sigyn and back before her shoulders slumped, ever so slightly. "No, no. I must speak with Father. Odin's fame will begin to spread now, embers sparking a wildfire."

So she believed his boast? Sigyn shook her head, and Frigg strode from the room, Fulla chasing after her as always. Killed a jotunn. Had he claimed to have felled a troll, she might have given it at least some credence. But a jotunn? She found that about as believable as men who claimed to have fucked valkyries.

Sigyn folded her hands behind her back and stared at the runes carved into the walls. Frigg, all the völvur, they thought to keep the secrets of old times among themselves, and thus they refused to teach any others to read the runes. Never even imagining a clever enough woman might begin to uncover their meanings on her own.

But symbols repeated in more than one place formed a pattern, and patterns were just puzzles with a few missing pieces. Find enough pieces and a woman could guess the shape, one answer leading unto the next until, with enough time, the picture of the whole clarified. The irony, of course, in Frigg's refusal to teach her the runes, lay in Sigyn now being unable to elucidate to Frigg the ones the völva herself did not seem to understand.

Her half sister had chosen this room to work in, knowing it important, and yet probably not even supposing why. In the chambers beneath Halfhaugr, the dvergar builders had recorded a history stretching back to ancient times. More surprising still, they seemed to predict or even prophesy events not yet unfolded. Something about the doom of gods, assuming she had correctly interpreted the other runes. A tale of destruction and of the someone or something that brought it about—a destroyer the dvergar feared. They wrote as if the gods were real, as if Vanaheim were a real place. If so, what could threaten Vanaheim?

Frigg's table stood against the wall, obscuring some of those final runes. Her sister rarely left her alone down here, and Sigyn could not exactly go creeping around the fortress on her own. She glanced over her shoulder, then crept over to the doorway. No one out in the hall. She shut the door, then dragged that table away from the wall to give her an unobscured view of the runes.

Ages of dust caked the lower wall. She knelt and brushed it away with her hand. Cracks had broken along the ancient stone. But these runes, here, they appeared at the beginning of the story as well. She traced them with her fingers. Eaters? Devourers? Beings born of chaos and driven to engulf the World in that same anarchy.

At the start of the tale, the Vanir, the gods, had struggled against these beings who would feast on men. And here, at the end, the dvergar wrote of the return of devourers.

Her heart began to race.

Sigyn rose, glancing from the upper runes to the lower ones. The Vanir had fought terrible battles against these devourers. Jotunnar? She tapped a finger against her lip. The Vanir defeat of the devourers marked the dawn of the World of Men. But naught lasted forever. So if these devourers were jotunnar, and if Odin *had* faced one ... then according to the dvergar runes, they stood upon the cusp of the end times.

A chill wracked her, and she blew out a long breath. What was she doing, getting caught up in this religious nonsense? She laughed at herself. She had more important things to worry over than the words of some fallen civilization.

$\mathcal{T}$he tribe's elkhounds heralded their return long before Odin and his brothers reached the Wodan town. By the time Odin reached the sentries, dozens of tribesmen and women bearing torches had rushed out to greet him. He was their jarl now, and they needed to see him as glorious. Especially if it meant no one looked too closely at Ve.

"The sons of Borr have returned," he said, spreading his arms as if to take in the entire tribe. "And they are *victorious*!"

His incautious shout echoed through Eskgard, and with it rose a cheer from all around. Most nights he might have urged control lest the vaettir in the woods be drawn to the town. But they needed a celebration. Ve needed one most. Maybe enough mead and a night with a woman, and he'd been spouting poetic insults at Vili afresh.

"The jotunn Ymir is dead!" Odin shouted and hefted Gungnir. "I drove this through his eye and split his skull. And I ask you—who is your jarl?"

"Odin!" the crowd cheered. Shieldmaidens pressed

forward, some winking salaciously at Odin, others eying his brothers. A pair of particularly voluptuous sisters each took one of Vili's arms around their shoulders and guided him away.

Odin raised his arms, waving down the commotion. Then he slammed Gungnir into the ground, letting it stand as a reminder to all of what they had accomplished. "Then I ask you ..." he said, when his people at last grew silent. "Where. Is. The *mead*?"

Another whoop filled the night, his people caught up in his own joy. On this night, let trolls and draugar and any other vaettir hear. Let them come and see the Ás tribe that had slain a jotunn. Let them know that on this night, men ruled. On this night, at least, Mankind would not fear the darkness beyond the flame, would not fear the cold or the mist. Especially not the Hel-cursed mist.

In moments, a stein of mead graced every hand, including Odin's, as a blonde girl slipped him a mug. The smith's daughter, he thought, and by the sinewy tendons on her arm, like to follow in her father's trade. If the look in her eye was any indication, she was a girl more than happy to serve her jarl.

Someone struck up a song, and soon the whole of Eskgard was caught in its fever, chanting along to ancient words calling back to ancestors long passed. They called their ghosts down from Valhalla, that their fathers and their fathers' fathers might look with pride on the tribe this night. And did Father see him? Did he hold himself avenged, or did he blame Odin for Ve's condition? Odin would not let Ve fall, not under any circumstance.

He'd only taken two steps when Heidr, the völva of the Wodan tribe, pressed a hand to his chest. "You grow too bold."

And here, the woman most apt to recognize the change in Ve. It made her a threat, but he forced himself to smile. He grabbed her around the waist and planted a kiss on her lips. Heidr probably had fifteen more winters than Odin's own twenty-four, but she was comely. Not that he'd ever bed a völva.

Heidr shoved Odin away. "You forget yourself, jarl!"

"Not yet, witch," Odin said, then took another swig of mead. "But a couple more of these and just maybe. You might try it. If not with me, then for the gods' sakes, with *someone.*"

He knew better, of course. A man would need more than a few drinks to risk falling under a witch's spell.

"You still behave like the child you always were," Heidr said and took another step away from him. Odin swore her glare ought to be enough to melt snow. "Your father was a man who understood—actions have consequences. You have a responsibility to your people now. Your gallivanting is apt to bring the wrath of the vaettir down on us, and though you *think* yourself prepared for the harsh realities of life, you are *not*, my jarl. Not even close."

Odin waved her away. He had no time for lectures. Besides, no doubt a lass or three would be eager to join him in his bed. Maybe he could still find the smith's daughter. He waded through the celebration, slapping his kin on the shoulders as he passed. All raised mugs to him. Good folk. Folk who knew life was short. Moments were all you had. Hel-cursed völva probably had her arse squeezed so tight she couldn't pop a fart to save her life. The World was what it was: cold and bloody. A good death was the best one could hope for—that and lots of fighting and fucking before one got there. Odin planned to make a fair account for himself before valkyries came for his soul—and he couldn't do that running scared of what might lurk in the night.

Times like this, in the heart of winter, nights were long. Cold.

Feral grunts sounded from Vili's tent, followed by the sound of one woman's giggles and another's cries of pleasure. Odin shook his head. His brother didn't waste any time. Vili had two bastard children already, which seemed to suit him nicely. The man often paraded through town, a toddler on each shoulder, boasting of his conquests on the battlefield and in his tent. Knowing Vili, he probably hoped some of the bastards would grow up to be berserkir like himself. Not that Odin would mind—the more berserkir a tribe had, the more influence they could win. Berserkir and varulfur were savage, but savagery had its uses.

A bonfire blazed in the heart of the town.

Nights like this, Father had sat in front of the fire, telling tales of the Njarar War, of his travels among the other tribes, legends of Vingethor and the Great March, or myths of the lost runeblades of ancient times. Father had been nigh a skald himself, and Ve took after him that way. Odin shook himself, trying to force the image from his mind.

Someone offered Odin a slab of elk flesh, which he took with thanks. The rest of the animal roasted over the fire. Grease dripped from it, sending sizzles of smoke into the sky and an aroma fit for gods wafting around. Odin bit off a hefty piece, savoring the steaming juices as they dribbled down his chin. Unlike his brothers, he didn't wear much of a beard, and for just this reason. He'd never liked feeling it sticky with grease and fat. Of course, Vili kept one for *just* that reason—he said if he got hungry in the middle of the night he need only lick his whiskers.

In the shadows, just beyond the firelight, sat Loki. The

same lass, the smith's daughter, seemed to be trying her wiles on Loki now. Poor girl wasn't having much luck, though, from the look of it. Loki acknowledged every word she said without ever meeting her gaze. He just kept staring into the fire as if it held more of interest than a woman's hips. Damned strange man, that foreigner. Odin's brother, now.

Mug in one hand, hunk of elk in another, Odin marched over to them. "What's your name, lass?"

"Jorunn, lord."

"Well, Jorunn, I need a few moments to speak with my brother here." He clapped her on the shoulder. "I'm sure you understand." The last thing he wanted was to make her feel rejected twice in one night. Nobody deserved that.

The girl blew out a breath but nodded. From the smell, she'd had more mead than Odin had. Good for her. Course, he'd have to fix that. No girl of seventeen winters was out-drinking him.

She strolled back toward the fire with admirable poise, only a slight sway in her steps. Or she could have been swinging her arse that way to get his attention. Which it had. He'd not mind a closer look, in fact.

"So," Odin said, then cleared his throat. "Don't you like girls? That lass seemed fair eager to share her warmth with you tonight."

Loki chuckled. "A drunk child, eager to share her warmth with any who would have her, just so she wouldn't have to feel alone in this world."

"That's pretty much what everyone wants, right?"

"After a fashion," Loki said. "But I doubt you came to ask me about my sexual appetites."

Odin snorted. "No." No, he'd left Ve wandering the town as a man in a daze. Eating, at least, but still it soured

Odin's mood. Let the people have their feast. They did not know, could not know, the fresh grief Odin had brought among them. In avenging his father, he had placed his own brother in jeopardy, no doubt further agitating Father's shade. "I have to find that damned amulet. Do you know of it?"

Loki poked the fire with a stick and stared at it a while before answering. "The wise man might have asked such a question before agreeing to the quest."

Odin groaned. "I already have a fucking völva to lecture me. Wisdom is for elders and witches. Men have to take action. Wait too long, and opportunity burns away." He took another swig from the mead and waggled his fingers over the fire. "Burns away like smoke. And you didn't answer the question."

"And here you claim not to value wisdom."

"Bah. Speak plainly, brother. You know these things, things about the Old Kingdoms, call yourself a student of history. Do you know of the Singasteinn, or don't you?"

Loki sighed. "There is a tale spoken of by but a few völvur, that long before the mist, the seas had swallowed our world. Men had little, but one made a deal with a mermaid. She drew up the most perfect pearl from the depths of the ocean and ensorcelled it, forged an amulet from it, one designed to grant the wearer power in a world so inundated. And when the seas had receded, still the amulet remained. Lost to the tribes that once held it, found by others, and lost yet again, down through the ages. But those who touch the Art are drawn to artifacts created with it, and such things rarely remain lost forever."

"Uh huh." Odin licked the last juices from the elk meat off his fingers. "That helps me about as much as a cock made of straw. What I want to know is what I'm supposed to do about the fucking thing. You're the one with all the answers, so tell me what to do."

"No man has all the answers, Odin. Some just have better questions."

Odin lurched to his feet, scowling at the foreigner. He leaned close. "I do not have time for games or riddles. You know what I'm dealing with, and if you can't or won't help me save my brother, I'll find someone who will."

At that, he spun and left Loki to stare in the damned flame.

The feast had served well enough to keep the others distracted, drunk and thinking little of Ve. But that might not last forever. If the people learned of Ve's condition they would banish him into the mist. Odin could not let that happen. And if he could just find these Niflungar, that ghost would solve his problems.

"I swear, Father," he mumbled under his breath. "I swear I'll save him."

He had not gone far when Tyr cut him off. Father's champion. And indeed, Tyr had helped train Odin with weapons, helped him grow into the warrior he was. Tyr's fame had spread throughout Aujum. Could he help Ve? Certainly his loyalty to Father had seemed absolute. And to Borr's sons?

Odin clapped Tyr on the shoulder, drawing him to walk beside him. "We did it."

"I heard. Skalds will sing of your feat until the end of time."

Well. Odin liked the sound of that. "Yes, but now I face another challenge."

Tyr nodded. "Glad to hear you say it. Consider Idunn's challenge to you. Your fame in slaying the jotunn will spread. Strengthen your claim to becoming king. Still, you'll need supporters. I spoke with your cousin Annar. The Athra find themselves in difficult times. If you were to—"

"What the fuck, man? I already told Idunn I have neither time nor desire to claim any throne." Was that what Tyr had been doing with his time? Odin scowled and shook his head. Being jarl was burden enough.

"You *must* talk to the Vanr, Odin. You cannot ignore the words of the gods. It is madness."

Idunn. Could she truly be a goddess? In the chaos of the hunt and of Ve's condition, Odin had given her little enough thought. But she had offered—had claimed to have an apple of Yggdrasil. One that would grant eternal life. Eternal life ... "Where is she?"

Tyr nodded, obviously pleased, then pointed to one of the outlying fires. "Speak to her. Then we must talk of the Athra."

Odin shook his head and stormed over to the fire where the supposed Vanr sat, laughing with a pair of shieldmaidens, passing around the drinking horn.

Idunn looked up at his approach and crooked a mischievous half smile.

"Walk with me," he said. "Please."

She whispered something to the nearest shieldmaiden, something that set the woman chuckling and winking at Odin. Idunn rose then. Odin snatched a burning branch from the fire as a makeshift torch, and wandered toward the edge of the town, Idunn drifting by his side.

"Are you a temptress?"

Idunn laughed. "For certain. Are *you* tempted?"

For certain. "In so many ways."

She laughed again, shaking her head. "If you are who you claim to be, I need a sign," Odin said.

"Oh? Huh. Why?"

What in the gates of Hel was wrong with her? "Because you walk into my life, ask me to do great deeds, offer me great boons, and claim to be a goddess. Would you believe such a person?"

"Ahhh." She smiled again, grabbing his hand and drawing him through the main gate, outside the town. "So you think I'm not really the same Idunn who gave your ancestors the spear. I understand. Why would you believe such a tale, after all? So instead, you turn to a stranger who takes you up a fell mountain, hunting a jotunn. And did that work out the way you wanted, did it sate the emptiness in your heart or solve your deepest worries?"

Odin frowned. Could she somehow already know about Ve? About what killing Ymir had cost him? He shook his head. "I want to trust you."

"Wonderful! I want that too."

Odin worked his jaw. How did a man deal with such a woman?

Idunn swirled around, finally pointing to the south, toward the Sudurberks. "So you climbed the peak with your foreign guide. What did you think of the mountain? Was it beautiful? Mysterious, unknowable?"

"I suppose so," he said, following as she led him toward the forest on the edge of the town. "I didn't think of it that way. I was there for a reason."

"Ah, that's the thing, my lord. You take it for granted because, for you, it's always been this way, hasn't it? Like this tree," she said, putting her hand on one. "Is this a normal tree?"

Odin shrugged. As far as he knew it was. Some of the trees might have their own spirits within. In summer, the sparse greenery of the forest would thicken, hiding increased game and sometimes even fruits. The weaker plants never survived the hoar, but some did. Some always did. Life adapted.

Long before summer, he'd have to honor his oath to the Odlingar ghost. Not quite three moons, and here, away from the terror the ghost invoked, that suddenly seemed a very scant amount of time.

Idunn pressed a finger to her lips, kissed it, then pressed it against the tree. A ripple passed under the bark, and ice fell away, shaking free from the branches. Leaves sprouted— moons before they should have. And then, unbelievably, flowers began to burst from the branches. An explosion of white and pink and red petals erupted across the tree.

Odin had seen flowers on occasion, but this ... He fell to his knees, mouth agape at the sight. A rainbow of colors. A warmth seemed to radiate from the trunk, from the flowers, from the very roots beneath the ground.

A long, cool breath escaped Idunn, and she steadied herself against the trunk.

"Wh-what *is* this sorcery?" Odin managed.

Idunn caught her breath a moment before answering. "What this world once looked like, before the Fimbulvinter. What it's meant to look like."

Fimbulvinter. He'd heard that term—what skalds called the time after the coming of the mists. This age. Then it was all true? Midgard had once been free of the mist? It had known warmth, and the nightmares visited upon Mankind —the trolls and draugar and aught else borne in the cold— were not meant to be.

"There was really a time before all this?" He waved his hand at the mist gathering just beyond the flames of his makeshift torch.

Idunn stared at something beyond his vision. When she spoke, her words came out slowly, albeit still with her unusual accent. "My grandfather died battling Hel, trying to keep her from spreading this mist across this world. He gave his life to stop the invasion of Niflheim, but much of the world of death had already spread into ours. And for nearly five thousand years, Mankind has been left out in the cold. Most of our Realm looks like that ..." she pointed first to the mist, then to the tree she'd set into bloom, "... when it should look like *this*."

Thoughts ran through Odin's mind too fast for him to call them to order. Five thousand winters ... did that mean Idunn herself was so old? She looked to be no more than twenty-five. And they were true, the stories that said the mists came from Niflheim itself? Men always said that, but Men were quick to claim Hel visited all the wrongs of the World on them. And völvur were so caught up in their own mystery he'd never given too much credence to their claims. Which made him twice the fool. All his life he'd spurned the lessons and warnings Heidr tried to impart, certain *she* was the one who did not live in the real world.

Odin swallowed, trying to get a handle on the situation. "Then why not use your power to fix all the trees?"

Idunn laughed, the sound high and echoing, clean as a brook in summer. By now, others had gathered to stare at the tree, just out of earshot. Afraid, no doubt. As was he, truth be told. Such sorcery was beyond his ken. Idunn had not lied when she claimed to be of the Vanir.

"It takes too much out of me, sweet Odin. I gave part of my own life to do this. It's different than sorcery. And even in a thousand lifetimes, I could never restore every tree in this world. They would die faster than I could finish my work. But there is a place where spring—true spring—reigns eternal." She waited for his questioning look before continuing. "Vanaheim."

"The islands of the Vanir ... they're real too?"

Idunn leaned close to his face, so close he could feel her warm breath. "Real enough. Like me. Do I seem like a dream to you?"

Odin swallowed and fell back a step. "A dream might be easier to believe." He shook his head. "What do you want of me? Why me?"

"Excellent questions," she said, holding up a finger. "As to the second, you're cunning, ruthless, and courageous. You've the potential to be a great king. You could go far, if you stop staring at my breasts."

Odin flushed. Right. Look at her eyes. Best not even consider other parts of her anatomy that had been on his mind. Odin rubbed his temples. "Can you, uh, give me a moment, please?"

"Of course. Sometimes we all need some time to think things through. Take as much time as you need. I'm immortal, so it doesn't bother me. For certain, though, it's nice to have someone to talk to. By the Tree, wandering the World you spend so much time alone, or hiding from different kinds of vaettir, trolls, and men of ill intent."

Odin stopped listening to her babble. She had spoken the truth. She truly was a goddess. No völva could have wrought the miracle with that tree. And if that much was true, then, too, must her tale about the apples be.

Apples of immortality.

"... because down in the far south, some places are still warm—not warm like Vanaheim, but warmer than here. And besides, my ancestors came from islands in—"

Odin cleared his throat. "Idunn."

She quirked a half smile. "Sorry. Was I rambling? I get lonely out here."

"My brother, Ve," Odin said. "He ..."

Idunn's face fell a little. "I spoke with him. The mists are deep inside him now."

"And can the apple stop him from going Mist-mad?"

Idunn pursed her lips. "An apple would certainly slow the process."

"Then give him the apple, please, I beg you."

Idunn glanced at the gathering crowd, then once again took Odin's hand and led him deeper into the forest. They wandered in silence a time, Idunn's steps slow, a little unsteady. She did seem weakened, drained. No wonder she he had hesitated to provide any demonstration of her power.

She leaned against a tree and blew out a breath. "I have an apple for you, and enough for those closest to you. But I already gave you my terms. You must make an oath to become king and to fulfill my wish once you have done so."

Odin clenched his fists at his side. For a brief instant he imagined himself strangling the woman. Goddess. No, even if he could have killed her—and with her power, who knew —he was not that kind of man. He had to be worthy of his father. With a growl, he unclenched his fists and stepped close to her. "So be it. I swear it."

"Swear an oath you cannot break."

Odin leaned a hand against the tree, placing his face a breath away from hers. "I swear on my father's spear, Gung-nir, and upon my father's name, Borr. I will make myself king, and I will grant you any favor within my power. Now, give me the fucking apples!"

She ran a finger over his cheek, and he trembled. Then she pushed him gently backward. She turned and knelt, then dug away at snow piled in front of the tree's roots until she revealed a hollow inside. From this, she drew forth a basket filled with apples that shimmered like gold. Even from the basket, their sweet scent wafted toward him, making his mouth water.

Idunn ran her fingertips over the apples before selecting one and offering it to him. "You will eat first; then I will take one to Ve."

His hand closed around the apple. Warmth filled his palm.

"Come," Idunn said. "Eat just one. And taste apotheosis."

Odin's breath had grown ragged. His heart pounded as he raised an apple to his lips. There would be no turning back. He didn't know what *apotheosis* meant, but if this worked, he would have to become a king. He would become more than a king. He would become a god. A thousand generations would praise his name. And by Hel, he'd be there to witness those thousand generations. Immortal as Idunn.

To be king of all the Aesir ... What glory. What honor to his father. What pride. Heidr had so often tried to warn him of the cost of his pride, and he had never listened.

But he had sworn an oath. He had to save Ve.

Slowly he bit down. Juice flowed over his tongue. Sweeter than any fruit he'd ever tasted. Sweet and bitter and spicy all at once. He swallowed, almost able to feel the bits flooding through his nerves. Explosions of sensation cascaded along his body, and he became only dimly aware he continued to eat. It was like eating the essence of life. Better than mead or sex or aught he'd ever known.

Stars swarmed before his eyes, and he fell on his back, watching as the mists cleared and revealed the glorious sun beyond. Midgard itself pulsed with life, as did every being on it. And he could feel them all. He shuddered in ecstasy until he had to close his eyes against the flood of sensations.

When he opened his eyes, he was looking up at Idunn, lying with his head in her lap.

"What happened?" he mumbled.

She stroked his hair. "You are changed now."

His pulse was pounding, his loins throbbing. Everything seemed apt to burst around him. Fire coursed through his veins as he rolled over, forced himself to stand.

"Ve?"

Idunn stood as well. "I will take him an apple."

"Vili too." Odin groaned. The World was spinning around him.

"That will leave you few apples left. Choose your remaining companions carefully, Odin."

He waved the comment away, panting, stumbling back toward the town. Gods! What was happening to him? Ethereal colors flittered at the edge of his vision. His gut had become a roil, twisting, writhing. His stones had become pulsing flames, so hot they seemed apt to burn through his trousers.

In the town, a riot of sensation coursed over him, the smells, the laughter, the taste in the air of smoke and food and sex. Jorunn was taking the drinking horn again. Odin staggered toward her, shoved the horn away, and kissed her. Her tongue was in his mouth, exploring, driving his senses to explode. Unable to stand it a moment longer, he grabbed the girl, threw her over his shoulder, and carried her off to his hall.

She giggled as he shouldered his way toward his bed. Wide-eyed slaves gawked a moment. It didn't matter. Odin yanked the girl's dress away, fumbled with his own trousers so clumsily he tore the laces.

Not sure whether he wanted to moan, laugh, or cry, he entered her. Part of him knew he used her more roughly than was his habit, but she only clutched him tighter. Gods, he couldn't get enough.

He would never, ever have enough.

Three times he took her, until she protested she could handle no more.

Then he beckoned one of the slave girls over to join them.

ODIN SHOT awake at the sound of the howl. It echoed through the town like a cry from Hel, setting all the hairs on his neck on end. The girl on his chest clutched her arms around his waist.

"My lord?"

Odin pushed her aside and snatched his trousers and a fur cloak. The screams began before he'd even finished fastening it with his brooch. Odin stumbled from the hall in time to see a massive black wolf leap onto a shieldmaiden and tear her apart. Its jaws ripped through her throat and shredded her flesh.

His spear. He needed his spear. He scrambled past the feeding wolf, struggling to reach Gungnir, unable to look away from the gruesome sight. Her death was his fault. He'd left his spear standing in the snow, a symbol of his pride. A symbol of his vanity.

A wolf circled in front of him, cutting him off. It turned its head toward Odin's spear, then back at him. And it pulled its lips back in a snarl.

Hel. It *knew*.

These weren't just wolves. Their eyes had the intelligence of men. These were varulfur. And the völva had been right. This celebration had caught their attention.

Someone shrieked in agony behind Odin. He kept his eyes locked on the wolf man. It advanced on him with slow deliberateness, a fell gleam in its eyes. Odin could tell it knew he was unarmed and was toying with him.

A man charged from the far side of the nearest tent, bellowing a war cry, sword high over his head. Tyr hadn't had time for armor or even clothes. Blood drenched him from the neck down—no little of it his own, judging from the bite on his arm.

The varulfur spun, leaping aside as Tyr swept his sword downward.

"My lord! Go!"

Odin nodded at his man. Tyr could take care of himself. There was no finer warrior among the Aesir. And the distraction gave Odin just enough time to reach Gungnir. He ran for it, skidding to a stop as his hand wrapped around the shaft. An immediate power filled him. His strength and fury amplified. The rage of the dragon coursed through his veins. These wolves had picked the wrong town.

Spear raised over his head, Odin roared a challenge to any varulf foolish enough to accept. Moments later, a pair of them bounded toward him. No single challenge. So be it. He whipped the spear around, turning about and using its length to keep both wolves at bay. One snapped at him. A twist of his wrist slashed Gungnir's blade across the beast's snout. The werewolf yelped in pain and fell to the snow, pawing at its half-severed nose.

The other varulf jumped for him. Odin snapped the butt of his spear into its throat. The wolf fell, gagging.

"I am Odin, jarl of the Wodanar! And I send you to Hel, shapeshifter!" He thrust his spear straight down. It pierced right through the wolf and into the ground. The creature gurgled, then began a slow shift back into man form.

A woman screamed as Odin yanked Gungnir free. That had come from the guest house he'd given Idunn. It had to be fifty feet away. Odin took off at a sprint, but it would be too late before he got there. He was human, and he'd never cover that distance before the varulf devoured her.

His breath came in shallow gasps, the cold stinging his lungs. He had to try.

He barged into the house in time to see a wolf jump at Idunn.

"No!" Odin hefted Gungnir for a throw.

The wolf passed through Idunn's form, which shuddered then vanished.

Odin's jaw fell open, the spear forgotten in his hand. Sorcery?

The wolf shook its head, sniffed the room, then turned toward the bed. Odin followed its gaze to a slight shimmer in the air, trembling among the covers.

The wolf leapt at the shimmer. Odin flung Gungnir. It flew fast as ever, impacting the wolf midair. The varulf crumpled and fell, a splatter of blood coating the shimmer before vanishing. Odin strode over to the wolf, now whimpering on the ground, planted his foot on its head, and yanked his spear free. The beast stilled and transformed back into a man.

"Idunn?"

"Hmm," her voice answered, coming from the direction of the bed. A heartbeat later, the shimmer fell away like a discarded shawl, revealing the woman beneath. Blood coated her face and dress, but it looked to be all from the varulf.

"Are you harmed, my lady?"

"No. I ... I'm fine. Thank you. By the Tree, I should have

known it could smell me, what with that wolf spirit inside it. A foolish mistake that could well have cost me my life."

Dare he leave Idunn alone? Odin backed toward the house's threshold but hesitated there.

"Go," she said, clearly reading his unease. "I've crossed from one side of Midgard to the other, foolish mistakes notwithstanding. I can take care of myself."

The sorcery. Odin nodded to her and darted out into the snow. The town had become a slaughter. Dozens of warriors and shieldmaidens lay wounded or dying. What a fool he'd been to disobey Heidr. She'd always urged caution, insisted the Aesir remain quiet and avoid attention. And he'd ignored her wisdom and thought *her* the fool for wasting her life in fear. She would know what to do now.

He started for her but caught Ve standing around, watching the varulfur with a blank expression on his face. Gods, not now. They could not afford this tonight. Odin slapped him on the shoulder. "Little brother!"

Ve turned toward him, eyes a bit too wide. For a brief instant they glimmered red. It was just a reflection of the fire. Had to be.

"Arm yourself, Ve!" Odin shouted, then took off running again.

He had to find Heidr, ensure her safety. Maybe her witchcraft could drive away these wolves. He bypassed several fights against the varulfur. Mankind might be disadvantaged against their superior strength and speed, but he had to—

A bear roared, a swipe of his claws taking off the muzzle of one wolf as another leapt onto his back. The Wodanar had their own shapeshifter, and Vili would help even the odds. Odin jumped into the air and flung Gungnir, impaling the wolf on his brother's back. The creature fell in a heap. Odin rushed over, yanked the spear free, and kept going.

Ahead, the völva's front door had fallen in. Fucking wolves. Odin scrambled over the snow, then slid to a stop when he spotted Heidr lying on the ground just outside the house. Her body lay still. A varulf had torn her throat out.

This was not supposed to happen.

Odin dropped to his knees beside her body. Her eyes were wide, staring up at the night sky, at the mists above and the perilous moon. The völva had served his father. In Odin's earliest memories, she'd just been an apprentice, but since he was a child, she'd become a font of strength for the tribe. The source of their wisdom. The völva told them when to move camp, where to hunt. And she'd been lost because of his pride. He'd brought the varulfur down on them. Heidr had tried to tell him ...

*Actions have consequences.*

Such simple wisdom, and he'd refused to hear it.

His hand trembled as he shut her eyes. "In the name of my father Borr, I promise you vengeance, völva." He rose, eyes sweeping the town for any further varulfur. There, on the edge of town, he saw one, struggling with a shield-maiden. Odin ran toward the pair, hefting his spear as he did. "Fly true," he said, then threw.

The spear soared through the night, cutting away mist as it soared and impaled the wolf. Odin continued his trot to retrieve the spear, battle-fatigue beginning to take hold of his chest. The moment he grasped the weapon, his strength and rage returned. How dare these wolves attack his people and kill his völva! Odin would see them rent and driven to the gates of Niflheim! He'd serve them in pieces to the minions of Hel!

"My lord," the shieldmaiden said.

He nodded at her, then turned to take in the town. Whimpers and screams of pain continued to fill the night, but there were no further signs of battle. Had they slain the last of these creatures? There would be more. He would hunt down the savages.

"Find my brothers," he told the shieldmaiden. "Send them to me."

"Yes, my lord."

He'd hardly felt the cold during the struggle, but as his battle frenzy wore off, an icy chill ate his bare muscles. From the deep darkness, dawn would come within the hour. Best get more fires burning to keep the mist away from Eskgard. Was the mist what turned the varulfur into cannibals?

He worked his way back toward Idunn's house. The Vanr seemed to know something of these varulfur.

Loki intercepted him, bloody sword in hand. The foreigner breathed heavily but showed no sign of injury. After a glance around, Loki tossed the sword aside. "Are you harmed?"

Odin shook his head. He was not harmed—he would do the harming. He would rend these monstrous wolves in half and leave their corpses for ravens. "Can you track them?" These creatures would pay for the lives they had stolen. Heidr would have vengeance.

Loki nodded slowly. "I can."

Idunn slipped out of the house now, eyes locked on Odin. "You don't want to do that."

Odin spun on her. "Fucking varulfur killed our völva, Idunn! I have enough to tend to without such raids, and no time for such fuckery. I will erase these beasts from the face of Midgard! I will cut out their hearts and send them screaming down to Hel!"

They would see what happened to those who attacked

the Wodanar. He needed make a point and make it fast. His oath to the ghost had settled around him like a noose, drawing ever tighter.

He grabbed Loki. "Find out where they came from. Now."

His blood brother nodded, cast a quick glance at Idunn, then took off into the mist.

"Gather the warriors!" Odin bellowed.

Wolves would bleed for this.

## 18

"There, in the ruins," Loki said, pointing toward the hilltop. The foreigner crouched on a rock, out of sight of the creatures.

Tyr knelt a short distance behind the foreigner, beside Odin. His fingers tingled, crisp like a winter storm. Always like that before violence. Battle had an energy that drew Tyr the way sex drew most men. When you were born to hold a blade, you felt it. Deep in the gut.

The crumbling wall might once have housed a stone fortress. Not all vaettir were hostile to Mankind. Just most. Enough to make a man avoid such places. More often than not, you found vaettir of one kind or another haunting the fallen places once meant to guard against them.

Sometimes, varulfur in the wilds let the animal take over. They grew full savage, leaving behind their humanity. So easy for that to happen. In desperation, men turned quickly from civilization. Chaos was the natural state, and to chaos all things returned. Unless a strong hand held it at bay. A strong hand and a heavy shield ... and honor. If Tyr hadn't known better, he'd have thought this such a camp. A pack turned feral. But the Godwulfs were expanding their reach in all directions. Annar and that traitor both agreed on that.

Vili would have wanted to attack at night, when he could shapeshift. Still had his strength in daylight, but not his full power. But if he could, so could their prey. So they'd need to strike soon.

Odin had asked Idunn to take charge of Eskgard in his absence. Idunn, not Ve. Strange, that. Stranger still he'd left one of his brothers behind at all.

"We have only a few hours of daylight left," Loki said. "If you want to do this, now is the time."

"Can we not wait?" Vili asked.

"The entities within them, and you, are Moon spirits. The animals are simply varying tribes of Moon spirit, manifesting in our Realm through possession. There are more of them, so waiting favors the varulfur."

Hel's frozen tits. Loki spoke like a völva. Surely it was unmanly to speak with such authority on the Otherworlds. Tyr spat, and a pair of shieldmaidens murmured concern at the exchange, but Odin silenced them with a glare.

"We should put out the fires," Tyr said. Hunting varulfur worked better without flame. That he could now say for certain.

"No!" snapped Odin. "Torches up." He looked to Tyr. "Take a small party around the back. Catch them off guard. But do not douse the torches."

Tyr grunted his assent. Odin made this harder. Tyr wouldn't have taken the man for being so superstitious, especially in daylight. Well, naught for it now. The battle beckoned. The tingling had grown to a throbbing in his veins.

He motioned the two shieldmaidens and a pair of other warriors to follow him.

They wound their way around back. No sentries. Arrogant. Varulfur thought men couldn't track them, or wouldn't with the snowstorms. That arrogance would be the death of them.

He was first through the breach in the wall. Odin's warriors would follow any moment. He was counting on Tyr to make sure none of these varulfur slipped away into the wilds. If that happened, they could wait for nightfall. Pick off the Wodan men one by one—

A low snarl sounded from just behind him. Tyr turned as a naked man collided shoulder first with his shield. The wood cracked under the varulf's strength, and Tyr's feet skidded backward, stopped only by the ruined wall. The varulf growled and punched before Tyr could get his sword up. The blow landed on his shield, splitting it in half.

The varulf wrung his hand for an instant as Tyr tossed his now useless protection aside. The wolf surged forward, intent to throttle him. Tyr rolled to the side and swung his sword. Blood sputtered from the varulf's side as the sword embedded just above his hip. Hot fluid sprayed over Tyr while the varulf screamed in pain.

The creature caught him by his mail and flung him against the wall. Tyr collided with the next man trying to enter the breach, and the two of them tumbled, one atop another. A shieldmaiden leapt over them, rushing the varulf spear first. The creature ripped Tyr's sword from his side. It stepped around her spear and planted that sword so deep in her skull the blade punched out the back of it.

Roaring himself, Tyr staggered to his feet. He dropped to one side and grabbed the fallen woman's spear. Thrust it up in a single motion. As expected, the varulf lunged at him, impaling itself on the shaft.

The varulf flailed there a moment. Grimacing, Tyr rose and hefted it upward. Then he drove the creature down to the ground and pinned it there. The varulf wiggled, spittle and blood dribbling from its mouth along with incomprehensible curses.

So they did have a sentry. Tyr spat on the dying varulf.

Shouts rang out from the other side of the ruin. Odin had joined the battle.

"There!" Tyr shouted, pointing some of his men in one direction. "Guard that breach. The rest of you, hold this one."

He spared a glance at the dead shieldmaiden. She had given her life to protect him. He didn't deserve it. And now, freeing his sword from her skull would mean dishonoring her corpse. That he couldn't do. Instead, he pulled a dagger.

"My lord?" a warrior asked.

"Stay here." They could handle this.

Odin might need him.

## 19

*T*here could be no survivors from this. Vengeance demanded blood. And Gungnir would provide. It always provided. These wolves would know the price of threatening the Wodanar.

Odin paused, giving Tyr time to get into position, then pulled his golden hair back into a ponytail, keeping it from his eyes. Other warriors flexed their muscles, or twitched weapons.

"They'll smell us," Loki whispered. "But with luck, they sleep and may not notice until we've descended upon them."

With a start, Odin realized Loki carried no weapon. "Where's your sword?"

"That wasn't mine."

All right ... "And now?"

"The varulfur will have weapons. If need be, I shall borrow one."

Odin snorted. His new brother was as mentally deprived as his others. Loki would fit right in. "It's time."

As one, his warriors rose and charged up the hill, not

letting out their typical war cries until they'd passed through a breach in the wall. Then shouts rang through the chambers, scattering an unkindness of ravens that had perched atop the ruins.

A pile of sleeping men and women leapt to their feet. They'd all been naked, sleeping on and under furs, one atop another. Like wolves. Odin slashed open one varulf's throat, then impaled another. A lop of Vili's axe beheaded a woman who went for a sword. Odin's warriors fell upon the unarmed wolf pack with ferocity. Well-deserved vengeance for last night's raid.

More shouts and war cries sounded from across the ruins. Tyr's forces must have found another congregation of the pack. Odin stalked through the snow-misted halls, cutting down stragglers. A large man—well over six feet tall —charged at him, snarling like a beast. Odin set Gungnir for the charge and thrust it up at the last moment. The spear shot clean through the varulf's chest. The varulf looked down at the shaft, as if stunned. Odin kicked him and withdrew the spear, then continued on.

A tunnel had been carved into the hillside, creating a cellar. After pausing to light a torch, he continued forward.

A body slammed into him from the side. Gungnir skittered away as Odin fell. The impact knocked all wind from his lungs. His vision blurred for one instant, then a man sat straddling him, hand on his throat. He grasped at the man's arm, but the werewolf's strength was Otherworldly. Odin couldn't breathe. Lungs were burning. He flailed weakly, trying to dislodge his assailant. The beast snarled, saliva dripping onto Odin's face. The foul spittle stung his eyes.

Someone slammed into Odin's assailant, knocking him aside. Tyr tackled the wolf, and the pair tumbled several times. Odin gasped, trying to get air through his bruised throat. When at last he rolled onto his side, he saw Tyr now atop the werewolf, raining blows down on the man with a dagger. As Odin rose, the werewolf got a grip on Tyr's wrists and flung him aside.

The varulf turned over, growled, and leapt for Tyr. Odin stumbled toward Gungnir. The instant his fingers closed around the shaft, he felt strength return to his limbs. The dragon's power filled him, and his breath came easier. A simple slash of the blade opened the varulf's back. The creature wailed, and Tyr kicked it off him. The warrior rose, then stomped his foot down on the werewolf's skull.

"How fare you?" His voice sounded raspy in his own ears. It would probably take days for the damage to his throat to heal. Maybe Heidr could have given him a draught to help—if his pride hadn't killed her.

"Damned sight better than you," Tyr said.

Odin grunted.

A child's wail caught his ear from the next room.

Odin exchanged glances with Tyr, then they made for the back room of the underground chamber. The place stank of uncooked meat and spoilt milk. Animal skins were spread over the floor in a kind of primitive rug. In the shadows of the room, a naked woman twisted, blocking his view of something. She snarled at him but made no move to charge.

She was one of them. One of the animals that had slaughtered his people, killed Heidr. A bitch for the slaughter. Was it the dragon's rage or his own? It did not matter. Blood for blood, and he'd made an oath.

He stalked closer, ready for her to move. She growled at him. Then he charged forward and thrust Gungnir through her chest. "Your menfolk await you in the Realm of Hel."

As she fell, he spied a straw-filled cart beyond. Inside

lay two babes, probably twins. One male and one female. Odin hesitated. Varulf children. His oath … Odin never broke an oath. These were werewolf children. He raised Gungnir.

Tyr's hand on his shoulder yanked him away. "My lord!"

Odin jerked. He damned himself for letting Tyr creep up on him.

"They are monsters!" Odin shouted.

These were varulfur. They were of the same tribe he'd sworn vengeance against for Heidr. If he failed to uphold his vow to its fullest extent, her spirit might well crawl out of Niflheim to haunt him for it. And yet, these children had done naught. They would have, of course. They would have grown up to be savage animals who raided the Ás tribes. Even then, that was not so different from what the Aesir did to each other, or to any foreign peoples they came across. The gods respected only strength. And some varulfur did serve in tribes, as berserkir did.

"They are infants," Tyr said.

Yes. The adults in the tribe had raided his village or condoned the raid. But the babes were innocent. Yet to spare them was to break his vow to Heidr.

Odin's mind swirled at the sight of the two werewolves. His throat had grown so dry. He had no desire to murder these babes. And it would be murder. He could not condemn them for what they *would* have done, had they grown up savage.

"I would not expect … sympathy from you."

Tyr folded his arms. "Because *I* was raised savage? I have more sympathy. Men can change. Your father gave me that chance."

His father. Yes, gods. Father had always tried to see the best in people. He had believed Mankind was slowly dying out. That chaos was engulfing Midgard, and only if humanity banded together could they forestall the end.

"Father trusted you." Odin let Gungnir fall from his grasp. The moment it left his hand, weariness wrapped its claws around his chest. His muscles ached from the battle, a fatigue he'd not even been aware of finally taking hold, even as the anger clutching his heart began to abate. *The spear is the strength of the tribe*, his father had once said. *But it is anger —a power to be unleashed or held in check, as the need arises.*

Tyr nodded, face solemn, slight hint of approval in his eyes. The thegn had gone on about the Athra and the Godwulfs just last night. The Godwulfs—a tribe ruled by varulfur. Did that prompt Tyr's request to spare these babes? Either way, the thegn had the right of it. Father would want him to check his anger.

Odin reached into the cart. "Forgive me." Heidr forgive him. He would not become a murderer of children. He handed one babe to Tyr and cradled the other in his own arms. "We'll take them with us." The Wodanar had a few berserkir, but no living varulfur. Maybe these twins would change that in future generations.

Right now, he had to find a way to save his brother. But still, he had sworn an oath to Idunn, an oath spoken on Gungnir and Father's name alike, and one he could never break. An oath to become king of the Aesir. "Tyr ... You served as champion to my father." Odin pulled off his arm ring—coiling dragons wrought in a twisting of silver and iron. He stared at it a moment before offering it to Tyr. "Serve as my champion now."

The thegn shifted the babe in his arm before taking the arm ring with reverence. He placed it on his wrist where Father's ring had once sat, and nodded solemnly.

Odin clapped him on the shoulder. "Good. I ask you not

to judge me harshly. I do what I can be worthy of Father's legacy, but I am bound by more than one oath now, torn in many directions. I have sworn to Idunn to become king, but first I must tend to another oath."

"What could be more important than the urd of all the Ás tribes?"

The urd of his family, of course. Odin shook his head. "Work with Idunn and do as you think best to draw the other tribes to our side. With word or blade, prepare the way and hold together what Father tried to build."

With a sigh, Tyr nodded. "If we are to return to the town before nightfall, we must leave now."

Indeed. Odin had someone he needed to see.

## 20

The sun had nearly set when they returned to the town, the werewolf girl cradled in his arms. She'd wailed all day with a hunger Tyr had no way to sate. Here, at least, he could find a wet nurse to care for the babes.

Though it was early for the night meal, Odin ordered the tables set in his feast hall. Much like his father, he kept his intentions guarded closely—too closely for Tyr's liking. Odin had asked for his trust, yes. And Tyr *wanted* to give it to him. He so wanted Odin to be worthy of it. But the man had refused to explain himself. Or explain what he intended, while asking Tyr to make him a king.

Worse still was that Odin didn't seem to want the fucking throne. He wanted something from Idunn, but Tyr couldn't say what. That didn't sit well.

Tyr headed for the feast as soon as he found someone to take in the varulfur twins.

Odin arrived after him, though. Up to something once again.

"Tyr," Idunn called from behind him. In her arms she

carried one of the varulfur twins. Took her away from the midwife already?

"Lady Idunn, welcome. Do you realize the child is a werewolf?"

"Of course she is, Tyr. Isn't that amazing?" She pinched the varulf's cheek. "It was so magnanimous of you to spare these two. It makes me proud to be your friend. And we will be friends, I promise."

She spoke rapidly. Tyr's head spun untangling her words. Hadn't even started on the mead. "I welcome your friendship, my lady. And I hope showing the wolves mercy proves a wise decision."

"Mercy is always wise," she said, continuing forward until she stood right at his side. "And what are we going to call these hungry little puppies?"

Puppies? "Odin said he'd call them Geri and Freki. He plans to raise them as his own."

Idunn clicked her tongue and rubbed Geri's chin. "Little Geri werewolf! I bet you'll have the most beautiful fur when you learn to shapeshift!"

"No doubt," Tyr said dryly.

"And now, darling Vili," she said and kissed the top of the berserk's head, "would you mind terribly looking after poor Geri a while? I need to steal your friend away for a private conversation."

Several of the men and no few of the shieldmaidens whooped and beat on the table.

Idunn smiled. "Seems they like the idea."

Tyr wouldn't mind some alone time in his house with the beautiful goddess. Did she know what those warriors thought? Was she truly oblivious, or just coy? Either way, ripping off her silky red dress was all he could think of.

After bloodletting, sex was all *most* men thought of. Shield-maidens, too. Killing made you remember living.

He offered her his arm, and she took it, walking out with him. Outside, the afternoon was setting. The mist had begun to thicken. Numerous fires around the town kept it away, as they kept away the worst of the cold. Kept it at bay for now. But all fires dwindled in time. Hymir was fond of saying so, and the jotunn did not lie. Not about that.

Idunn led him around the town a bit, chattering about the goings-on while he'd been away. How a shieldmaiden was now with child. How a hunter had found a bride in town. About the dwindling food stores and how lean the winter would grow.

Tyr grunted at each story, never certain what to say. At least not until she led him into her house and beckoned him sit before the fire pit.

A pot hung over it, boiling some odd-smelling brew.

"What is that?"

"Hmm? Tea. Would you like some?" She scooped out a mugfull.

He took a large swig of it. Scorched his mouth, tongue, throat. Left him gasping. "Bitter as a troll's arse! Some völva medicine? I am not ill, goddess."

She giggled, then gingerly sipped from a mug herself. "To your continued good health then. So tell me, champion of the Wodanar, how did you fare in the Athra lands?"

"Uh. Godwulfs are pressing out all their borders. Athra are falling one by one." He recounted his tale while she listened, only occasionally asking questions.

"So," she said when he had finished. "This Hallr Stonecrusher would be the new jarl. And would he fare better than Alci?"

"Alci's ambitious, but Stonecrusher is a fucking traitor. Less honor than a troll."

"Hmmm. Interesting thing about honor, viewed from the long perspective. It can be everything, and it can be naught at all. The Vanir made many choices for the sake of expediency. Wrong choices perhaps, but only history can judge, if even then. Men look at the World from but a single vantage point."

Tyr cracked his neck. "I know naught about such things. I know Borr taught me honor is the one thing no one can take from you."

She raised a finger, sipped her tea, then nodded. "Perhaps. But then, if you hold to it so stubbornly that your world freezes around you, and your people falter and die, that honor will not warm you in the lingering cold. Then, perhaps, your persistence in taking the high road becomes a matter more of pride, and from there but a short stop to reach hubris."

"Huh. So ... Placing my honor above the needs of the people is ... arrogant?"

She shrugged. "I don't know, Tyr. But if you refuse to stop Alci on grounds of your honor, you must live with the ghosts of his victims. Offer them what explanation you will; tell them how they had to die so that you might remain clean."

Tyr scratched his head. Something about all that sounded off, but then, Idunn was a goddess. She ought to know best. He had to put his trust in *someone*, after all. "So you would have me send Hallr back to his people to kill Alci?"

"For now, I think, you may be better using him as a spy. Learn what you can until the time is right."

He groaned. Intrigue. Lies. Treachery. "Tastes foul."

Idunn nodded. "Then I have something sweeter to offer. Odin asked you to be his champion, and thus, asked me to give you this." From her dress, she drew forth a golden apple.

From the World Tree. Immortality.

His breath had quickened. He didn't remember reaching for it, but he held it now. Warm in his palm. Pulsing like his own pounding heart.

"If I ..."

"You can live forever," she said.

What a thought.

He bit down. Tastes exploded in his mouth. His throat. His eyes swam. Whole fucking house spun. More. More! Juice dribbled over his face. He was lying on his back. How had he gotten here? Another bite. Another. Fire and ice and life surging through his veins. His heart ready to explode.

Every muscle tingling.

Alive.

So alive.

The core fell from his half-numb fingers. He rolled to his knees. Room whirling. Round and round, up and down, like a ball. Idunn sitting there, half a smile on her face, watching.

Her pulse beating fast, in time with his own. Showing through her skin. Through that thin dress.

He crawled to her.

"Are you well, Tyr? It can be ... overwhelming."

Frey's flaming sword! Whole body was going to fly apart. So alive. And he needed more and more life.

He launched himself atop her and tore at her dress, hiking it up over her hips. She laughed. Made no attempt to stop him.

Stroked his cheek as he fumbled with his trousers. "I

know. It happens to everyone. But if you choose me you'll face consequences. Maybe see things you didn't—ugh."

She grunted as he pushed inside her. He pounded again and again, choking in fervor. Not able to find release. Frey! He just needed to let go. To be with someone again after so long. To hold her.

"Zisa," he mumbled.

"No." Idunn shoved him backward, then straddled him. "I am not her."

She grunted, panted. And then screamed, laughed. Waves of it hit him. Made him spasm. Time stopped.

Idunn sat in the shadow of a tree that touched the heavens. Sat with an old woman, deep tan skin, short hair. Talking, arguing. And somehow setting the course of the future.

And the old woman died. Idunn carried her ashes across the World, beyond the Midgard Wall—where it should have been—and vanished into the snowstorms. The chaos Realm. She had walked into Utgard.

"I've eaten some bad mushrooms ..."

Idunn leaned her face, glowing face, radiant, close to his. He lay on his back. "I warned you."

## 21

*I*dunn emerged from Tyr's house, flushed, her dress torn.

Odin watched her, arms folded over his chest. She jumped just a little when she saw him, then flashed her wicked half smile.

"When I asked you to give him an apple, I did not expect you to give him so much more."

She shrugged. "We all have needs. The apples are so imbued with the energy of life they tend to bring those needs to the forefront."

Odin quirked a smile. "You weren't concerned about my needs when I ate my apple."

Idunn grinned. "You didn't ask." She winked and returned to the dance.

Son of a bitch. Did she mean she would have ...?

Now there was a missed opportunity he'd regret for eternity. He shook his head. "Walk with me, Idunn."

She smoothed her dress and fell in beside him, apparently trying to ignore the rip running up the red silk. Odin stifled a chuckle. In his fervent lust, Tyr had ruined fabric no doubt worth more gold than the thegn had ever seen.

When they had passed away from the other houses, he turned on her. "I have agreed to your terms, Vanr. I must soon choose the rest of my companions. Give me the last three apples."

Idunn quirked a smile. "Have someone in mind?" She drew the apples from her dress, and he dropped them in his satchel.

"I might. But before I can become king, I have something more I need."

Idunn sighed. "By the Tree, Odin, I beseech you for the good of all, let this thing go."

He scowled. Already knew what he'd ask then. Ve was blood. And for him, Odin would never let go. "Where do I find these Niflungar?"

"Such ancient peoples are best left forgotten. They serve as a distraction from your true goal."

He clenched his fist at his side. His true goal was saving his brother, and if the ghost could do that, he'd take any action on her account. "I have an oath to uphold, one made before my oath to you. Help me fulfill that oath, then I will tend to yours."

"These people worship *Hel*, Odin. They draw strength from the Otherworlds, and it changes them, turns them into something you cannot imagine. They were driven from these lands long ago, and even if I knew were they now hid, I would not tell you. Do not disturb their rest. Better for you, for us all, if they are left to slumber."

Odin slapped his fist against a tree trunk. "Enough! If you won't help me I will find someone who will."

"Odin!" she shouted after him. He did not stop, did not turn back to face her. The goddess was quick to offer assistance—when it suited her—and withhold it when it did not. And that refusal reeked of betrayal. Or his own delusion in allowing himself to believe she cared aught for the anguish suffered by Odin or his kin.

Leaving her behind, he trod to where his new blood brother took shelter. The man sat awake, staring into the flames of his fire pit almost as though he expected company. "Do you know where the Niflungar lurk now?"

Loki motioned for Odin to sit across the flame. "Welcome, brother. Still you seek this amulet, and it so vexes you, but at last you begin to realize the questions you ought to have asked before embarking on this undertaking."

Odin groaned but did take the seat. "Damn it, Loki. Can I not have a straight answer?"

"Would you know one if you stumbled upon it?"

"What the fuck does that mean?"

Loki dug a finger into the ash around the fire pit, drawing a line. "The simplest way to reach from one place to another is a straight line." He dropped a stone in the middle of that line. "Unless of course a mountain blocks your path. Then you must assess whether to go around, under, or over —all to reach a destination you cannot actually see."

"I'm not looking for a metaphor."

"Perhaps that's the problem. You assume that, despite the mountain in your path, the simplest road must still be a straight one."

Odin snatched the rock and flung it out into the snow. "Who are the Niflungar? Where do they dwell?"

Loki sighed. "What do you know of the Old Kingdoms?"

Odin groaned. Now *more* lessons. "They dominated the North Realms for a long time. You said they all fell apart some eight hundred years ago, left a bunch of ruins. Oh, the Odlingar were one of them."

"One of nine kingdoms. Also among them, the most feared, most treacherous, were the Niflungar. They tried to conquer all the North Realms, and though they were defeated, it was not before breaking many of the Old Kingdoms, and not without great cost to those who remained. The Niflungar fled from these lands and retreated into myth, into restless sleep, awaiting the day they might return."

Gods, what had he agreed to? How was he to find these people at all in three moons, let alone retrieve the ghost's stolen amulet? In a moment of desperation, he'd made any bargain he could to save his brother. Once again, he'd been a fool to give no thought to the cost. But he no longer had a choice. He had to save Ve.

"Brother ..." Odin blew out a breath. "In the time I have known you, I have come to rely a great deal on you."

"You honor me with your trust."

"Then tell me how to find the Niflungar. I understand what you say. Even Idunn tells me to turn away, that these people draw strength from the Otherworlds. But I cannot turn back, surely you understand that. I will not abandon my brother to Mist-madness. The ghost is the only salvation I have left to turn to."

"Salvation is not the province of ghosts," Loki said, then sighed. "The Niflungar's power comes from an Otherworld —Niflheim, the World of Mist and domain of ... Hel herself." Loki almost seemed to choke on that. Frightened? Him? "They are sorcerers, Odin, masters of the Art who would leave your völvur trembling in pools of their own urine and begging to wake from nightmares without end. And you are so resolved to seek them out?"

"I have to!" Odin leaned forward. "Do you not understand family, man?"

"Yes, brother, I understand family." He looked to the fire pit and shook his head. "There are those who can answer any question, should they be so inclined. They can speak of all who walk on Midgard and even those who dwell beyond, for they watch from outside the bounds of time as we see it. You call them Norns. And they will have your answers, if you can ask the right questions."

Norns. Weavers of urd, mistresses of Fate. Every step he took carried him deeper into Mist-madness. Into Realms beyond those of men, beyond where any sane or living soul ought to tread. And still, there remained no way back. Only forward. "So be it. Take me to them."

"I will arrange it." Loki rose.

"Wait, brother. I ... I owe you more and more with every passing day. Idunn has asked me to become King of the Aesir. I would have you by my side in this."

Loki folded his arms over his chest and cocked his head. "I already swore a blood oath to you."

Odin fished through his satchel and pulled out an apple. "You know what this is? Eat it when you find yourself free to take a woman." Or three.

Odin's foreign brother stared at it before taking it and slipping it into a sack at his side. "Even if you find the Niflungar, even if you steal the Singasteinn back from them, still you have made other oaths that bind you."

"Yes. That's why I need you to help me become king. I gave apples to my brothers, too, and to Tyr."

"A few immortal warriors alone will not put a crown on your head."

Odin grunted. "No. But with them and Gungnir, it's a damned good start. I'll bend the people to my will if I must, and offer them a better future."

"Offer them? Or thrust it upon them for their own good? Thus speaks many a tyrant."

Odin's fist clenched at his side. Who in Hel's name did Loki think he was? Odin had just given him fucking immortality, and his brother compared him to a tyrant? "Is that how you see me?"

"No, but others will. If you choose to follow Idunn, then consider carefully *how* you do so."

Odin worked his jaw. In truth, Loki was probably right. As usual. But Loki also understood the twisted urd cast upon Ve. "I had to make this bargain."

With a sigh Odin rose and left to walk the grounds. In the day, the mists weren't as bad, and one need not fear the vaettir—at least not as much. According to Idunn, he should now be immune to the effects of the mist. He was one of a lucky few, while the rest of the Aesir suffered under a plague stretching back five thousand years. But still, he'd be careful to heed Heidr's words on caution. It was a mistake he would never repeat.

In the woods just beyond the tents, a horse neighed. Odin jerked at the sound. Horses were rare and valuable beasts, and the Wodanar had few enough that no one would let one roam free. He crept forward to the edge of a copse.

Despite Odin's attempt at stealth, Loki beckoned to him. Odin rose to join him, then balked. The horse Loki led had eight legs, a pair jutting from each shoulder and hip joint.

"What in Hel's frozen underworld is that?"

"This," Loki said, guiding the horse toward Odin, "is Sleipnir. Finest steed in the lands, and one who can guide you anywhere in Midgard and beyond."

"It's a fucking monster."

The horse snorted at him, eyes seeming to flare red.

Loki nodded. "Yes. Legend says before the World was formed, there slept great primeval monsters of chaos. Their offspring became dragons and monsters. Before the mists, many had been driven into hiding or hunted to extinction. Long ago, great winged horses were common, and such a beast could have taken you anywhere. Now few, if any, remain. But Sleipnir is ancient and wise. Earn his trust, and he will earn yours."

Earn the damned horse's trust? Like a troll's rocky arse. "And the horse will take me to the Norns?"

"They are keepers of the past, present, and future. Sleipnir has seen the secret places they dwell and can carry you there. But I urge you to use caution among them."

Loki was a bit too full of his own mystery. "You speak like a völva, man. Can you not just guide me yourself?"

"Trust me, brother. And trust Sleipnir."

Odin sighed and shook his head. Truth was, he could afford to waste no time. Three moons sounded long enough to find a tribe or kingdom nigh to Aujum. But a foreign people, driven into hiding? And sorcerers. Human warriors Odin could best, monsters he could slay. But magic was a thing not meant for men.

Nor could he leave Ve for long. By Frey's flaming sword, he would *not* lose his little brother. Odin's mother was gone, and now his father. No more. There was no time.

"Tell the others where I have gone."

The horse had no saddle, so he slung himself over bareback and tucked Gungnir in front of him. A hand on the horse's mane to steady himself, he turned to Loki. "Tell them I will return soon." Odin hesitated. "Brother. I need you to guard the last two apples well. Save them until I decide who most to trust."

"I will."

Odin tossed him the satchel.

This was madness, more like than not. But Odin needed answers. He could not save Ve without knowledge. He kicked his heels into the horse, and it bucked.

Odin slipped from the sudden motion and spilled over the horse's arse, landing behind. The deep snow cushioned his fall, leaving him dazed only a moment.

"Gods-damned beast!" he spat.

Loki shook his head and stood with hands behind his back, saying naught, but raising an eyebrow when Odin looked to him. Earn the horse's trust. Stupid animal.

After brushing himself off, Odin moved to Sleipnir's head and placed a hand along it. "Please."

The horse neighed. Hopefully a good sign.

He leapt back on the horse again and pressed his knees together. "Take me to the Norns, Sleipnir. *Please.*"

The horse took off at a sudden trot, forcing Odin to lean low and clutch his mane. Sleipnir darted around trees and obstacles with no guidance from Odin. It was fast—much faster than a horse had any right to be. On and on it charged. Trees swept past in a blur.

His mount moved at unearthly speed.

Apt, as his quest was like to take him beyond the bounds of Midgard.

AN HOUR'S TRAVEL, and Odin recognized an old ruin as they passed it. Impossible—that place was eighteen miles from the town. It should have taken nigh unto a day to reach it.

Sleipnir charged onward, never slowing. The horse ran up the steep incline of a hill and leapt right off it, clearing the distance to an icy precipice ahead.

"Whoa! What in Njord's name are you doing?" Odin yanked the horse to a stop. "I want to get there in one piece. If that means we get there a bit slower—"

A low growl rumbled through the hills, cutting him off. Odin turned to the side in time to see a snow bear rise up on its hind legs. He fell backward, trying to clear the bear's claws, but they swept across his shoulder. The claws ripped through his furs, mail, and skin like stew. Sudden pain blurred his vision, and the force of the blow hurled him aside.

Sleipnir snorted, raising hooves to kick the snow bear. It backed away under the assault, then roared. Gods, he should have been more attentive. He crawled forward, pulling himself toward Gungnir where it had fallen, twenty feet away. He was never going to make it.

The bear roared again, moving in on him. Odin pulled himself to his feet, fighting the pain in his shoulder. He would die standing, a man of the Aesir. The animal reared up on its hind legs, bringing both paws down on Odin. Odin screamed back at it in defiance. Its forelegs fell on him like boulders.

And he caught them.

His feet dug into the snow as the impact drove him backward, but he held up the bear's legs. His arms ached with the struggle of keeping the beast away. It snapped its jaws at him, snarling. Gods ... He was holding up a bear. He was holding up a fucking *bear*! Odin roared right back at the animal.

"I am Odin! God among men!"

For a brief instant, the beast recoiled, as if shocked a

man was matching its strength. In response, rage and power boiled inside Odin.

Sleipnir reared up, kicking the bear in the back of the head. Dazed, it shook its maw. Odin dropped the bear's legs, and it slumped down. Damned animal could have killed him. Odin punched it right in the nose. Bones crunched under the blow, and the bear whimpered. Odin roared at it again and landed a wild haymaker atop its skull. The impact stung his fist and actually cracked open the bear's skull. It collapsed into the snow, blood oozing from its mouth.

Hel's frozen tits. He'd just punched a bear to death.

His legs gave out from under him as his newfound strength seeped away and he fell to the snow. Sudden pain in his shoulder raged. His hands had gone numb. He'd probably cracked his own bones with that absurd stunt. He was losing blood from the gouges in his shoulder. Thanks to Sleipnir's speed, he was far from Eskgard.

He had to get up. The horse nuzzled him, eliciting another grunt of pain. "Yeah. Thank you."

Sleipnir was offering his head, wasn't he? Odin grabbed on, and Sleipnir rose, pulling Odin to his feet. Then the horse knelt down in the snow, allowing Odin to mount more easily. First, he paused to retrieve Gungnir, then mounted.

He'd seriously underestimated his new friend. "Thank you," he said again.

And would the apple stop him from bleeding to death? He supposed he would soon find out.

------

## 22

*T*he ice spread out over the Gandvik Sea for a
dozen feet or more. It created a shelf Tyr now
walked on, with Annar. His journey back to Athra-held
lands had felt different. Easier. A new strength rose in him,
an endurance. As if the apple had reinforced his muscles.

Not only would he live forever, but be more than human.
How was he supposed to feel about that?

In the distance, a whale breached.

Both men drew to a stop, watching.

"Whalers are too far out. They'll be cursing themselves
for missing that beauty. Would have fed us through the rest
of winter."

Tyr grunted. Though they stared at the deep, no other
sign of the whale arose. Mist covered the sea. You couldn't
see far anyway.

"You'll have to send him back there," Tyr said at last.

"So Odin agreed to it?"

"Ugh." Odin had barely heard two words about the
Athra and the Godwulfs. *Make me king*, he'd said. Well, Tyr
would do it.

"I thought you hated using the lying traitor."

"I do." Tyr spat on the ice. "Fucker should be hanged. But we have more to lose by not acting."

"Suppose we do. Doesn't seem like you, though."

And how well did this jarl think he knew Tyr? With a scowl, he turned to look back at the town. "It's not just me. There's a hand guiding mine and Odin's both."

"Oh?"

Men might deny it. Call him a liar or a madman. But some might believe. Maybe it would give them an edge. And Hel, Tyr needed to tell *someone*. "A Vanr is driving this."

"Ah. You mean a völva. That Heidr, yes?" Annar started back for the town, Tyr following.

"She's dead. I mean an actual Vanr came to us. Asked Odin to do something."

Annar faltered now, looked back. "Troll shit. What are you playing at?"

"Not much of a tafl player." He paused. "Idunn, she came to Odin."

"The goddess?" Annar chuckled. "Next you'll tell me my cousin fucked her too."

Ah. Well, not Odin. Not so far as Tyr knew. He frowned, shook his head. "Whether you believe or not does not matter overmuch. Something does matter. World is changing, Annar. Odin's going to change it more."

"Meaning?"

Tyr walked in silence until they reached the fence around Annar's hall. He leaned on that fence. Go inside. Let the traitor go free and hope he spoke the truth. Bold move. And as Tyr had said, he wasn't much for tafl.

"I'm here for Odin, helping you save your people. One day soon, Odin will come himself. Come and call the Althing. Not to try any great crime. He will stake his claim as King of the Aesir. You will support him."

Annar coughed, looked around. "He is my cousin, yes—"

Tyr looked down at the log forming a horizontal beam of the fence. Anger swelled in him. Heat. Power. He slammed his fist on it. The log cracked and splintered. Whole chunk of the fence crashed down.

Everyone in earshot paused, staring.

Tyr had wanted Annar's attention. Hadn't really expected that dramatic an effect.

"Odin is chosen by the Vanir. And if you would have us as allies, I will have your oath."

Annar swallowed, looked at the fence, at his people. Shook his head. "Gods. So be it. I give my word. Stop the Godwulfs, and Odin will have my voice at the Althing."

That put two tribes in line.

Seven more would need to be won over.

## 23

*S*leipnir carried Odin far and fast in the morn, and the next day beyond that, and again. The days blurred as much as the miles, and they passed far beyond aught he had ever known. The eight-legged horse carried him far to the east, beyond all Aesir lands and back through Bjarmaland where the tribes had lived before the Great March of Vingethor. And beyond, in mountains that stretched into the sky and covered the land as far as he could see. On one of those peaks he'd paused, looking out at the World above the mists, a world stretching so much farther than he'd ever imagined. And over that mist, running through the heart of the mountains, rose a wall of impossible height and thickness.

The sight left him trembling, shivering atop the monstrous steed. Skalds and völvur spoke of the fortification with the reverence of the works of gods one never expected to lay eyes upon. But the stories were true. Out of these mountains, the Vanir had raised the Midgard Wall to enclose the middle world, shut it out from Utgard, the outer world. Beyond that wall lay the Realms of utter chaos, the wilds of Jotunheim and Njord alone might know what else. And to serve its purpose, the wall must run for thousands of miles, around the Hyrcanian Sea and beyond.

Far-wandering travelers told stories of Serkland, a Realm of savage foreigners across a mighty sea and thus outside the sphere of Midgard. If those Serklanders were human, did they worship other gods? Were there other gods besides the Vanir?

At last, they climbed a mountain peak he would have called impassible on his own. But the horse's every step fell surefooted. Icy winds bit at Odin. They had passed through the chill of the mist and above it, and now he clung to Sleipnir as much for warmth as to keep his seat.

His stomach growled. The apple sustained him, even while his supplies dwindled, and he found himself eating but a few mouthfuls at a time. Even once he found these Norns, still he would have to return to the known lands.

"I truly hope Loki knows what he's doing."

The horse snorted.

"Yes. I trust you." Absurd, one-sided conversation.

His breath frosted the air, and his cheeks had gone numb. This place would be the death of him, apple or not, unless he found warmth quickly.

The horse followed a winding route up the mountain that had begun to look suspiciously like a path. At last a hall came into view—a hold carved right into the mountain. An ice-crusted overhang kept the snow from gathering too heavily before iron double doors taller than he was. Runes like those he'd seen in the Odlingar castle covered them.

Odin raised his fist to knock, but the doors creaked open on their own. Given the choice, he'd have preferred to avoid sorcery. But then, he needed these sisters. Loki claimed they were keepers of past and future. Perhaps that meant they could guide him toward his destiny. Like as not, though, they might try to steer it. Either way, if they could tell him of the Niflungar, he had no choice but to descend into the foreboding passage.

Inside, a row of braziers lined each side of the hall, which descended farther back into the mountain than he could see.

Gungnir in hand, Odin glanced back at Sleipnir, who neighed. "Right. Get on with it, huh?" He clenched his fist at his side and strode through the threshold. He'd gone no more than a dozen steps before the doors swung closed behind him.

"Show yourselves, völvur!" His voice echoed down the hold, making him cringe.

No answer returned to him.

Even with the doors shut, he could see, thanks to the braziers, though he didn't relish wandering through the dark hall. The flickering flames cast pitiful light that gave way to deep stretches of shadows, all dancing to an unheard song.

Were these Norns human völvur, or were they vaettir? The latter, he began to suspect, as he pressed on down the sloping path. He walked longer than he could track the time. Hours, perhaps. Still the path went on and on; still the braziers continued. He should have been well under the mountain by now.

The apple had given him stamina beyond mortal limits, he knew, for despite the hunger and the distance, he still had energy to carry on.

"Go up the mountain, go down the mountain," he mumbled. And he'd have to repeat the whole process to get out, wouldn't he? Had Loki known about this when making his fool metaphor with the rock? Most like he did.

Odin could boast of his journey here, but the tribe
would think it just that—a boast. A hall carved into a mountain, and the Sisters of Fate? Indeed, why anyone would
choose to live here was beyond him. What was it Loki had
said? That Sleipnir would carry him across Midgard and
beyond, to the lands of the Norns. Did this mean he had
somehow passed outside the Mortal Realm into on Otherworld? He had reached perilously close to the Midgard
Wall, so he might well have crossed some other boundary
between worlds.

Though the hall was shut against the mountain wind, a
sudden chill passed through him, and he pulled his cloak
tighter. More than once Odin caught himself looking back
over his shoulder. Maybe it was a mistake to seek out these
Sisters of Fate. Maybe he should return to Sleipnir. But if he
did so, if he abandoned this path, he had no way to find the
Niflungar. Not in the time the ghost had given him. Already
the days had begun to slip away from him. This remained
his best chance. Fast as his new steed could run, still it had
taken nigh unto half a moon to reach this mountain.

He had to save Ve. He had to.

Finally, the path leveled out, opening into a wide
circular chamber. At the heart of the room stood a massive
well, and around it, three hooded women.

"You are the Norns?" Odin asked.

"We were," said the nearest.

"We are," said the next.

"We will be," the final answered.

Odin tried to release the tension in his muscles. "Your
location is hard to reach."

"That was the point."

"Location is irrelevant."

"We shall be where we need to be."

Odin glowered. The women were *worse* than fucking völvur. Odin approached the one to his left. "Can you tell me where to find the Niflungar?"

"You do not know who you are, or who you've been."

Odin shrugged. "I don't even know what that means."

"Correct. Son of Borr, who felled the jotunn who once ruled this Realm. Eldest of three, descendant of Wodan."

He shifted his footing. They knew him already.

"All the powers went to the thrones of Fate," the middle woman said, "there to ruminate on the thoughts of stones, and the urd of a withering tree, whilst they await the roar of Jotunheim and the writhing of nine serpents."

"Now you fancy a child of the Vanir, grandchild of the far eastern isles," the first woman said. "New moon and dark moon. Dream of one who dreams of you, never the two dreams to meet. Still you wait for the one to hold your heart."

"Find your heart you shall," the third sister said, "and lose it, too. First, the burning child ignites a pyre you cannot staunch. A price must be paid for every gain, a hefty weight for each wisdom. Sight for sight, breath for breath. The seed of the one-eyed king falls in betrayal and languishes in Hel. The beginning of the end, time of fire, time of flood. The land trembles and weeps before the ravages she knows are to come. Axe-time, sword-time, come the sundered shields, wind-time, wolf-time. Never shall men each other spare. The sun turns black, and the land sinks into the sea, while a conflagration feasts upon the heavens. Only fires burn pure, only ash will remain."

Odin grunted, more unnerved by their nonsense than he'd have liked. "Sisters, you speak in riddles that mean naught to me. I have an oath to keep. Can you guide me to the Niflungar?" Or was all this a waste of time?

"Old places the people of the mist favor," the first sister said. "Places touched with ancient past where waits the doom of men. When all lands have fallen do children cross the seas and dwell in sorrow, waiting upon the dimming of the sun. Night falls, and darkness wakens."

More riddles. People of the mist? Did that mean the Niflungar were somehow connected to the mists of Niflheim? Why not—they seemed to have named themselves after it. And if the Norns thought them perilous, the doom of men, he had to expect them deranged by overlong exposure to those mists. But the rest, what did it even mean?

Odin rubbed his face. "Speak plainly. I need answers, a location!"

"Knowledge has its price," the middle sister said.

"What price?"

"The knowing," the third sister said. "It is not easily unknown."

Odin opened his mouth but had no idea how to answer that. "Your riddles serve no purpose."

"We have spoken."

"We will speak."

Odin groaned. He hoped he had no reason to ever seek out these Norns again. Loki had said they held the answers, but instead they had given him more questions. Maybe his foreign brother would understand their words, but Odin surely did not. Be these sisters goddesses, vaettir, or mere deranged völvur, they were too removed from the World to reach. And far too unnerving for him to wish to hear their counsel.

Best he returned to Sleipnir and got off the mountain. He glanced back over his shoulder as he left their chamber. The well stood alone in the darkness.

And though he wanted to dismiss their words, in the

hours trudging back up the mountain, he could not escape them. They rang through his mind like a funeral dirge. They blazed his consciousness like the pyre the sisters had spoken of.

None of it made any sense. None except ... *A price must be paid for every gain.* The pit of his stomach would not let that one go. Not even when he at last crested the slope and reached the icy mountain where Sleipnir waited.

*E*skgard offered a welcome sight after his time away. It seemed every time Tyr came home he'd had to leave almost as soon. Back into the mist, into the cold. Such went kingmaking.

Much had changed, if not here, then in Athra lands. Much Odin needed to hear. This time, Tyr would force him to listen. The jarl could no longer push aside his duties.

Tyr headed straight for the great hall. The doors stood half open, despite the chill. Vili reclined on Odin's throne. Fumbling with an empty drinking horn. Other men and women sat at the tables, passing around horns. Talking. Bored.

"Where is Odin?" Tyr demanded.

Vili chuckled. "Ask the goddess. Maybe she knows. Or his new blood *brother*." He nigh spat the last word, pointing to the corner where Loki sat alone.

Tyr ignored the foreigner. "Odin is away?"

Vili snorted. "Long away. While the rest of us pass a dull winter." He thumped a large index finger against an armrest. "Come summer, I say we raid somewhere."

"Borr spent his life bringing peace between the tribes."

Vili shrugged. "Father's dead. Besides, we can raid into Hunaland, Reidgotaland, anywhere. Fuck a troll if I care." He slapped the armrest. "We can join the Friallafs against Miklagard!"

Men called the southern empire soft in one breath. Undefeatable in the next. Decadent, but vast.

Tyr slumped down on a bench before Vili. Not the most articulate of Borr's sons. Strong, though. Brave. Maybe more honorable than Odin. Tyr sighed. "Your cousin Annar finds himself beset by the Godwulfs."

"You want us to fight werewolves?" Vili banged his fist against his armrest again and grinned. "Now that's more like it. I can rip a wolf clean in half. Owe them too, after that raid."

"Huh. Maybe. But it's not about us. It's about some rivalry between the Hasdingi and the Godwulfs. I aim to maintain the peace your father built. Not break it."

Vili scoffed, waving the thought away.

If Odin wasn't here, then maybe Idunn would know what to do next. Tyr rose, turned to find her. Instead he nigh crashed into Loki a half step behind him.

"What do you want, foreigner?"

"You are keen to bind the tribes to Odin. Some can be bound with silver, some with sword, but one bond holds stronger than either."

Vili chuckled. "He always talks like that. Should've been a skald."

"What are you on about?" Tyr asked.

"Jarl Hadding of the Hasdingi is old and dying, and with a sole heir, the woman, Frigg, who remains unmarried. Nor does Odin have a wife. You might well bind the tribes together with a marriage. And with the Wodanar joined to

the Hasdingi, do you think the Godwulfs might well recon-
sider their course of aggression? Especially facing three
tribes united against them."

"A wedding!" Vili roared. "By Hel, yes. That would
finally give us some fucking excitement. Get old Hadding
busting out his finest mead." Vili pointed at Loki. "I thought
I didn't like you. Becoming a brother to Odin and so forth.
But you helped us kill Ymir, and now this. You are a good
man."

Tyr had serious doubt on that account. Nevertheless, the
plan did sound workable. A marriage alliance between the
heads of two tribes would secure another tribe under Odin.
And possibly an end to the Godwulf tribe's attacks at the
same time.

"All right. I will visit Hadding and propose this."

"I will accompany you," Loki said. "I know the jarl, and
they know me there."

"Good, good," Vili said. "Be quick about it. I want that
damned feast."

He had only just returned once again. Tyr grumbled
under his breath.

IDUNN SAT on the fence outside her house. Balance should
have been awkward. She was like a cat. Tyr blinked, tried to
not imagine her naked again. Writhing. Her pulse joining
his own. Her warm trench wrapped around him like …

No!

Gods. Get it out of his head. He'd had a wife. And he'd
lost her.

Idunn was right. She wasn't Zisa.

She was a goddess, though.

"Tyr!" Warm smile. Warm arms. So perfect wrapped around him.

He nodded at her. "I have a plan. I'm going to Halfhaugr. I'll arrange Odin's marriage to Frigg, the jarl's daughter. Should swing that tribe our way. Might give the Godwulfs pause, too."

"Oh, wonderful. That's a lovely plan. I almost wish I could go as well, but he'll expect me here."

"Uh. Wasn't my plan, really. Loki suggested it, even insisted on coming."

"Loki?" Idunn frowned. Expression ill suited her. Aught that made the goddess frown set a vein throbbing in his head. "The foreigner."

"Yes. Why? You know aught of him?"

"A little, maybe. A wanderer, that one, dabbling in the affairs of others where he ought not."

Tyr scowled. He'd known that bastard would bring ill fortune to the Wodanar. Idunn fretted over him, too. Almost enough to make Tyr crack the man's skull and be done with it. Save for his oath to Odin. To Borr. "Is there more?" No way he could act against Odin's blood brother. Not without serious charge.

Idunn sighed, then shook her head. "I don't know, really. The marriage might still serve our ends, Tyr. Odin needs the support of the Hasdingi, and Halfhaugr is central to control of Aujum."

"Then come with me. Help me keep the foreigner in check."

"Hmm. I wish I could. I have a ... a duty here, a promise made to Odin."

Shame that. Tyr grunted. "All right. We will speak when I return."

THEY LEFT IN THE MORNING, trusting to a dog sled to carry them far. Fewer nights spent in the wild the better. Tyr guided the sled. While Loki stared off into the mist like he could see aught through it.

After long hours of silence, the foreigner looked at him. Smirked. Brash trollfucker.

"What?" Tyr demanded.

"Some questions are best held close to one's chest, true enough, but ask naught and you may learn even less. Vast ignorance is apt to disguise itself as common wisdom."

Tyr shook his head, looked to the dogs. "What the fuck does that mean?"

Loki chuckled. "It means you wish to ask something but still your tongue. Deep down, part of you realizes that uncovering the answer means exposing your worldview to scrutiny it might not endure."

"You talk like a damned völva. You took Odin to fight this Ymir. Sons of Borr might've died up there. And now you've sent him off Njord knows where. Why?"

"Are you so certain Njord knows so much?"

Tyr spat over the side of the sled. "You insult the Vanir now?"

"Has it occurred to you that you ask me questions and then complain when I have the answers?"

"What fucking answers? You led Odin to fight Ymir. He tells it like you even aided him. But you tell no stories of your glory."

"I'm not interested in glory."

"And that's the fucking problem. You can't trust a man who doesn't care for honor."

Loki was staring off into space again. What did he see

out there? A trap? Was the foreigner leading him into an ambush? "You think glory and honor are exactly the same thing?"

"A child still on the teat knows that much, foreigner."

"The pursuit of glory may one day cost you much."

Tyr scoffed. "Are you a coward?"

Loki offered no answer. The bastard. Tyr's accusation was unfounded, of course. The foreigner *had* gone up against the jotunn, even if he downplayed his role. He had gone where *Tyr* should have gone. But then, Loki had somehow tricked Odin into sending Tyr away. He must have.

And now, Loki had convinced him to have Odin marry Hadding's daughter. The foreigner must have some greater scheme. But Idunn was the only one clever enough to unravel it. And she had said to arrange the wedding.

Tyr would do so. But he'd keep an eye on Loki. A careful eye.

## 25

*T*he deer wouldn't venture beyond the copse of evergreens. It was rare to spot one at all this close to town, and Sigyn was determined not to lose it. She was no hunter, as Frigg insisted on reminding her every time she went out alone, but she was a good shot with a bow. Her calves ached from crouching still so long, waiting for the animal to give her a clean shot. Her father had not named her a hunter, true, but she *could* be a hunter. Maybe that was her place—the same place Hermod had once held.

She'd left Snow Rabbit tied to a tree a quarter mile away, afraid the horse would spook the deer. Poor mare thought she'd been getting a gentle ride, but then Sigyn had seen the tracks. She would be the song of the town if she brought the animal down. Game had grown sparser and sparser around Halfhaugr, especially in winter. Bringing home fresh meat certainly wouldn't hurt her marriage prospects, either.

Her father would have her pretend to be simple, demure, and spineless. Then maybe he'd find a man for her. "No man wants a wife smarter than he is." Troll shit on that.

The deer lifted its head sharply.

Damned beast had heard her. It was going to bolt. She could feel it. It was going to—

The deer bounded off, darting between trees. Sigyn rose and drew her bow back in a single motion. She narrowed her sight along the shaft. Steady. Steady … She loosed.

The arrow whizzed over the deer and thunked into a tree.

"Son of a troll!"

She blew out a long breath. She ought to have stuck to just the riding today. Her dress was damp with melted snow as she trekked back to Snow Rabbit, making the journey oh so much more enjoyable. When she finally reached the mare, the animal shook nervously. Leaving her tied to a tree outside the wall might have been foolish, but no harm had come of it, nor would she expect any during daylight, though that light was fast fading.

"Come on, girl," she said as she untied the rope. "Best head home."

Snow Rabbit started back the moment Sigyn mounted her, setting a pace just shy of a full trot. Sigyn wouldn't hold her back. The poor animal knew what lurked out in the mist at night probably better than humans did.

The wind blew against the back of her neck, so she pulled her hood up. For a time, she kept the pace, then set Snow Rabbit trotting. They'd both be less on edge behind the town wall.

Moments later, another rider approached from the direction of town. A man, by his bearing, and pressing hard —in the wrong direction if he wanted to reach anywhere safe by nightfall. She could get off the road to avoid the traveler, but he would have seen her already. If he meant her ill, she'd rather meet him with bow ready. Besides, a man in that much of a hurry wouldn't be like to stop for a lone woman. She dismounted, unslung her bow, and nocked an arrow without drawing back.

It took only a few breaths for her to recognize the man— Agilaz. "Sigyn. What are you doing out so late? You should be behind the wall."

Sigyn tucked her arrow back in her quiver. "Well, *you're* out here."

"I'm a trained hunter and scout. You're a wellborn lady."

Yes, wellborn—after a fashion. "Where are you going, then?"

"Scouts reported trouble spreading between the Athra and the Godwulfs. The jarl wants me to learn the truth of the matter."

She climbed back on Snow Rabbit. "So I'm coming with you." She cared not overmuch about the Athra, but any threat to the Godwulfs was a threat to Hermod.

"No."

"But I—"

"No, Sigyn! Go home. The jarl has guests from the Wodan tribe. You should be there to meet them. You can catch the night meal if you make haste."

Guests? Had Odin returned after all?

Sigyn winked at Agilaz, letting him know she knew he'd manipulated her. It was fine—she *was* curious about the jarl Frigg and their father so desperately wanted to win over. "Just take care, then." With that she took off toward the town.

A guard called out at her approach, then others opened the gates for her, albeit briefly as they ushered her inside with disapproving glares. With her luck, she'd probably just added a slew of rumors for the town to whisper about her. 'Did you hear about Sigyn? Out riding at twilight like a crazed völva. Tempting the vaettir, that one.' She shook her head. Actually, the fear of vaettr possession was strong enough she shouldn't risk further implicating herself. Suspicious fools wouldn't need much goading to think she'd become host to something or other. A few winters back, the town had driven out a woman they claimed was alf-ridden. Poor woman had probably frozen to death in the wild.

Sigyn hurried on to the stables and handed Snow Rabbit's reins to the boy there. "The Wodan jarl, he's here?"

"No, my lady. One of his thegns went to see the jarl, though. And the foreigner came back with him."

"Foreigner?"

"Am I so foreign?" a voice said behind her. "I have walked these lands often enough."

Sigyn's shoulders hunched reflexively, and she blew a quick breath to calm herself. She'd not even heard anyone approach. Slowly, she turned to face the man—a sandy-haired stranger. His eyes, blue as sapphire, widened for a heartbeat when they met hers—so briefly she might have imagined it. Except she knew well enough the effect her pretty face could have on men who didn't know better. This man dressed simply, like a common freeman, but his elocution was too fine for an uneducated man.

She lowered her eyes from his. She couldn't seem too bold. "Does walking in a land make you a native there?"

The man nodded slowly, then stood straighter, hands behind his back. "Given enough time, I believe most would argue it does." He spoke with such deliberateness that Sigyn felt her cheeks flush. Gods, he was probably imagining her naked.

And did that even matter? Not really. Had she not just been looking for a husband to distract her from Hermod? With such thoughts in her head, it mattered little what went on in the heads of others.

"Are you with Jarl Odin?"

"Yes. You can call me Loki. If you wish to see Odin, though, he is not with us."

And if the jarl of the Wodanar had not come, why had he sent his thegn here? Surely not to thank Frigg for her aid in avenging his father. Such a purpose required he make the trek himself. The thegn might have come alone bearing a demand or threat, if Odin sought pretense to make war on the Hasdingi—the last thing Frigg or any of them needed.

"You speak volumes in silence," Loki said.

"That's ..." Disturbingly perceptive. "... the gift of women."

"Hardly a universal one. I've known many women—"

"No doubt."

He raised an eyebrow, and Sigyn flushed a little, praying it was merely that she'd interrupted, rather than that he'd caught her implication. With a lean body, a handsome face, and refined manners, he could well have had *many* women.

"I ... I should go," she mumbled and edged around the man, careful not to brush up against him.

What in Hel's frozen world had she been thinking? Letting herself get flustered by a man just because he looked her way. It wasn't like she'd never known a man's touch— she'd taken her pleasure from a few in her time. But deep down she'd always known they'd never take her for more than someone to warm a bed on a cold night. If she wanted a husband she'd need to ... to what? To not interrupt a man when he was speaking, maybe. Freyja alone knew how to please a man. Legend said the love goddess could have any man who drew breath. It shouldn't be that hard for Sigyn to claim just *one* for herself.

She pushed open the door into the great hall, forced to put her shoulder into it because of its weight. It creaked on its hinges, revealing the warmth of the hall. Inside, a feast was laid for a night meal. Jarl Hadding had gone to great lengths to impress his guest: plums, apples, roast squirrel, and at least one whole reindeer. Not that it surprised her. Her father wanted to win Odin's support just as much as his daughter did.

All had gathered around the feast table, with Odin's thegn sitting across from her father. Sigyn's chair stood empty next to Frigg, so she settled into it, offering only a nod to those around her. The Wodan thegn took no notice of her, and most of her own people pretended to take even less. Frigg, however, clasped her hand in welcome.

No sooner had Sigyn sat than Odin's thegn rose, hefting his goblet into the air. "Jarl Hadding. Your hospitality is worthy of song. We come unannounced, and you honor us with a feast to make your ancestors proud. And I ..." the thegn looked to Frigg before taking another sip of his goblet. "I would like to propose a more permanent alliance between our peoples."

"What did you have in mind?" Her father folded his arms, obviously trying to hide his interest.

"What alliance is stronger than one of marriage? My lord remains unmarried, as does your daughter."

A slight silence filled the hall, before several Hasding warriors whooped in approval. Sigyn lowered her gaze to hide her own shock. Odin *knew* Frigg was a völva. While her sister had plotted to sway or seduce Odin, he'd come to her on his own. What man married a völva?

Sigyn would have put her sister's chances of a good marriage at even less than her own—which was to say about as the same as finding a mermaid atop a mountain. By Hel, Sigyn would have made a better match for Odin, though she had never met him, and he probably knew naught of her. It wasn't as if Hadding boasted of his bastard daughter, but she could have made a wife fit for a jarl. She sipped her mead. Not that she cared.

Her father stroked his chin, though whether in consideration or just because he wanted to cover his own surprise, Sigyn couldn't quite say. "You honor us, Tyr. Please, convey my acceptance to your lord."

Tyr sat, banging his hand on the table as though he'd won a great victory. Loki slipped in during the commotion and sat close to Tyr, those too-blue eyes watching Sigyn.

This was a man with an agenda, a deep plan. One more puzzle.

## 26

*W*hen Odin returned to the Wodan town, his people were waiting for him. Scouts must have reported his arrival ahead, because Vili already had mutton roasting on the fire, though it was early for the night meal. The thick aroma was intoxicating as heady wine. Odin had eaten little since he'd left the Norns' mountain.

"Thank you," he whispered to Sleipnir before dismounting and joining his brothers.

Vili ambled over the moment he spotted Odin. "Sons of Borr together again," his middle brother said.

Odin clapped him on the shoulder. "Indeed." He cocked his head at the mutton. "And how well you know me."

He snagged a leg of mutton and bit deep, shuddering with pleasure as its hot juices dribbled down his chin. He took a swig of mead, then looked around.

"Where's Ve?" He had dared hope the apple would have revitalized the boy.

Vili belched out a raucous laugh. "Little brother's been plowing the goddess's trench, putting the two of us to shame. Spends all his time in her house."

A pit opened in his stomach that had naught to do with hunger. He handed Vili the mead skin and mutton. "I'd better check on them."

"You think he'd let us join in?"

Odin glared at Vili, who jerked back and then let out another rumbling chuckle. Odin stormed off toward Idunn's house. Vili was an oblivious fool and always would be. And if things had gone badly, maybe that was a mercy.

He paused on the threshold, listening. Just in case Vili was right. Inside, a girl sang softly, though not Idunn. What in Hel's frozen underworld was going on?

Odin stuck his head in the tent to find Jorunn sitting in front of Idunn, singing of valorous battles against the jotunnar long, long ago. Ve sat on a cot, skins wrapped around himself, gently rocking back and forth to the melody, eyes staring vacantly ahead.

Idunn had positioned the smith's girl such that both the small fire and Idunn herself blocked clear view of Ve. The goddess crooked a half smile at Odin's entrance. "Did you know this girl has a *lovely* singing voice, Odin?"

He shook his head. He'd had no idea. "Indeed you do, girl. Why don't you grab some mead at the feast hall? They've started the night meal early tonight."

"What's happened?" he asked the moment Jorunn left.

Idunn ground her palms into her eyes. "I should have given you the apples sooner. I'm always too late. I keep trying to be like her, and it's never enough."

Odin knelt beside Idunn and reached a hand to her shoulder. "Be like who?"

"My grandmother. She was a hero, Odin. You'd have liked her, I think. A warrior like you—"

"What is happening to my brother?" he demanded.

Odin had no patience left for Idunn's prattle. "You said the apple would halt this!"

"I think … part of him wants it."

"What? What did you just say?" She grimaced as his grip tightened on her shoulder. He knew he was hurting her, but he couldn't make himself stop. "You were supposed to be taking care of him, Idunn! I trusted you. Half the tribe thinks you're in here fucking his brains out. And … and you're saying he wants to lose his mind? So what in Hel's frozen underworld—"

Idunn's face darkened, and she shoved him so hard he tumbled over. "Do *not* use those words. My grandfather *died* to stop that frozen underworld from becoming *this* world. And I … I would have gladly slept with Ve if I thought it would have saved him. Do you think I want to watch this happen?"

Odin rose slowly, gathering himself, before stalking to his brother's side. Ve's eyes glimmered red, and he gnashed his teeth as though they pained him. "What are the mists doing to him? And what do you mean he *wants* it to happen?" When Idunn didn't answer, Odin turned back to her only to find her looking away. "Idunn?"

She shuddered, clutching her head in her hands. The goddess, looking so vulnerable. Afraid. Such a thought did not comfort him. "A person can fight the mists—for a while, at least. He's not fighting hard enough, and they're swallowing him up inside. Leaving room for something else."

Something else? Gods, she meant a vaettr was possessing Ve. "Use your sorcery. Cast it out."

"I *can't*. For Ve, it's as if whatever is inside him is filling a void. Part of him wants it there."

Odin placed a hand on Ve's head. It burned as with fever.

"I just need time! Time to find the Singasteinn and earn favor from that ghost."

"Are you so certain she can halt the transformation?"

Transformation? Hel's frozen ... Odin let the thought trail off. When he stood, he almost fell over. The ground seemed to sway beneath him. Was this his fault? What would drive Ve to such loneliness that he'd rather be possessed than face it? Ve had always been ... just there. Odin watched out for him, never let him get over his head in a fight. What more did the boy want? A woman? Had Ve needed a wife? He'd never asked Odin to arrange a marriage, but maybe Odin should have broached the topic himself. Vili had been content to foster bastards on every willing maid in the tribe. Odin had just assumed Ve would be the same.

Or was it something else? Had Odin and Vili pushed Ve aside? No, no damn it. All he had to do was honor his oath to the ghost. She would stop this.

"Fuck me," he mumbled. Unable to look at Idunn or Ve any longer, he staggered out of the house, wandering until he at last collapsed before a fire.

Someone offered him a stein of mead, and he kicked it back, hardly tasting it.

"So, brother," Vili said, "tell us of these völvur you went so far to see."

Odin turned slowly to the berserk. He was completely oblivious to what was happening to Ve. Gods, they *had* ignored their little brother. And now ... now Odin was going to fix it. No matter what it took, he was going to save Ve. No, not just Ve. He was going to save *all* his people.

"Well?" Vili asked. "These Norns?"

Odin hesitated. The Norns spoke in riddles, but what he'd understood of it left an unpleasant taste in his mouth, like a splinter in the back of his mind. Talk of fire and flood and betrayal would only distress the others, and even if it were all true, they could do naught about it. "You know völvur. Stuck on their own mysteries. Now is the time for drink."

Vili chuckled and nodded. "Meat and mead both!" Just like that. The World was so simple to Vili—action without consideration of consequences. Odin tried to share his joy, but there was no joy in him. He could feel the emptiness in his own heart, borne of his failures and weaknesses. Failures he could not repeat. And it wasn't his brother's counsel he needed, was it? For a time he sat with Vili, before slipping off to find Loki.

He had not gone far however, when Tyr intercepted him. Part of him wanted to wave the thegn away, to push forward toward the only thing that mattered. Loki might know where to go to save Ve. But Odin himself had made Tyr his champion and his voice, and he had made an oath to Idunn as well. "What is it?"

Tyr grunted, dropping whatever greeting he'd intended. "I did what you asked. Found a way to draw the Hasding tribe to our side."

"Good. Yes." Halfhaugr was central to all the tribes. If he controlled that, winning support at the Althing became that much easier. "What did you offer them?"

"You are to marry the jarl's daughter."

Odin sputtered. "Marry the ... She's a fucking völva, you fool!"

"Everyone will fear you. Respect you."

The king with a witch bride.

"Jarl Hadding is not long for Midgard," Tyr said.

Odin groaned. And Frigg was his only heir. The plan had the barest hint of sense to it. Enough to keep him from smacking Tyr for his folly. "You overstep your bounds."

"You said to make you king. Few drops of blood on the wedding bed. Save you rivers of blood on the battlefield."

Odin clenched his fists at his side. Gods but he wanted to hate Tyr for this. "I have other things to tend to."

He left Tyr standing there, no longer caring what the man had to say. Only Ve mattered now.

Odin's blood brother had climbed a hill some distance outside the town and sat alone beside a small fire. The trek was short, and after so long on horseback, any chance to stretch his legs was welcome.

"Welcome back," Loki said when Odin reached the top. "Did you find what you were looking for?"

Odin slumped across the fire from Loki, then kicked at some of the loose kindling. The fire sputtered and seethed. Like Odin, recoiling from outside forces. Every step he took seemed to carry him further into damnation, all while Ve dwindled. "I'm not sure. But for certain Sleipnir was an aid. Thank you for that."

"Then keep him. He'll be loyal to you for as long as you return it."

"A fine gift." Not so long ago he'd seen the horse as monstrous. Now he knew better. Sleipnir was glorious. And everywhere Odin rode, men would look on with awe. Maybe that had been part of Loki's plan all along. "And I want you to have something ... Another of the apples, brother. One to give to whom you choose as your companion in life."

Loki opened his mouth, then swallowed without speaking.

Odin raised his hand, forestalling the need for thanks. Loki had earned all Odin could give and more a dozen times over. And now Odin needed his counsel more than ever.

The foreigner had a way about him, and if anyone could handle the details of his visit with the Norns, Loki could. Odin's blood brother had become his last hope to save his true brother.

He told Loki all he could recall of the Norns' prophecies and riddles. And at last he told him what Idunn had said of Ve.

And when he had finished, Loki nodded. "So what do you want to do?"

A part of him wanted to simply ask Loki what to do. But if Odin was to be King of the Aesir—a role Idunn had forced upon him, true, but one he had pledged to accomplish—he needed to make such decisions himself. He drew in a deep breath and blew it out before speaking. "Tyr would have me marry Frigg Haddingsdotter. A völva. But the Niflungar ..."

"You don't know where to find them."

"I was hoping you would tell me." The ghost's curse coiled around his heart, crushing it, threatening to steal away those he cared most for. His brothers were all the family he had left.

And all of this because of his damnable pride on the mountain. Had he not gone after Ymir, Ve would not have caught so much of the mists. He'd not have needed sanctuary in the Odlingar castle. The varulfur would not have come to the feast. Like a wretch, he brought misery upon his tribe and his own kin. Or was he but a fool for not considering the consequences? For not heeding Heidr's warnings about the cost of all actions. No way remained to him, save forward.

"What of Tyr's plan, then?"

"Marry Frigg?" The woman was attractive, for certain, but Odin was hardly ready to settle down with a wife. "Marriage would mean passing up on a great many willing girls. Why settle for one love when you can have many?"

Loki raised an eyebrow. "Is that love?"

Odin shrugged. "Physically speaking, anyway. Besides, the woman is a völva. How could I marry someone like that?" Legend said to sleep with a völva was to risk falling under her spell. To say naught of dealing with a wife who'd always have to act like she knew more than she really did. That bit was like to grow tiresome about three days into the marriage. If that much.

"A völva touches the Otherworlds, and is touched by them in turn. The marriage might serve more than one end, should you let it."

Now it was Odin's turn to raise a brow.

"What do you know of seid, brother?"

"A völva's magic. They see things, know things, can bespell a man's mind."

Loki nodded, then stirred the fire. "There are two kinds of energy at play within us, Odin. One kind is stronger in men, one kind stronger in women. When men and women are intimate, they can draw out a small portion of the opposing energy, balancing our own. When you bring her to fulfillment, part of the energy she gives you will be that that feminine energy."

Odin scoffed. "You're saying I can fuck the magic out of a witch?"

Loki frowned. "That was vulgar. If you are to be a king, you must rise above vulgarity, no matter where you came from. What passes for the jarl of a small tribe will not pass for a king. And, no, that wasn't what I was saying. Naught is lost, just shared. Her vital energy passes into you as yours passes into her, and from it you may gain a hint of seid."

"That's a power for women."

Loki raised a finger to forestall the objection. "You want to unite the Ás tribes under your banner, and you're going to be swayed against gaining power and insight because it's *unmanly*? Perhaps Idunn did not choose her champion carefully enough."

Odin's fists clenched, but he forced himself to keep them in his lap. "How dare you? *I* will lead our people." He would do *aught* to save Ve.

"Then lead. Take the power from her, and you may gain a glimpse of the things she sees. With it, you might understand riddles that otherwise leave you out in the cold."

Odin grunted in disgust. Tyr had little love for Odin's foreign brother, but they both of them agreed on this damned wedding. And if it could tell him where to find the Niflungar …

Gods, Loki was right. Marrying Hadding's daughter would give him so many things he needed. And maybe, one day, there could be something more between them. She was regal, intelligent. She *would* make a fine queen. And other tribes couldn't help but fear the man with the monstrous horse and the völva queen. He sighed and let his face fall into his hands.

Finally he stood. "Prepare yourself. We leave for Halfhaugr in the morn."

## 27

*C*lay pots, metal vials, and bowls of Freyja alone knew what all came crashing onto the floor as Frigg swept her arm over her work table. Sigyn's sister wailed and leaned against that table.

After blowing out a slow breath, Sigyn moved to Frigg's side and set a hand on her shoulder. Very few people ever saw a völva lose her composure. The respect their titles carried demanded they hold themselves above others, above petty human emotions.

Frigg turned toward her, and Sigyn embraced her older sister.

"Naught I try helps him."

Sigyn held Frigg at arm's length so she could see her face. Their father had had a long life—longer than most jarls could hope for. It was the way of things. But now that Frigg could no longer stave off the inevitable, she seemed to take it harder than she should have. Or maybe Sigyn would have felt the loss more poignantly had she not been pushed aside and cast out by nearly everyone she'd ever known.

"Perhaps no brew *can* help him." Sigyn squeezed her arms. "If it is his urd, he will die."

Frigg scoffed. "I didn't think you believed in urd."

Sigyn shrugged. "You do, völva. That's really all that matters here. Not that I think that's all that weighs upon your mind this afternoon. You've hardly left this room since Father agreed to have you wed. For all your plans to sway Odin, you never actually expected to get him, least of all like this. You went hunting for a bear and, on finding one, only then realized you have not armed yourself for such prey."

"Odin isn't prey."

"And yet you pursued him as such. Had you slept with him, could you truly have swayed his mind with your trench? Or is that all völvur bombast meant to discourage men from raping your kind?"

Frigg's face fell, touched by a hint of fear that tugged at Sigyn's heart. She had not expected that.

"You don't know. You're a virgin, aren't you?"

Frigg turned from her then, leaned back on the table, shoulders slumping.

Damn. She never had learned to mind her tongue. "Don't fret over it, all right. In fact, forget such things. You spoke with this man. Tell me of him."

"Angry ... He is so angry." Frigg turned to look at her now. "Consumed with it, like his insides were caught aflame. A fire rises in him, one fit to consume Midgard."

"Is that your vision?"

Frigg sighed. "It was difficult to make sense of it. But I saw myself as his wife, side by side, ruling over a great city like the ones in tales of ancient times. And there was fresh water, greenery, plants—like summer. A summer that didn't end. I think Odin won't be a mere jarl—I think he will be a king. And there was war, yes, famine, flame."

Sigyn tapped her finger against her lip. What was she to say to something like that? Frigg seemed so convinced of herself, it almost made it hard to doubt her. So *had* she seen a vision of her future with Odin? And why was Sigyn even here, forcing her to talk of it? The decision definitely had naught to do with a masochistic need to see Frigg, of all people, find a marriage while Sigyn remained alone. "The Ás tribes have not had a king in a long time, but even if they raised one, what has that to do with summer?"

Frigg considered for a moment, her eyes latched onto Sigyn's face. "What if theWorld could change? The Vanir are said to live in islands of spring—of warmth that does not wither and fade after a few moons. What if somehow Midgard could share such a destiny?"

Sigyn shook her head, then rubbed the bridge of her nose. Now they had devolved into true völvur pomposity. Breathe in the smoke of a few strange plants and call the hallucinations visions. If that's all it took, she could be a völva herself. But these women convinced themselves what they saw was truth—albeit not always literal truth. It could be a metaphor. And since no one could really disprove a metaphor, a völva's visions could hardly be disputed. All very convenient.

But Frigg clearly would not allow herself to be easily dissuaded about this. Sigyn sat on the cold stone floor. "This Realm has been covered by the mists of Niflheim for as long as anyone remembers. These stories about a time before the mist—they're probably just stories. Who wouldn't dream of a better World? No matter what world we live in, people will look around and imagine it could be or could *have been* better."

If Frigg thought some rage-mad jarl could change all of Midgard, she was thinking with her heart over her brain.

And Sigyn was beginning to think Frigg *did* have feelings for Odin. Perhaps those feelings had been born of Frigg's visions—a self-fulfilling prophecy of her love for him. And though Sigyn had not met him, he didn't sound fit to be king of aught.

"What if I could be a queen?"

What if she could? She'd be like to spend the rest of her life watching for knives in her back.

Frigg eyed her, as she sometimes did, clearly trying not to reveal what was going on in her mind. Sigyn knew well enough, though, even if Frigg would never admit it. She knew because her own thoughts had gone there—that Sigyn herself might prove a better heir to Jarl Hadding. She was younger, more beautiful, and not a völva. She'd have been a decent match for a marriage alliance—if any man would have had her.

Frigg, though, had had her first visions as a child. Visions damned a girl, forced her to look into the darkness and allow it to seep inside in the name of cultivating seid, in service to a tribe that would fear her. The tribe's old völva had taken Frigg away—and no father, not even a jarl, could deny a völva her chosen quarry. And thus began the slow poisoning, the transmogrifying a girl into a witch, who, in moments of weakness, clung to shreds of a life that might have been.

Sigyn tapped a finger against her lip. "Do you believe Odin has such ambitions?"

"I don't know, perhaps. Whether he has them or not, I believe he carries a weighty urd." Frigg paused a moment, then sighed. "Father is ... not long for this world. All my potions have only staved off the inevitable. I will need a strong husband if I am to hold leadership of this tribe. And that is to say naught of the numerous threats we face from

without. The Skalduns, the Godwulfs, and the Vanir-
damned Sviarlanders. And those are only the nearest threat.
Were Father to have refused Odin, then we'd have made
enemies of the Wodanar as well."

There. Frigg had accepted their father's death, at least in
some part of her mind. But Odin had sent his man here
unbidden, offered marriage before Frigg or Hadding had
finished sowing those seeds. And even Frigg realized that
for the man's actions to line up serendipitously with her
plans—and her vision—ought to raise a few doubts. More
than a few.

"And you want me to find out where Odin's true intentions lie. If he already plans to strive for kingship, and if his
offer for your hand holds any ulterior motive."

Her sister sighed, looked back at the empty table. "You
have a way of uncovering the truth of things, yes. But, Sigyn
..." She turned, serious as ever. "Tread with care. Our whole
tribe hangs in the balance."

For a heartbeat, Frigg's calm trembled, her poise threatened as it so rarely was. Sigyn had seen her sister's tears
when her mother died, but she was so afraid to show
anyone her true feelings. Was that völva training? Was that
need to hide herself something that had been beaten into
her sister? Sigyn remembered running through the town
square, laughing, chasing after a smiling Frigg, but that was
so many years ago. Before the visions and the training and
the loss.

"Don't worry," Sigyn whispered. "I'll figure it out."

---

## 28

*T*he baying of elkhounds greeted them as Halfhaugr drew nigh. Odin rode Sleipnir out ahead of his people. More than a third of the Wodanar had come. Warriors, berserkir, shieldmaidens, washerwomen, tradesmen. All he had invited to see his wedding. The numbers would serve as a message to Hadding, as well—a reassurance, perhaps, of the value of their alliance, or a threat should the jarl have second thoughts. Odin had little time to worry overmuch on his oath to Idunn until he had saved Ve. But if the key to that lay between Frigg's legs, he needed make damned sure her father could not change his mind.

A scout approached as he drew nigh, a hound at his heels. Agilaz Farshot. He took in Odin's entourage but made no comment. Not even a visible reaction to the eight-legged horse. A steady man this, perhaps a thegn.

"We did not expect so many guests. I'd ask them to wait outside the town while I inform Jarl Hadding. He can make arrangements."

Odin looked back at his people. "I understand. We are eager to celebrate, of course."

"Of course." Not even the hint of a smile. Stern bastard.

But that name ... Agilaz. Odin had not much considered it when they first met at Father's funeral feast, but wasn't Agilaz some famed archer from back in the Njarar War? Ve would have known. He learned all such tales.

"Jarl Odin, I welcome you inside Halfhaugr, however. Frigg Haddingsdotter awaits you in the fortress."

So they wanted him to enter alone, separate from his warriors. A reminder of their own strength, of the strength of their walls. Hadding was a fool if he thought he could hold Halfhaugr against Odin's men. The jarl could not have even guessed what Odin had become. Something far more than a man. So infused with the glory of Idunn's apple, Odin could fight his way through a dozen men or more.

He snorted, then dismounted. "Lead the way."

ॐ

INSIDE THE FORTRESS, Frigg stood, hands behind her back. She wore the most elegant of green dresses, embroidered with golden knotwork that might have represented the boughs of Yggdrasil. Ironic, that the fruit of that very tree had made Odin immortal. The woman nodded respectfully as he drew nigh.

Yes, she had beauty, grace, poise. And to save his brother, all he had to do was satisfy her. In his mind he tore the dress from her shoulders. Held her down until she shuddered beneath him, crying out in pleasure. The image seemed so real, he flushed. At least with his thick fur cloak, she probably couldn't see the swelling in his trousers.

"Welcome to Halfhaugr, my lord," she said. A blonde girl stood beside her, as well as a burly man. A guard, perhaps. Agilaz had wandered off to meet Hadding.

Odin smiled. He'd wooed many a girl in his time, though never had he considered claiming *it will save my brother's life* as a reason to overcome a woman's resolve. "Thank you for accepting my proposal."

Frigg half bowed, then beckoned for him to follow. "My father has arranged a private room for you in the fortress. I hear you bring a great many retainers with you. We will try to arrange lodging for them in the town."

"Wonderful."

Would she agree to sleep with him before the wedding? Unlikely. Still, knowing why he had come here made it hard to think of aught else.

Odin followed behind her, taking in the fortress. Old dverg work, and stronger than men could hope to build.

"Did you truly ride here on an eight-legged horse?" the blonde girl asked.

"Indeed. And I don't believe I caught your name."

Frigg looked to the other girl. "This is my half sister, Sigyn."

Half sister. A bastard child, perhaps? Elsewise, why had he never heard aught of another daughter of Hadding?

"Well, Sigyn, the horse is called Sleipnir. And he has carried me across more miles than I can count into lands you cannot imagine."

"I have a great imagination."

Odin chuckled while Frigg raised an eyebrow at her sister. The girl bit her lip, as if suddenly realizing she might have overstepped herself.

Frigg led him down a hall, past several wooden doors,

before stopping at one. "Please make yourself comfortable here. I need to check in with my father."

Sigyn hesitated as if she intended to linger, ask more about Sleipnir. Frigg grabbed her sister's wrist and pulled her along after her, followed by their guard.

Odin grunted, then stopped in the room long enough to cast in his satchel. He too had things to ask the jarl of the Hasdingi.

JARL HADDING SAT in his darkened hall, coughing and sputtering while Odin waited. The jarl cleared his throat once more. "We're arranging a few private houses for the nobles among you. The others will have to stay in communal lodgings."

As long as his brothers got their own houses, Odin cared little. The others would be used to living in close quarters. Well, Idunn, of course, she would need her own space.

Odin shrugged, trying to seem amicable. "Anything you can arrange will serve. Come, let us speak of the wedding date." The much more pressing matter.

"Yes." He coughed, then spit out some thick vileness on the floor before his throne. "The new moon will prove auspicious. Frigg herself has divined this."

"The new moon! By the Vanir, man, you'd have us holed up here halfway to the solstice."

The jarl snorted, whether at Odin or because of the thickness, who could say? "A strain on our supplies, yes."

"So let's set the date sooner. Surely tomorrow or the day after would—"

"Tomorrow!" The jarl shook his head, then raised a finger. "I remember being young. That eagerness. You won't grow old in a single moon, Jarl Odin. Tonight the mead will flow freely. Bring your men and enjoy it. Savor this time."

Odin scowled. He would certainly partake of the mead. He doubted, however, he would enjoy the jarl so delaying his more urgent quest.

## 29

*S*ure enough, the eight-legged horse occupied a stall in the stables. Hands raised in supplication, Sigyn crept toward the strange animal. It snorted at her approach, its black eyes never leaving her own. The depth there spoke of worlds beyond Midgard and secrets no mortal had uncovered. Where did he come from? Somewhere beyond her reach, no doubt.

"Shhh," she whispered. "Easy. I'm a friend."

"Sleipnir chooses his friends with care," a voice said behind her.

She spun to see Loki had crept up on her, silent as a shadow and twice as mysterious.

"And is this horse truly the jarl's mount?"

"Insofar as Sleipnir could belong to any person, he belongs to Odin at the moment."

She smiled, turning his words over in her mind. Loki must mean the animal was too intelligent to be owned, which told her something in and of itself. Perhaps the horse was possessed by a vaettr. She'd heard spirits could alter a being's physical form, given enough time. That could explain it. But still, questions remained. If it was a vaettr, why would it want a horse? What kind of vaettr was it? Did it serve Odin out of mutual beneficence, or did it have some ulterior designs the jarl hadn't even considered?

"They are holding a feast inside," Loki said.

Sigyn laughed. "Feast might be a stretch, I think. The winter draws on, and Father cannot hope to feed so many of Odin's people. Certainly not if he hopes to hold a proper celebration for the wedding soon. Maybe that was Odin's plan—to shame the Hasdingi or else force us to overextend ourselves."

Loki stared at her with those too-blue eyes, the hint of a smile on his face. "A wise jarl has many plans, without doubt. But to what end would Odin wish to shame Hadding and the Hasdingi?"

"I don't know that yet. But whatever he intends, I will find it out."

The foreign man broke into a true smile now. "Of that I have no doubt. I must join the others inside."

So would she. Drunk men were apt to say more than they ought, especially to a pretty girl. Loki, much as she wanted to speak with him, did not seem the kind to easily unveil his secrets. She'd make time to talk with him later, though. He was almost as much a puzzle as Sleipnir.

TALKING to Odin's people had proved less illuminating than she might have hoped. They claimed Idunn herself walked among them. Such fancy made them seem gullible, entranced by a deceptive völva. And yet, still the jarl had come here on an eight-legged horse, so she could not afford to rule out aught.

By now, many had passed the drinking horn around a half dozen times. A brawl had broken out, turned into a wrestling match, and ended with both men agreeing they needed more mead. A commodity that would run out soon enough at this rate.

Sigyn drifted among the guests, engaging in idle chatter while keeping ever conscientious of the conversations around her. Drunk men might still let slip their secrets, and any detail, however ostensibly unimportant, might prove the key to understanding Odin's ultimate purpose.

Still, such an undertaking did not require her to remain sober either, and she'd accepted the horn a few times herself. Odin's men offered it to her more oft than her father's, who pretended she did not exist. Tonight though, that did not bother her—not much, at least.

In one corner of the hall, Loki sat in front of Olrun, playing tafl. Sigyn's foster mother had a mind for the game, indeed had been the one to first teach Sigyn many winters back, though Sigyn had long since surpassed the woman. Intent on the game, she edged closer, until Olrun looked up.

"Here now. My daughter may give you a better challenge, foreigner. We both know where this game is headed."

A glance at the board made that obvious. Loki would have her in five moves.

Her foster mother rose and motioned for Sigyn to take her seat. She did so while the blue-eyed foreigner reset the board.

"Dark or light?" he asked.

Sigyn settled into the chair, trying not to grin. "You choose."

Olrun leaned against a nearby pillar, watching them. Like as not, she wanted to see Sigyn thrash the man who had just defeated her.

Loki leaned forward. "How interesting a question, especially when you leave it to another to decide."

"As you just did?"

He smiled ever so slightly. "Then I would give you the light."

"You'll play dark, then?"

"One must learn to play both sides to truly master the game."

Sigyn quirked her own smile and moved her first piece. "What game are you playing, then?"

He moved in turn, motioning for her to play. "I've studied most games across Midgard. Some are instructive, some entertaining—the best are both."

They traded a few more moves. She couldn't quite pin down his strategy. He blocked off her easiest plays but had not made any advances that might actually win him the game.

"You play very cautiously," she said.

"It's the long game that matters most."

She took one of his pieces. "Too much caution can cost you."

He seemed remarkably unperturbed, continuing to shift his pieces out defensively, not even making counterattacks. After several moves, he finally spoke again. "Sometimes one has to make sacrifices to win."

She chuckled. "From where I sit, you don't seem to be winning much of anything." She claimed another piece.

"Perhaps you sit too long in one place. Everything is a matter of perspective. The changing of viewpoints can illuminate the World in ways we could not have imagined before." He shifted his king, cutting off her plan to hem him in.

Instead, she claimed yet another of his pawns. She

opened her mouth to taunt him then shut it and leaned back, taking in the whole board. Had he just ... No. There was no way he could have planned that far ahead. What, twenty moves? And yet, he moved his next piece, leaving her with no choice but to fall back. To precipitate an endless series of counters that would end with him the victor in another ten moves.

Sigyn tapped her finger to her lip. Did he *see* this? Had he set this up on purpose? She moved again, testing.

Once again, he shifted another piece, forcing her hand and smiling ever so slightly about it.

She rose, shaking her head. "That was ... I'm impressed."

"Wait, what happened?" Olrun asked. "Is he giving up?"

"No. He's already won."

Loki leaned back, saying naught, but Olrun sputtered.

"H-how did ...? You were winning."

No. Maybe she never had been. How fascinating. An opponent who could plan even farther ahead than she could. She'd have to improve her game. For now, though, she nodded at Loki in respect. Maybe one more drink after all.

THE FEAST HAD LONG since dwindled away.

The guests were most like to be asleep, but she could use the time to snoop through their belongings. Sigyn crept about the hall, inspecting the drunken warriors. Chances of finding something were slim, but you never knew. The things people carried could tell you a lot about them. Hadding had provided Odin with a room to sleep in, but the rest of the guests lay sprawled around the great hall. Some lounged on benches or slept in chairs, others on the floor.

Odin's massive brother lay facedown on a table, snoring into the wood.

Sigyn snorted at the sight.

Behind her, someone stirred. She spun to see one of the warriors—Tyr—watching her with one eye open. He'd slept leaning against a pillar, as if guarding his fellows. Actually, that must be exactly what he was doing. The way he stared at her made her skin crawl. Not much chance for snooping through anyone's things now.

She hadn't seen Loki in here. He would have the most answers, but this Tyr was Odin's thegn and champion. He might know Odin's heart well, and it might prove easier to pluck answers from him than from one as clever as Loki.

Heart pounding, she approached the warrior, then spoke softly. "You're the one who offered the proposal on Odin's behalf."

Tyr grunted.

She knelt beside him. "It surprised us all."

He snorted. "Him, too."

Oh? So he had come here without orders from his jarl? How intriguing. Odin had not sent Tyr, and yet the jarl had come here with all his people, ready for a wedding set to unfold in but a few days. The jarl must place unwavering trust in his thegn, then, enough to accept the man's choice as his bride. Unless, of course, Odin plotted betrayal, adapting his plans to the opportunity Tyr had thrust upon him.

"You never truly said what Odin hopes to gain from this."

"A wife."

Sigyn smiled and shook her head. "Perhaps, but he could have found one anywhere. You came here, to Halfhaugr."

Tyr grumbled something under his breath. "Godwulfs are on the move. Threatening the Athra."

Sigyn frowned but nodded. So Odin, or at least Tyr, must know Jarl Alci was her father's brother. Maybe he thought he could pressure his new father-in-law to restrain Alci. If so, Odin was in for profound disappointment. Her father could not protect his own people from Alci, much less some other tribe. "Where can I find Loki?"

"Can this not wait until morning?" he whispered, though the crook of his mouth said he thought he knew exactly why a woman would seek a man at this hour.

Sigyn flushed, no doubt confirming his suspicion. Let the man think what he wanted. Never mind a part of her longed for just that. For anyone who would want her for her.

Tyr jerked his head toward the main door. Loki had gone outside? Into the mists? That was ... unfortunate. Sigyn nodded at the warrior, rose, then approached the door herself. Damned thing would creak on its hinges for certain. With luck, though, all these men were twice over too drunk to wake from the sound.

She should be safe enough, here within the town walls. As long as she had fire, she need not worry overmuch about Mist-madness.

She edged it open, then slipped through the crack. Outside, the bitter night air stung her cheeks. She pulled her cloak tighter, but it wouldn't be enough. She needed a warm bed and a few hours' rest. Maybe Tyr had been right. Maybe this should have waited for morning. And yet she found herself continuing on.

A breeze blew through town, stirring a drift of snow. Sigyn grunted against the cold and took a few steps outward before she spotted the man sitting in front of a small fire, staring at it. The flame was between the two of them, but he seemed to be looking at her, or at least in her direction.

Was that enough of an invitation?

It would have to be. She trudged over, then sunk by the fire, across from Loki. Not even the flames granted enough warmth out here.

"Why did you leave the hall?" she asked.

"That's not what you came here to ask me."

No. Again, he was a bit too perceptive. "And yet, it remains a valid question."

"So it does."

How very illuminating. If he wasn't going to cooperate, this was pointless. "Do you want me to leave you alone?"

"No," he said, as though shocked at the question.

He didn't want to be alone, and yet he'd slunk away from his fellows to sit out in the cold. The man himself was starting to seem as mysterious as the horse. And Sigyn treasured a good mystery.

"Your jarl, he knows Frigg is a völva."

The man simply smiled at her from across the fire—the merest hint of a smile, really—but she found herself returning it. He waited for her to ask an actual question. How clever. Fine then.

"Why does he want to marry Frigg?"

"Is a political alliance not reason enough?"

"You've implied an answer without actually giving one. Does that work out for you?"

"Most of the time, yes," Loki said, his smile growing.

"And if I request you give me straight answers?"

He sat with hands resting on his knees, legs crossed. The position looked uncomfortable, but he seemed at peace. "I suppose you won't know until you try."

If he wanted to play, she'd indulge him. She liked a puzzle. "Please answer my questions directly."

He didn't respond to her imperative, just stared at her with those deep blue eyes.

So she hadn't actually asked aught. "Will you please give me direct answers to my questions?"

Oddly, he blinked, then stared up at the stars for a time. He seemed so entranced with them she feared to interrupt, as though he communed with the gods themselves. "I'll make you a deal," he said at last, finally returning to stare into her eyes. "I will answer a question directly, if you will do the same."

"Deal," she blurted, then realized her mistake. She'd agreed to a single question only—which meant she'd have to choose very wisely. Something that would answer all Frigg's concerns at once ... or at least allow Sigyn to deduce the answers to the remaining questions.

Sigyn folded her hands in her lap, smiling while she turned possible questions over in her mind. *What is the real reason for the marriage? Does Odin truly care for Frigg? What was Loki's secret?* Her smile grew. What she wouldn't give to know that. The man undoubtedly had many, but she couldn't afford to waste her one question on them. Not after she'd promised Frigg. Still, she hated to leave a mystery unsolved ... No! What could she ask? *Is Odin trustworthy? Why did Frigg dream of spring at Odin's side?* No—he could well answer some nonsense about a völva's visions being metaphors. But then, that would tell her something, as well. If the vision was a metaphor, and Odin would not become a literal king, that might well sway Frigg's choices.

"Once again your silence speaks well of you, Sigyn Haddingsdotter."

"How do you know my name?"

"I—"

"No!" She raised a hand and almost leapt to her feet. "That is *not* my question." Damn. He could have easily asked after her with any local. Maybe Olrun had told him after their tafl match.

Loki smiled and nodded. She narrowed her eyes at him, but couldn't quite hide her own smile.

She had to ask something about spring. If Odin's future was somehow tied to that, then the urd of all Midgard rested on him. But the question had to be about Odin. Any question she asked specifically regarding Frigg's vision could be vague or unhelpful, even in a direct answer.

"I have my question," she said at last. "What is so special about Odin that he might shape the urd of Midgard?"

Loki's mouth opened as if he hadn't quite expected that, but his eyes still seemed warm. Almost proud. "What a well-thought question. One, I suspect, that has more depth than even you realize. Since you have requested a direct answer, I'll try to give one that will make the most sense, rather than be the most complete. Odin was chosen by one of the Vanir, Idunn, to receive the apples of Yggdrasil, making him immortal—a gift he can share with a few select others. This gift, and the power and responsibility it entails, would naturally allow—in fact, all but force—him to challenge the current state of the World."

Sigyn's mouth hung open a crack. Of all the things she'd expected he might say, that was not one of them. Her first reaction was to dismiss the implausible claim. The idea of a goddess traveling to a small Ás tribe and offering the gift of immortality was absurd. But then, so was a man riding an eight-legged horse or slaying a jotunn. If the gods had truly chosen Odin, then the man was destined for a life of greatness, be it great glory or great tragedy. Sadly, the two so often went hand in hand.

She tried to speak, but only a pathetic gasp of breath escaped.

Loki raised a hand as if to forestall any further questions. "I believe I have upheld my part of our bargain. Now I have a question for you."

Sigyn blew out another breath. "A deal is a deal."

"So it is," Loki said, his eyes locked on hers. "Consider this. Odin now faces the question of eternity. Ask yourself whether the life you live is one you would be content with for the rest of time, or if, in his place, you would find your existence wanting. Tell me, Sigyn, have you not felt aught missing from your life, as though some part of your soul sought for something you could not quite name?"

"I ..." She swallowed. What did that mean? That she was lonely? Without doubt she was. How could she not be when most people, even her own father, had never understood her? At best she was tolerated, at worst feared and mocked for the very talents the gods had blessed her with.

Loki rose, still smiling. "Thank you for the direct answer, Sigyn. We should probably return to the warmth of the hall."

But for a while she sat there, shivering, unable to stop running his words through her mind.

## 30

_T_he pounding inside Odin's head was even louder than the pounding on the door. For a moment he pulled the furs over his face, as if that could cut out the banging. Too much mead last night. Or perhaps not enough —a few more pints and maybe he'd have slept through this interruption. Instead, he stumbled over to the door and flung it open.

"What in the name of Hel's frigid crotch is going on?" he demanded.

The servant, a chambermaid, reeled back, her mouth agape. Poor girl was probably no more than fourteen. Gods, Loki had been right. Odin was a vulgar man. It appeared that was something he'd have to work on.

"Uh, apologies, my lady. You woke me from a pleasant dream."

The girl stared at her feet. "Jarl Hadding summons ... er ... requests your presence."

What now?

"Fine. Run along and tell them I'll be there shortly."

Odin rubbed his palms against his eyes then stumbled

over to a wash basin and dunked his head in the chilled water. Gods! That'd wake him well enough. He shook his head, flinging droplets of water around the room before donning his tunic.

Finally he strode out to the great hall, where Frigg and Sigyn stood by Hadding's side. The jarl shifted in his throne with poorly disguised pain. The old man squinted at Odin before speaking. "Jarl Odin, let us not mince words. You have been holding out on your prospective allies. It has come to my attention you hold a great gift, the greatest gift a man could hope for."

This was not mincing words? Odin folded his arms. If the jarl wasn't going to be direct, neither would he. "Indeed. My sexual prowess is legendary, so I shouldn't be surprised word has reached this far. Your daughter shall not be disappointed."

Frigg pressed her lips together, barely hiding her displeasure. Sigyn blushed and stared at her feet.

Hadding glowered and rose from the throne, his knees popping as he did so. "I know you have apples that grant eternal youth! Don't you think your allies deserve such—" A cough wracked the man's chest, then he rubbed it before continuing, "such considerations?"

How in the burning flames of Muspelheim did he know about the apples? It was too much to hope Odin had kept the secret from his own people, but who would have told the Hasdingi? Of course, every one of them had been drunk last night. For all Odin knew, he himself might have let that slip in his boasting. Dammit, this was not what he wanted to face. Even if the apple would cure Hadding of his ailments —and Odin didn't know if they worked that way—the man wasn't just old, he was a coward and a weakling. Hardly someone Odin wanted to spend eternity with. Besides which, he had only one apple left, and that was meant for Frigg. He needed his queen by his side.

Odin clenched his fists at his side for a moment before answering. "Rest assured, Jarl, I will treat my allies right. Those who earn my friendship will get what they deserve."

Hadding nodded, apparently satisfied with Odin's words, though Sigyn frowned. Odin tried not to look at her. The girl had recognized his words actually promised naught. She was a clever one, one worth watching. And if she told Hadding, would he listen?

Hadding coughed again. "Well, then."

"Once the marriage is concluded, our alliance becomes formal. Why stand on tradition? We could well hold the ceremony tomorrow."

When Odin turned from Hadding he caught Frigg smiling at him. It was well she was pleased with the union. Eternity was a long time to spend with an unhappy wife. Odin returned her nod. She whispered something in her father's ear, and he grumbled about it.

"I'm afraid we need at least one more day to arrange the feast."

Odin tried not to let the irritation mar his face. Every moment he wasted with this frivolity was a moment Ve slipped farther from him. If the only way to save his brother was to bed Frigg, that was hardly an onerous task. But they needed to get on with it. Still, arguing over it would only lead to suspicions and quarrels. Odin waved his hand in acquiescence. "If you'll excuse me."

He then strode off to find Tyr. The warrior was outside, despite the early morning hour, shirtless and working through forms with his sword, a daily regimen Odin wished he still had time and discipline for himself. Once, growing up, he'd trained like that with Tyr every morning.

"Come to join me?" Tyr asked without looking his way or even pausing in his strokes.

How the fuck did he do that?

"The jarl has set the wedding for the day after tomorrow."

"Good." Tyr continued swinging his sword, not even looking at Odin. A master of the blade, for certain.

"I'm going to ask for a house here, for my brothers. Watch over them."

Now Tyr paused mid-stroke, and turned to face him, sweat streaming down his face. "They are men grown."

Odin stepped close to the thegn. He had to trust someone with this. And he *had* named Tyr his champion. How far did the man's loyalty stretch? "After the wedding, I will have to leave, to find these Niflungar. Hadding has learned of the apples and thinks I'll give him one. I have none to offer him, nor would I if I did."

"Not a strong man. Not anymore."

Odin grunted. "I see you understand me. The jarl will not be well pleased. He might even encourage the Wodanar to leave Halfhaugr."

"We need it."

They did. Odin had sworn on Gungnir and his father's name to make himself king. And that meant holding a fortress like Halfhaugr.

"Most of our warriors, half the tribe, they dwell inside the town walls for the wedding. If Hadding pushes too far while I am away, do what you must, but do not lose this place."

Tyr's grumble sounded almost like a growl, but he nodded.

## 31

*S*igyn pulled the golden headband from Frigg's brow, staring at it a moment. Unmarried noble girls wore these as a symbol of purity. And now she would be wed in mere hours. Traditionally, this ceremony should have taken place the day before the wedding, but both Hadding and Odin seemed all too eager to speed things along.

Their father because he was too blinded by greed for the apples to think of aught else. Odin because ... well, Sigyn had to assume Odin had reasons beyond simple lust for Frigg. The man sought power. And while he had promised naught definitive in his clever wordplay, he *would* be locked into alliance if he married Frigg. Nor could she imagine he'd want an enemy of the Hasding tribe, not after going to such lengths to gain them as allies. And if Sigyn aired her fears to Frigg, it would only further agitate her already apprehensive sister.

"Why are we rushing all this?" Frigg asked again, while the maids pulled away her dress.

Sigyn wrapped the circlet with care. If Frigg had a daughter, she'd present this to her one day. "Father is just overwhelmed. You know he's not well."

"And you really think those apples might save Father?" Frigg suddenly seemed aware of the other women around.

"I don't know," was the only answer Sigyn could offer. She had no reason to doubt Loki's statement, but it all seemed too fantastical. She'd found Loki a few more times over the past day, and though every conversation had been fascinating, none had truly revealed much. "Come."

Sigyn took Frigg's hand and led her to the bath the others had drawn. Rocks heated in a brazier decorated the room. Sigyn dipped her hand in the water. It was almost too hot to bathe in, but it would cleanse Frigg of her old life in a ceremony every girl dreamed of, and one Sigyn would never be like to know herself. She flicked drops of water from her fingers on the heated stones, starting a curtain of steam throughout the room. The other five girls did the same while Frigg eased into the bath. Before long, Sigyn was tempted to remove her own clothes as well. The room had filled with so much steam a sheen of sweat built on her forehead and damped her blouse. It wouldn't take much of this for her to miss the damned snow.

If she was honest with herself, Sigyn envied Frigg for all of it. The rituals, the ceremony, the honor, having a man between her legs ... Frigg, völva that she was, was getting it all. And Sigyn *should* be happy for her sister. She *was* happy for her. But being part of all this forced her to confront her own distance from everyone else. Now she'd lose one of the only people in the whole tribe who understood her. Sigyn knew part of Frigg had feared her, feared she would replace her as Father's heir. Sigyn could only hope this marriage alliance would ease that fear, because Frigg was also one of the few people she truly cared for.

At last they led Frigg to another bath, this one unheated. The icy water would wash away the sweat and warmth and the old life Frigg had known. Sigyn did *not* envy her that ritual. Her sister shivered as she sunk into this tub. She dunked herself underwater briefly, then rose. One maid handed her a towel, while Sigyn watched the other maids gathering Frigg's dress, its deep green fabric embroidered with red knotwork.

Frigg's mother should have been here to do all these things. Though Frigg was two years older, it had been Sigyn to comfort Frigg when her mother died. Agilaz and Olrun had been the only parents Sigyn had ever known.

After Frigg had donned her new gown, Sigyn placed the bridal crown on her head. It was real gold, taken in a raid centuries back, before the Hasdingi had settled at Halfhaugr. Völvur spoke of those days, living in Bjarmaland, raiding villages for plunder. Odin's people still lived that way. Sigyn liked to think abandoning the savagery represented progress. Would Odin take them back to such days? Unless, of course, she were to truly believe Frigg's vision of spring, Mist-madness though it sounded. But Loki had said the Vanr goddess had chosen Odin. And much as she wanted to dismiss it as superstition, the foreign tracker had a way about him, one that bespoke wisdom and truth.

Frigg straightened the crown on her head and examined herself in the reflection of a washbasin. She blew out a slow breath, then stared at herself in silence for a long moment—a silence Sigyn dared not break. What tensions and joys did her sister feel this day?

"I am ready," Frigg said at long last, eyes still locked on her reflection.

Sigyn took her by the hand and led her out through the great hall.

"Jarl Odin has already given the bride price and brought a sword," a servant told her.

This was it, then. She led Frigg out into the yard. By now, the sun had risen. Most of the townsfolk had gotten little sleep through the night, but the excitement filtering through town was intoxicating.

Odin's people stood in front of a table laden with gold and silver ornaments. There were necklaces wrought like winding serpents, arm rings of twisted gold, a headband depicting Yggdrasil. Hadding would probably have accepted an offer of half as much. For the apples, he'd have probably taken a tenth of it.

For a dowry, he presented two goats, two horses, and two cows. If Odin took offense at the offer, he gave no sign, nor had he during negotiations. He was so eager for Frigg, Sigyn almost had to wonder if he truly had feelings for her sister. A marriage for love was uncommon at best, despite the tales skalds told of such things. No, impossible. Odin would have come himself if he had … And Tyr had acted without his jarl's knowledge.

Hadding and Odin clasped hands, accepting the exchange. Odin turned to wink at Frigg. Sigyn couldn't see her sister's face beside her, but she assumed she gave no reaction. Frigg was so poised. So responsible. For the sake of her marriage, Sigyn hoped her sister could show a *little* emotion when Odin was bedding her. The last thing a man like Odin probably wanted was a woman indifferent to his attentions.

Already, laughter filled the air, mingling with raucous shouts. Someone had opened the mead.

THE PROCESSION CONTINUED on to the grove just outside town. Marriages were always held here where the fertility spirits could bless it, most especially Freyja, the goddess of sex. If she heard them at all, Sigyn wasn't convinced Freyja would care. At least she'd never listened to any of Sigyn's prayers.

Odin presented his ancestral sword to Frigg, a finger ring resting on its hilt. Sigyn's sister hesitated only a moment before taking the sword and putting the ring on her finger. A maid in turn came and gave Frigg a ring and sword, which Frigg handed to Odin. The jarl took both, slipping on the ring and sliding the sword into a scabbard already prepared for it. He'd wield that for the rest of his life, using it to defend his family—or so the tradition went. In turn, Frigg was meant to hold the ancestral sword in trust for their first son. Sigyn was no sap, but she liked the custom. The tribes were now bound by rings and blades, their urds entwined.

"Now let us feast!" Hadding proclaimed.

The crowd cheered and raced back toward the great hall. Sigyn grabbed Frigg's hand, pulling her along. Unsurprisingly, Odin and his warriors were first back to the hall, meaning the bride's party would serve the mead. Sigyn didn't mind. As everyone sat around the table, she moved from one warrior to the next, taking their measure while she poured drinks. Odin's two brothers could not be more different in appearance—the one a mountain bursting with vivacious laughter, the other a short man who stared vacantly ahead. Then there was Tyr, the champion, always solemn, always watching everything. And, of course, Loki, whose eyes followed her every step. She felt them searing into her back as she walked around the table. Her cheeks burned at the thought of it.

When everyone was seated and had a drink, Frigg sipped the bridal mead daintily. She wiped her lips, then handed Odin the drinking horn. The Wodan jarl chuckled, and Frigg frowned. Then Odin downed the mead in one swig and slammed the horn on the table. At that rate, the drink would run out before the honeymoon. Still, Sigyn had to smile at his exuberance.

Servants brought course after course of food to the table. There were platters of wild vegetables gathered in the woods early that day—celery, radishes, spinach. Troughs of butter, curd, and cheese, flatbreads, apples, and plums decorated the table ... If Hadding had skimped on the dowry, he made up for it in hosting the feast. He had dipped deep into the winter stores, as she well knew. She and Agilaz had done much of the gathering, after all. As the day drew on, slaves brought out oysters and mussels, pike and bream, and all manner of fish harvested from the nearby rivers.

By this time the guests had begun rearranging themselves, finding companions to share drink and talk. Sigyn had sat with Frigg while her sister seemed at odds with Odin, but they sank into deeper political topics, and Frigg at last seemed to find her place.

Sigyn took the chance to bring Loki a plate of radishes. He was the most interesting guest at the party, after all. Few men she had ever known would match wits with her, much less seem to enjoy doing it.

She sat across from him and slid the plate over.

"A peace offering?" he asked.

"Are we at war?"

"I should hope not. Where I come from, this was once offered to rivals to stem hostilities."

"You're not of the Aesir."

"Not originally."

She waited for him to elaborate, but he said naught else, just watched her.

"Why did you tell me about the apples?"

"Because you were clever enough to figure out how to ask."

Sigyn smiled, shaking her head. That had sounded like a compliment. How refreshing. "There'll be trouble for those apples."

"Trouble follows all things worth having and many worth less. It is the way of Mankind to fight over scarce resources. And when there is naught scarce enough to fight over, they invent conflicts of philosophy, ideals worth killing and dying over."

"You make humans sound like violent animals—or trolls."

Loki grunted. "Trolls? They have more in common with men than you might like to think. But, no. Mankind is more devious and more glorious. To be capable of villainy, one must first be capable of heroism. Do you call a bear that mauls a child a villain? Of course not. The bear lacks the capacity to be other than it is. But a man who did the same thing made a conscious choice to do so and made that choice with an understanding of its meaning and consequences. And trolls ... they are somewhere between bears and men—twisted and given over to vicious instincts, neither animal nor any longer human. Victims of their own natures."

Sigyn leaned forward, hands on her cheeks. "And are you a villain or a hero?"

Loki shrugged. "That probably depends on who is telling the story, does it not? Most of us try our best to seem heroes to our allies and villains to others. The best you can hope for is to look back on your actions and the intentions behind them and know you did what you did for the right reasons."

"And can you?"

"Mostly."

Sigyn tapped her finger against her lip. "Naught … selfish? Naught you would take for yourself, and damn the consequences?"

"Is that selfish, or mere self-interest? Should we not claim something of life for ourselves? We are so often asked to sacrifice all we can give and more for … for the future, for the people around us, for the needs of the many. But if everyone spends their life giving and giving and never thinking of themselves, what is the point? There must be balance in all things."

Her cheeks felt hot and her stomach unsettled, the way he stared so deeply into her eyes made her want to back up and move toward him at the same time. If he was saying what it sounded like, if he felt the same as she did … "And what would you claim?"

Before he could answer, Hadding stood and clanked his goblet on the table. "The time has come to consummate the marriage. Attendants, escort the bride."

Well, damn. Sigyn watched Loki with regret. Now she'd never know what he'd have said. "I … I have to go."

She scampered over to Frigg and escorted her to her bedroom. Frigg said naught while Sigyn helped her out of her dress and into her nightgown. If she was nervous, she didn't let it show. Sigyn stood a fertility idol by the bed, then hugged her sister. Though Frigg's expression remained collected, she clutched Sigyn's hand a moment. Sigyn embraced her.

For a moment, it looked like her sister would say something, ask something. But then Frigg just nodded. Sigyn sighed and returned the gesture as Frigg settled back on the bed.

Sigyn slipped out the door.

## 32

Tradition required witnesses see Odin remove the bridal crown as symbol of consummation. The sex was assumed after that. All ridiculous, but people lived and died on their traditions.

Frigg sat stiffly on her bed, eyes locked in one corner of the room. Was she afraid?

Odin sat in a chair across from her, hands resting on his knees. All the women he'd lain with, it had never quite felt like this. He'd always known what to say before. He sighed. "I'm glad your father agreed to this union. I hope you are pleased as well."

"I am ... most pleased."

"Good." He banged his palms against his knees. "Good."

He looked around her chamber. Rather than a brazier, she had an actual fireplace, casting warmth and a pleasant smoky aroma through the room. A weaving hung on the wall, depicting a dragon rising from the sea. He pointed at the tapestry. "You've visited the Gandvik Sea?"

"I've never seen it."

"Ah. Shame. Well, we'll go one day. My cousin lives on the shore. It's very ... impressive. Very impressive."

"I'm sure."

He rose. "So. Should we, uh ..."

She stared into her fireplace like it would give her the answer. Uh huh. He drifted over to the bed.

Now she did look at him, eyes haunted. A völva bride. As soon as he lay with her, she'd have him under her spell. Why then, did she look to be the one afraid?

"Stand up." He guided her up, then slid the dress over her head.

She stood there in her shift, hugging herself. "Urd is a heavy weight."

"Yes." She had no idea. The weight of destiny crashed down upon him, holding him to so many oaths that threatened to tear him to pieces.

He unlaced his tunic and tossed it aside, then yanked off his trousers. After removing her shift, he laid her back on the bed. When he looked up, she had her fists clenched around the sheets. Eyes staring off into the darkness again. Seeing things, perhaps.

She cried out in pain when he entered her, even gentle as he tried to be. She wiggled under him a bit, but not as he imagined. She'd gone so stiff this had begun to feel more like work than pleasure. When he finally spilled his seed, chest heaving, she went limp.

Odin frowned. He didn't feel any different. Maybe because she hadn't taken her pleasure from him. Damn it. How was he to give pleasure to a woman so intensely uninterested in it?

For a while, he lay there beside her, tossing around words in his mind and discarding each. Without her climax, this whole marriage meant naught. He hated himself for thinking that, but there it was. Ve's life depending on him drawing out her power. Besides which, a lifetime—or many —married to a woman this pent up, this reserved, would serve him ill.

But he had married her.

After blowing out a long breath, he reached over to the sack that lay with his discarded clothes and pulled out the final apple, the last fruit of Yggdrasil. He rolled over, offering it to her. His wife.

"Is that ...?"

"Yes."

Her hand trembled as she reached for it. "From Vana-heim ..." She mumbled something unintelligible, then grasped his hand with her own and took a bite of the apple. In an instant she sat upright, no doubt shocked by the over-whelming sensation. Her eyes rolled back as she chewed, savoring every moment. Would she experience the same things he had? Bite after bite she took, eating as though driven by some compulsion.

And then the core slipped from her fingers and she threw her arms around his waist. Odin let her push him back down on the bed and straddle him. Her body burned with heat, and the look on her face told him she felt the need as pressingly as he had back then. Frigg planted kiss after kiss on his face and chest before mounting him.

It seemed the apples had much the same effect on women as on men. The urgency of her need hardened him far more than the first time.

Finally, some fire in her.

And then she screamed. No, he was screaming. A wave of energy hit him. Shadows moved in the corner of his room like ghosts watching him and his wife. The air shimmered, flickering back and forth between colors too vibrant to be real and too dull to hold his attention. Like a draught of the strongest mead, her release had left him dizzy, euphoric, and taunted by strange visions.

His eyes glazed over, and shadows danced at the edge of his sight, cutting off his view of Frigg. Nor did he need sight. Somehow she was as much inside him as he was in her. Whispers plagued his mind, like secret conversations just out of eavesdropping range.

This was something else, like he'd seen beyond Midgard to the Otherworlds. Could Frigg explain all this to him? Could she understand the choices and decisions he now faced? She had the qualities of a queen, if he could but trust her. And he had to—he'd married her because he needed her. And he needed her forever as his queen, as a partner.

At last she collapsed and fell into a daze. Odin stumbled from the bed, eyes burning with the mercurial nature of his new reality. Color bled from the walls. Reality rippled around him, pressed in on him with a profound sense of the wrongness of the World, of the barest glimpse of alien Realms hostile and angry.

Much as those who touched those Realms. Sorcerers, like the Niflungar, trading away their humanity bit by bit for powers drawn from corrupt and twisted worlds. Powers of Niflheim. A maelstrom of visions swirled before his eyes, of battles, wars, death. And terrible magic. The source of such powers lay in the frozen wasteland of the dead, its icy and perilous queen watching him now.

As she had watched her children, broken in fire. And they fled north. Into the islands of Reidgotaland. To one island where they slept for centuries and now wakened.

They called that island Samsey.

And he knew. Knew where to find the Niflungar.

He stumbled on the floor, blinking, trying to shut out the

blurring, blinding procession of madness. In the shadows, his brother Ve ran. Raced in bent and twisted woods. Odin chased after him, or thought he did, and Ve spun, eyes glowing red. His teeth had become tusks.

Odin screamed in horror.

## 33

_S_igyn had lingered by the door until all the other attendants, those on both sides, had returned to the party. Then she drifted away. Frigg would be fine, and Sigyn could do no more for her.

Still, a vexing wildness roiled in her gut, one not even the mead seemed to soothe. Frigg was married now, and still Sigyn walked alone in the World. Her sister wanted to be queen. Sigyn would have settled for being _anyone_.

No, she didn't feel much like more drinking. With everyone at the feast, no one would wander the lower halls where the dvergar had hidden their secrets. She glanced around the corner, then headed for the stairs.

Frigg's workspace remained strewn with mess spilled over the floor and filled with foul odors. Her sister must not have allowed any slaves down here—rightfully so, they'd like as not poison themselves—nor had she come back to clean up herself.

She stared at the runes on the wall, but they slipped round and round in her mind, unwilling to divulge their secrets. Maybe she was drunker than she'd thought.

"I have an answer for your question." The voice came from behind her, causing her to stiffen. She turned slowly. Loki stood in the shadows of the threshold, not quite in the light of the sconce here and blocking that of the one in the hall. "If you have an answer for mine."

His question? He had asked her if she was content with her life. In truth, before today, she had thought of little *other* than that question. So simple, really, and yet so difficult to quantify. So few ever stopped to ask such a thing.

"I'm lonely," she said before she could stop herself. The words seemed to escape on their own. "I'm surrounded by people who don't understand or appreciate me, who resent whatever help I offer them. My own sister loves me. I know she does, but she can't show it ... And I ... I just want somewhere I ... fit." Gods, that sounded ridiculous. "Why are you so interested in this?"

Now he drifted into the room, looking a moment at the runes before turning sharply on her. "Because I am drawn to you. You are not like other people, Sigyn. And sometimes you think it's your curse, but it can be a blessing. And I would claim you, if you let me."

Sigyn swallowed, uncertain what she had just heard. Was he saying he wanted to bed her? Freyja, she'd take it even if that was all it was. If he wanted more ... No. She couldn't afford to delude herself. He would go away with Odin and leave her here. But even if for a night, she wanted something more than this life. Frigg would have her dreams. And Sigyn needed to pretend to have her own, if only for a single bright moment.

She took his hand, trying to still the trembling in her own. She shut the door to the workshop then fell back against it. "I want something *real*."

Loki leaned in, his cheek brushing hers. "So do I."

His hands were warm on her face and shoulders as he pulled away her dress, warm as he caressed her breasts. She shuddered from it all. She hadn't lain with a man in too many moons, and now, this one ... She leapt up on him, wrapping her legs around his back. She didn't want to be a proper noble lady. She wanted to be *her*. He didn't recoil, just hefted her up, against the wall, kissing her with such urgency she couldn't breathe.

His whole body felt aflame as he pushed inside her. Sigyn almost wept for the closeness so long denied. She threw her arms around his shoulders and pulled him closer, trying to drink in every moment until her body at last surrendered. She felt his release, too, hot inside her.

And then something happened.

Like a surge of energy passing through her, forcing her to arch her back as she climaxed again. She looked into his eyes and saw stars there. And she fell into the sky, watching the World change and change again beneath the eternal cosmos. Shooting stars crashed through those skies and pummeled the World. Fires burned, and tides surged, until at last she stood beneath the greatest tree she had ever seen. Its trunk stretched up toward the heavens, seemingly connecting all the worlds of the World. Along its boughs ran a silver squirrel that watched her with knowing eyes.

And from the branches grew a golden apple. She could see within it, not with her eyes, but with something deeper. That apple glowed like sunlight, shimmering with the light of life itself.

Sigyn reached for it, and her hand clasped around its smooth surface. It pulsed like a beating heart, tantalizing and intoxicating. She shook herself, suddenly realizing she and Loki lay on the stone floor. But she truly held a golden apple in her hand.

"I asked you what life you'd want to live for eternity," Loki said. "Odin gave me one apple to give to whom I pleased. One chance to offer someone I wish to spend my immortal life with."

Sigyn's hands trembled around the apple. "Me? You just met me." She couldn't even swallow. Such events did not even unfold in skalds' tales, and even such tales always ended in tragedy. The heroes died, oft as not, betrayed. Life offered naught but hardship and a bitter end.

Except for this time. He wasn't asking her to marry him —he was asking her to spend the rest of time with him. Dizziness swept over her, and she nearly fainted. Eat this and she would become something more than human. She would be a goddess herself ... She held in her hands the chance for immortality. And if she took it, there would be no turning back. There could be no return to the life she'd known. The uncertain future would lie before her, stretching on and on, titillating and terrifying in equal measure.

But then, maybe it was already too late. Maybe knowing what she held in her hands, what life *could* be like, would already make this little town seem stifling, even suffocating, to know that she could have had more, could have embraced an urd beyond the ken of mortals. And with Loki, she could truly be herself—and he wanted her for who she was. Never in her life had she met anyone like him. And, in truth, she knew she'd never meet his like again, never have another chance at such a perfect match for herself.

"Perhaps I just met you," he said. "Perhaps I knew you in another lifetime. Maybe, just maybe, I have *always* known you, and I've waited so long just to find you again."

A tear formed in her eye, but she blinked it away. She wouldn't let aught spoil this moment. If it were a skald's tale, then let the drama unfold as it would.

She bit into the apple.

## 34

Odin gasped, his knees slamming into the floor. He was in Frigg's chambers, his new wife tossing fitfully. A vile surge in his stomach sent him crawling to the chamber pot, where he heaved up all the mead he'd drunk at the party. Panting, he glanced back at Frigg. His sickness had not disturbed her in the least, it seemed.

Gods, had Loki known this would happen? Was that how the man had gained such insights—had he too fucked a völva? No wonder men feared the witches' seduction. Such visions would haunt the bravest warrior.

Odin yanked on his clothes and wandered out to the great hall, stumbling twice into the walls. While some still slept off the party, it seemed the sun had risen, because outside he heard music. Sleeping in Frigg's isolated, windowless chamber had disoriented him. How did these people manage without seeing the sky?

In the town square, some of the men chanted a song to their ancestors, while another played the lyre. In their midst Idunn danced, her thin red dress swirling in the air. It caught currents of the winds, flying about like her dark hair, entrancing almost every man and woman in Halfhaugr. If all Idunn said was true, did these same apples make the Vanir immortal? What was a goddess if not a woman untouched by time, blessed with powers others could never understand? He'd seen her vulnerability with Ve that day.

But Idunn was an enchantress. Maybe Loki should have suggested *her* for Odin's wife. Odin shook his head at the thought. Frigg was his wife now. Indulging in such fantasies dishonored a woman who didn't deserve such treatment. She would be a fine queen.

Idunn turned, smiling at Odin, almost like she knew what he'd been thinking. His ears flushed. Damn.

Not like every man in the whole town wasn't thinking the same thing about her.

She glided over toward him, placed her hands on his chest, then kissed his cheek. "How was the wedding night?"

"Idunn?"

"Yes?"

"You don't seem like someone who's lived for thousands of years."

She laughed. "Because I talk too much? Or because I'm not afraid to call you out for staring at my tits? Which, by the way, you've been doing again. Not that I really mind. I know they're nice. Anyway, how many immortal women *do* you know? I know a few. Mostly, priorities change when viewed against a canopy of eternity. False modesty falls away, and you're left with a clearer view of the things that matter in life—happiness, laughter, companionship. Or else ... or else you become so caught up in your own existence you forget the lives of those around you. Some of the other Vanir are like that. To them, your lives go by so fast they no longer take notice at all. It's kind of sad."

Odin worked his jaw, uncertain what to say to all that.

He *had* been admiring her breasts. Again. And she did talk more than he expected a goddess to. But then, so often, her words seemed to hide more depth than her flippant tone would suggest.

"So did you give her an apple?"

"Yes."

"I assume you remembered she'd be needing your sexual attentions right after … You should probably be with her instead of me. We all have needs."

"Yes." He shook his head as he walked away, trying to clear the lingering shadows, though he did not head toward Frigg. He needed to find Loki. He didn't know how, but somehow he understood. Secrets of the World had unraveled before him. Maybe his blood brother could explain the visions. And what he'd seen of Ve, what did that mean? After scouring the town, he found Loki and Sigyn both sitting on the roof of a house. How and why they had climbed up there Odin couldn't guess.

"Loki! Come down here, I would speak with you."

The man shared a secret smile with Sigyn. Sleeping together, were they? Odin couldn't blame Loki's choice— Sigyn was a beauty, for certain. Ironic, that his blood brother would choose his wife's sister. Irony, or urd, perhaps. Loki jumped off the roof, landing in a crouch in the snow beside Odin.

"How was she?" Odin asked before he could stop himself.

Loki frowned, sparing a glance back at Sigyn. "I've warned you about vulgarity, Odin. I've given Sigyn the apple you granted me."

Odin's jaw hung open for a moment. Loki had just met the girl. He restrained himself from asking if she'd really been so good in bed Loki needed her for the rest of time.

And it meant the apples were truly gone. "I ... forgive me, brother. I spoke out of turn. If you wish to spend your immortal life with Sigyn, I wish you happiness."

"But that's not why you've sought me out."

"No. I bedded Frigg, as you suggested."

"And you've absorbed some part of her seid."

"I saw my brother ... his eyes had turned red. His teeth had become like ..."

Loki sighed. "Like a troll's."

"What?" Odin stopped in his tracks. "What does that mean? Do you know what's happening to Ve?"

"I know. Odin ... where do you think the trolls come from?"

Odin shook his head, taking a step back. "No. No! Trolls are the spawn of jottunar."

"Do you confuse what you wish to be true with reality? They are men, twisted and warped by too long in the mist. Why do you think they still seek human wives, brother?"

"No!" Odin lunged forward and grabbed Loki's tunic, shoving him back against the house. "Why! Why didn't you tell me this sooner?"

Loki gripped his hands but didn't attempt to pry them loose. Instead his crystal blue eyes bored into Odin's, as if seeing his soul. "Because if it happened, there was naught you could do to stop it. This is a war within him, a process not easily halted once begun."

"You. Should. Have. Told me!"

"And what would you have done differently? Do you think I would let you suffer if I knew a way to prevent it? We have no way to stop this."

"I have a way! I will retrieve the amulet, and the ghost will end this!"

Odin shoved Loki against the house again, then stormed

off. The ghost had threatened Odin, warned him the price of failure would be those he loved. So this had to be her work. It had to ...

Hadding had given Odin's brothers a house in town. Odin broke into a run, dashing there and flinging the door open. Vili lay sprawled on the floor, a naked girl under each arm. One groggily looked over at Odin as he burst in. He didn't even bother to look at her, instead spinning until he spotted Ve, sitting in the corner.

He held one of the babes—Geri, assuming the embroidered blankets hadn't been switched—in his arms, rocking the child. In the darkness, his eyes were glowing red. He opened his mouth too wide, revealing pointed teeth, a tongue slightly bulbous.

Hel and Freyja, this could not be happening.

Odin staggered over and reached down. "Ve. Give me Geri." His voice sounded so hoarse in his own ears. A bare whisper. Pain built in his chest until he wanted to weep like a maid.

Ve's eyes darted down to the babe, and his tongue licked the edge of his teeth.

"Give her to me. Now."

At his commanding tone, his brother handed him the child. Odin took her gently, then backed out of the house. It was all too much. He'd failed again. He'd been doomed all along, maybe. He would not sit by and watch this happen. He would not allow this!

"I'm trying!" he shouted at the sky. "I'm fucking trying! I haven't given up! I won't!" Villagers had begun to stare at him, but he didn't care. "I will get your damned Singasteinn back!"

At that, Geri began to cry. Gods, where was the other babe?

"Lord Odin?" Frigg asked.

He spun to find his wife, fully dressed, watching him along with the other concerned villagers. Odin shoved Geri at her, and she took the babe with a slight hesitation. She tried to speak, but he dashed off, back toward his brothers' house. This time, Vili woke as Odin crashed inside.

Ve remained in the corner and actually backed farther into it when Odin opened the door. He backed away from the sunlight. He now feared the one thing all men counted on to protect them from the vaettir. Odin shook his head.

"What the fuck is your problem?" Vili demanded.

"Where is Freki?"

Vili looked to a blanket on a nearby cot. Odin dashed over without waiting for his brother. The child lay there, pawing at the air like a wolf in a dream. Mercifully asleep.

Pausing only long enough to sweep up the babe, he stormed over to Vili. With one hand, Odin yanked Vili to his feet by his beard. The big man yelped and looked as though he might have punched Odin if not for the babe in his arms.

"Watch. Your. Brother!" Odin glanced at Ve to make his point.

For the first time, Vili seemed to notice the red glow in Ve's eyes. "Frey's flaming sword! What happened?"

"Watch him. And let no one else call upon him until I return."

"Where are you—"

"Just do it!" Odin stormed out to see Frigg, Sigyn, and half the gods-damned town staring at him.

"Are these your children?" Frigg asked.

What? Odin glanced at the babe in his arms. She thought the twins his bastards. "No." But they were his, weren't they? He'd taken them from their mother and spared them. And he could no longer count on Ve to watch over them. "I mean, they are not of my blood. I adopted them. They are mine now."

"I see." Frigg's face gave no indication of what she thought about her new husband taking on wards. Wait until she found out the babes were werewolves. "I would speak with you, Lord Odin?"

Lord Odin? "Gods, woman, you're my wife now. I would have thought ..." Odin bit his tongue. He was going to say he would have thought he might have loosened her up a bit last night. But Loki was right—vulgarity had to be beneath him. He had to be a man worthy of kingship. A king to save the Aesir from this madness Hel had visited upon them. "I would have thought you'd be resting, my lady." Odin had no time to talk with her. He needed set out for the Niflungar without delay. "I have to ride from here. I may be gone long."

Frigg frowned, seeming to examine every detail of his face. "I see. And the apple for my father? It was ... kind ... of you to offer one to me, but his need is immediate."

Odin pushed the other babe into Sigyn's arms. "Take care of this child as if it were your own." With that, he grabbed Frigg's arm and pulled her away from the others, who continued to stare. "I gave the apples to those who were best suited for them, wife. Be satisfied you and your sister were among them." Even had he another, he wouldn't waste it on a weakling coward like Hadding. And he had already delayed too long in fulfilling his oath to the ghost. There was time left, but not so much. The solstice crept ever closer, now less than two moons away.

"I am grateful. But now you must give one to my father."

Odin folded his arms over his chest. She was telling him what to do, was she? "Those apples were entrusted to me, personally, by the goddess Idunn. *I* decide what to do with them, wife."

Frigg stiffened, her lips very still before she spoke. "You promised an apple to my father."

Odin shook his head. "I promised to treat my allies right. The best way I can do that is by giving apples to those with the most to offer."

"My father is the jarl of the Hasdingi!" For once her words came out blurted, her calm broken. But only for a moment, then she looked aghast at her own outburst. "*He* is your ally."

"Frigg, I know this is a hard truth to face, but your father is not a well man."

"Yes, my lord. That is why he needs an apple immediately."

He shook his head sadly. "We don't even know if an apple would reverse the ravages he's already suffered."

"Well, you have to try!"

The woman had best get control of her temper. "I am a jarl, and soon I will be king. I will not be told what I *have* to do, not by you nor anyone else! Your father hides in fear behind his walls, complacent and weak. He has no place in the future I will build."

By now a crowd had gathered around the two of them. Damn her. She'd raised her voice first. Now he couldn't back down even if he wanted to.

"You *will* save my father, Odin," she spat, her voice pitched low enough that others couldn't hear. "Or I will place such a curse on you you'll wish you had!"

Odin's fists clenched. He caught himself raising a hand toward her and restrained himself. Curse him? He'd had far too much of witches and ghosts and curses. Ve was losing himself, perhaps because of a curse, and now his own wife threatened him with another? "Do not presume to threaten me, woman! You ate the last apple yourself," he whispered back. "Consider that."

Her face grew pale, and she fell back a step, shaking her head.

"I ride for Reidgotaland!" he shouted to the assembled crowd.

Without another word he stormed off and shouted for Sleipnir. Moments later the horse came trotting over the hills. Odin leapt into the saddle.

"Take us north," Odin said. "Far north, hard and fast."

He did not look back as the horse galloped away from the camp. Not at first. Not until he already knew it would be too late to see any of the people he had just left behind.

# PART III

———————

Fifth Moon

## 35

*T*he runes in lower Halfhaugr swam before Sigyn's eyes, taking on new shapes, winding and unraveling in a clarity she had never before hoped for. Hand to her temple, she panted, desperate to stop the motion of a swirling World changing around her. But the World had not changed, she had. Whether from the apple or her hallucinatory experience with Loki, something inside her had shifted, had opened to view the World in new light, as with the parting of mists. She swept her hair back from her face.

And how had that all occurred? She'd had her pleasure of men before, and might have even called it a spiritual experience. This time, though, had reached a whole new magnitude of transcendence, had prompted visions in her, perhaps not unlike those her sister experienced. But how? Had the apple made Sigyn a völva as well?

So often Sigyn had doubted the tales, the stories, the many beliefs men held about the Otherworlds. How could they possibly know what went on in places they could not see or touch? But she saw something now.

She shoved the table aside once again, clearing away any

obstruction before these runes. Apples of immortality, seid, visions, Otherworlds—if such things existed, then perhaps too the dvergar had come from those Otherworlds, perhaps they did indeed carve a prophecy down here. One no one else among the Aesir read or understood. If so, it then fell to Sigyn to unravel the secrets lost to men.

She brushed dust from the wall.

The end times. She had seen it before, but it now it seemed to sing in her mind, the voice of the stone booming like a herald of darkness. The runes, taken as a whole, rather than one at a time, began to paint a clearer picture in her mind's eye, an unfolding play in the shadows while she stood transfixed, letting her present surroundings fall away.

The end times. The doom of the gods. *Ragnarok ...*

*Brother would fight brother ...*

*Sisters' sons would break the bonds of kinship ...*

*The World falters ...*

*Axe time, sword time, broken shields, wind time, wolf time ...*

Her heart slammed against her ribs. The words seemed to echo all around her from the unending shadows. The crash of iron. Her legs sinking in a sea of blood.

*The Destroyer wakes ...*

Sigyn slipped to her knees, hands splashing down in the blood. She raised them to her face, staring in horror, unable to quite get the scream past her throat. Stretching into infinity spread row upon endless row of corpses, now waking, grim and merciless. Marching under the heel of the Queen of Mists. Hel was coming for Sigyn, coming to feast upon her soul.

Tears tumbled down her cheeks. Blood seeped from her fingers. She trembled, shook, freezing from the inside out.

Was Hel the Destroyer? Was she to break free of Niflheim and end Midgard?

"Sigyn?" A voice, far away. "Sigyn!"

Strong arms enwrapped her, jerked her to her feet. She shuddered, shut her eyes. Blinked. Agilaz held her in his arms, tight grip on her biceps. Concern on his usually emotionless face.

"Papa?"

He pulled her close into an embrace. She almost never called him that. He had never claimed to be her father, nor encouraged her to think of him as such. But sometimes, in the darkest nights, a girl wanted her parents. Cast out by those who had birthed her, she would draw solace from those who accepted her. They understood, especially Olrun.

"What happened to you?"

"I ..." Sigyn glanced at the runes then quickly turned away, lest their embedded story consume her mind once again. "I fear for the future."

"As do I. Word has come through our new allies. King Otwin of Njarar sides with the Godwulfs, or at least with Jarl Alci."

Sigyn stilled herself with a slow breath. "Otwin. The same king to whom Father owes debts of old?"

Agilaz nodded. "Otwin was his father Nidud's hand in Aujum during the war. He drove Hadding and the others into it. That's why we call it the Njarar War. His father may have been the cruelest king the North Realms have ever known. He tortured my brother, Sigyn."

Agilaz had a brother? She opened her mouth to ask, but he waved it away.

"I do not speak of him. All I can say is I fear for Otwin's allies almost as much as for his enemies."

"Hermod. Hermod is with the Godwulfs."

"Indeed. And I must ride for the Godwulf lands with all haste."

"I'll come with you."

Agilaz shook his head and fixed her with a stern gaze. "Your presence might make things worse. Stay here and keep an eye on our Wodan guests. Already your father grows agitated that Odin fled without keeping his promise."

"Odin did not actually promise to give Father an apple."

"Perhaps not, but we cannot trust men who rely on clever words to avoid keeping faith." He put a hand on her shoulder and squeezed. "Sigyn, you and Olrun, you must work to keep this new alliance from fracturing. We cannot afford war with the Wodanar. Stay close to them and, if they plot against us, make sure Hadding knows of it."

Sigyn sighed but nodded. Keeping an eye on the Wodanar was not difficult. Finding a way to help Hermod, that was a problem. But she would think of something. She had to.

## 36

*A* shelf of ice rimmed the shore of the Morimarusa, stretching perhaps a quarter mile out. That sea wrapped around Reidgotaland where it joined with the Gandvik Sea. Some said the ice grew so thick you could sometimes walk from Reidgotaland to Sviarland.

Reidgotalanders around the sea took fishing boats out beyond that, some hunting fish and sharks. Out here, the mists never seemed to part. Every boat Odin could see had a torch pole mounted to both ends in a feeble effort to keep the perilous vapors at bay.

Odin had watched them long enough to realize they spoke a dialect of the North Realm tongue, but understanding them proved a challenge. Besides, there were few enough in any event. More ravens haunted this town than people.

He patted Sleipnir's neck. "How are we going to cross?"

Perhaps he could barter for a boat. Even if the locals didn't understand his words, they might understand an offer of value. Perhaps Odin's arm ring, or ...

Sleipnir started off again, down toward the icy shelf.

"Whoa," Odin said. "You crack that ice, and we'll be taking a very cold swim."

The horse paid him no mind, holding a steady gait right toward the water. Odin pulled back on the horse's mane, but Sleipnir just jerked his head forward and kept on. Then the horse trod onto the water itself. His hoofs hit the sea like solid ground. Odin let the reins go slack, too shocked to even try to control his mount. The moment he did, Sleipnir took off at a gallop.

Odin clutched the horse's neck. "Gods above!"

He should have learned by now not to underestimate this animal.

Sleipnir charged across the Morimarusa, waves lapping at his many heels. The mist out here grew so thick Odin couldn't see past Sleipnir's snout. "I hope you know where you're going," he mumbled.

The horse snorted.

They charged out, far past all fishing boats and beyond. A few shouts rose as he went by, fishermen no doubt fearing spirits out in the mist over the sea. Perhaps he'd give rise to a new legend here.

ODIN HAD no way to judge distance, but he guessed a quarter hour's ride and he heard hooves on solid ground again. The island of Samsey. At last.

The path Sleipnir trod inclined upward, and soon Odin passed high enough that the mist thinned, revealing a treacherous path winding along a rocky mountainside. Beyond, through the mist, stood the outline of a castle stretching far up into the sky. It had to have been eight stories tall.

As they neared, the sound of rushing water began to fill his ears. No vegetation grew on this mountain, though moss had sprung up on some of the rocks. When Odin drew closer to the castle he at last caught a glimpse of the water. It fell in a steady unfrozen stream that ran from the base of the castle in a cascade that pitched over the mountainside. The stream looked like it emptied into an inlet below, though the mist prevented any vision of that.

"What kind of madmen would live in such a place?" he asked.

Predictably, Sleipnir gave no answer.

Odin kicked the horse forward toward a bridge crossing the stream. Halfway across he paused. No soldiers guarded the gates ahead, which stood open but hardly inviting. No men walked the crumbling battlements above, though an unkindness of ravens watched his approach. Where were the Niflungar themselves? Had they fled this place?

The mists congregated into an almost solid mass at the castle's threshold, cutting off any vision of what might lie beyond. The mists were born from Niflheim, all men knew that. They carried the whispers of the dead and gave rise to the draugar. But never had Odin heard of them forming a wall like that. A fell sorcery lay about this place, as if Hel herself lurked within.

A fool he'd been to come here, and twice a fool for agreeing to the ghost's quest in the first place. He'd leapt at any chance to save his brother, never considering she might send him on such a perilous errand. Never considering her curse might cost him more than he was willing to pay. No, that was foolishness. Any price was worth it to save his brother.

Almost of their own accord, his fingers drifted to stroke the runes carved along Gungnir. At last his fist tightened around the shaft, and he climbed from Sleipnir's back, drawing strength from the dragon spear. Now he had no choice—now Ve depended on him. And he would be his brother's salvation. He would fulfill his oath to that ghost, and she would halt Ve's … transformation. Whatever darkness lay beyond, he had tasted the fruit of Yggdrasil. He had slain a jotunn. He, a man become god, would fear no sorcery.

"I am Odin!" he bellowed into the mist.

Above, ravens cawed in answer.

Odin pushed forward until his fingers brushed the cloud. It had no more substance than any other vapor, but frost iced his hand as he drew it back. "I am a lord of the Aesir! I come for audience with the lord of the Niflungar."

His voice echoed off the high cliffs and the castle walls, disappearing too soon, as if swallowed by the mists. And then the fog in the threshold parted, forming a vague corridor into the courtyard.

Odin swallowed. Despite his bravado, such a display did not reassure him.

Though, there was no turning back.

Which meant the only way was forward.

He pressed inward, and the path ahead turned. If he strayed from it even a few feet he'd find himself in a wall of blinding mist. He would probably wind up walking right into an icy well for his trouble—assuming it could do no worse. He glanced behind. The mists had enclosed the way he'd come—even now they continued to fold back to their original shape, driving him forward. A simple gesture to show where the power here lay? Or a deliberate course to force him into a trap.

Either way, he had no real choice.

Gungnir leveled before him, he pressed onward,

watching each step, training his ears for any sign of his surroundings. He'd sworn he heard whispers coming from the mists themselves. But he could make out no words. It was not a language he knew—or perhaps it was several he didn't, a cacophony of souls bemoaning their urd. A shadow passed through the mists to his side.

He spun, spear brandished toward the sight. But it was gone, vanished so quickly he could have imagined it. Or perhaps the Niflungar enjoyed playing with his mind. But then there was the other possibility. The glimpse of visions he'd inherited from his union with Frigg seemed to show him the Otherworlds that lay beyond the eyes of men. Could it be, then, that he saw not illusions planted in his mind by others, but a reality they would have tried to conceal from him?

In either case, Odin had had enough of these games. He knelt, snow crunching beneath his knees, and shut his eyes. Fear had never been his problem. Heidr would be like to have said lack of fear was his problem. She would have been wrong, of course. Odin felt fear the same as other men. But he knew it for what it was—a challenge to separate the weak from the strong. The weak would back down, broken by their own nature, while the strong rose above themselves. His brothers needed Odin. All of the Aesir needed him. So he let the fear go.

A völva could train for years to harness her gifts. Odin didn't have years right now. But if he could see beyond this world … He waited until his heart had slowed, slow as a man sitting before a fire with his friends. Then he opened his eyes, careful to keep them relaxed. He needn't fear the mists. He needn't even see them.

Slowly, the World around him dimmed, fading into a haze, and with it, the mists. They became transparent, revealing the shadows moving within. Some were shades, drifting on the currents of the mists, seeming as lost as he had been not a moment before. Ghosts trapped in this place. Odin could do naught for them. But other shadows, they moved with intent, their shapes more defined, like his own.

One paused right beside him, bending over to inspect Odin's kneeling form. Odin rose and looked straight into the shadow's eyes. The figure froze, then glanced side to side and even behind itself.

Wondering what Odin was looking at—they had no idea Odin could see them. These sorcerers were too clever for their own good.

At last, through the parting mists, Odin spied the main gate and strode purposefully toward it. The whispers around him intensified as he ignored the winding path the sorcerers had set for him through the mists. Frost gathered on his sleeves and cloak. To a mortal, breathing in such thick vapors could be hazardous. Odin was no mere mortal. He was, he suspected, naught like what these sorcerers would expect.

He flung open the doors to the keep.

Shadowy forms jumped at his entrance, a woman dropping a platter with a shriek. She ran, dashing toward a spiraling staircase. Other shadows moved about the hall, edging around him. These must be the Niflungar—men and women of this Realm. Odin shut his eyes again, willing away the Otherworldly sight. When he opened his eyes, still the World seemed hazy, colorless and out of focus. He could tell the mists had not seeped inside, but he couldn't get his eyes to return to normal.

"Hope that's not permanent," he mumbled, before pressing his eyes closed again. Again he shook himself, the

World cast in shadows. A sudden weight settled on his chest. Had he been too hasty in turning to this Otherworldly sight? He could not well save his brother if his vision were so obscured.

A raven cawed behind him then soared right over his shoulder, so close a beat of its wings brushed his cheek. The shadows of men and women in the hall parted for the bird as though accustomed to it, making way for its flight. The animal alighted on the shoulder of a man who stood at the end of the hall. He turned to the bird for a moment before drifting toward Odin, wisps of shadowy matter seeming to trail behind him. The figure's eyes gleamed, the only distinct feature in a maddening blur of shadows that seemed to bleed off into the background. The man had more substance than the true ghosts, but less than the common servants that fled at his approach.

Odin planted the butt of his spear in the ground and stood firm. He would offer no threat, but nor would he grant honors to a man who treated his guests to mazes and mysteries. A proper king would introduce himself, not hide behind the mists.

When the man at last neared, he paused and spoke. "It is not permanent, Odin of the Aesir." His voice was thick, as though he were tasting the words for the first time, his accent strange and unplaceable. "Of course, once you open the door, it is never truly shut. You may choose not to look through to the Otherworlds, but you will always know more waits just beyond your sight."

"Who are you?"

"I am Gjuki, King of the Niflungar, High Priest of Niflheim, known to some as the Raven Lord."

"Can't imagine how you got that nickname."

"You are yet nascent in your powers, young lord, but not without potential."

"What potential?"

"The potential for greatness, of course. The chance to take this Realm and make it our own. The power to shape our own destinies and those of the common folk beneath us. And I have watched you, Odin. I know your heart longs for that power. You will be content only when the World kneels at your feet. And I can give that to you. Come." With that, Gjuki turned and started down the hall.

Odin's grip on Gungnir tightened. When the World knelt at his feet? Odin had no such lofty dreams. Idunn had forced kingship upon him, and he would claim it, if only to save Ve. He could not, however, deny Gjuki's majesty. Still Odin was *not* accustomed to being summoned like a slave. Being called to an audience with the coward Hadding had been bad enough.

Gjuki did not wait for him, however, disappearing around the corner. With a grunt Odin started after the Niflung king, more disturbed by his words than he'd have liked. The man spoke of kingship like tyranny, just as Loki had warned. Was that the power Odin sought? And could he accept such a gift, should it come from these sorcerers?

These people seemed to hold control over the mists. Men and women alike, clearly wielding seid. They were more than just völvur. They were true sorcerers as Loki had said. Ones who had delved into the powers of Niflheim more deeply than any should, and yet ... and yet they showed no fear. Men like Gjuki could rule Midgard if they so choose. Or rather, Odin could, had he such powers. And Gjuki offered them freely?

The king led him through a great hall lined with thousands of candles. Another raven came to alight on the king's right shoulder, while the one perched on his left took flight. Scouting ahead? Did this sorcerer truly speak to the birds? The so-called Raven Lord had as many as secrets as Loki. The man spoke of the Otherworlds as if he knew them. Völvur told tales of those worlds, but they spoke in whispers, hinting at Realms unknowable to mortals. But Odin was no longer mortal, and, he suspected, neither was Gjuki —if the man had ever *been* human.

At the end of the great hall, Gjuki paused. An altar stood on a raised dais. Runic carvings covered the top and sides of the altar, their meanings hidden from Odin. Gjuki spoke without turning to face him. "The winds carry word of you far, young lord. A mortal man who slew Ymir. No mean feat, even for one of us." He held up a hand, and the archway beyond the altar trembled. Dust jetted from cracks in the wall, stinging Odin's eyes. Then the stones sank into the floor, revealing another hall beyond.

Odin swallowed. How powerful were these sorcerers? Could they match the magic of the Vanir?

"Come," Gjuki said again. "I will show you to your chambers."

"My chambers?"

"My ravens have watched you for some time now. More than long enough to prepare for your arrival."

If this man thought to keep him prisoner, he would find himself sorely mistaken. Odin followed, eyes darting down every side passage. All the people of the keep watched him as he passed, though none seemed intent on threatening him. But then, they were mere shadows to him. It was hard to tell which ones were alive and which were shades trapped in this fell place, much less judge their intent.

Odin followed Gjuki up seemingly endless flights of stairs. Odin's superhuman stamina let him take all those flights without becoming winded, but then, neither did Gjuki breathe heavily. The stairs wound around in a spiral, carrying him up a tower until at last they reached the highest landing. The king strode toward an iron-banded door on one side, but Odin drifted over to the window. Below ran the stream he'd seen before, jutting around rocks in a violent torrent before pitching over the cliff. Now that he could see through the mist he could make out where it hit the Morimarusa far below.

"Beautiful, is it not?" Gjuki said. "There are so many things we can teach you."

Odin turned from the window, trying to look the Raven Lord in the eye. But the man remained a shadowy form, his facial features blurred. "What do you want from me?"

"The only thing that matters. Power."

Odin chuckled. These *sorcerers* wanted his power? What could he teach them? He shook his head and took a step toward Gjuki. He had come here for the Singasteinn, and he aimed to take it, whatever power it might hold. The Raven Lord was alone now. If the king didn't have the amulet on him, he'd at least know where it was. Whatever these people might teach him, Odin had given his oath to the Odling ghost. He would live and die by that oath. And that would fix everything.

It had to.

Before Odin could even ask, Gjuki opened the door, revealing the lush chamber beyond. A four-post bed dominated the center of the semicircular room. A dresser, wash basin, side rooms—this was no prison tower. It was a chamber for an honored guest. A woman stood by the window but turned when the door opened.

"My daughter is quite an adept at the Sight. She can help you regain your normal vision. When you have rested, we will speak of the future." He turned to the woman. "Odin forced part of his mind into the Penumbra and—unless I am mistaken—has yet to be able to shut out the visions that now haunt him."

The woman snorted and stalked toward Odin. Transfixed, Odin watched her then jumped at the sound of the door shutting behind him. This king trusted Odin with his daughter. Moments ago Odin had intended to overpower Gjuki and take the amulet by force. His neck heated. These people might have deserved better than he'd intended to give them. They did not seem so bad.

The woman pulled off gloves and tossed them aside, then placed her shockingly warm hands on Odin's cheeks. She stood nearly as tall as he did. She leaned in closer, so close he could feel her breath on his face. Still, her eyes were naught but shadows. "Let it go," she whispered. "The mortal world has much to offer."

"Who are you?"

"Gudrun." She pressed a goblet into his hands. "Drink, my lord. Find yourself."

A draught of mead to relax away the Sight? Odin would gladly take it. He downed the liquid fast, gasping as it burned his throat.

Gudrun pulled him to her and pressed her lips against his, ignoring his half-hearted protests. She was soft, unhardened by the bitter chill. Odin started to pull away. However he and Frigg had parted, Odin was a married man. He should ... She wrapped her arms around his shoulders and drew him closer. All thought fled his mind as Gudrun massaged his lips. He shut his eyes, lost in the sensation.

Gudrun shoved him. Odin stumbled backward, falling onto the plush bed. The World shot back into focus as he opened his eyes. After so long gazing at shadows, the colors seemed almost too vibrant, and he blinked at the sight. Gudrun was dressed in an embroidered blue dress and a cloak lined with thick fur. Long blonde hair flowed over her shoulders, escaping past a large golden headband wrought with intricate patterns. And around her neck hung an amulet of gold that seemed to shimmer with its own faint light.

"Yes," she said. "The Singasteinn. I know what *she* wants of you. But I can give you so much more. I can break the curse that vaettr placed on your soul. I can give you *everything.*"

Odin tried to speak, but a lump formed in his throat. Dimly, he realized he had dropped Gungnir when she kissed him.

Gudrun released the clasp on her cloak and it fell away. With two fingers she pulled at the laces of her bodice, exposing her breasts. Her nipples stood erect in the chill air, bright pink against her pale skin.

"I'm a married man," Odin stammered.

"Married to a völva? You hold yourself tied to a woman whose powers are as a child's compared to mine, and you dare to imagine she might give you a shadow of what I can offer?" Gudrun's voice dropped, becoming huskier, almost hypnotic. It seemed to echo in his mind until he could hear naught else. "She cannot satisfy your lusts as I can. You hunger for flesh, for knowledge, for power ... I offer all the secrets of the World." The Niflung princess straddled him on the bed, forcing him backward.

Odin's arms trembled. This was wrong. Part of him insisted it was, but that part could barely be heard over the all-consuming volume of her voice. She issued commands with the authority of a true queen. A fire built in his loins, ready to devour him alive unless he sated it.

"Take what you want," Gudrun whispered in his ear. "Take it all. Forever."

Odin grabbed her shoulders so tightly she cried out, and he rolled atop the princess. Some other thought had been in his mind. Something on the tip of his tongue—he couldn't remember. The fire kept building until he roared like a beast. He snatched two sides of her bodice and ripped the dress in half.

The gods had made her for him. And he could not deny them.

## 37

*C*astle Niflung lay on the fringes of Midgard, wedged on an island separating the Morimarusa from the Gandvik Sea. This island, Samsey, had become their hidden sanctum, where the greater part of the Niflungar had slept away the ages. Gudrun's grandparents had built it some eight hundred years ago, after the Niflungar were driven out of the mainland by the now-fallen kingdom of the Lofdar. It had long since served as the last refuge of the greatest descendants of Halfdan the Old. If Gudrun's parents—Gjuki and Grimhild—had not lived through these events themselves, they must have at least firsthand accounts of it from *their* parents. And that meant they themselves had survived for many centuries.

They had used the Art to sustain their mortal forms long beyond the time allotted to Mankind, using secret knowledge denied to her, at least thus far. At just past twenty-five winters, she had aged about as much as she cared to. Grimhild could have passed for her—slightly—older sister. The queen's most treasured spells were housed in a grimoire said to be written by the hand of Hel herself—there was none greater. Hel, Queen of Niflheim and Mistress of the Art. And through those spells, Grimhild had somehow maintained her youth down through the centuries.

In her bed, the Ás man stirred, rolling over before collapsing on his stomach like a sea lion on a rock. Gudrun smirked to herself. The love potion had worked more than well enough to enthrall him. His will was weak enough she might have even drawn him to her bed *without* need of alchemical assistance, but her father had insisted she leave naught to chance. Insisted, most like, *through* Grimhild's orders. Though her father was the king of all the Niflungar, Grimhild was Hel's high priestess and claimed to hear the voice of the goddess in her dreams. Anyone who questioned that claim seemed to disappear, probably into the Pit, Grimhild's nigh-bottomless dungeon beneath the castle.

The queen's unnatural longevity must derive from feasting on the souls of her victims, much as a vaettr fed upon its host or even upon other entities from beyond the Mortal Realm. The secret to that would lie in the grimoire, but Gudrun had never been able to lay a hand on the tome. It never went far from the queen and, as far as Gudrun knew, not even her father was allowed to touch it. Only the queen's vile servants could—the Bone Guard, Grimhild's former enemies in life, damned to eternal servitude in death and acting as a reminder of the urd of any who dared stand against the queen.

As now, when Grimhild had taken the Bone Guard and ridden for Sviarland, intent to secure her puppets there. Grimhild had sworn not to repeat the mistakes of her predecessors to the throne—as if it were her bloodline and not Father's directly descended from Naefil. But so long had the vicious queen ruled the Niflungar, perhaps even Father had become one of her innumerable puppets. The queen had built an army of pawns spread across the face of Midgard, moving only a few pieces at a time, ever waiting for an endgame that would ensure that, when the Niflungar returned, no one would be able to stand against them.

Their waking had come slowly at first, but now they moved with greater surety. And the Vanir did naught. They no longer watched Midgard, nor cared for the urds of man.

Maybe that was why her father had tasked her to seduce and train Odin. To create another pawn, a would-be king among one of the numerous barbarian peoples left in Midgard. Not that the task was odious. He was handsome and an apt lover. Moreover, his body surged with vital energy that coursed into Gudrun every time he climaxed. She felt stronger, vibrant, her own life force fortified by Odin's. Given enough of such power, she might even one day challenge the queen.

All things in time.

Wool cloak slung tight around her shoulders, Gudrun slipped from her room. Father would be in his study. Such intuitions were inherent blessings of the Sight. Oh, she was not given much for prescient dreams or visions of the past, as some blessed with the Sight were. But instincts, intuitions, those she excelled at. That and communing with spirits. Ghosts flittered at the edge of her vision even now, though she ignored them. To acknowledge their existence was to invite their ire or pleas, and Gudrun had time for neither.

Instead, she stalked the halls, making her way down to her father's study in the basements deep under the castle— though not half so deep as the Pit. A circle of candles lit the room. All servants of Hel disdained fire, but not even the royal Niflungar could read in the dark. As always, countless musty tomes and scrolls cluttered the shelves ringing the chamber, and a bowl of water sat on the table.

Not for drinking. Water had numerous other uses—it was liminal, fluid both literally and spiritually, and thus served as an excellent medium for focusing the Art. Her father didn't look at the bowl now, though. He watched her, head cocked to the side as he listened to whatever secrets the raven on his shoulder whispered in his ear. The ravens proved more effective spies than the spirits Gudrun or even Grimhild had to use for gathering information. Less costly now, though Father had hinted he had once paid a great price for such servants.

All sorcery came with a price. You drew power from the Otherworlds, and the Otherworld took back from you tenfold. The mere thought wakened spirits writhing beneath her skin, clamoring at the back of her mind, always eager to take from her. They would take her body, mind, and soul, given the chance. Such was the urd of all sorcerers who lived long enough.

"Your mother will return within the moon."

Gudrun leaned over the table, demanding her father meet her gaze. "The Ás is somewhat more than human, is he not?"

Father looked to his raven as if the damned bird would answer the question, then finally raised an eyebrow at Gudrun. The one thing he had always demanded from his daughter was intelligence. Unlike Grimhild, who demanded *everything*, oft as not, more than could be borne.

"What are his secrets?"

"Are you not equipped to pry such things loose from him?"

Gudrun scowled at him. Obviously she could get the man to tell her all he knew. "I doubt the Ás has any inclination of Grimhild's purpose for him." The queen wanted Gudrun to make him a pawn, because in her mind, Gudrun was *her* pawn. All pieces in the grand game she played. A tafl board on a scope encompassing all Midgard. Maybe even beyond.

"Your *mother* has her instructions from Hel herself—there is none greater."

"There is none greater." Why would Hel want Odin?

Her father stroked the raven's head and leaned back in his chair. "A Vanr came to him. Brought him a gift."

A Vanr. From time to time, a few of those self-proclaimed gods still wandered the World, but most had not left Vanaheim in a thousand years. Any gift they brought would be laced with double-edged purpose, and ... in Hel's name ... Odin's vital energy. Every time he climaxed inside her it was like standing under a waterfall. Because he was infused with the energy of life. "An apple of Yggdrasil?"

Given such power, no wonder Gudrun felt so invigorated. And had Grimhild been here, no doubt the queen would have seduced Odin herself. Perhaps she still intended to. That thought left an unexpected sourness in Gudrun's stomach. She was not going to share the man with *anyone*, much less the queen. If Grimhild thought to claim this pawn for herself, she was in for a shock. Gudrun had lost so much because of the woman.

She was not going to surrender Odin.

He was hers.

## 38

*O*din shot awake, gasping for air as though he'd been drowning. The winds were chilly against his bare skin. A glance around told him the previous night had been no dream. Gudrun lay sprawled naked across the bed, a glorious goddess. Splinters of the dresser littered the floor. They had smashed it when ... Gods, how many times had he taken this woman? The bed, the wall, against the window ...

Her voice seemed to coil inside his mind, as though demanding he come and ravish her sleeping form once again, and already his body began to rise to the challenge. Only a slight hesitation held him back. Wasn't there some other woman in his life? He tried to picture another face, but none came to mind.

Some force pulled him closer to Gudrun, her scent growing heady with the nearness, until he could not stop himself. And why should he? She giggled and jerked awake as he buried his face between her breasts. He felt his kisses grow so fevered he thought he would faint, then flung her legs apart so he could enter her. Any sense of time fled him.

WHEN NEXT HE looked out the window, the sun had set again. He stared out over the mist and the icy castle beneath him. In the moonlight it felt even more removed from the World of Men.

An uneasiness settled over him, like something he was forgetting tingling the edge of his mind.

"This place is steeped in sorcery," he said when Gudrun put a hand on his shoulder. "Like something time forgot."

"Not entirely inaccurate," she said. "What do you know of sorcery? Of the worlds beyond Midgard?"

Not enough, that he could say for certain. When he turned to her she was fully dressed, as was he, though he didn't remember dressing. A fog seemed to have settled over his mind. Hunger, perhaps.

"I could use something to eat," he mumbled.

Gudrun pressed a goblet into his hands. Odin drank the burning liquid once again, then sank back onto the bed. At the edge of his vision, those shadows had drawn up again, trying to creep into the room through cracks in reality.

"There are ghosts in here."

"Shades are everywhere, Odin." She held out a hand and pulled him back to his feet.

He was so tired. He wanted only to feast, to fuck, to sleep. What had he been doing before this that had left him so exhausted? The thought seemed to flit through his fingers.

Instead he followed her out among the halls. Other Niflungar greeted him by name, nodded at them. He knew them, he realized. He'd spoken to some over the night meal, met others out in the courtyard. He knew them, but most of their names escaped his grasp.

The little one, no more than ten winters, that was Gudrun's brother Gunnar. Always running about with a sword, training, testing himself. Hadn't he asked to spar with Odin once? Yes, yes. But Odin had refused him.

"Gunnar wants to become a master, like his big brother," Gudrun said idly.

"Big brother?"

"Guthorm. He's away with ... our mother. Not one of Father's heirs, so he avoids Castle Niflung most times. Come." She led him further down halls that blurred before, obscuring thought and time as in a dream. All of life had become a dream. "You have awakened to the Sight, Odin, and with it, you see and feel things others cannot. You see past the Veil into the other side, the shadow of this Realm where ghosts and spirits dwell when they watch us. We call this shadow the Penumbra. Beyond it lies the Spirit Realm, where further Otherworlds orbit us."

"So I ... I'll always see these shadows now?"

"You'll always know they are there. The Sight has other uses—those strong in it can pierce the veil of time, forward, backward, gazing upon the strands and fetters of urd. Your völvur, the strongest of them, possess the barest hint of such a blessing. Any sorcerer likewise must gain at least some level of Sight, for sorcery is the power of the Otherworlds."

"So seid."

She paused. "A name for harnessing the energy suffusing your body and the World around you. Through force of will and expenditure of that life energy, you can change the World around you by calling upon spirits. *That* is the essence of sorcery."

Gudrun led Odin farther into the castle, to a wall that folded in upon itself at her approach, revealing an opening. It led to a long hall, and he followed her down it, eyes latched onto her arse. Would anyone dare speak against them if he took his lover right here in this secret passage?

No.

None would dare challenge Odin. Lord of the Aesir. Prince of the Niflungar.

He grabbed both of her arse cheeks and pushed her against the wall.

She chuckled as he lifted the back of her dress. "I have something to show you."

"Show me," he demanded.

Instead, she spun around in his arms and pushed him backward. "Say you love me."

"I ... I ... love you."

At that she kissed him, then pulled away far too soon. "Midgard is but one of many worlds, Odin. A small, weak world compared to those beyond. Tell me of Niflheim."

They'd had this conversation before, hadn't they? The words came to his mouth as if by rote, and he knew them. "The World of Mist, of cold. The world of the dead, ruled by Queen Hel. There is none greater. From Niflheim comes the power of sorcery, the power to unmake the Realms of man."

"Yes." She smiled. At that she grabbed his hand and pulled him forward until they paused before an iron-banded door. Inside, a man shrieked in pain. The sound ran through Odin like a wash of icy water, the mist in his mind clearing a moment. And then Gudrun's lips were on his again, her breath mingling with his, returning the peace.

"How many Otherworlds, Odin?" she asked, a breathless pant against his cheek.

"Nine worlds in the Spirit Realm. Nine worlds as there are Nine Spheres of Creation ..." He was forgetting something important. There was something he was meant to do. "Nine worlds that are not places but ..."

"But more like states of consciousness," she prompted.

"Consciousnesses, shaping reality. Shaping our world, every world. The Otherworlds and the …"

"The Penumbra—a layer of the Astral Realm." She pursed her lips. "Hmmm." She then opened the door, revealing a scene of horror beyond.

An obsidian altar marked with strange runes rested at the head of the room. Gjuki, the Raven Lord, stood before it, ravens on each shoulder. But it was the naked man strung above the altar who held Odin's eyes. Blood dribbled down numerous cuts along his abdomen, the blood stains all but invisible on the black stone beneath.

"What is this?"

"Sorcery," she said. "Sorcery is the most dramatic form of the Art. Sorcery calls forth the power of spirits, enjoining them or bending them to our will. And what greater spirit could there be than almighty Hel?"

"There is none greater," Odin said.

"Yes. So now is your chance to practice it. Kill him—offer his soul and body to Hel and complete the ritual."

Odin's stomach lurched at the thought. Even as his hand drifted toward the victim.

Bile scorched his throat. Something was wrong. Who was this man? He shook himself. Sorcery called up power from vaettir out of Niflheim. It ate away at body and soul, by its nature and by its cost. Why would he want to harm this innocent man? No, no this was wrong. Odin opened his mouth, trying to find words to explain to his love she had taken a wrong course.

Gjuki slapped the altar. "He is not ready."

Gudrun spun Odin around and kissed him again. She drew him from the room by his hand. "He will be," she called over her shoulder.

Odin followed as she led him back toward their bedchamber. Fear threatened to drown his lust until he found himself disgusted by the reaction of his own body, unable to stop himself from rising again at her call.

## 39

*S*houting from beyond the smithy. Angry cries, grunts of effort.

Damn it.

Tyr raced around the building. Three of Hadding's men surrounded Vili, fists raised. Another lay in the snow. Blood pouring from his broken nose and split lip. Damned berserk.

"What in Njord's name is this!" he demanded.

One of Hadding's people leapt on Vili's back, wrapped an arm around his neck. Vili lunged backward, slamming the man into a post of the smithy. Force of it cracked the post—damn nigh split it in half.

Another man stepped in, swinging.

The crack of his fist against Vili's jaw.

The berserk turned to face his attacker. Grinning. Fucking grinning.

Bears don't look fast. But they can be. Berserkir too. Vili had the man by the throat, hefted off the ground before anyone else had moved. The Hasding man's eyes bulged. He clawed uselessly at Vili's grip.

Tyr wasn't a berserk, but the apple made him strong. He seized Vili's wrist and shoulder and shoved the man. Borr's son released his victim. Spun on Tyr.

"Enough!"

Vili glowered.

"These are our hosts."

"Poor fucking hosts." Vili spat. "We're not fucking wanted here. Let's be gone, and Hel take these trollfuckers."

Would that they could. Odin had ordered them to remain here, hold Halfhaugr. Even against its own ruler.

Angry shouts agreeing they ought to leave. At this rate, the whole town would rise against them.

Tyr scowled at the gathering crowd. "Everyone calm down. Go back to your work."

They didn't.

More of the town arrived with each passing moment. Watching, simmering. Ready to boil over.

Tyr's hand drifted toward the sword on his back. Not the way it ought to go.

Vili grinning again. Fucking imbecile. Cracking his knuckles.

Wodan warriors had begun to form a crowd on the other side. A few had drawn blades, axes. Blood would run these streets.

And then the Hasding crowd began to part. Making way for someone.

A woman, bearing sword and shield. Tyr had seen her a few times in the past moon. Olrun, wife to one of Hadding's thegns. A shieldmaiden, and clearly one these people respected a great deal.

Olrun planted her sword in the ground—mushy snow and mud now. Looked from Tyr to Vili and back, barely acknowledging the rest of the crowd. "Jarl Hadding has grown displeased with this alliance."

Because Odin had fucking betrayed him. Denied him the damned apple and then run off.

Olrun locked his gaze. Understanding. Warning. "The jarl believes it is time for the Wodan tribe to return to Eskgard or wherever else suits you." Shouts of agreement from the crowd. Anger was rising fast, but they deferred to her.

Vili spat.

Tyr cracked his neck, barely stopping himself from scowling at the man. Fool berserk wanted a war. "It suits us to remain here. Until our jarl returns."

Some of Hadding's people began to beat weapons against their shields. Odin's warriors immediately started doing the same.

Damn it.

"I'll fight you," Tyr said.

"What?"

Some of the Wodanar laughed. Tyr ignored them. "A duel. I win, we stay. You win, we go."

Olrun glanced at her people, and at the Wodanar. Glowered. Yes, she was aging. Past her prime. And he'd given her an unworthy challenge, damn him. She had no chance, and they both knew it. So why had he said such a thing? Hel, this scheming for Odin's throne was wearing him down. It was the kind of thing he'd have said long ago, as champion to Hymir. As a jotunn's bloody sword arm.

The shieldmaiden sighed. Wrapped her hand around the sword. Now he'd have to fight her. Not to the death. He'd try to spare her, best he could.

Hel take him for this.

The girl, Sigyn, raced to Olrun's side. Put her hand on her shoulder. Whispered in her ear.

Too late for warnings. Too late. Blood boiled in both crowds. Boiling blood led to blood staining the snows.

Olrun said something back. The women argued a moment. Then the shieldmaiden looked to her people. "All of you, disperse. Hadding's daughter commands it!"

At her sharp tone, the warriors faltered. Angry murmurs about a bastard child. About Mist-madness or alf possession.

Tyr looked to his own people. "In Odin's name." He pointed away. "Get gone. We will not strike the first blow against our hosts."

Vili grumbled. Looked apt to challenge him. Instead, the berserk spun, walked over one of the men he had felled as he left. Ground the poor bastard into the snow.

As both crowds began to disperse, Sigyn strode forward and grabbed Tyr's arm. Dragged him away from the smithy and toward another house. Same house where Olrun stood out front.

"What's going on here?" he demanded.

"Come inside, please."

He joined her in the house, and she settled down on the one of the bed shelves.

"I cannot believe Odin would marry my sister only to invite war with our people."

Odin did a lot of things Tyr couldn't believe. Unsure what to say, he watched the girl.

She tapped a finger against her lip. "You asked me what's going on. I was fostered with Agilaz and Olrun. But Jarl Hadding is my father, and I can try to speak with him and with Frigg, try to persuade Father against this course. War benefits no one."

"The losers least of all."

"If you intended to take Halfhaugr by force, I think you would have done it already." She leaned forward now. "Why did Odin ride off to Reidgotaland? What does he hope to gain in the north?"

"Odin keeps his own counsel." A half truth made one nigh as bad as a liar. What was he becoming? "You share a bed with his blood brother. Why not ask the foreigner about Odin's mind?"

Sigyn neither flinched nor denied sleeping with Loki. Smiled even. "Was that supposed to distract me from my question? Or do you not even know the answer?" Sigyn tapped her lip again. "It's no matter. While he is away, you seem to want to prevent bloodshed, yes?"

Tyr folded his arms.

"The Hasdingi stand on edge because of the Godwulfs."

"I've heard." A tribe ruled by varulfur was apt to bring chaos. Tyr's spy among them should have reported back to the Athra. But from here, Tyr had no idea if that had happened.

"We sent my foster brother among them, in marriage, hoping to secure peace. Only now we learn the jarl there conspires with the King of Njarar to seize some or all of Aujum. Perhaps this makes Jarl Alci a common enemy."

"He's your uncle."

She shrugged. "Sometimes the family who chose you matters more than blood."

Tyr did not even know who his blood relatives were. Some had whispered Hymir himself had spawned him on a human woman. Tyr refused to believe, save in his darkest moments. "What would you have me do?"

"You're Odin's champion. If you were to aid the Hasdingi in this issue, it would go far toward smoothing over the injury Odin did here. The people only know that Odin angered Father and Frigg both and then fled. But you and I know about the apples. My father is going to die because Odin would not part with one. If that happens as matters stand now, Frigg will be like to divorce him in her grief."

He grunted. Such a divorce would cost Odin any support among the Hasdingi. Maybe cost him the throne. "So you want me to go to Alci."

She shook her head. "I don't think Jarl Alci wants to hear of peace now. He is drunk on dreams of glory. No, find Hermod—my foster brother—and Agilaz. They are among the Godwulfs now. To have peace, the Godwulfs must have a new jarl. And you are known among all the tribes as a champion of Borr. They cannot turn you away."

To murder a jarl. Tyr groaned. "Your father approves of this?"

"My father would not act against the bonds of brother-hood. But Alci leaves us with little choice now. Do this, Tyr, stop Alci. And I will stay here and do all *I* can to maintain the alliance between our peoples. My father and sister both are ill disposed to the Wodanar at the moment, but I can sway their minds. But you must save ..."

"Save?"

She shook her head. "Just save us all."

More schemes. Plots. A warrior ought to meet threats with a sword in hand. A song in his heart. Instead, to make a king, Tyr worked in shadows and lies. Betrayals. He'd ask Idunn, but he knew what she'd say. Odin must become king. And it sounded like that meant Alci must fall.

## 40

*M*ore than a moon had passed since Odin had come to her, and they now had fallen into an easy rapport. He had not yet managed to evoke or bind any spirit, but he would. He would learn the Art and become a sorcerer of Hel, as Grimhild had commanded. He needed only a bit more time.

They walked through a garden of ice sculptures in the central courtyard. Gudrun did not know where these statues had come from, for they had rested here her whole life, but she knew what some few of them represented. The nine sons of Halfdan the Old, the progenitors of the Old Kingdoms as Odin called them. He drifted along beside her, a man half dreaming and so eager to escape his life she needed fewer and fewer of her potions to keep him here.

Without a sense of time, he murmured about all the things he would do, how he would become King of the Aesir, how he would stop his brother Ve from transforming into a troll. The former, perhaps, he could have done, and made a better life for his people. The latter ... no. Probably not even this Odling ghost could stop the changes the mist wrought in Odin's brother.

Gudrun's own brothers, her two younger brothers, sparred through the garden. Hogne leapt upon the fountain's lip, flipped around, teasing their youngest sibling to chase after him. Gunnar did so with admirable gusto, never showing the barest hint of fatigue. Ten winters. Very soon the boy would be inducted into the mysteries of the Art and, if he survived at all, would lose what remained of his childhood. She drew to a stop, watching as her little brother laughed, running, playing, though he'd have called it training. And she could no more save him from his urd than Odin could save his own brother.

But she could dream of it, as Odin dreamed.

"You love them."

She turned to Odin, unable to quite find the right words to explain to him. "Love is ... complex. They are my brothers."

"And you love them. I know, I love my brothers. They ... they should be here too. We're all family."

Gudrun stiffened and ground her teeth. Oh, to have a family where love came so simply. Odin had no idea how much urd had blessed him. Could she even afford to love her brothers? Guthorm, her half brother and Grimhild's eldest—he was their mother's favorite, for which he had suffered almost as much as Gudrun, though he did not seem to realize it. He and Gudrun shared a bond, true enough, though she would not have called it love. More a mutual devotion to the pursuit of the Art and the return of the days of glory.

"Hogne still treasures Gunnar," she said. "And I ... care for them."

"Why do you hesitate to embrace the bonds of family? What greater connection exists between people?"

She swallowed. "You do not yet understand." Each of them was, or would become, a tool in Grimhild's arsenal, a weapon aimed at Midgard and the descendants of the enemies of the Niflungar, all while the queen plotted and schemed to claim all the world in the name of Hel. "You would be king of a single people. My … *mother* will take the throne of all Midgard." And her father, too, of course, by her side.

"You are lucky to still have your parents."

Gudrun chuckled. "You have not met Grimhild. But you soon will. Tell me then, if you still think any of us lucky to have her."

Odin paused then. "You … *hate* her."

This Ás was more perceptive than a man under her spell ought to be. He had a strong will, an iron in his soul that would bring him all the more pain as Grimhild broke that will, ground him beneath her heel. The thought of it opened a hole in her stomach as deep and dark as the Pit beneath Castle Niflung. What had come over her? She grieved at the thought of Hogne and Gunnar slowly falling into the abyss of darkness that consumed all sorcerers. But thinking of Odin like that, of him becoming one more victim in Grimhild's unending machinations to claim all lands, it hit her like a physical pain, squeezing her heart.

A disgusting sensation, as if … as if she had drunk of her own draughts. In Hel's name … She had let herself feel for this man. Grimhild had sent her to him as a whore, intent to capture this king, though why she cared so much for one more pawn, Gudrun did not know. Except, Odin was not a pawn—he was a king on the tafl board, and Gudrun could no longer bear the thought of losing him.

Hel damn her for her weakness.

As the Queen of Mist would damn Odin and devour his soul.

## 41

*L*oki had an inexplicable love of high places. That and fires. Often when Sigyn sought him out, she found him either staring into a flame or perched atop a building, a rock, or some other precarious place. Actually, she sort of loved that about him. This time, he stood at the cusp of the spiked wall surrounding Halfhaugr, staring out north so intently she'd have almost thought he could see something she couldn't.

And she could see farther and clearer than ever since he had given her the apple. What else would the apple do to her? Would she gain magic powers like stories claimed Freyja or Idunn had? Would her other senses enhance to match her vision?

He didn't turn at her approach, but his posture loosened almost imperceptibly. How did he know it was her? One more mystery she'd have to unravel. And now she had all the time in the World to do so.

Everything about him was a puzzle. Strange, mismatched tattoos covered his arms, obviously from more than one foreign culture. He knew things no man should know. And he had this way about him ...

"He's been gone too long," Loki said at last.

Odin. After the fight Odin had had with Frigg, part of Sigyn expected him to never return. Indeed, part of her *hoped* he never would. Already the Wodan jarl had brought such upheaval to her life, and though grateful for the bounties he had endowed her with through Loki, she feared the greater changes he seemed to have in mind. Perhaps that was selfish—after all, if not for Odin, she would not have become an immortal, nor found someone to share this new life with.

Instead of answering, she slipped her arms around Loki's and tucked her chin over his shoulder. "What do you see out there?"

Through her embrace, she felt him swallow hard before answering. "The future. Always."

What did that mean? Did Loki also fear Odin's plans? Or could he mean it more literally? The apples seemed to affect each of them a little differently. Was it possible Loki now suffered the visions as Frigg had?

"And what is the future?"

"He is."

"Then why didn't you go with him?"

"You know the answer."

Sigyn suspected she did. Loki seemed inclined to see himself as a teacher to his blood brother, though he looked little older than Odin. He obviously wanted Odin to learn some things on his own. Agilaz had often said a lesson learned for oneself was worth ten lectures. Did Loki then send Odin off alone on this sojourn as a means of preparing him for something grander still? If so, the lessons seemed cruel and lonely. But then, maybe all the strongest lessons were like that.

"I have to go after him."

Sigyn sighed. Somehow she'd known it would end with that. "I'll come with you."

"I wish you could, but I need to travel swiftly, and I can best do that alone. I cannot allow Odin to fall into the shadows or succumb to the mists, however alluring their calls might seem."

She squeezed him tighter, savoring his warmth. "You'd better come back to me."

"Naught would stop me from it."

At that, he slipped from her arms, kissed her forehead, and leapt over the wall. Sigyn leaned forward to gaze at where he had landed, crouched in the snow nigh fifteen feet below. Damn. Could she do that? Would the apple prevent injury if she tried such a foolhardy maneuver? Part of her wanted to try it, to feel the rush. Yet enough people in the village thought her mad already.

A chill wind swept over her, as Loki disappeared off into the mist.

Sigyn's father had forestalled his decision to cast out the Wodanar at her behest, though his patience seemed nigh at an end. As did his life. The ever creeping thickness clouded his lungs and his eyes while Frigg and Fulla fretted over him like the invalid he was fast becoming. And Sigyn had no more words of comfort for her sister.

She sat upon the low stone wall surrounding Agilaz's house in Halfhaugr, staring out at naught and somehow still seeing more than she ever had. Her eyes kept getting stronger. Her ears too. Footsteps crunched snow as someone made his way around the corner of another house.

Shortsnout rounded the bend and took off at a trot when he saw her, drawing a smile from her even as the hound leapt about below her knees. A moment later, Hermod slogged forward, burdened with a heavy pack and Njord knew what other weight.

Sigyn leapt from the wall and raced over to her foster brother, pausing just long enough to cuddle the hound. "What are you doing here? Where is Agilaz?"

"Father remained at the Godwulfs to keep an eye on things." Hermod embraced her, then held her by the arms.

He still held her like a brother, and yet, somehow, that no longer hurt. She was happy to see him well, for certain, but … it had changed. Or maybe she had never really loved him like that. Maybe she'd convinced herself that any mutual affection between her and a man who accepted her must represent a romantic connection, and, in so doing, had failed to acknowledge the value of other bonds. Because being loved as a sister did matter, after all, and not every woman had that.

Loki had opened her eyes even as his apple had enhanced them.

"I feared for your safety."

"I know. I met your friend Tyr on the road and sent him on to meet Father."

Sigyn guided him back toward the house. Olrun had gone out wandering the town in an unstated but obvious hope her mere presence would induce calm and prevent another altercation between the tribes. The longer the strife went on with the Godwulfs, though, the more likely her hope would prove futile. The Wodanar had not lit the first fires of the Hasding anger, but their presence fanned those flames.

Hermod dropped his pack inside and slouched down, warming his hands by the fire. "I cannot stay long here. My wife awaits my return."

"I didn't think to see you here at all."

"Alci himself sent me, Sigyn. He thought, given my connection between the tribes, I would prove the perfect emissary."

"Emissary to what end?"

Hermod glowered at the flames as though he could avoid whatever he intended to say. And he need not say it, for his coming could only portend a single end.

Sigyn sucked air through her teeth and shut her eyes. "He sent you here to demand his brother surrender Halfhaugr to him. He's coming to take our home."

Hermod's wary gaze offered all the answer she'd need.

## 42

When they spoke of sorcery and the Art, they did so in nigh total darkness that frayed Odin's nerves and invited in the sibilant whispers of the vengeful dead. Shades were so thick on this isle that Odin could all but choke on their invisible rage.

He and Gudrun sat huddled in a windowless room below Castle Niflung, the only light from a dwindling candle on the floor between them. Odin's legs ached from sitting with them folded beneath him for hours. Bare chested, he shivered in the cold. Not even the apples of Yggdrasil completely blocked out such chills. Or maybe it was not the cold alone that froze him this night, try as he might to block the sensation of being watched. And hated.

"Tell me," Gudrun said.

Odin cleared his throat. "On the far side of the Penumbra lie the nine worlds of the Spirit Realm. Each home to vaettir, timeless beings of thought and power."

"And?"

"And malice. They are not friends to Mankind." That ire

settled upon his shoulders now like heavy mail dragging him under a river.

"But they can be bargained with, cajoled, or dominated, whence comes the power of a sorcerer."

He almost could not swallow. Hearing this over and over did not make him inclined to want to bond such a vaettr to his flesh and soul. Gudrun knew more of the vaettir than he'd have ever thought a mortal could know—or should know. She herself had bound more than one to her flesh, making a pact with beings she knew were powerful and hateful beyond mortal ken. And yet, even she admitted her knowledge was but the surface of a sea of unknown, of beings ancient long before the rise of the Old Kingdoms, even before the coming of the mists. With the Sight, they could see into the Penumbra, true, but not into the Spirit Realm beyond it. What they knew of those worlds came from hints and intimations of the vaettir themselves.

And the vaettir lied.

Seething in timeless enmity, they manipulated, used, and possessed mortals foolish enough to cross their path.

And now Gudrun wanted him to call one forth, pull it through the Veil and let the formless, hostile entity into him. Through a pact with a servant of Hel—there is none greater —he might come closer to his goddess and, indeed, gain some measure of mastery over her domain. The Niflung sorcerers thus controlled mist and cold, used it to conceal themselves, to spy, to kill. To wield influence far beyond that allotted to Mankind, at a price men could not begin to fathom.

A man's soul would shriek from it, at least until it withered into a useless remnant. Such was the price for the godlike power of true sorcerers.

Gudrun had painted a complex symbol on Odin's chest. She called it a glyph, though it looked to him much like völvur runes, only more intricate in design. Other such designs decorated this room, forming a circle of arcane symbols designed to ward against the very vaettir she wanted to evoke.

"Are you quite certain this is wise?" he asked.

The princess sighed and shook her head. "Wisdom factors little into powers from beyond the Mortal Realm. Every use of the Art comes with risk—every time you pierce the Veil, you might lose yourself. Even after you bind a spirit and gain its power, using that power gives over more and more of yourself to the spirit. The wise sorcerer uses the Art as the last resort, not the first. It is, however, better to *have* a last resort to call upon in desperate extremes." She placed a reassuring hand on his wrist. "Now. Do you remember the words?"

Words of a bargain, a pact to make with the unknown, spoken in language that meant naught to him and every-thing to vaettir. He would call out names of fell vaettir. To name a thing was to evoke it. Even common men knew that much, or thought they did. Still they invoked the name of Hel in feeble curses, not realizing the goddess—there is none greater—might actually catch it. She was not always listening, but she might be, and only a fool would invite the eye of the Queen of Mist to fall upon him.

His breath came in rapid, irregular pants. He pressed his palms together. Steady. He could do this. Hel commanded it. He must become like the Niflungar. He would gain their power, and then he might lead them in battle, help them reclaim their rightful place as rulers of …

The door crashed open, and a man strode in. He bore a

sword at his side, though he placed no hand on it. With a single glance, he took in everything.

Gudrun rose. "This is an evocation chamber, brother. You know better than to barge in like that."

"No incanting—you had not started."

The princess frowned. "I take it Grimhild has returned."

"Mother will see you. Both of you."

She looked to Odin, working her jaw with some unknown emotion. Brother. Her elder brother, then, Guthorm. The man's resemblance to Gudrun was undeniable. Blond hair just like hers was bound at the nape of his neck, and they had the same pale blue eyes.

Gudrun avoided speaking of her mother. She feared the woman. So what now, would Queen Grimhild want of Odin?

THEY MET the queen in a throne room Odin had not realized Castle Niflung even had. Two thrones sat in the back of a long, mist-shrouded hall, though Gjuki's sat empty. Grimhild, however, looked like part of hers. It shimmered, like black ice, multispined spikes jutting from the back of it. The armrests looked like onyx, carved in the shape of skulls, and the queen herself wore a skull mask—though too large to be a human skull. A troll's, perhaps.

Guthorm stood off to the side, but otherwise, the queen had no guards. A woman possessed of extreme confidence, at least within her own castle.

Gudrun, on the other hand, stood rigid at Odin's side, so stiff she seemed apt to shatter. Her only movement the slow grinding of her teeth. He meant to pat her on the shoulder, reassure her, but somehow found himself not quite able to move while Grimhild silently inspected him.

After a prolonged pause, the queen leaned forward, hands on the armrests. Those skulls had ruby eyes, gleaming. "Has he become one of us?"

"He ... would have. We were in the process of evocation when you returned."

"Long as you've had, and that is all you have achieved?" Grimhild cocked her head ever so slightly. "A disappointment, I'm afraid."

Gudrun managed to grow even stiffer in posture.

"You speak harshly to your own kin," Odin said.

"Odin," Gudrun whispered through gritted teeth.

The queen rose, looking at him now. As she stood, she pulled off the mask, revealing a smooth face beneath. She looked but a few winters older than her daughter, a woman in her prime and so radiant in beauty he could not look away from her eyes.

She drifted toward him as if floating on the mist, at once motions of fluid grace and immeasurable sensuality that caused a sudden swelling in his trousers. He knew he stood there, eyes and mouth wide, but he could not move. Not as she drifted ever closer. Not as she stroked a finger along the line of his jaw.

"You will love me." Her voice sounded off, echoing against his skull in low, pulsing tones.

"I ... I ..."

His hands shook. He loved Gudrun, not this woman.

"You will love me and serve me until the end of your days. And beyond ..." It came out as a whisper that rang inside his head with the force of a peal of thunder. Of a lightning strike.

Odin gasped, struggling to breathe. He loved her, the beautiful queen. He loved ... Gudrun ... his princess who he ...

He shook himself. "I ... I ..."

Married? Was he not married already? To Gudrun?

No. No he had married someone else.

He groaned, backed away, clutching his head. So many voices ringing out, pounding against his temples. Laying claim to him.

*Love me.*

*Serve me.*

*Love me.*

*Serve me.*

*Love me.*

"Your Art is interfering with the brew I gave him."

"Fool child. Were your sway half so strong as you think, you would have had naught to fear."

Odin had fallen to his knees. Where was he? Who was speaking? He needed to rise, to do ... something. What had he come here to do?

"My own Art has done well enough thus far. Odin is mine. Must you truly claim everything?"

"Daughter. You—"

"Please. Let me do this. Let me have *this* one damned thing for myself."

Silence lingered a moment. Odin struggled to rise, to shake himself free.

"I must ride for Hunaland very soon. Dear Volsung needs my attention. When I return, you had best have swayed him fully. Fail in this, and you will regret it, daughter. You will force me to take more than one barbarian man from you."

Odin staggered to his feet. "M-my wife ...?"

Gudrun seized his cheeks and kissed him hard, with such hot passion all thought fled from his mind. "Come," she said at last. "You must be thirsty. Let us have some mead."

Mead. Yes. He needed mead to clear his head.

# PART IV

Sixth Moon

## 43

*G*udrun lay in their bed, asleep and naked beside Odin. He stroked her hair.

Was this love? This was what he'd been missing with his wife. Odin shook himself. Wife? Where had that thought come from? He wasn't married.

He was meant for Gudrun alone. He should marry *her*. This very day he'd ask her father for her hand. The Raven Lord was powerful, a true king. Except ... except ... Hadn't there been something wrong with him?

He'd being praying ... to Hel—there was none greater.

A sourness rose in his stomach. He needed mead. He reached for the goblet that always sat by their bed. It felt cold to his touch, chilled. He wanted to drink.

But somehow, the thought of that burning liquid just made his stomach turn again.

He shook his head and rose, trying to make no sound as he pulled on his trousers.

Hel—there was none greater—there was something about her. Something he needed to remember. She was queen of the underworld. She'd brought the mists of Niflheim. She'd given their power to the Niflungar, allies of Odin's people. And the mists …

Hel, none greater, had brought them … five thousand years ago … Idunn's grandparents had fought her. Why would they fight Hel? The woman, Idunn, haunted his vision. Beautiful, with exotic, rich skin. Was she not an ally to his people? She'd given him Gungnir, the spear that had rested in the corner of his room for … moons. How long had he been here?

Odin shook himself, then turned back to Gudrun. She'd taught him so many things. Secrets of the World, though he had trouble focusing on them. He could see into the Penumbra now, he had the Sight.

Something was wrong.

He'd come here to find the Singasteinn … because he'd promised the ghost. The ghost who had cursed Odin, who had … Ve! Son of a troll-fucking whore! Odin spun, his fists clenching at his side, taking in the woman in his bed.

No. Not his bed. His wife lay alone in his bed. This was the sorceress's room.

And it wasn't love. It was sorcery. Gudrun had literally enchanted him. She must have. He'd heard völva could do such things. And the mead … a love potion?

The conniving bitch had seduced him with flesh and foul Art drawn from Hel.

But … her words were clearly the truth. She could give him everything. The Niflungar and the Aesir together might well rule Midgard. Was that what Gjuki intended? Was that reason enough for him to throw his daughter in Odin's path? The sorcerer might have sought more than this frozen kingdom at the edge of Midgard. And Odin could give it to him—together, they could take everything, conquer all the North Realms and beyond.

Odin shook his head again. Whatever they intended mattered naught. They'd bewitched him, used him. Perhaps Gudrun *could* break the curse the ghost had placed on Odin, but that was not enough. Because Odin would live for eternity knowing he had broken his oath and sacrificed his honor. And Ve, gods! Ve! Odin would save his brother himself, without relying on such people. How easily he forgot Heidr's lessons. Gudrun's help would have had a price, too. Everything did.

He'd almost let himself fall for her. And for what? An enchantress who had worked her Art on him. A people who worshipped Hel herself. Hel—there was none ... No! Gods above and below, Hel had *done* this to the World. She was a queen of nightmares, an enemy to Mankind. His enemy!

He clutched his head. The sorceress's seid beat at his temples, demanding he return to her bed. To deny it felt like ripping his own skin off. Odin had to be gone from this place before his mind fell under Gudrun's spells again.

He donned his tunic and stood over Gudrun. She still wore the Singasteinn as well as her golden headband. And to look on her there, barely stirring in the depths of some dream ... was it more than lust? He could spend eternity by this woman's side. His heart sped at that thought. He could do it, but for the price of his honor. And his brother's soul. Or maybe it was her magic, still working at his mind, trying to draw him back. He barely stifled his groan.

Maybe the apple had given him resistance to her powers. Maybe any mortal would have been helpless in her thrall. Or maybe even the brief respite from her potion had been enough to clear his thoughts. But fuck, did he want this woman. And for that, he loathed her almost as much as he hated himself.

Odin clenched his teeth. He had to return that amulet.

Not much time remained, of that he was certain. The Odling ghost would lay her curse upon him if he did not move from here.

Gingerly he unclasped the amulet from Gudrun's neck, careful not to wake her. Despite himself, he planted a light kiss on her forehead. "I'm sorry."

Odin hated this bitch. And loved her.

Perhaps he'd never untangle the truth of his heart, the truth of whether his feelings were real or the results of her power ... Every moment he stayed increased the temptation to crawl back into that bed. He knelt to retrieve his spear—for moons he'd let his ancestral weapon lie on the floor, as if it were naught but common iron. What shame he'd brought to it. And to his father—perhaps one of the shades looking on Odin—languishing in despair at the failure of his son.

Shaking his head, Odin slipped out of the room. Back on the landing, he slid the door closed and backed into a man waiting there.

"My lord?" the man asked. "Was there something you needed?"

"I, uh ... just some food. I'm famished." If the man had been waiting in the hall, he'd no doubt heard all that had gone on the night before—all the nights before—and couldn't help but believe that.

The Niflung, a man dressed finely and armed with a short sword at his side, nodded at first. Then his eyes drifted to the amulet clutched in Odin's left hand. "Very good, my lord. I'll just check with her ladyship to see what I should arrange."

"She's sleeping. You don't want to wake her."

The man took a step toward the door. "I'm afraid I—"

Odin slammed his fist into the man's gut. Before the servant could even double over, Odin grabbed him and wrapped his hand around the poor bastard's mouth and nose. The servant flailed, clawing at Odin's arm with his nails. Odin just tightened his grip, drawing the man down to the floor. A few heartbeats and those struggles lessened until the man slumped into unconsciousness.

Odin shook his head.

Fuck.

There would be more servants down there. Guards, sorcerers ... and Gjuki. Odin would never make it past all of them if they were intent on stopping him. And if they tried, he'd be forced to kill them. Maybe a lot of them. These people didn't deserve his slaughter. Despite the seduction and sorcery, they had done naught to physically harm him. He could not repay their hospitality with violence any more than he could remain and break his oath to the ghost or abandon his brother.

"Odin?" Gudrun called from behind the door.

He could go back in there. Stay.

And lose himself forever.

And gods, would he have wanted that. Part of him still did.

Instead he turned to the window. Eight stories down and then icy rapids. But he was immortal. Maybe he could survive such a fall. And it might be the only way to avoid killing these people. Odin started for the window when Gudrun's door opened.

"What are you doing?" she demanded. "Stop." Her voice dropped in pitch. "Stop!"

It echoed in his mind. He should listen to her. Remain. Be the man she needed ... He flung himself out the window before he could think more. Icy wind stripped away whatever words Gudrun shouted after him. The air tugged at his clothes and stole his breath. And then he plunged into the river.

A shock like a bolt of lightning shot through his body. All thought fled, and he barely held on to the amulet and his spear. The current slammed him against a rock. Breath exploded from his lungs, and his vision blurred.

Don't let go.

Do not let go.

He could lose neither Gungnir nor the Singasteinn.

Another rock slapped him in the shoulder.

Then he was falling again. He sucked in another lungful of air as he pitched over the waterfall, finding himself with just enough time to realize it was a fuck of a lot taller than he'd thought.

The Morimarusa slammed into him like solid rock.

He sank beneath the waves, mind swirling and unable to focus. His legs were surely broken, though it should have hurt more. The cold was too much. He was going to drown.

The thought cut through his rapidly numbing mind and body.

His immortality would mean naught when he was drawn beneath the sea, caught in the net of Rán. Perhaps he would rise as a draug, hatred fueling him with a desire to consume those he once loved.

His legs wouldn't work. He swam toward the shore, his strokes clumsy and growing slower. For a moment he managed to get his head above water, sucking in a single breath before he sank again. This was how it would end …

Something bit his shoulder, jerked him toward the land.

A rough tongue grazed over his eyes. Odin gagged, sputtering up water. Sleipnir stood above him, scuffing the icy ground with his hooves.

The horse had pulled him from the sea? That was impossible. No horse could do such a thing.

But Sleipnir was so much more than just a horse. Where had the horse been? Hiding from the Niflungar?

He tried to speak, to offer thanks, but his throat only rasped. Sleipnir knelt beside him, insisting he mount.

Yes. They'd be coming for him.

In the sky above, a raven circled once before flying back toward the castle.

Gjuki's little spies.

A gasp of pain escaped him as he pulled himself onto Sleipnir's back. His legs were broken. He was certain now. And that should have hurt more than this. His body trembled. Could an immortal die of deathchill? If so, he surely would. He'd seen the toughest warriors in the World brought low by the cold, especially when wet. They would lose fingers, toes—lose their lives.

Sleipnir took off, running across the sea the moment Odin had managed to mount. Odin slipped the amulet around his neck and tucked Gungnir across his lap. He needed sleep. He needed to rest.

Rest.

Except a man dying of the cold had to stay awake. Odin bit his tongue, trying to focus his thoughts and remain alert. Sleipnir's ride across the sea had become a dream. He'd lost any sense of time, but whenever he looked up, he saw a raven above. Following.

Gjuki would know. The Niflung king would know Odin's every move.

A sickness welled in the pit of his stomach. Gods, he had made a terrible enemy, hadn't he? In trying to hold to his honor, he'd no doubt deeply offended Gjuki's.

Mists swelled up before Sleipnir, taking the shape of a

serpentine head. A dragon. Sleipnir jerked violently to the side, changing directions to avoid the apparition. Seawater splashed up under his hooves, further soaking Odin.

Fire.

Fire would keep the mists away and let Odin warm himself. If he wasn't dead yet, he should heal. The apple had made him that way, at least. He suspected he'd recover from aught that didn't kill him. The thought left him both slightly comforted, as Sleipnir sped toward the shore, and unsettled.

A wall of mist seemed to harden before them, cutting off passage to the shore. Sleipnir leapt into the sky, soaring over the wall and kept running. He was fast, maybe faster than the damned ravens. But the speed only served to further chill Odin to the bone.

"Fire," he mumbled to the horse.

While it was unlikely the animal could start a fire, if he could understand Odin's need for it, maybe he could find a place.

Sleipnir snorted and galloped toward the village they'd passed through on the way here. The people there, even if they couldn't understand him, would surely see a man in need and offer hospitality. But they scattered like the wind as Sleipnir approached. One man rushed inside a house, slamming the door.

A monstrous horse might have some disadvantages, too.

"Please," Odin croaked. "Fire."

No one answered.

Sleipnir trotted up to a hut with a smoking chimney. Odin grunted. The horse was right, as usual. He needed warmth to survive, and if it frightened these people, they would have to live with that. Sleipnir kicked the door. When no one opened it, the horse kicked it again, this time hard enough to make the frame shudder.

Odin climbed off the horse, then slumped to the ground. A fresh agony shot through his legs the moment he put pressure on them. Maybe that was a good sign.

"Please. Help me." The words meant naught. If the people inside heard his tone, though, it might move them.

At last a man opened the door and stared down at him. The foreigner had blond hair past his shoulders, a thick beard, and a long mustache. He looked upon Odin's bedraggled form with a hint of wary sympathy in his eyes.

Odin pantomimed rubbing his hands together and warming them on a fire.

The man eyed the horse with fear, then Sleipnir backed away.

Odin patted his leg to indicate it was broken.

When Sleipnir had backed out of sight, the foreigner helped Odin up, supporting Odin's weight on his shoulder. The hut was small, and a woman, plump with child, already sat by the fire, another little girl clinging to her skirts. Both backed away as the husband deposited Odin on the floor by the fire.

The man opened a trunk and pulled from it a dry cloak. He tossed it at Odin, then spoke to his family, who scampered into a room divided from this one by a fur curtain.

"Change my clothes?" Odin nodded and pulled his wet garments off. They clung to him like a second skin, sealing in the chill. His teeth chattered.

The man was shorter than Odin, so the trousers and tunic he offered fit much too snugly. But they were far better than Odin's freezing garb. The man called out for his wife, and she came and hung the wet clothes on a rod before the fire.

Odin shut his eyes, soaking in the delicious warmth of the fireplace. Just a short respite. A reprieve before the fury of the Raven Lord sought him out and sought to strangle him for his temerity. Gjuki would send Odin's soul screamed down to Hel that the goddess might draw out his suffering for eternity. A punishment for rejecting the all-powerful queen of death.

Odin had left behind foes more powerful than any people he had before encountered. And they would hunt him. Soon.

## 44

The whole of the Godwulf camp rustled. Bristling with the energy. Tyr knew it, when battle drew nigh. They were eager, almost ready to move. To march on Halfhaugr. Tyr had come here to stop a war. And found war underway without him.

But Alci had not turned him away either. Had even allowed him to call on Agilaz, who stayed with Alci's thegn Hoenir. No one had truly welcomed him. Not Agilaz, thegn to a jarl whom Odin had alienated. Not Hoenir or his daughter Syn, a shieldmaiden awaiting the return of her husband. And perhaps least of all Hallr. The bastard stared at him with open distrust.

The traitor to his own jarl. Man ought to hang from a tree instead of sit around a fire pit with them. Talking of treason and murder. Maybe they all ought to hang, Tyr included.

"Hadding will never surrender Halfhaugr," Agilaz said.

Syn scoffed. "Doubt Alci expects him to. He sent Hermod as a pretense."

"That means war is inevitable," Tyr said.

Hallr shook his head. "Not if we kill Alci. I've been sending messages back to Jarl Annar. He will agree to strike, give us a distraction."

Tyr scowled. "So you'd rather start a war with the Athra." With Odin's cousin, who already supported Odin.

"Just long enough to give me the chance to end Alci."

Tyr spat. "You want to assassinate your own lord."

Hallr just shrugged. "Only way to become jarl."

Tyr barely resisted the urge to seize the man. "Other than a proper challenge."

"No one beats Alci in a fair fight."

Then none of these people *deserved* to be jarl. "So I'll challenge him."

Hoenir sighed and rubbed his temples. "We all know your prowess, Tyr, but you have no claim to leadership in this tribe. Only a thegn of the Godwulfs can become the next jarl."

Syn rose with a huff. "And what of you, Father?"

"I'm too old to take down Alci, even by surprise." And probably too honorable to try. Hoenir would make a damned sight better choice than Hallr. But he was human. As a varulf, at least Hallr had a chance.

"Very true," the traitor said. "It has to be me. And as soon as your husband returns, dear Syn, Alci will order the march on Halfhaugr. Assuming he even waits that long. We all know Hadding will tell his brother to go to Hel. So, if we want to do this, I need to send word to the Athra. *Now*. They must attack before the chance is lost."

This is what he had been reduced to. In all his years of service of Hymir, Tyr had never plotted assassination. He had done murder more oft than he cared to remember. Had pillaged and razed and raped his way across Aujum and

Bjarmaland. Under the tutelage of an incarnation of chaos. But he had not schemed. Not as he now did for Odin.

For a throne the man did not truly want.

Tyr growled, drawing stares from the others. Let them look. Let the fucking traitor look upon Tyr. Who, by agreeing to this, became no better himself.

Tyr. Champion of a jotunn. Champion of Borr. Champion of Odin.

Assassin.

Plotter.

Schemer.

Wretch.

Was Borr's legacy worth so very much? Borr had saved Tyr from the darkness. And to honor the man, Tyr descended back into that mire. Covered himself in muck, so he could hold Borr's son up above it all.

He spat. "Just get it done."

## 45

*S*igyn's sister stayed so often alone in the moons since Odin had left. Publicly scorned, shamed by her new husband, perhaps Frigg feared to show her face. No —that wasn't like her. She doubted Frigg's dignity would allow that. It was worse, Sigyn suspected. Her half sister was actually hurt by Odin's rejection.

When Sigyn knocked on Frigg's chamber door, there was a slight pause before she called for her to enter. Most people would never have caught the reddening around her sister's eyes, so faint in the dim light of the brazier. But Sigyn's eyes were too sharp now. Frigg had been *weeping*. Gods. *Frigg,* of all people. That bastard was lucky he wasn't here, else Sigyn would have found a way to shame him so completely he'd be the one hiding in his chambers.

Her sister sat on the floor, herbalist instruments in front of her. Weeds and plants no doubt intended for one völva ritual or another. Or perhaps to dull the pain of a broken heart by enveloping the mind in haze.

"What happened?"

"Naught, Sister. I was just preparing a poultice for the hunters."

"And the fumes stung your eyes?"

Frigg sighed, then pushed away the poultice bowl in front of her. "There are times one can be too perceptive, Sigyn."

"Why let him discomfit you so?"

"Lord Odin is my husband, Sigyn."

"A political alliance. If you want another lover it's not as if he could fault you."

Frigg murmured, shaking her head. "You don't understand."

Sigyn knelt by her side. "I understand you had a vision of you and him ruling together, but then you became infatuated with the vision, not the man. He may well be a future king, but he's also a—"

A bellow that shook the walls echoed, chased by a crunch of splintering wood.

"What in Freyja's name?" Sigyn asked.

Frigg started to rise.

"Stay sheltered!" Sigyn shouted and dashed from the room. Screams rang through the town, and the walls shuddered again. Sigyn raced from the fortress. What could make such sounds?

More bellows echoed, sending shivers down her spine. It must be something out of the mists. The sun had just set, but even so, vaettir attacking the town? It seemed impossible.

She ran to Agilaz's house and snatched up her bow. Her foster father was still with the Godwulfs, and Olrun had gone, taken her sword out to meet this threat.

Sigyn ran outside in time to see men and women scattering around the town square. She needed to see what was happening. She sprinted up the stairs to the wall. The thatched roof of a house below the keep trembled, then exploded upward as a massive form crashed through the wall, flinging debris in all directions. The creature that stumbled through stood over eight feet tall, its hide covered in rocky protrusions and moss. A nose as thick as her wrist dangled from an elongated snout, hanging just past boar-like tusks.

Trolls!

Her father's soldiers launched arrow after arrow at the beast. Most ricocheted off the thick hide as though they'd hit a stone wall. Sigyn launched a shot herself, but it flew wide as the monster burst through another house. An instant later, it came crashing back out, a woman over its shoulder.

Oh Hel. They sought troll wives.

A man chased out of the house after the beast, pounding ineffectively against the troll's back with an axe. The troll spun, a sweep of its massive hand sending the poor man crashing back through the walls of his house.

Again and again Sigyn loosed arrows at the monster. A few stuck in its hide, barely slowing its rampage. Another troll stomped into view, a woman slung over one shoulder and a sheep tucked under the other arm. With one foot, it kicked a hunter who charged it. The poor bastard hurtled back through the air and slammed into a house.

Gods, Sigyn couldn't do this—she was used to hunting deer. Agilaz and Olrun were the warriors. But she had to do something or that woman would be ... She nocked another arrow, this time slowing her breath as she sighted along it. That thick hide covered most of the troll's body. She wouldn't pierce it except by luck—but maybe she could find a spot more lightly armored.

Like the back of the creature's knee. It would be a hard shot on a moving creature, even one of that size. But if she missed, she risked the woman's life. She had one chance. Adjust for the wind, adjust for its movement, its gait awkward but constant ... Sigyn's eyes narrowed, her focus drawing in deeper and deeper until she saw naught else. Was it the power of the apple?

She loosed.

The arrow soared, almost off mark. Almost, but not quite. The creature toppled forward with a shriek, the woman flying from its grasp. She tumbled along the ground through three rolls before being lost in a snowdrift. Sigyn let out a whoop. Several other guards turned to look at her— whether shocked at her impossible shot or her outburst, she didn't care.

The wounded troll pushed itself to its hands and knees, jerking its head around with murder in its eyes. A few warriors advanced on it, clearly not eager to close the distance. The first drew too close—the troll lunged forward. Its claws rent right through the warrior's armor and tore out his guts, flinging them steaming onto the snow.

A woman screamed a war cry, charging the beast. Olrun! The troll tried to turn, but before it did, she had scaled its back. She drove her sword straight down where spine would have met skull, igniting an eruption of ichor that coated her face. The troll stumbled around, flailing wildly and unable to dislodge her. Olrun threw her weight onto the blade and drove it further down until the troll fell to its knees. Then she leaped off it and rolled along the ground.

Well, damn. Her foster mother seemed to have that one well in hand. Ordinary blades couldn't do that. One day, she need to ask about how Olrun had pulled that off.

More bellows sounded from across the village. Sigyn

was no warrior, but she'd tasted the apple of immortality. She would not stand by, so she ran toward the sounds, knowing it was about the stupidest thing she could possibly do. She sprinted around a corner in time to see another troll crush a villager with a single blow. A horse ran from the troll. The monster overtook the animal in three strides and flung it to the ground, then proceeded to jump up and down on the poor beast, shattering bone and flesh.

Another bellow sounded inside the house given to Odin's brothers. Shit, she couldn't leave them. She darted around the troll and burst in through the door.

"Ve!"

A grunt sounded in the corner. Sigyn turned to see red glowing eyes there, as a crouched form rose. The thing that strode forward looked somewhere between a troll and a man. Rocky protrusions had erupted from its face and elbows, though it wore what had been Ve's tunic.

"Oh, gods," Sigyn mumbled, backing away from the creature. Was this even possible? Could a man become …

The troll-man was on her in two strides. Sigyn tried to knock an arrow, but with one hand, it snatched her bow and crushed it, the other grasping her bodice. It ripped it away, the momentum flinging Sigyn right into its arm. She shrieked, pounding the rocky skin with ineffective blows.

The troll-man flung her over its shoulder and trod out into the street. Sigyn hung with her chest against its back, screaming, trying to twist around and reach the dagger at her waist. Its grip was iron, her weight not even slowing the troll.

"Help!"

"Sigyn!" her father shouted.

Hadding wore his mail, as he had not done since she was

a child. Broadsword held in both hands, he rushed toward her.

"Father!"

He swung, connecting with the troll's midsection, drawing forth a roar of pain from the beast. A gout of black blood spurted over his face as he reared back for another swing. The troll was faster. It twisted, slapping him with a claw. The blow sent her father flying through the air. He slammed into a support pillar inside the house, splintering it and continuing onward.

"Father!" Sigyn shrieked.

A bear roared on the other side of the troll. Sigyn never saw the impact, but she was flung free of the troll's grasp and tumbled end over end through the snow. Cuts and bruises stung her arms and chest and back. When she finally pushed herself up again, one arm trying to cover her naked breasts, a bear was grappling with the troll, pummeling it into submission. A berserk. Was that Vili?

Did he realize the troll was his own brother?

Another house exploded as a troll charged straight through it, shoulder-slamming the bear. The troll-man shook itself, glared at the bear for an instant, and then charged off. Sigyn rolled to one side, trying to get out of its line of sight. Instead, it just snatched up the first woman it came upon. She shrieked as it flung her over its shoulder to the position Sigyn had occupied a moment before.

Sigyn saw her face—Fulla.

By instinct she reached for her bow before remembering it had been destroyed.

"Fulla!"

The trolls crashed right through the now-splintered main gate.

Pulling her cloak around herself, Sigyn ran back to

search for her father. There had to be a chance! He couldn't have been gone just like ... The moment she saw his body, back bent nigh in half, head lolling to one side, she knew the truth.

Hadding had been dead the instant the troll struck him.

Unable to form any other thought, Sigyn sank to the ground beside his body, wailing.

*T*he next thing Odin knew, the villager shook him awake. The smell of hot, fishy soup wafted through the house. Of course, this man was probably a fisherman. He pressed a bowl of soup into Odin's hands.

"Gods, thank you," Odin said.

Despite the scorching heat, Odin began to gulp the soup like he would a mug of mead. Its warmth filled his throat and settled his stomach.

The man said something in his foreign tongue and motioned for Odin to slow down.

"Yes, yes." He was right. Take it too fast, and it would just come back up, not tasting nearly as good the second time.

Slowly, he sipped the soup, letting it warm his insides. These people had saved his life. One day he'd find a way to repay that.

A dog barked outside, joined by another, and another. Soon, human shouts followed.

Odin knew the sound of abject terror when he heard it. For a moment, the man turned toward the commotion. When he looked back to Odin, his face had blanched.

A lump formed in Odin's stomach. The Niflungar had come after him. What had he brought down on these people?

"I'm sorry," he said, handing the man the bowl.

The fisherman knocked the bowl aside and shouted, pointing at the door.

"Yes. I'm going. Sleipnir!"

Odin grabbed Gungnir and stumbled to his feet. Throbbing pain ran through his legs, but they had already begun to mend. Walking was torment, but at least possible. He wobbled his way to the door, but he hadn't even reached it before the horse kicked the damned thing in.

If he stayed here, he'd bring Gjuki's wrath down on this village. But even the brief respite they'd given him would be like to save his life. "We ride," Odin said, and pulled himself atop his mount.

Outside, the mist had thickened, engulfing whole houses. Whimpers ushered from some, screams from others. And those mists crept ever closer to Odin. The sorcerers were hurting these people to find him. These innocent fishermen were suffering because of Odin. And he had almost let himself join the Niflungar. No. He'd been right before. These people were not human. They had embraced Niflheim and its dark queen Hel, and in so doing, they had lost themselves.

And if he could, Odin would stay and fight, protect this village. His eyes met those of a raven perched atop a nearby building. Gjuki's scout.

Even if Odin were at full strength, he could not fight an army of men, much less one of sorcerers. The best thing he could do for these people was to be gone from their midst. And thanks to the ravens, at least Gjuki would *know* he was gone.

"Take us home," he said to Sleipnir, never taking his eyes from the raven.

The horse trotted away from the house, then galloped over the hill. Mists swirled after them, trying to box them in. Sleipnir turned with the agility of a snow rabbit, charging down another path.

Odin had been right. He had made himself a powerful enemy.

But then, so had Gjuki.

One day the Raven Lord would pay for what he had wrought here. This Odin swore.

SLEIPNIR RACED THROUGH THE WILDS, the wind tugging at Odin's hair. Perhaps a day they rode, leagues passing as Odin drifting in and out of consciousness, his body struggling to heal from the damage he'd inflicted upon it. Maybe he should have fought his way out. Killed as many of them as he could have.

Or was that the spear's rage filling his mind? The dragon blood that forged it did seem to incite violence.

They must have passed out of Reidgotaland and into Hunaland, but still, many miles stood between him and Aujum.

When he could take no more, he begged Sleipnir to stop. The horse led him to a vale, sheltered from the winds by cliffs that rose up on three sides. He dismounted and slumped against a rock. The pain in his legs had faded to a dull ache. It couldn't have been even two days. Two days to recover from broken legs.

Idunn had made Odin something inhuman. It seemed he could recover in days from any injury. He had strength and stamina beyond mortal man. And now he had the Sight, as Gudrun called it. Odin swallowed hard and shut his eyes. His quest for power, his mission to do as Idunn had asked, was transforming him. He'd wanted to honor his father. Now, Odin was becoming a being his father would not have even recognized. He was becoming a vaettr himself. He was becoming a god. And he'd have given it all up if it meant saving his brother.

But that would accomplish naught. He had to fulfill his oath to the ghost, and then he'd attend to his oath to Idunn.

But given what power had done to the Niflungar, what it had made them, would that become his urd as well? Would he one day ride through a village and torment the common people to achieve his aim? He'd thought he wanted men to fear him. He'd thought that alone might let him face his quest. But that fear, too, would have its price. Just like everything else.

He shut his eyes. The ravens would find him soon. Gjuki might well chase him all the way back to Aujum. Odin would return the Singasteinn to the Odling ghost, break the curse on Ve. Then he would deal with Gjuki. Before that, he had to claim what rest he could.

Dreams—or perhaps visions—haunted his mind. Odin was bombarded by sights of the Penumbra and shades that populated it. Ghosts of the slain, unable to escape to final rest. It was a world filled with the restless dead, like Midgard, a world taken over by the mists of Niflheim. And he had almost let himself be drawn in by their power.

He jolted awake at a hand on his shoulder. He snatched Gungnir and shoved the man away before recognizing Loki.

Odin coughed, clearing his throat. "Should have known Sleipnir wouldn't let anyone else sneak up on me."

"You've been hard to find."

"Brother, I ..." How could he even begin to explain to Loki the things that had happened of late? If anyone could understand, it would be his blood brother. And yet, so much had changed. Most of all Odin himself. He had so many doubts.

"We must make haste back," Loki said. "I have an ill feeling for our people."

---

## 47

*G*udrun glared out the window from which Odin had leapt two days before, as if she might somehow still spot him emerging from the river.

The Singasteinn was the only true gift Grimhild had ever given Gudrun. Wearing it, and speaking the proper incantation, she could take the shape of a seal and swim even in the freezing Morimarusa, freed from the limitations of her mortal form. Grimhild had given her the amulet the first time she had bled as a token of her newfound woman-hood. And Gudrun had spent hours upon hours swimming in the depths, lost in the elation of her seemingly boundless Realm.

On her return, Grimhild had, of course, insisted she lay with a male sorcerer. It was tradition, a means to awaken her Sight and her heritage while inducting her into the Art. Neither the fear nor pain of that bedding had eclipsed the glory of swimming in seal form.

Old scrolls spoke of the Singasteinn in legends, even before it came to the Odlingar kingdom from which Grimhild had stolen it. Some said it was crafted in the mythical mer kingdom of Hiyoya, forged from the souls of finfolk. The finfolk—wereseals—had oft tried to recover the amulet, a few even tracking it to Castle Niflung some years back. They had failed.

No one would take it from her.

Except Odin had done so.

He had stolen it from her. And he had *left* her.

And why in Hel's name did that hurt so much? After all, she had seduced him with a love potion. A little alchemy, a little mead, and a look at her breasts, and he was hers. *Should* have been hers forever.

Gudrun slammed the shutters on her window. Damn it. Damn him! How could he leave her? Was she not enough for the Ás king? Had they not shared something beyond words? He said he loved her. He said he … She rubbed unexpected moisture from her eyes. What in Hel's name was wrong with her?

Her arm ached, a glyph branded there itching. Yes, she had several vaettir bound to her, the most terrible among them a wraith. She could send her out, have the vile creature suck out Odin's soul and leave his corpse a withered husk. And the thief would deserve it!

Except then he'd be dead. And that tasted foul, empty, and bitter.

She should not care so much for the loss of a pawn. That was what pawns were for.

But he wasn't a pawn. Not to her. Maybe not even to Grimhild.

He'd said he loved her.

She clutched the glyph on her arm. Why had he left her? Why?

It had to have been some mistake, some lapse in his judgment. In his time with the Vanr woman, had she also ensorcelled him? If so, perhaps the Vanr's Art had interfered with Gudrun's own. That must be it. Odin loved her; he would not have left her here, alone, unless he felt he had no choice. She just had to show him ... show him the truth. Which was that he need not be her pawn at all. He could be her king. They could rule together one day.

She had to find him, had to bring him back. And a wraith was not the way to do that.

For such a task, she needed someone with more tact and more sympathy than any spirit would show. All beings from beyond the Veil resented Mankind, even the Niflungar. Especially the Niflungar, who enforced their mortal wills upon immortal beings.

In the back of her chamber, a heavy shroud hung on the wall, concealing one more Niflung treasure. One Gudrun did not often care to look upon, despite its uses. She stood before that shroud, running her fingers through its thick, black wool. Coarse. Rough, like what lay beyond. Maids had embroidered it, of course. Naught plain decorated her chamber. Yet she had insisted on black embroidery upon black fabric, on designs intended to avert the eye rather than draw it.

Water was liminal, but sometimes a medium needed something stronger. Something wrought in the darkness of Nidavellir, the land of the dvergar, who had forged such devices of quicksilver in earlier ages when they yet took interest in the Mortal Realm. While they yet reached out from their strongholds, intent on conquest, before the Niflungar drove them into hiding. Before the Lofdar did the same to the Niflungar.

Gudrun yanked the curtain away.

The mirror beyond it gleamed, its surface almost like water. So deep a person could lose herself forever looking into it, as though it might reflect the shattered depths of one's own soul. It so drew the eyes that she had not even noticed the intricate silver border the first time she saw the mirror. Only days later had she been able to examine the dvergar craftsmanship, the rune-adorned dragon framing the quicksilver.

A shudder seized her, and she let it run its course.

Denying such things frightened her was foolish. Because they *should* frighten. The quicksilver would reflect and amplify her own Sight, acting as a focus. It would not, necessarily, show her things she wanted to see. Worse still, it might show her *to* things she did not wish to be seen *by*.

Whispering incantations under her breath, she pressed her palms upon the surface. It was icily cold. Thicker than water, and viscous rather than solid. The chill spread through her hands and arms until her knees shook.

"Odin," she mumbled.

The quicksilver surface shimmered as she jerked her hands away. To anyone else, it would have seemed merely to reflect Gudrun. But for her eyes, Odin rode over snowy hills, mounted upon his monstrous horse. A stranger accompanied him, a man intuition warned her lay steeped in his own secrets, perhaps even versed in the Art. Together they made way back toward Aujum and the Aesir lands.

"Damn it." Hel take that Vanr trench and her sorcery, drawing away Odin from his true home. Gudrun ground her teeth. She needed to stop him from getting back to the Vanr, and now Odin had left her only one recourse to achieve that. "Show me Guthorm."

Though ever his mother's faithful son, Gudrun's brother had, on occasion, shown her affection, even sympathy. Had she been born a man, she might have found Grimhild a more tolerable mother. Such was not her urd. Guthorm walked with steady purpose, mists clinging to his every step. Those were forests in Hunaland, meaning Guthorm had only recently left one of the numerous petty kingdoms south of here. Grimhild had her pawns in nigh every one of those kingdoms in Hunaland and a fair number spread in Valland besides. Not so many in the Aesir lands in Aujum.

Guthorm froze in place, his neck stiff before slowly looking around. An adept sorcerer himself, he sensed her scrying. Which was expected.

"Brother."

He grunted, then turned to the side, walking a short distance until he came to a frozen stream. Guthorm sank to his knees and pushed snow from atop it, revealing the smallest reflection, one that would allow him to see her. She could not pretend to understand quite how this mirror worked, but it did. And the window it opened between places could sometimes reveal both directions.

"Gudrun," he said. Guthorm didn't speak much. He spent most of his time alone, stalking the mists as Grimhild's assassin. Those she could not sway to her cause through bribery, blackmail, or seduction, Grimhild had her son eliminate. A task for which he was exceedingly well suited, even before she had gifted him with a runeblade, one more dverg-forged relic. In truth, a great many of the Niflung treasures came from the Earth spirits, who had a way with metals. They had forged Gramr for the Niflungar in the days of the Old Kingdoms, perhaps as a peace offering, though Gudrun suspected she did not want to know what price they had asked for such creations.

Gudrun worked her jaw, trying to find the right words. Admitting her failure tasted foul. And yet, maybe Guthorm could help her. He could find almost anyone, after all. "Odin took the Singasteinn from me and fled from here, heading in your direction, I think."

Her brother frowned and looked up, as if he might catch sight of the Ás even now.

"I ask you to find him, bring him back to me."

"I will find him. And he will pay for his betrayal."

"No, no ... I want you ..." Her face was falling toward the quicksilver, as if the World had shifted and now the mirror had become *down* and drew her toward it as surely as the ground would. Her hair tumbled toward the shining surface.

Gudrun caught herself on the silver rim with both hands. And still she kept falling inward. Quicksilver shimmered around her, blocking all peripheral vision. Clogging her eyes and ears and mouth and nose. Suffocating, closing around her. In Hel's name!

It wrapped her in its chill embrace. Until all she saw was Grimhild. The queen had an icy beauty, with fair skin and hair like spun gold, all concealed loosely behind a mask of bone. A troll skull she wore when she wanted men—and women—to fear her. And everyone did.

"You failed, daughter."

"No, I—"

"You were to draw Odin to Hel's service. Not only did he leave, he took from you a treasure of the Niflungar. We do not part with our treasures, Gudrun. We do not let others take them. And so where you failed, your brother will succeed. Odin's soul will be sent screaming to the gates of Hel."

She was going to send him to kill Odin. That wasn't what Gudrun wanted at all. Odin had said he loved her. He had said ... He was supposed to be her king. "You don't have to—"

"Fear not, daughter. I will deal with you on my return. Until then, think on your failure."

A force slapped her across the face, severing the connection and sending her reeling.

Gudrun crashed down onto her chamber floor. She lay there, head spinning, trying to catch her breath. Hel take Grimhild. Guthorm would never dare disobey his mother—no one dared disobey her. And that meant Odin was a dead man.

## 48

*H*ermod had returned.

And the Godwulfs marched to war. Marched, or rather rushed forward. A horde of men and werewolves. Slavering for blood.

Ready for a slaughter.

But not for their own. The Athra attacked from upwind, raining arrows upon the Godwulfs. Daylight attack. They had to win before the sun set or the Godwulfs would tear them to pieces.

Sword in hand, Tyr watched the unfolding carnage. Alci had arrested Agilaz and Hermod, but Tyr was neutral. Or so the jarl thought. Perhaps Alci had hoped Agilaz would resist and give him an excuse to murder the man. The thegn had not, forcing Alci to hold him for trial at the Thing. If Alci took Halfhaugr, he'd be like to execute Agilaz and maybe Hermod as well.

Tyr couldn't let that happen, but they had a plan.

And so Tyr stood by. Let men die on both sides. Waiting for his moment. Waiting to give Hallr a moment.

Blood and screams. Guts and shit spilled on the snow.

All so much like his days under Hymir. Carnage a jotunn would have loved. All a reminder of the man Borr had saved him from becoming. But urd was cruel. Drew a man back no matter how hard he fled.

Alci bodily flung one man into another. Grabbed a spear and impaled them both. Still strong, even in human form.

And Hallr did not strike. Drew closer to Alci, yes, but did not strike. Looked to Tyr, looked to Alci's nearby champions. A pair of varulfur nigh as tall as Vili. Big bastards, with a vicious streak. One of those champions hewed through an Athra shieldmaiden's skull with an axe.

Tyr hefted his shield. Only one choice then. Forward.

Roaring, he charged into the fray. Right at the champion who'd slain the woman. The man balked, as if not sure of Tyr's intention.

Raised sword and war cry ought to have told him that.

Tyr feinted left, then swung low. The varulf got his shield down an instant before Tyr would have claimed his kneecap. Tyr jerked out of the way of that axe, swung again. Chips and splinters broke off the shield. The varulf hesitated.

Didn't expect a human to match his speed, his strength.

Tyr whipped his own shield forward, shoved it into the man. The varulf pitched backward a step. Tyr caught him with an upswing of the blade. Shattered his chin, tore through his nose. Showered himself in blood.

The other champion bellowed, charging Tyr as his brother fell.

Tyr spared Alci a glance. The jarl had felled a half dozen warriors on his own. Men, shieldmaidens, their corpses decorated his feet. He laughed, awash in blood.

Grimacing, Tyr met the charging champion, rushed forward himself. The man leapt in the air. Intent on bearing him down with sheer weight and momentum. Tyr rolled under him and twisted around. Launched himself forward and smashed his shield into the varulf's face. Bastard fell. Dazed.

Tyr dropped down on him knees first, drove his blade through the man's throat. A geyser of hot blood sprayed in his eyes. He jerked his sword free. Turned to Alci.

Another warrior rushed him. Tyr blocked a blow on his shield, whipped his sword around. It sheared through the man's face.

Jarl Alci shrieked at him, mindless with rage. Batting aside Athra warriors like they were made of straw. So. Tyr would kill him after all. Maybe he had no claim to jarldom of the Godwulfs. He would still end this varulf, here, now.

Alci tossed aside his shield to pick up an axe. Sword and axe together. Very aggressive. Dangerous.

Tyr gave ground as Alci launched a wild flurry of attacks at him. The axe embedded in Tyr's shield. Alci jerked it back, splintering the shield in the process. Tyr swung his sword, but Alci's move threw him off balance. The jarl easily parried. Turned to riposte. Tyr twisted, tried to dodge, but the blade bit his shoulder, scraped off his mail. Tyr fell to one knee from the impact.

He flung the tattered remains of his shield at Alci's face. The varulf batted it away with his axe, but it gave Tyr a breath. Time to rise, fall back.

"Greatest warrior of the Aesir?" Alci spat. "I'm glad you betrayed us. Gives me an excuse to crush your legend."

"You die today."

Alci chuckled. Advanced, sword out front, axe high. Ready to strike.

Hallr caught Tyr's eye. Readied a spear. Tyr shook his

head. Alci was his now. Urd had brought him here. And he would finish this himself.

Alci charged again. Tyr parried aside the sword. The axe whooshed by his face, almost took off his nose. He swung, scored a nick on Alci's sword arm. The man barely seemed to notice. Again he swung. Tyr parried.

Then Hallr's spear burst through his lord's chest. The traitor hefted Alci up, into the air. Planted the butt of the spear in the snow. His jarl flailed, dying. Blood running down his lip.

The traitor nodded at Tyr. He bent to pick up Alci's sword and raised it in the air. Ready to declare himself jarl of the Godwulfs.

They had done it.

Tyr growled. And he swept his sword up in an arc that lopped Hallr's head right off his shoulders.

The body tumbled down like a doll.

Tyr spit on the corpse as it stained the snow crimson.

Hoenir stood amongst his people, arms held high. Many fires burned, ward flames and pyres alike. Pyres for the Godwulf jarl. For half his thegns.

Some other thegns yet lived, might have challenged Hoenir's claim to the jarldom. Might have.

Hermod strode to his father-in-law's side. "Jarl Hoenir, on behalf of my father, thegn to Hadding, I offer you the support and friendship of the Hasding tribe."

The old man clasped his son-in-law's arm, then nodded at Agilaz, who stood apart from the Godwulf people.

A few more days, and Halfhaugr would have fallen under siege from these people. Now they offered friendship.

What else could they do? They needed a friend among the Godwulfs. And now, Hermod's marriage might actually mean something. But Odin needed these people as well.

Tyr looked to Annar, nodded, and they both strode forward.

"On behalf of Jarl Odin of the Wodanar, I offer my support," Tyr said.

Annar stood beside him. "And as jarl of the Athra, I offer mine."

A message. A warning to any of Alci's former thegns. Three other tribes now stood behind Hoenir.

Maybe the old man could hold his place. Hermod would help him, without doubt. And because of Tyr, they would both owe Odin.

Because Tyr had embraced assassination. Betrayal. Murder.

He strode away from the fires, out into the night. Some would celebrate. Some would mourn.

Tyr had the stomach for neither. Was this truly what Borr would have wanted? Back in Halfhaugr, Idunn waited, urging Odin to become king of the Aesir. To guide them all to a better future. Like this? Through blood and treachery?

Men became no better than jotunnar.

Someone chased after him, footfalls crunching the snow as he ran. Hermod drew up short as Tyr turned, glowering.

"Your wife must be pleased."

Hermod nodded. "She just became daughter of the jarl."

"And we murdered a great many men to make that happen."

"Neither of us has to like this road, Tyr. But we did what we had to, what men like Alci and Hallr forced upon us. Neither one of them deserved to rule."

Did Odin? The eldest son, the heir of Borr. Tyr cracked

his neck and groaned. For Odin, Tyr had become a monster once more. For the son of Borr, he had cast aside the honor and teachings of Borr.

Tyr advanced on Hermod until he stood close enough to feel the man's breath. "Very soon, Odin will call for the Althing. He will seek kingship of all the tribes."

"My sister thought as much. First king since Vingethor …"

Sigyn was too clever. Much like her lover.

"You and your father-in-law will support his claim." Tyr's fist clenched, daring the man to deny it.

But Hermod did not deny it. He bowed his head. "You saved us all from war. Odin may count on us."

At last, something turning his way. "Ride back to Halfhaugr with me. Tell Odin yourself. And convince your gods-damned sister to agree. She has the ear of Frigg and Hadding." Tyr raised a finger in warning. "It is best for all."

Hermod murmured something under his breath.

"What?"

"I hope you're right."

By all the gods, so did Tyr.

## 49

*O*ut over the river, the boat carrying Hadding's body burned, lighting the night with an eerie glow. Sigyn stood apart from her half sister, who watched from the shore alone, the wind flapping her dress about her legs. Ice had built inside Sigyn's chest—a cold ache that naught seemed to fill. And though she knew Frigg probably needed her, Sigyn had not been able to comfort her sister, nor even to speak.

Her father was gone.

And he had died saving *her*. The daughter Sigyn would have sworn he cared less than *naught* for. Her whole life she'd thought herself a burden to him, a reminder of an indiscretion that was like to sour his marriage bed, and later, a child too willful to find a husband or do her family proud.

And when she was in danger, her father—old, crippled, and in pain though he was—had rushed out like a man half his age, glorious and valiant in a fight he'd known he could not win. Her father had died for her.

A tear streaked her cheek.

She'd thought she knew everything. She'd thought she was so good at reading people, so godsdamned clever. So how had she missed something so very basic? Had he ... loved her? The father who had never favored her with even a smile had not hesitated a moment to attack a troll for his daughter.

The dozen small fires in the boat grew into one mighty conflagration. The river would carry her father's ashes far away, and maybe—if all the other stories proved true—maybe valkyries would take his soul to Valhalla. For such a death, he deserved to feast alongside his ancestors, rather than rot beneath the heel of Hel.

If Odin had given her father an apple, would he still live? Perhaps not. Perhaps naught would have let him survive such injuries, but they would never know, and Frigg was never like to forgive her husband for denying her that.

Sigyn could not blink as the boat vanished into the mist. Her father had vanished with it, gone forever, taken from her before she had ever known him. And with his departure, she could now never ask him the truth of his heart, the truth she had so long feared.

The Wodan warriors stood apart from the Hasdingi. It would fall to Frigg now, deciding whether the alliance would hold. Odin's people had fought with valor against the trolls, and many who lived today owed them their lives. If not for those warriors, many women—Sigyn included—would now be troll-wives, ensnared in a fate worse than death.

But then, those trolls had come for Ve, of that Sigyn no longer had any doubt, even if she would not share the thought with others. The trolls had come for one of their own. It would be too much a coincidence for the creatures to attack the town after years of silence, on the same day Ve became one of them, if they had not somehow known. The implications were disturbing, and severely so. Did that mean all trolls had once been human? Were they now possessed by vaettir, or were they something else, something corrupted by the mists themselves? Or ... were some trolls created as such, and others born of troll-wives?

She wanted to hate Odin and his brothers for all that had happened. Maybe part of her did, though it almost meant hating his blood brother Loki as well, and that man had been the best thing in her life. He was the one person she'd found who could truly understand her, match wits with her, and more, be grateful for it. Perhaps Ve was the victim here as much as the rest of them. And if Frigg's vision was true, and Odin's quest was something more than a madman playing god ... then could the mists be banished? Could the World know the true spring of children's stories? Could these men-turned-trolls be saved?

Sigyn thought she loved mysteries. Now she just wanted some answers. None lay on the riverbank. She hugged herself and went to her sister, taking Frigg's limp hand to lead her away.

Neither spoke.

❧

THE PROCESSION HAD MARCHED through the town and back to the fortress. The now-silent great hall where once her father had ruled.

For a time, Frigg stared at her father's throne. Then she sat in it. A murmur rose among those in the hall at her presumption. And yet none rose to challenge her. She looked every bit the queen.

"Our people have been taken by trolls," Frigg said at last. "Who will go to rescue them?"

"Go to the Jarnvid?" someone asked. "That's suicide. Not even the Godwulfs venture within."

Tyr strode forward. "I will go, my lady." He and Hermod had returned only this very morn, while her foster father had remained to help ease Jarl Hoenir's first days as ruler.

Odin's brother Vili joined him a moment later. "And I."

"And I." Odin's voice boomed through the hall from where he stood at its threshold.

Frigg rose from the throne at his entrance. Then Sigyn noticed Loki in the shadows behind Odin, watching her.

She drifted from Frigg's side to meet Loki, even as Odin approached to converse with his wife.

"I should never have left you alone," Loki said.

"Did you know about Ve?"

"Yes."

Son of a troll. She raised her hands to slap him, though he didn't flinch. "You don't think that was something I should have known?"

"Perhaps. I'd hoped to have more time ... Things are progressing more quickly than I anticipated."

What in Freyja's name? "Well, *that's* a shame. Does it bother you that I was almost raped by a fucking troll?" Others turned toward them at her outburst.

In answer, Loki placed a palm against her cheek, his eyes pained. "That would not have happened."

"If we're going to spend eternity together, you'd better start trusting me!"

"Sigyn, I—"

She silenced him with a finger pointed at his nose. "Don't think this is over, either." She spun on her heel to stalk back to Odin and Frigg, even as she realized what she'd just said. Eternity. Even angry as she was, she could not imagine spending forever with anyone save Loki, and perhaps that boded well for their future. That thought made her boil even more inside. Damn him. He deserved her anger, and she was *not* going to let it go because of some warm coziness he managed to engender inside her.

She found Odin and Frigg leaning into one another, whispering in tones no one should have been able to hear. Yet Sigyn caught their words, her ears seeming to filter out the rest of the noise of the hall.

"I'm sorry," Odin was saying.

"My father is still dead, husband. And where have you been?"

"I was ... detained."

"Detained? Is that what you will tell our child, Odin? You failed to save his grandfather because you were *detained*?"

"Our ... child?"

Frigg pulled his hand by one finger, placing it over her abdomen, her face grim.

"You mean the child we will one day have?"

She shook her head. "It's a boy. A völva knows these things. We will have a son. What kind of father will you be?"

Sigyn tapped her finger on her lip. That explained Frigg's earlier emotional state. To carry Odin's child while he'd ridden off in anger .... She hoped never to face such a situation. And how keen her ears had grown. Would she one day be able to track scents like a wolf? See in the dark? The possibilities seemed so intoxicatingly endless she felt giddy.

"I will be a father our son can be proud of," Odin said at last, his voice sounding hoarse.

Frigg leaned closer still. "I will *never* let you forget that

[350]350350350350350350350350350350

promise, husband. You've failed your family once. You will not do so again."

To Sigyn's surprise, Odin didn't challenge her claim, instead nodding with utmost sincerity. "This I swear." Then he spun and strode down the hall. "We ride for the Jarnvid! We ride to save our people!"

$\mathcal{N}$o words escaped over the lump that rose in Odin's throat as he rode toward the Jarnvid. A son. His own child. Frigg was right. This child would hear tales of all Odin had done in his life, the good and the bad. And his son would know the World through those deeds even as he would learn right from wrong by lessons Odin never intentionally set out to teach. The boy would learn honor, as Odin's father had tried to teach his own sons. Odin's son would be worthy of the line of Borr.

A grandson Borr would not see, unless he looked down from Valhalla. Odin prayed he did.

And Odin hoped his son would learn to be a better husband than Odin himself had been. He had betrayed Frigg, and he would have to live with that, though the knowledge he had been ensorcelled did offer some slight comfort.

Tales had spread of the troll attack even before Odin had reached Hadding's hall, tales that spoke of trolls bursting into the village. And Ve was gone. Odin knew that before he'd even spoken to Vili. He was gone to the Jarnvid, gone to his own kind, and he had taken women with him. Odin would warm Hel's bed before he let those women suffer such a life. He would get his brother back. He would save them all. He had made an oath, and though Gudrun's games had cost him much time, he could still make it to the Odling castle if Tyr's reckonings were right. There was another day, at least, before the solstice. He'd make it. He had to. He had to break this curse.

The Jarnvid was the long-rumored home of the trolls, and thus Odin's destination. If past experience was any guide, these monsters would be like to sleep away the daylight. With sunset they'd wake, they'd feed, and then they'd fight over the women. Odin could not change what had already passed, but if he could spare these women even one more night of it … And judging by the sun, time grew short.

He glanced back over his shoulder, at the war party behind him. It was comprised of Tyr and Vili, and the others, as well as several Hasding hunters. But they could never move as swiftly as he could. And those women—and Odin's brother—had no time.

"The Jarnvid, Sleipnir!"

The horse twisted his head around, watching Odin with his inky black eye. It lasted only a moment before Sleipnir again took off at a gallop.

MILES BLURRED by until he and Sleipnir passed into the Jarnvid. The trees here twisted back on themselves, their roots grown in a tangled mess of crisscrosses that often resembled spider webs. Legends said the bark was hard as iron, and trolls sometimes sharpened the edges of the roots into razors. This was not a place for Mankind. Not even the Godwulfs drew too close to this cursed place, much as they claimed to ward Aujum against it. Sleipnir's pace slowed to a walk inside the wood. The sharpened foliage was simply too dense to allow a faster pace. Ravens perched on the branches watched his every move.

Odin glowered at Gjuki's spies.

The horse climbed a hill, at last stopping before a tunnel dug into it. It must have been a troll burrow. It was too low for him to ride through or even bring Sleipnir, which was a shame, since his mount would help even the odds against the trolls' superior size and strength.

Troll hide would deflect most weapons, but not Gungnir. Odin dismounted and hefted the spear, immediately feeling its power flow through him. His legs had healed, and his strength returned. All that remained now was the task at hand. This weapon, this spear born of dragon's blood, would give him the strength for that task. Naught in Midgard, not even trolls, could stand against it. Ymir had fallen, and so would these monsters. Odin lit a torch. He would have preferred having both hands for his spear, but he needed light more than the trolls did. Maybe it was pride that made him come alone. Maybe he would find naught but valkyries waiting for him this night. But he'd made so many mistakes … he could not let this become another.

He crept forward. The burrow delved deep, perhaps fifteen feet down. Ahead, deep snores echoed off the walls. The tunnel opened up into a central chamber accessed by a maze of side passages. Odin knelt at the entrance, taking stock of the scene. Huddled masses that looked like mossy boulders slept, piled atop one another. Six trolls perhaps, though it was hard to be sure given their sleeping arrangements. More might well dwell deeper in the burrow.

In the center of the room, iron roots had ripped through the ground like claws rising from the dust. Those roots bent into a cage where a half-dozen naked women lay huddled in each other's arms, bruised and bloodied. The nearest he recognized as one of Frigg's maids. Her hair was fiery red, even in the torchlight—probably what had led the troll to choose her in the first place. The root cage had sprouted thorns that looked sharp enough to shred skin and sinew if the women tried to slip through the cracks. Troll magic? It didn't matter. One way or another, he would set them free.

No sign of Ve ... unless he had become indistinguishable from the other trolls. Odin refused to believe that.

Odin laid the torch on the ground and rose, both hands on Gungnir as he snuck forward. The red-haired maid looked up abruptly at him and started to whimper, drawing the eyes of the other women. Odin silenced her with a finger to his lips and continued toward the largest mass of trolls. Three of them in here—it had looked like four from the entrance. So with the two on the other side, five trolls occupied this warren. And gods knew how many beyond.

Too many. But the only other choice was to wait for Tyr and risk them waking. He could be here in less than an hour, most like. No. The element of surprise was an advantage he couldn't surrender. He just needed a way to diminish their numbers ... They lay sleeping in a pile. All three of them lumped on top of one another in a mass, like dogs in a litter.

There.

He hefted his spear over his head and slammed it straight down, roaring with the effort. Gungnir sank through one troll's skull, into another's chest, and apparently through the arm of the third. And it kept going, embedding right into the stone. The wails of the wounded trolls were a nigh-deafening cacophony.

The other two leapt to their feet. Odin grasped his spear but didn't pull it free. The first troll was dead, the second dying, but the third was just pinned under them. If he removed the spear, he'd free that troll.

"Fuck."

The troll's flailing became frantic as it tried to dislodge itself from its fallen brethren and the spear.

Odin spun to face the remaining two. He drew his sword —a sword given to him by Frigg to protect their family—and readied against the charge. He could only pray the sword held true to its promise.

Trolls had weak spots, albeit not many. The joints, the eyes, the noses ...

Odin stepped in front of the cage. The first troll rushed at him, all fury and animal aggression. Odin leapt to the side and rolled as the troll swung a meaty hand at him. The creature slammed its palm into one of the roots, a thorn punching through its flesh.

It wailed in agony, bending the root as it yanked its hand away, further shredding its palm and spraying the women with black gore. Odin came up swinging at its knee with enough force to cut to the bone. The troll toppled forward, clutching its wounded hand, howling like a fiend of Hel. A heartbeat later the other troll slammed into Odin.

The impact knocked all wind from his lungs and sent him flying backward. He crashed into the burrow wall and fell, smacking his chest on the ground. Vision blurred, he gasped. Fiery surges of pain rocked his body with each ragged breath. Broken ribs.

Dimly, he heard the troll bellow. Odin pushed his face up, half expecting to see the troll ready to rip his head off.

Instead it grabbed him by his tunic and slammed him up against the burrow wall, sending fresh jolts of pain coursing through his body. Distorted as the troll's face was, he recognized it.

"Ve!"

Again the troll slammed him against the wall, knocking all wind out of him, before flinging him away. Odin crashed along the floor and rolled up against another wall. Pain blinded him. He couldn't rise.

For a moment he'd matched strength with a snow bear and fought through the pain of his wounds like a berserk. That power was in him. He reached for it, falling inside himself, desperately grasping for it. Something inside him seemed to rupture, filling his limbs with more strength than he'd ever known. The troll—his brother—charged forward and swung a claw down at Odin.

Odin flung himself out of the way. The pain of his broken bones faded in the surge of power rushing through him, and he drank that power like mead. Before Ve could turn, Odin charged him, wrapping his arms around his brother's midsection. His momentum and enhanced strength allowed him to heft the troll's weight and charge forward, slamming him into a wall. Rather than grant him respite, Odin rained blow after blow upon his brother.

Ve could take it.

He'd had an apple, too.

Odin pounded his fist again and again into Ve's ribs until they cracked. An uppercut to the troll's jaw sent his brother stumbling backward, head colliding with the wall.

Dazed himself, Odin backed away, then wrapped a hand around Gungnir. The dragon's power filled him, fueling his own, blending until he could no longer see the difference. The pinned troll wrapped a hand around Odin's leg. He yanked the spear free and slammed it into the last troll's head, then whipped it around in front of him, pointing it at Ve.

Ve watched him, gleaming eyes locked on Gungnir. The troll was wounded, stunned. Odin could close the distance and finish this. They both knew it.

Tyr and the others would be here, ready to clear this burrow and end the threat. And they would hunt down and kill Ve, never knowing who he was.

"I'm so sorry, brother," Odin said. "I swear I will return the amulet and restore you. I'll force that ghost to break this curse." He glanced back at the women he'd come to rescue, then turned back to Ve. "Run!"

Ve needed no further prompting. He took off, lumbering down a side tunnel.

Odin slipped to his knees. The power he'd drawn seemed to flee the moment his heart began to slow. With it gone, the renewed agony of his wounds hit him like a fresh torrent. He fell over, dimly aware of the women shouting.

His vision blurred.

## 51

The twisted Jarnvid lay before them. No horses inside. Even the hounds wouldn't venture there. Dogs were wiser than men in such things.

Hermod rose from where he knelt. "He passed this way, maybe an hour ago."

"You have your father's gift at woodcraft."

The young man scoffed. "I'm fair certain that's the only eight-legged horse in the area." He switched his torch to his left hand so he could draw a sword. "No woodsman enters the Jarnvid. At least not until now."

Vili strode forward, axe in hand. "Wish the fucking sun would set."

Tyr spat. "No. You don't. Trolls won't come out in sunlight." He drew his sword. This would be bloody. But his lord—his *king*—had ridden in there alone. Tyr would not leave the son of Borr to face this by himself. He ought to have seen what was happening to Ve. Had he remained, maybe he could have stopped this from happening. Maybe not.

Tyr lit his own torch off Hermod's. He edged his way into

the thorny wood. Had to be careful. Trees here could shred a man right through his mail. Vili pushed past him. Berserk tore a gash open on his side but didn't slow.

"Odin!" Vili bellowed. "Where the fuck are you, brother?"

Tyr cringed.

"This way," Hermod said, pointing off to Vili's left. "Deeper inside."

Vili raced off blindly, axe clanging against the iron-like trees. After a dozen strides, he paused, looked around. Huffed while Hermod caught up and pointed in a new direction.

"Vili," Tyr said. "Guard our backs."

The berserk grunted. "Soon as the fucking sun sets ..."

And that would be in mere moments.

They pressed on, even as darkness spread over the wood. Fast as if someone had shuttered a window. And then only torchlight remained. In the dark and the mist, a man couldn't see five feet.

"Stay close," Tyr commanded.

Vili had already doused his torch. He fell to his knees, groaning and roaring as he shifted. He tore off his clothes as the bear burst forth.

A louder bellow rang out from off to the left. A moment later, a massive form lumbered through the trees. It crashed into one of Tyr's men. Impact flung the man's body into a tree. Impaled him on a thorn bigger than Tyr's arm.

Tyr roared at the beast. Troll turned to meet his charge but not fast enough. Tyr leapt into the air, clanging his sword against its skull. The troll recoiled, stumbling backward, before slamming its claw atop the spot where Tyr had stood. Tyr rolled forward between its legs. Drew a knife in the same motion. He slammed the knife into the back of the troll's knee. It pitched forward.

Tyr mounted its back. Grabbed his sword. Jerked it free. He rained blows on the troll's neck. Blade clanged against rocky protrusions and skin tougher than armor. But a few blows bit. Geysers of black ichor spurted out of those wounds, drenching Tyr.

A bear collided with the troll. Tyr tumbled off backward, dropping his torch. Bear bore the troll down, clawing out its face. Its guts.

Another troll came crashing through the wood an instant later. Tyr snatched up his sword and raced in. Dodged to the side. Troll's hand slapped a tree, cracked it. Tyr's blade hit it in the abdomen. Blade snapped in half. Arm numb with the impact, Tyr stared a heartbeat at his broken sword. Damn. Not good.

The troll seized him by the tunic and hefted him off the ground. Tyr beat at its wrist with the hilt. Troll roared in his face. His stomach lurched. He dropped his weapon and clutched the troll's arm. Just before it tried to fling him free into a thorn.

Tyr's brain rattled around in his skull as the troll shook him about. The troll slammed him against a tree. Knocked all wind from his lungs. His arms lost their strength, and the troll flung him on the ground. Bellowed at him.

Tyr tried to roll over, to grab a weapon, torch, something. To catch a breath.

Troll was going to smash him, maybe step on him.

Hermod hewed at the back of the beast's knee with his sword. Troll wailed, spun on him. The young man thrust the torch in the monster's face. That sent the troll reeling backward.

Tyr scrambled to his feet, grabbed his fallen sword hilt, and raced to Hermod's side.

By now, Vili had risen from the other one. Swaying, bloody snout. Still charged right in to the next troll. The bear shoved the troll backward, driving a thorn through its shoulder.

The trolls' own twisted wood could hurt them.

Tyr drew all the supernatural strength he could. Everything the apple had given him. And he slammed his shoulder into the troll's gut as it tried to pull off the thorn. The troll shook the tree. Half the wood seemed to tremble with it.

Then Vili's claws began to rend its neck. Black blood sprayed everywhere.

Tyr retrieved his torch. As he let his strength go, pain flooded back in. His back felt like a giant welt. He was lucky the troll hadn't snapped his spine.

"Can you continue?" Hermod asked.

"You saved my life."

He shrugged. "You probably saved mine too. Sleipnir went this way."

ODIN LAY unconscious in a troll burrow.

Sleipnir had waited outside, leaving no doubt where his master had gone. Fool son of Borr had waded in there alone. It was like storming the gates of Hel, going into a troll's lair.

And within, so many dead trolls. Odin had single-handedly slain twice as many trolls as the three of them together had taken.

The women had fled their cage but still huddled

together. Weeping. Trembling. Nigh broken by the violence and horror.

"Get them out of here," Tyr said to Hermod. "Stick close to Vili."

He knelt by Odin's side. Tyr's place was here, until he could wake his king.

## 52

Odin's head felt apt to burst as Tyr shook him awake. "My lord!"

Odin grunted, then rolled over to spit out a mouthful of blood. "What happened?"

A fool's question, as Tyr's gaze clearly stated.

Odin pushed himself up, fresh shots of pain scourging every part of his body. The trolls would have pulverized a mortal man. As it was, even the apple had barely allowed him to survive the beating that … Ve … that Odin's own brother had dealt him.

And how much time had he lost?

"You must wait for your wounds to heal," Tyr said.

Odin pushed the warrior away, grunting with the effort of it. He'd wasted too much time already. He'd meant to ride all night to reach the Odling castle, but his time lost to the trolls and unconsciousness would cut deep into that period.

"I must be gone," he said. "See the women safely back to Halfhaugr."

Night was in full swing before Odin rode from the Jarn-vid. Ve had lost himself to that monster, and Odin would do whatever it took to restore him. His injuries meant naught compared to that. Sleipnir ran like the wind as if he understood the urgency too well. Singasteinn had become a hot weight against Odin's chest. He needed this to be done. He needed to be free of ghosts and curses and the mist.

The weight of it all threatened to suffocate him, an avalanche of urd, crushing him and leaving a poor imitation of a man in his place.

Odin had made an oath to Idunn to become king, and in so doing, had accepted responsibility for all the Aesir. The throne was one more burden, but one he had agreed to shoulder. He had to give them a better World. He would not allow anyone to suffer Ve's urd again.

A sharp hiss filled the air to his left a heartbeat before the mist slammed into Sleipnir like a solid wall. The horse tried to bank but was knocked through the air end over end. Odin, bareback, tumbled off and hit the ground hard.

"Sleipnir!" he gasped.

His mighty steed hit the hill, tumbled end over end, and lay still.

"Sleipnir!"

"The horse cannot save you this time, traitor," a voice called from the mists.

Odin pushed himself up, searching for where Gungnir had fallen. It had landed some distance away, down the slope of a hill. "Who are you?"

Mist clung to the man as he trod through it, revealing himself at first in silhouette, then in truth. Guthorm. Gudrun's brother, Hel's assassin—Grimhild's favorite.

Odin edged toward his spear, not taking his eyes off this newcomer. He struggled to claim the power within, that strength that let him lock out pain. A rustling sounded behind him. Someone moving through the mists. Many someones.

"You have betrayed my father, Little King. You've turned away from the Lady Hel and spurned the gifts that were offered to you. And you have shamed my sister! And that we will not abide." With agonizing slowness a sword crept from his scabbard. The mist seemed to chill around it, as though it radiated cold. Runes decorated the length of a woven steel blade. A runeblade. The stuff of legend. Guthorm held the sword before his face, as if saluting Odin. "This was forged by the dvergar. No finer blade graces Midgard. Retrieve your weapon, Odin. Die like a warrior."

Odin swallowed. He desperately wanted to check if Sleipnir lived, but Guthorm would give him no such chance. Instead, he resumed edging toward his fallen spear. He'd practiced gazing into the Penumbra with Gudrun. Gjuki had said that once the door was open, he would always know it was there. Well, now Odin needed to know. He needed to see the sorcerers creeping through the mist, seeking to surround him.

His eyes glazed over, and an instant of dizziness swept him before he righted himself. It grew easier each time he embraced the Sight. The shadows in the mist leapt into clarity. Many were wandering ghosts, trapped on Midgard long past their time, but Guthorm did have a half-dozen warriors with him. A hunting party seeking their prey.

Odin knelt and retrieved Gungnir. As he clasped it, its power merged with his own, making it easier to hold onto his strength.

"Are you quite certain you want to do this?" Odin asked. He leveled the spear before him, as if inviting Guthorm in.

The man stalked closer, sword before him. "Oh, yes."

Before Guthorm could reach him, Odin spun, slashing

out the throat of one of the not-so-hidden sorcerers in the mist. Blood gushed from the wound, and the falling corpse appeared clearly. He reversed his momentum and jutted out the butt of his spear, breaking the nose of another man. The sorcerers scattered, suddenly realizing how vulnerable they were. Odin hurled Gungnir like a bolt of lightning. It crashed through a man's chest and exploded out the other side, piercing into a boulder beyond. The dragon was thirsty for blood this day.

Guthorm roared, charging him. But Odin wasn't finished, nor did he intend to face the prince with other sorcerers at his back. He dove into a roll, slipping under Guthorm's furious swing. The strength the apples gave him made him fast. He easily chased down another man and slammed into him, the impact sending the poor bastard rolling along the ground.

Odin sprang forward, snatched Gungnir, and spun around to meet the Niflung prince. He raised his spear to parry the prince's downward chop. Sparks sheared off Gungnir at the impact. The runes on that sword glowed. Odin had never seen another weapon of ancient power besides Gungnir. This sword was extraordinary, seeped in eldritch energy and hungry for blood. Again and again he parried Guthorm's onslaught. This man was a master to rival Tyr.

Odin fell back, quickly losing ground. Left, right, and again he jabbed, trying to drive the prince backward, to gain maneuvering room. But Guthorm forced their bodies ever closer, gave him no chance to use the spear's superior reach.

The prince swung low and, when Odin tried to parry, suddenly altered the direction of his swing. The feint earned him a gash along Odin's left arm. A hot burning lit up and down his fingers, almost immediately replaced by a sudden chill as his arm began to numb. Was it the power of that sword? Odin tried to fall back again, a maneuver that only earned him a shallow cut across his thigh. That too began to go numb.

He was going to lose.

The realization of the inevitable hit him like a blow to the gut. Guthorm was simply a better warrior. The prince would slay Odin. His corpse would rot and his soul would writhe under the lash of Hel.

Odin gave over trying to attack, focusing instead on keeping the prince at bay. He'd lost all track of the two remaining Niflungar. Perhaps they had fled, or perhaps they knew their prince could handle this battle.

His damned leg threatened to give way with each step. It was too numb. But feeling had begun to return to his arm. His body, his own immortality would heal the wounds, even those caused by the runeblade.

Guthorm launched another onslaught, a series of cuts and thrusts Odin narrowly avoided. The prince panted, nigh snarling with rage. He mustn't have expected Odin to last this long—because a normal man never would have.

Odin might not have Guthorm's skill or speed, but he had the strength and stamina to outlast the trollfucker. The thought must have shown on his face, because Guthorm, now streaming sweat, snarled again and began another series of attacks. This one Odin recognized. Guthorm had that speed because he had probably practiced a handful of forms ten thousand times.

Odin made no attempt to attack. He gave ground freely to the prince's foray, his leg already regaining its strength. The prince's chest heaved, but still Odin let him come on, making no retaliation. Guthorm tried another series he'd already used, this time his attacks a little slower, his feints more predictable. Knowing exactly where the blow would land, Odin twisted aside, letting a sword stroke graze his arm rather than trying to parry it. At the same time he thrust forward, driving Gungnir through the Niflung prince's chest.

The prince looked down at the spear impaling him as if in shock, eyes wide as his blood gushed from his ruptured chest. Odin glanced around, spying the remaining sorcerers lingering on the edges of the battlefield. These Niflungar were not used to men seeing them, much less slaying them. They had transcended mortality but still feared it. That was their weakness.

"Go back to your king!" Odin shouted at them. "Tell them a new king rules Mankind! Tell them a new god rises!"

That was what he had set himself up to become. Only then could he do what he must to save this world. To save Mankind, he must rule them all. Gudrun had been right about that.

With a last look of disgust, Odin cast Guthorm down into the snow, pausing only to claim the runeblade, then trod over to check on Sleipnir. The horse neighed at his touch, gingerly trying to climb to his feet. By the way Sleipnir favored two of his legs, they must be broken. The horse was lucky he had so many to spare.

But Odin certainly couldn't ride Sleipnir, not now.

"Can you make it safely away?" he asked.

Sleipnir snorted. As usual.

Odin nodded. Then he had a hard run ahead of him. He dashed up the hill and ran on toward the old castle.

STEP after merciless step he ran, until even his superhuman stamina waned. Until his chest burned and broken ribs ached even through the mask of power he'd used to block the pain. Breathless, he climbed the steps before that castle. He'd made it. Moons of struggle, and he'd at last save Ve. Before he reached the top, the sun crested over the mist, warming his skin. He had made it only just in time.

And then the warming became a burning, a searing, like his arms and chest were aflame. Steam rose from beneath his cloak. Odin screamed in horror and pain, hurling his garments away. His cloak, tunic, and gloves—all he tossed aside, revealing the singed skin beneath, still smoldering with wisps of smoke. The acrid, sickeningly sweet smell of his own burnt flesh filled his nostrils, and Odin vomited.

When he looked down, he saw the burns were not random. They encircled his arms and chest in a ring of runes. From the pain, he could only guess they covered his back as well. Covered all of his chest but the spot where the Singasteinn hung.

Weak with exhaustion and agony, he crawled on his knees up to the entryway. Then he flung the amulet into the castle. An echo rang through the empty hall as it clattered across the frozen floor.

"Ghost! I have returned your amulet!"

No answer came.

"Odling!"

Odin panted.

No.

No, he had done it. He'd had one more day. Surely she could not have begrudged him the first rays of dawn on the solstice itself. Mere moments ... He looked again at the runes marking his skin. What did they mean? The old languages, the old words were said to have power. Völvur knew such things, but Odin did not.

*All you build will turn to ash, your children shall die, and your dreams shall burn.*

"Damn you!" he shouted at the empty castle. His voice echoed through the halls.

He stormed upstairs and beat down every door, searched every corner. No sign remained of the ghost. She held him to her curse, and he had failed her, even if only by a moment. And this ... this meant ...

He'd thought her curse was what was happening to Ve. He'd thought that had been the price, the warning. But it was never that. The awful urd his brother faced had naught to do with the ghost, did it? It was merely the price of a spurned and neglected brother left too long in a cursed world.

Odin had failed. He'd failed his brother and thus failed his father. Whether this ghost could have ever healed him or not, Odin had failed Ve. He had failed up on that mountain, way back, when his pride put vengeance for the dead before the safety of the living.

Now Ve's own body had betrayed him and made him a monster. A thing. And Ve had taken the apple ... he would be as a god among the trolls. A king among their kind as much as Odin was among men. The realization settled on Odin with overwhelming certainty. Frigg said völvur just knew some things, and he now he had a fraction of her power. He just *knew*, with a prescient certainty born of the Sight.

At last, at the threshold to the castle, he stared down at the golden amulet. All of this for a piece of jewelry. For greed. For pride.

He slipped to his knees. The avalanche of urd had finally

buried him and left him in the abyss of despair, powerless and broken.

Urd. Vast and terrible as the World itself.

Urd, that stole all worth having and left behind ash.

Or perhaps, to blame urd was but one more way to try to evade his culpability for all that had passed. Odin's failings, his anger and his hubris, *they* had ravaged his brother as much as the mist. And rather than face it, he had deluded himself, or allowed a ghost to delude him, even knowing that vaettir lied. That they hated the living.

And at long last, Odin could return their enmity.

No blow could strike the ghost who had so betrayed him, nor had rage yet availed him of any benefit. His anger had cost him everything he cared for.

Odin rose, trembling, and let the Singasteinn fall to the floor, heedless of the echoes its clattering made.

So then, let this be the last of his anger. The final act, to count himself and Ve avenged against Odlingar and Niflungar alike, in the only manner he was ever like to achieve.

Roaring, he drove Gungnir's point through the Singasteinn. The amulet shattered beneath the dragon spear's blade, shards of it skittering along the frozen floor. A wail erupted around him, not in the Mortal Realm, but just beyond the Veil, audible only because of his gift. Whether the parting anguish of the spirit at last freed from the amulet, or the grief of the ghost denied its treasure, it mattered naught.

Odin did not look back. Naught remained for him in the castle. Naught, in fact, had ever waited for him here.

He was left only with an oath to take a throne he had never wanted. And a final obligation to protect what remained of the Aesir, from now until his last breath.

# PART V

Year 118, Age of Vingethor
Second Moon, Summer

## 53

*T*he summer solstice had come and gone, bringing a new year. Eight moons of work. And now, nine tribes had gathered in Halfhaugr. Odin had called the Althing, and every tribe had come. He and Tyr and Idunn had passed among each tribe. Fighting. Bargaining. Killing.

They had gone too far to turn back. Tyr had gone too far. No matter how many battles he had to fight, he would see this through. And now they had.

"Will they choose him?" Idunn asked. The Vanr goddess stood behind him, peering at the circle of jarls.

Tyr didn't answer her. Really, it was not for them to speak now.

Now came the time for the jarls to speak.

Hoenir stepped forward, into the circle, the aging man taking in each of the jarls now. "We stand here, the heirs of Loridi. In his honor we hold the Althing." He looked at some of the other jarls. Arnbjorn, the jarl of the Itrmanni had proved especially difficult. "Some of you have objected to this Althing. Loridi said we were to hold it but once every nine summers. And this was not that summer. So then, I ask you brothers, why are we here?" He did not pause long enough for anyone to answer. "Because times of change require us to change as well. More than a hundred winters back, Vingethor called the Althing. And that was also not the ninth summer. Yet he called it, and our ancestors answered. Because times had grown harsh, because we needed a new way. As we need again now."

Hoenir pointed at Odin. "Our ancestors named Vingethor king that he might lead them into better lands. Now the time has come to once again call forth a king who will lead us."

"Lead us where?" the jarl of the Itrmanni demanded.

"Wherever the fuck he wants," Vili said. Odin had named Vili the new jarl of the Hasdingi. Frigg did not seem over pleased at it. But Vili was a son of Borr, too. Odin had to honor his kin.

Hoenir scowled at the fool berserk, as did Odin. A son of Borr, yes. Without any measure of his father's cunning.

"To lead us into a future where we stand united," Odin said. Hoenir fell back into his place, allowing Odin to stand in the middle. "United against our common enemies. I say to you, our enemies are the enemies of all Mankind. The mist, the ever-encroaching chill. No longer will we watch our numbers fall with each passing winter. Moreover, raiding together, we can challenge the rulers of any other land. They will tremble before our strength, and we, all the Aesir, shall know fame across Midgard. Fame, and wealth beyond measure."

Several men whooped at that.

"I would be your king and give you this future." He raised a hand for a silence. "Name me."

"I name you King Odin," Hoenir said.

"I name you the fucking King of the Aesir," Vili said.

"I expected more formality on such an occasion," Idunn mumbled.

So had Tyr.

Annar stepped forward. Odin's cousin had stayed here in Halfhaugr over a moon, helping him prepare. "King Odin."

Jarl Steinar of the Friallaf tribe stepped forward. "King Steinar."

Everyone fell silent.

Odin turned slowly to face the jarl. "You wish to be named?"

Steinar spat on the floor. "Men say you're a living god. That you've killed jotunnar, trolls, and all manner of vaettir. I shit on your tales, and I piss on your fame. I say you're a man and a liar. Where were you when we sacked Kaunos and gutted the Miklagarders? Was your spear beside mine? Did you break the shield wall? Or were you too busy fighting—or fucking—a troll?"

Gasping filled the hall.

Odin worked his jaw. Tyr strode forward, hand on his sword hilt. But Odin held out his hand. Good then. Some things a man had to do himself. Especially a leader.

With a long sigh, Odin drew the sword from his shoulder. Frigg's family sword. Strong, well wrought. Some said forged by Volund himself during the Njarar War. Blade worthy of a king.

"Your words leave no space for compromise, Jarl Steinar."

The jarl drew his own sword. Advanced on Odin, who stood very still, sword pointed at Steinar.

The Friallaf jarl lunged forward, batted away Odin's sword. Or tried. Odin moved much faster. Twisted the blades out of the way and caught Steinar by the throat. With one hand, he hauled the man off his feet. Then he drove his sword through the jarl's belly. Odin flung the man onto the ground.

Steinar's skull cracked on the stone. He lay still, blood streaming from head and gut.

After that, no more jarls challenged Odin.

Odin took the throne. A throne that had once belonged to Hadding. His daughter Frigg now sat in a throne beside Odin, her belly thick with child. A procession of völvur entered, bearing a golden crown worked with the likeness of Yggdrasil.

"By the Tree," Idunn said. "Beautiful."

The eldest völva placed the crown on Odin's head. The hall erupted in cheers. A people bursting in joy. In hope.

Idunn spoke, but Tyr couldn't make out her words. Her hand touched his shoulder, and he turned to her. Her smile was warm, yet almost ... afraid.

"Congratulations," she said. "You did it. Odin is King of the Aesir."

"You do not look as well pleased as you might."

She laughed. Another, almost true smile. "I am quite pleased."

"Will you ... remain among us still?" It was the question he had feared to ask all these past moons. Under the apple's effect, he had lain with her. Now he desperately wanted to hold her again. But how does a man ask a goddess to stay by his side?

Before she could answer, Frigg gasped. Clutched her belly. Screamed in pain.

Her maid, Fulla, rushed forward to her side. "The babe is coming! Make way, make way!"

## 54

*A* peal of thunder rang out over the night. Odin stood upon the ramparts atop Halfhaugr, crown on his brow. Below, his wife wailed in labor. But some places remained forbidden to men, even to kings. So he watched the night over Aujum, heedless of wind or rain.

Aujum. His Realm now, all of it, as all the Aesir bent before him. He'd kept his oath to Idunn, though it had not bought him the one prize he had truly sought. Ve was gone, lost forever because of Odin's failings. Neither he nor his father had sought a crown, and now, with it done, part of him wanted to cast it out into the night. But more than his oath to Idunn held him now. He had made an oath to himself, to make a better World for the Aesir.

This storm had raged long, all through the labor, as if wakened by the pain of his wife. If she knew of Odin's disloyalty to their marriage bed, she did not speak of it. Nor comment when he woke in the night, flush with dreams of a sorceress who held a piece of his heart he could never recover. He leaned against the ancient dvergar stone and sighed. He had made enemies of Niflungar, and they would come for him. He'd need to prepare Aujum against them.

"Holy lords of Vanaheim, it's wetter than the sea up here," a woman said behind him.

Odin turned. Frigg's maid stood on the threshold, under the fortress eave, peering out at him and blinking into the night.

"The babe is born?" he asked.

"Oh! Indeed, and right well he was. More than healthy and good as new." Fulla's fiery red hair blew in the wind. She trembled a little as Odin approached. She'd always trembled a little, ever since her time with the trolls. He'd feared to ask how they had used her. It was not his place, in any event, though more than once he had found her weeping in Frigg's arms. And still, she did not give up, did not give in to despair.

Even a simple maid had something to teach him.

Odin could not afford to surrender to this melancholy, this miasma suffocating him. He was a father himself now. That alone ought to have left him elated and calling for unending mead. Ought to. If he could forget for one moment that neither his father nor brother could ever share his joy.

He patted her on the shoulder and hurried inside, half running down the stairs to the ground floor. Frigg had refused to move into her father's old room, so they stayed in her own chamber. Odin paused there a moment before easing the door open.

Sigyn stood inside, a babe cradled in her arms. A tuft of red hair crowned a head peeking out of a bundle of blankets.

"M-may I?" Odin asked.

His sister-in-law smiled as she handed him the bundle.

Odin took his son gingerly. Bright eyes, so like Odin's own father's. Looking back at him. Odin sucked in a breath that stung his lungs. Father *was* here, he knew he was. "Uh ... What shall we call him, wife? Have you given it thought?"

Frigg nodded. "I have given it much consideration. His name shall be Thor."

*Thunderer.*

A crash of lightning rang outside.

How appropriate.

"Rest a bit," he said to Frigg. Tradition demanded he show off the boy.

He carried little Thor out into the great hall where jarls and thegns and warriors of nine tribes gathered now, feasting and toasting their new king. Not an honor he had sought, but one he had claimed, nonetheless, and could not now shirk. Not now, nor ever. Let them drink deep of the mead and take what joy they might—these people had earned it ten times over. They had bought it with blood.

Odin raised the baby high. "Behold Thor! Son of Odin! Prince of the Aesir!"

The cheer that rose through the hall overshadowed even the continuing rumbles of thunder. Would Father be proud now, to see Odin on a throne of the tribes? He had wanted an end to the internecine wars. Odin would give him that lasting peace, in Borr's name. Thor could become a symbol of his grandfather's dream.

The varulf twins crawled about on the floor around the throne, as Fulla chased them around. His other children, and he had to do right by them as well, by all his people.

Odin nodded to Fulla, who came and took Thor from him.

As he turned back to his people, Loki strode up to him.

Odin clasped his blood brother's arm. "I suppose I owe this birth to you, in a way."

Loki smiled, shook his head.

"I wish that I ... well, of course he's far too young for an apple, anyway."

Loki nodded. "Undoubtedly. But, my friend, if it would ease your mind ..." Loki produced a golden apple from a pouch on his belt. "I might have saved *one* more for just this occasion."

Odin took the apple, his hand almost seeming to shake. A hollow opened in his chest. No words seemed worthy of such a boon. "Brother, I ... You did this for me?"

"You're welcome."

"But if you had an apple to spare," Odin asked, "why did you not give it to Hadding?"

"It would not have saved him. A man cannot change his urd."

Odin grunted. He had mused over and over on that very topic. Perhaps Loki blamed urd, but Odin could not. Still, it was always hard to know his brother's thoughts. This brother, at least. Vili raised a drinking horn in salute, before downing the whole thing in one swig, earning him raucous laughter and cheers from those about him. Odin nodded at him, then passed among the rest of the hall, accepting the well-wishes and embraces of men and women from nine tribes.

Nine tribes, bent to his will, united under his rule, as Idunn had bid. And the Vanr woman herself? She moved in and out of the light of braziers, eyes watching him like a weight on his soul.

Once satisfied all here had seen him, Odin drifted away, followed Idunn down the hall and down stairs. The Vanr goddess led him to the room Frigg used to brew her potions and salves and stood there, staring at the wall.

The brazier down here cast the room in heavy shadows that tightened around his throat like a noose. Long ago, someone had worked the Art in these depths, and the foulness of it still tainted these stones.

Odin was about to ask what she did here. But something was ... odd. Those runes on the wall. He couldn't read them, but they ... looked much like some of the runes now wrapped around his chest and arms. After pulling away his tunic, he looked down. Yes, some of the same verses marked his body.

His stomach lurched. His palms had gone clammy. He did *not* want to ask the question he knew he must. "What is this?"

"Five thousand years ago, the Vanir were a tribe much like the Aesir. Not quite so primitive, but similar."

Primitive?

"This was before I was born, of course. My grandmother came to them, after the breach to Niflheim released the mists and their chill. She thought she could lead them to a better future. So she led them across this world and to the island we now call Vanaheim. She was looking for something—the Tree of Life. Her people had called it Djambo Barros, but to the Vanir it was called Yggdrasil.

"Imagine a tree stretching up to the heavens, with roots reaching far down into the earth. And imagine it had golden fruits. The tree itself held the mists and the chill at bay, giving my people—including my mother, who was nigh grown by then—a shelter from the Hel-cursed place this world had become. And when they ate the fruits, it changed them. It made them immortal and gave them insights, along with powers much like you yourself have begun to develop.

"My mother ate the fruit, and I was given one when I was old enough, too. By that time, we already knew the apples didn't grow quickly. There would never be enough for everyone in the World or even all of our own people. My grandmother, she never took one. I guess ... I guess she missed my grandfather and didn't want to face eternity alone."

Idunn hugged herself, and Odin couldn't stop himself from taking her hand. The goddess knew more of loneliness and despair than even Odin. Facing long centuries as she had, he would no doubt endure the same heartache. And if he survived as long as Idunn, would his hope have finally withered, or would he become what she was now? Lost and alone and clinging to one last, desperate dream of redemption?

"It was a long time ago," she said, but shut her eyes for a moment. "When she was old—very old—she called for me and told me all the stories of her life. Wonderful stories of a world before the ice and the mist, a world I'd never known. She spoke of beautiful islands so hot you had to rest in the middle of the day, of waters so warm and clear that swimming was a pleasure ... And she told me she feared she might have made a mistake in bringing the Vanir to Yggdrasil. She'd wanted to save Mankind, not elevate a single tribe to godhood. And the Vanir jealously guarded the tree and its fruit, denying other tribes the warmth of the lands of spring.

"I don't know. Maybe if they had tried harder, they could have found a way to banish the mists. But they didn't. They cast themselves as gods. And they fought the chaos, yes, but eventually they cut themselves off from the rest of the World and let it languish. Our king, the king before Njord, he walked away from his throne and vanished, and the rest of us, we just withdrew. And for a long time, I watched. I watched with the eyes my grandmother had opened, as Vanr society became so isolated from the rest of Midgard we might as well have lived on another world.

"And maybe that was *my* fault. I let centuries, millennia pass, lost in doubt and unsure what to do. And then I started making pilgrimages to Midgard, determined to see the people who lived there. To find the strongest."

Odin shook his head and released her hand. "I don't understand why you're telling me all this, Idunn. Or why you wanted me to take this throne, but I held my oath. I made myself king."

She shuddered, then tapped a finger on the runes branded on his chest. Her touch left him tingling, and he backed away, pulling his shirt closed.

"I told you once you had become king I would give you one more task as the price for those apples."

"And what would you have me do?"

Her eyes flashed with intensity he did not often see in her. "You will gather the tribes, all the Aesir people and march them to the west. Far, far west, beyond all lands you know. You must march on Vanaheim itself, and there, dear Odin, you must fulfill the greatest of your tasks. You must cast down the gods, overthrow the Vanir ... and take their place."

# EPILOGUE

The town could not hold all the Aesir, and thus a thousand fires dotted the land around the hill, warding against the mist. The revelries carried on long into the night, ringing out the cheer of the moment, the people unaware of the tribulations so soon to befall them. Loki drifted among those fires, just out of sight, never quite one of the Aesir, never quite able to allow himself such an indulgence.

Instead he claimed a lone torch and wandered out into the wild, climbing the next hill over from Halfhaugr. There he kindled his own flame before settling down beside it.

The woman made no sound as she approached, though he felt her presence. She flowed about the hill like the wind, circling as if waiting for an invitation, even as she knew he would not offer one. Nor did he flee from her. The time for that had passed. Were they to march across Midgard together, as her plan entailed, he could not avoid her forever.

And so finally Idunn drifted over to his fire and knelt before it, the flame separating them, as it ever had.

"You do not savor the festivities," she said.

"I've seen a great many festivals. One is not so different from the next."

Idunn nodded slowly, then looked off in the direction of Halfhaugr. The fortress was just visible, rising out of the mist. "It is he, is it not?"

"You suspected that quite some time ago, I imagine, even before you first came to him."

"He's not your puppet, you know." Her anger, so carefully concealed before the others, now simmered just beneath the surface, so palpable he could almost taste it.

"Nor yours, Idunn. You play a very dangerous game if you think to manipulate the Destroyer." Loki might have searched for words to placate Idunn and still the flame burning in her breast, but anger, held long enough, became a poison one mistook for a shield. And no word, least of all from him, would drive Idunn to cast away her beliefs.

The Vanr woman grew silent for a time. "I know who you are, Loki. I know why you had an apple left. You had no need to eat the one Odin gave you, not after you tasted one long, long ago."

"Longer than you can imagine." She wanted to blame him—people always needed someone to blame for the tragedies of urd, as if, by pointing a finger at a cause, one might somehow obviate the result. Loki was used to it. Sometimes, it served to allow oneself to become the subject of rage. Sometimes, no other choices remained.

"My grandmother *never* forgave you for what happened to my grandfather. You know that, don't you? I'm not going to let you do it again. Not here."

"Chan—" Loki stopped and cleared his throat. He would not let her draw him into an outburst, especially not with their audience, lurking in the shadows. "Your grandmother was an amazing woman. But she saw the World as a simpler place than it really is. As someone who has lived as long as you have, you ought to realize that. And Idunn ... if you come between me and Odin, you will regret it."

Idunn rose, glaring at him. "How many worlds must burn before you?"

Loki shook his head. "Fire is life."

The Vanr snorted and stalked away, back into the night, casting a last, spite-filled glance his way as she went. Her anger, her shield, would carry her far. At least until some final catastrophic event forced her to acknowledge the agonizing truth that it had not protected her, had only allowed her to accumulate more wounds that, unnoticed, were left to fester.

Loki waited until she had drifted out of earshot. "You can come out now."

At first, no one responded. Then, with a sigh, Sigyn rose from where she lay on her belly nearby and sauntered over to the fire. "I was trained by a master woodsman. How did you know I followed you?"

"Is that the best question you have?"

Sigyn snorted as she sank down beside him. "Tell me what burden you carry."

Would that he could. "Take comfort in knowing your mere presence eases all burdens." He stared into the flames, watching the dance, the pattern. Such an excellent medium for the Sight and all the terrible weight that accompanied it. The flames could speak to those who would listen, could reveal the past and future to those willing to suffer blindness and agony for it.

Sigyn slipped her fingers into his hand. So warm, so filled with life ... and so much like *her*, so very clever, perhaps even more than Sigyn herself realized. She was putting pieces together in a puzzle she had only just begun to understand. And to not tell her everything was like having a serpent gnaw at his heart. But to tell her all … that would be worse, not only for him, but for her. He would not cast her into the ocean of darkness he was forced to look upon, not while any choice yet remained to him.

"I saw Yggdrasil. The first night we made love, I saw a vision of it, in my mind. Are you one of the Vanir?"

"No, Sigyn. I am … something else."

"A god?"

"No. Nor truly are the Vanir. The space between gods and men is perception and arrogance, pride and foolishness. Naught lasts forever. All empires fall; all Eras burn down to cinders."

She squeezed his hand. "I *love* you. I do. But I want the truth."

"Some things cannot be given, only taken."

She tapped her finger against her lip. "I know what you did in that tafl game, but I can't see *how* you did it, planning so many moves in advance. But now I'm left to wonder, if you have not done the same thing here, moving pawns here and there, down through the ages toward an endgame no one else has yet glimpsed."

"Tafl has a finite number of moves available at any given junction. Life offers much more intricate designs."

Sigyn sighed and fell silent a moment. "Tell me what it meant, your conversation with Idunn. Try to explain."

He returned the squeeze of her hand. So clever, so certain. But missing some of the pieces and never imagining how excruciating uncovering the obfuscated truths might prove, not only to herself, but to all the World. As always, one faced the choice to shelter one's loved ones and earn their ire, or weigh them down with knowledge they fooled themselves into thinking they desired. And as always, the middle path offered at least the illusion of asylum from either extreme, if only a temporary one. A half truth, to spare her the depths of despondency.

He sighed, but she squeezed his hand, demanding an answer. "It means the past cannot stay buried forever. It means the future will haunt our every step. We are, all of us, set on a path that has only just begun. A spark ignites embers in the darkness that, tended well, become a flame. The flame spreads like a living being, writhing and feasting, engorging itself into a conflagration that sweeps across the land and swallows all in its path until only ashes remain."

Before she could ask more, he reached into the campfire and from it drew forth a fistful of flame, dancing around his hand, illuminating the awe on her face. "The fire is lit. Now we tend it. And we wait, for the inevitable inferno."

**THE CYCLE CONTINUES …**

**Next Book:** Odin has become King of the Aesir. Now he must begin the more dangerous task of guiding his people across the frozen wastes of Midgard.

*The Mists of Niflheim:* books2read.com/mlmists

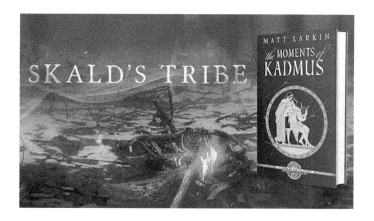

Join the Skalds' Tribe newsletter and get access to exclusive insider information and your FREE copy of *The Moments of Kadmus*.

https://www.mattlarkinbooks.com/skalds/

# ABOUT THE AUTHOR

Matt Larkin writes retellings of mythology as dark, gritty fantasy. His passions of myths, philosophy, and history inform his series. He strives to combine gut-wrenching action with thought-provoking ideas and culturally resonant stories.

Matt's mythic fantasy takes place in the Eschaton Cycle universe, a world—as the name implies—of cyclical apocalypses. Each series can be read alone in any order, but they weave together to form a greater tapestry.

Learn more at mattlarkinbooks.com or connect with Matt through his fan group, the Skalds' Tribe:

https://www.mattlarkinbooks.com/skalds/

# AUTHOR'S NOTE

What I'm doing, what I've been doing for some time, is working to retell and reimagine real-world mythologies within the context of a single dark fantasy setting spanning multiple Eras. This Era, the Ragnarok Era, is a mythical past set in an ice age brought on by the presence of mists escaped from Niflheim. So you see things like dire wolves and mammoths, mixed with the Norse and Germanic epics. I had a lot of sources, but the most prominent you'll see here are the eddas and the *Volsung Saga*. Some day, if enough people cared, I could come up with a list of other primary sources—my writing cave is littered with tons of them. One of the most substantial influences was the *Prose Edda*, in which Snorri supposes Odin was a mortal man living in ancient times, one who travelled west from somewhere in Asia and gave rise to many legends.

I published the original version of *The Apples of Idunn* in early 2014. At that time, it was about half the length of this book, in part because I had wanted it to be a fast-paced adventure story, and in part because I decided to trim out parts of what I originally wrote. And it was well received—I

got invited to a podcast interview, had a college professor
want to teach it in her class, and otherwise was pretty
pleased with it. I published the sequel (*The Mists of
Niflheim*). I wrote the third book (*The Shores of Vanaheim*).
And I just kept going on, planning the fourth one, but I realized more and more, I had not quite done what I'd wanted
with the first book. Book 1 was around 50,000 words. Book 3
was around 100,000 words. That was my first clue.

I had always planned the series to span three trilogies,
each with a different focus, but I first conceived of them as
these fast adventures. And the one thing everyone wanted—
including myself—was just more. Historical fantasy, all epic
fantasy, really, has the reputation for being doorstoppers,
and I came to realize there was a reason for that. Tales of
this scope need it. They need the time and depth, and often
things need to be seen through different characters' eyes.
After agonizing with the decision—and this is a hard decision for any author—and consulting with my editors, my
mentor (thanks Sean), and others, I finally decided I was
going to go back and redo this series the way it should have
been all along.

The other factor that changed for me, was that I lost my
dad. I had written this epic about Odin trying to avenge his
father and had done the best I could to express his feelings.
But frankly, until you've been through losing someone really
close, you just don't know. That loss demanded I come at the
series with a deeper emotional resonance than *Apples* originally portrayed.

So what changed? Each book now features a prologue
and an epilogue told from Loki's point of view. In addition,
the first book did not originally feature Tyr or Gudrun as
point-of-view characters. I also pulled back the opening to
show more of the events leading up to Odin hunting down

Ymir. Mainly through Tyr, it shows how Odin becomes King of the Aesir, which was largely glossed over in the original version. Besides all that, the book went through a huge number of editorial revisions to plot and text (big thanks to Clark and Fred for all the help here). The overall plot is not changed much from the original version, though there are some subtle differences.

I wanted to stay as close to the spirit of the original sources as possible, while still not only putting my own spin on the tales but also fitting them into the framework I was creating for that dark fantasy setting I mentioned. It means, of necessity, some things changed to fit the setting or the story. The end result, *The Ragnarok Era*, is something I'm immensely proud of, and I truly hope everyone enjoyed this first taste of it. There's a lot more where this came from.

I could not have done this alone, too, so I want to take time to say thanks to everyone who helped me with this. So thank you Brenda, Eryn, Hanna, Sean, Clark, Fred, Clarissa, Jena, and Juhi. And most of all, thanks, Dad, for everything. I miss you.

Thank you for reading,
    Matt

*For Juhi. For believing.*

Lightning Source UK Ltd.
Milton Keynes UK
UKHW010715080222
398372UK00002B/339